"AZRAEL. IT IS TIME . . ."

"Who are you?" Nate yelled into the darkness at the voice. The sound seemed to die as it left his mouth, to vanish without an echo.

Something had changed in the darkness around him. It wasn't void any longer, there was a thick sense of presence around him, as if he might reach out a hand and feel slick skin and undulating flesh. He felt as if any moment something heavy and damp might wrap around his throat, strangling him.

"Which road?" The words were heavy, cloying, and came from organs that were not meant for human speech.

The darkness resolved into something. Two some-things. Behind him, he could dimly see a corridor in the classroom building. In front of him was what might have been a hill or a lawn, backed with blue sky. Both views seemed incredibly distant. At the same time they felt intense enough that he need only reach out to one or the other to touch it.

The sense of alien presence was overwhelming, on all sides, as if cascades of rippling flesh were about to engulf him.

"CHOOSE!"

BROKEN CRESCENT

S. Andrew Swann

DAW BOOKS, INC.
DONALD A. WOLLHEIM, FOUNDER
375 Hudson Street, New York, NY 10014

ELIZABETH R. WOLLHEIM
SHEILA E. GILBERT
PUBLISHERS
http://www.dawbooks.com

First Printing, May 2004
1 2 3 4 5 6 7 8 9

DAW TRADEMARK REGISTERED
U.S. PAT. OFF. AND FOREIGN COUNTRIES
—MARCA REGISTRADA
HECHO EN U.S.A.

PRINTED IN THE U.S.A.

This is for Mu, who insists
on sitting on the Manuscript

BOOK ONE

Long after the great and terrible battles, long after the world had been broken by the forces Ghad himself had created, Ghad walked between the world and the shadow of the world to see what there was to be seen. At length he came across a man-child crying in the wilderness. Ghad took on the form of an old woman and approached the man-child.

"Why do you cry such bitter tears?" asked Ghad.

"I cannot work the fields, and the College will not take me. My parents abandoned me here."

Ghad frowned. "Listen, child, and I will teach you what the College will not." And, because it pleased Ghad to do so, he taught the man-child words of power beyond the knowledge of the most learned of men.

The man-child returned to his village and spoke such words that the houses of his parents, his uncles, and his grandfathers were consumed with fire.

And, because Ghad hated man, Ghad was pleased.

—*The Book of Ghad and Man,*
Volume II, Chapter 105

Chapter One

ARMSMASTER Ehrid Kharyn was the highest civil authority in the city of Manhome. His offices reflected that authority. They occupied an entire floor on top of the tallest tower in the city outside the College itself.

Either side of the Armsmaster's office opened onto a balcony circumnavigating the tower. The great balcony overlooked the mainland on one side, the ocean on the other. From this spot, Ehrid Kharyn had almost complete autonomy to act in the Monarch's name, deploying forces, guarding the borders, enforcing the laws of man in an area that stretched beyond either visible horizon.

Almost.

Standing in front of Ehrid was an elderly man, masked and robed, who was busy demonstrating the limits of the Armsmaster's power.

"Need I remind you that you are pledged to aid the College of Man in all things?" The old man's voice was flat and lacked emotion. It was a tone that the scholars of the College tended to affect. The masters more so than the acolytes. And this old man wore the elaborate inlaid mask of a master.

Ehrid knew the mask, if not the person behind it. The jeering demon face fixed a crimson scowl at him, inlaid with gold and ivory. It was the unique mask of the Venerable Master of the Manhome College—by extension, the entire College of Man.

"I understand the prerogative of the College in matters of theology. But your request goes beyond that prerogative." Ehrid was a bear of a man, nearly six feet tall and, dressed as he was in the full crimson and black regalia of his office, at least two thirds as wide. Diplomacy did not come easily to him, and if he had faced anyone else, the hard edge of his words would cause opposition to shrivel, and his adversary to make an abrupt obsequious retreat.

Unfortunately, to the College of Man, a chosen representative of the Monarch was only slightly better than a ghadi servant.

Worse, the ghadi have no pride to swallow.

"There is no call for emotional displays, Master Ehrid."

There were no appeals, even to the Monarch himself. Something both of them were quite aware of. Ehrid knew that he was lucky that they allowed him even the illusion of power. The Venerable Master Scholar could, literally with a single word, remove Ehrid from his position as Armsmaster of Manhome, if not from existence itself.

But it wasn't in Ehrid's nature to simply acquiesce.

"This isn't emotion. It is good sense. I cannot have my men searching for demons under every ghadi rock. Who will man the gates, keep the watch, maintain the peace when I have half my force scattered from here to Zorion?"

"You will manage normal operations."

Much as Ehrid might pretend differently, he knew that even the Monarch himself would not directly oppose the College in anything. Still, Ehrid tried to influence his visitor. "You expect a stranger, but you cannot describe him. With the powers you have, I would think you could find this stranger yourself."

"Think what you may. We need your men."

Ehrid bit back his words. He wasn't a diplomat, but he did know where the limits were. No one could achieve any secular rank, especially in Manhome, without knowing exactly how far the College could be pushed.

He had reached that point. "Of course, my guard is fully at your disposal. I just wished you to be aware of the consequences of reassigning so many guardsmen." The words were conciliatory, but it was beyond Ehrid to sound pleased with the outcome.

"We are aware. The College will finance the hire of additional men if they are needed. However, the men on patrol outside the city must be experienced, competent, and know well the law."

"Of course." Ehrid gritted his teeth. "Is there anything else the College desires?"

"No." The Venerable Master turned and strode from Ehrid's chambers, descending the stairs without once looking back. Not even offering a token gesture recognizing Ehrid's authority or the authority of the Monarch.

Please, may Ghad avert his gaze.

When the Venerable Master was gone, another figure appeared, walking in from the balcony. He wore the robes of an acolyte, and a featureless mask that normally indicated someone of the lowest caste of the College of Man—though, even if Ehrid did not know the man, he would have known better just from the acolyte's confident bearing.

"The College asks for no small service," spoke the acolyte in a half amused voice.

"You observed?"

"You expected any less from me?"

Ehrid grunted. "I will defer to you in the arcane arts, but it strikes me as reckless for you to stand so close to an officer of the College. Much less the Venerable Master himself."

"Trust, dear Ehrid, they are so comfortable in power that the opposition of one such as I simply does not occur to them. Even should old Red Mask suspect any treachery, I am more adept and longer studied than he is. Settle your fears."

"I have been wrapped in your web too long to have those fears. But I fear losing use of my guard in a half blind ghadi hunt. What phantoms do they chase nowadays?"

The plain-masked acolyte shook his head. "Do not dismiss the College's phantoms lightly, Master Ehrid."

Ehrid frowned and walked past the acolyte and leaned on the railing overlooking the ocean. Below him, half of Manhome sprawled and spilled over itself, crowding the plateau beneath Ehrid's feet. "I have seen much lost because the College fears the invisible. I believe in threats I can touch and see. But the College will go to the World's End to capture a thought, a myth, a dream. How should my guards arrest a dream?"

"I know what they seek, and I suspect it should be more tangible than a dream."

"What should the Monarch have me do, then?"

"Do as the College bids you. But, of course, inform me of anything your guard might find on their behalf."

"What do you expect us to find?"

"Perhaps nothing. Perhaps something."

Chapter Two

S OMEONE was stalking Nate Black.

What do you do now? Nate thought while he stared at the flickering screen. The apartment was dark, his roommate asleep. The only sounds were the soft whir of the trio of fans on Nate's over-clocked Athalon PC, the sound of Chuck snoring to himself deep in the bowels of the apartment, and the soft purr of Tux curled up in Nate's lap.

It was three-thirty in the morning, and the windows were all dark, except the one window facing the street. From that window came the sterile mercury glow of a streetlight.

Nate read the e-mail for the tenth or fifteenth time.
Subject: warning
Date: Thu, 10 Oct 2002 00:00:00 -0400 (EDT)
From: @
To: Nate Black <nb4@po.cwru.edu>
    they know azrael, take the road that is offered.
A single one-line message.

Nate's hands shook, and he rubbed his temples. *It's been over six years . . .*

Tux stretched and let out a feline yawn before snuggling deeper into Nate's lap.

"Mind games, it's only fucking mind games."

Nate carefully looked at the header of the message, to assure himself that, like the last two, it had no header information at all. Nothing.

@ was good at covering his tracks. Not only did he

delete everything but the cryptic "@" sign from his return address—no grand achievement, any idiot could spoof the From: line in an e-mail—but he also methodically erased *all* the header information. That was scary. It also shouldn't have been possible. The only way Nate could imagine someone eliminating *all* the routing information from an e-mail would be to hack the mail server at Case and write the message directly in Nate's inbox.

That meant that either @ was a good hacker in his own right, which did not reassure Nate. Or @ was on the Case Western IS staff, which would probably be worse.

Nate was very careful to delete the message from his machine. Then he telnetted to the mail server, and checked to make sure that it had been erased from there as well. Just having the name, Azrael, on his hard drive—*anyone's* hard drive—made Nate nervous.

Azrael had done stupid, dangerous things and hadn't been caught. Even though Azrael had ceased to exist six years ago, getting caught was the thing that Nate was most afraid of.

He shut down the computer. Firewall or not, he wasn't leaving his box up on a live DSL connection unsupervised, not with @ out there.

"Mind games," Nate whispered to Tux.

Chuck was still snoring in the back somewhere.

He shooed Tux off his lap and walked over to the kitchen. He opened the fridge and stared inside. On his shelf was a two-liter bottle of Mountain Dew, rye bread, cold cuts, and a box of Velveeta. On Chuck's shelf was a 12-pack of Budweiser, a bottle of Heineken, a six-pack of Zima, and a paper bag from Taco Bell.

Nate grabbed the Heineken. He didn't drink, but for once he felt he needed one. Besides, Chuck still owed him a five spot for the gas bill.

Since the bulb was out in the kitchen, Nate held the

fridge open with his foot so he had light to hunt down a bottle opener.

He walked out into the living room and sat down on the couch, under the glare of the streetlight. He popped the top off the beer and it bounced off his knee to rattle on the hardwood floor. Tux shot by him, chasing after the bottle cap as if it was suddenly the most urgent thing in his life.

Nate took a long pull from the bottle, then he held it up against his forehead.

"What do you do?" he asked no one. "What do you do when someone is after you and you can't call the cops?"

Damn @.

Damn Azrael.

• • •

"I'm fine, Mom," Nate lied. He shouldered the phone to his ear as he pulled on a pair of black jeans.

"I just haven't heard from you all week."

"I'm in the middle of midterms, you know that."

Nate rummaged in the pile of clothes next to his bed and pulled out a red T-shirt that looked the least grungy. It advertised a local band called "The Electric Flaming Jesus Baby." The initials E.F.J.B. hovered over a Derek Hess rendering of a burning nativity scene.

"You're still planning on coming home for Thanksgiving?"

"Yeah." He wanted to get off the phone, but he didn't want to let on that he had anything on his mind other than midterms.

Mom, you know all those years you were worried that I spent too much time in my room? Well, you see, I was committing a whole host of felonies, some of which might carry a twenty-to-life sentence since they rewrote the rules after 9/11.

"How's Sis?" Nate said, desperately changing the subject.

"Oh, Natalie just got acceptance letters back from Antioch and Oberlin. She's so excited. . . ."

Nate nodded and made appropriate monosyllabic noises as he listened to his sister's academic progress. There was a surreal element to it. The six-year gulf between them had seemed vast all his life, and now it struck him that some of the girls he'd dated recently were only a year older than Natalie, at most.

That realization actually made him feel farther away from home.

"She'll be there, right?"

"Where?"

"Thanksgiving dinner."

"Of course? Why wouldn't she be there?"

"She's eighteen now, she might have made other plans."

"Are you sure you're okay?"

"Sure I am, Mom. I got to get to class, though. Love you."

"Love you, too. Are—"

"Bye, Mom."

"Bye."

Nate hung up half convinced that his mother knew all about Azrael.

• • •

Azrael was dead, six years dead.

Nate kept telling himself that.

He had methodically erased all his own records of Azrael, down to formatting and overwriting all his hard drives—twice—as well as shredding and burning the hard copy associated with his alter ego. Nate even hacked on to the ISPs where Azrael kept accounts, deleting all record of the handle. He had delved into archives, trying to erase any messages that had him as a sender or recipient.

Nate had killed Azrael three months before his eighteenth birthday, when it had finally sunk in exactly how much prison time he could face if he was ever charged with the shit Azrael had done.

No one had ever known that Azrael was Nathaniel Black.

Even when Nate was young and reckless, he had more sense than to allow Azrael to divulge his real name to anyone, however trustworthy. No one in the small hacker community knew Azrael was a sixteen-year-old kid named Nate who was going to Shaker Heights High at the time.

All anyone knew was that Azrael had a road map to get root access to systems owned by folks from AT&T to the federal government. Azrael had modified the web sites of half a dozen foreign governments. Azrael had coded a virus that had made it on the national news. He had once even hacked Microsoft's own web server and replaced the link to customer service with the e-mail to the attorney general of the United States. You name it, Azrael had the bragging rights.

But Azrael was six years dead! No one should give a shit anymore.

Apparently @ did.

Nate was sitting on the arm of an overstuffed chair in the corner of the student lounge. He hunched over his PDA, prodding it with a matte-black brushed-metal stylus. He brushed unruly strands of hair away from his eyes as he stared at the little glowing screen.

What do I think I'm doing?

The little device in his hand was Internet-enabled, and he had just downloaded his e-mail. That had been a mistake.

The new message from "@" had the subject "Last Warning."

Don't open it. Mind games. He's fucking with your head.

"Hey, man? You all right?"

The voice jarred Nate. He looked up from his PDA to see someone he barely recognized from his networking class. Nate looked at the guy's buzz cut and thick glasses and couldn't remember his name. For a long paranoid moment, Nate felt the pulse hammering in his neck and wondered, *Is this guy @?*

After a moment he shook his head. "No. I'm fine." He said it a little too sharply, driving home the fact he wanted to be alone.

"Sorry, you just looked a little—" The guy backed off when he saw Nate's expression. "Right, none of my business. See you in class."

Sam, his name's Sam. As he turned to go, Nate called after him. "Hey, Sam?"

"What?" He turned around. He looked more clean-cut than Nate had ever attempted. Button-down shirt, slacks, loafers . . .

"You ever commit a felony?"

"What?"

"You know, a felony. Something so serious that if you got caught we're talking ten to twenty years."

"Hell, no."

"Come on," Nate said. "Never sold drugs, boosted a car, broke into a house—"

"You're kidding, right?"

"What about hacking? Ever been in a mainframe you shouldn't've been in? Fiddle with a virus?"

"Look, I'll see you in class, Nate. Please don't get weird around me." Sam turned and left Nate alone in the lounge.

It was less than a minute to class, and Nate hadn't opened the e-mail yet. He clicked on the header and watched the message window open. Just two sentences in @'s pithy style.

"They're coming for Azrael. Take the road when it is offered."

"What the fuck do you want?" Nate cursed at the screen.

The first message from @, six days ago, had said, "They shall know Azrael's name."

That one sentence put Nate in a panic. He almost hopped a Greyhound right there. But he had a life, a family, and an education that had him ten grand in debt. He couldn't just disappear, no matter how scared he was.

So he walked through the next day, verging on

panic. But there hadn't been any knocks on the door, no dark limos had slowed down to drag him inside—

But the messages kept coming.

He almost thought @ was taking out some sort of revenge. Nate told himself that he was falling into @'s trap by letting the mind game get to him. If the Feds actually had anything on him, they would have nabbed him long before now. There was a difference between suspecting that Nate Black was the late Azrael, and *proving* it. Nate knew for a fact that there was no physical evidence connecting him to Azrael.

That line of thought did as much good for his peace of mind as it had when he opened the last five messages. In other words, no good at all.

There were other possibilities.

Blackmail for one. Nate had precious little in the way of assets, but he still had a wealth of information buried in his head, things Azrael knew that Nate Black shouldn't. . . .

But there was another, more frightening, possibility.

What if these were legitimate warnings from a fellow hacker?

The nightmare scenario had the FBI, Secret Service, CIA or someone, arresting some schmuck from six years ago who hadn't learned Azrael's lesson and had gone on with the "black hat" hacking past the time where his luck ran out. A schmuck who had known Azrael back in the day. A schmuck who'd known enough to connect Azrael to Nate.

It would take time; the schmuck and the Feds negotiating their deals; the Feds checking the schmuck's background details to assure themselves that if they pleaded this fish it would hook them a bigger one.

Nate stood up and shakily put his PDA in his pocket. "I'm freaking *myself* out." He looked up at the clock on the wall of the lounge and saw it was ten after one. "And late for class."

Nate shouldered his backpack, left the lounge, and started walking down the corridor toward his networking class.

It wasn't fair. He'd been a "white hat" for six years. He shouldn't have to spend every waking moment worrying about ancient history.

The halls felt eerily empty to him. The squeak of his boots on linoleum was too loud and echoey. His breath tasted of copper, and he felt his pulse in his neck.

He was thin and wiry, high-strung at the best of times. More than one past girlfriend had compared his body—not his face, thank God—to Iggy Pop. Right now his body was tense and trembling, as if someone had taken pure caffeine and had injected it directly into his hypothalamus.

When he passed a classroom, he had the urge to thrust the door open and yell at them, *"Yes, I was Azrael, damn it! I did things that would make you never trust your social security number again!"*

It was almost a relief when he turned the corner and saw a guy in a cheap suit standing outside the door to his classroom. He didn't even slow his steps at first. All he could think of was how mundane the guy looked. Just a rumpled brown suit. Not even a pair of shades, or an earphone . . .

The guy turned to look at Nate, and for a moment Nate thought that he might be wrong. This guy could be here for something completely different. He might not be a Fed, or even a cop.

A blare of incomprehensible static echoed through the hallway and the guy raised a walkie-talkie to his mouth, taking a step toward Nate.

That was more than enough to get Nate to turn tail and run away as fast as he could.

All the adrenaline that had accumulated since @'s last warning let loose in a single spastic jerk. He spun around so fast that his boots nearly slid out from under him. He slammed into the corner and started running back the way he had come.

He tried to tell himself that this was insane. The guy couldn't be a cop waiting there for him. Not *now*.

But Nate was close enough to hear the words the

guy was shouting into the walkie-talkie, "—pursuit of Caucasian suspect, six feet, one sixty, brown hair, brown leather jacket, black denim jeans, red T-shirt—"

Where the hell was he running? It was over now. Even if he got away. They would have his apartment. He couldn't use an ATM or a credit card without letting them know where he was. He couldn't go home to his parents. He should give up now, take what was coming. It would be what? Ten years a prisoner against a life as a fugitive. . . .

And what would his life be like after that?

He kept running.

Nate slammed his way into a stairway and looked behind him. Brown suit was right on his heels, less than ten feet away. Nate swung his backpack behind him, at the guy's feet. The suit tried to jump it, but he got a foot tangled in a shoulder strap. Nate turned his head away when he saw the guy falling. He heard him plow face first into the linoleum as the stairway door hissed shut behind him.

Nate headed up, because that wouldn't be the way they'd expect him to run.

Only because it's idiotic not to head for an exit right now.

Nate couldn't fool himself. The cops probably had the exits pretty well covered right now. Paranoia gripped him. He *knew* they'd have a helicopter watching the escape routes. The Feds would be here. Any moment now they'd start lobbing tear gas at him.

Two floors up, he slammed though the door.

"It was just one guy." Nate said, panting. "He's spitting teeth out on the second floor. You're away . . ."

Right.

If there weren't dozens of cops here now, there would be in three minutes. And if anyone knew anything about what they were doing, every guy on campus security was converging on this building.

And on top of everything else, they had him on

assault of a police officer. They weren't going to be gentle when they caught up with him.

His thoughts were running as wild and spastic as he was. He turned corners on the corridors, heading toward the opposite end of the building, and the exits farthest from the guy in the brown suit.

His feet pounded along the corridor. His breath burned as he sucked in lungful after lungful of air. His head and his side throbbed in time to his machine-gun pulse.

Uncontrolled and frantic, he couldn't quite stop when the world went black.

One moment he was running down the hall, the stairway and the glowing red exit sign tantalizingly within reach—then it all was gone. Classrooms, exit sign, fluorescent lights, linoleum. Everything was replaced by a flat unbroken blackness as if he was suddenly struck completely blind.

The shock made him lock his legs, but momentum carried him forward to fall . . .

And fall.

And fall.

Eventually he stopped falling. At least, it seemed as if he stopped falling. There was no impact. No *ground* as far as he could tell.

Oh, my God, something's just gone seriously wrong in my brain.

He could picture it all too well—a vein balloon swelling between pieces of thinking meat, waiting for the stress of the moment to blow like a hand grenade buried in a cow's dead carcass. Tearing away vision, touch, even the sense that there was a world around him . . .

For a few moments he kept hyperventilating and his pulse raced even faster. By increments he calmed down, his gasping breath slowing, pulse easing.

There was absolutely no sense of motion, no breeze, no sense of where up or down might.be. He could move his arms and legs freely; they met no resistance, no ground or wall. It was almost as if he floated in water, but his breathing was unaffected. He touched his body with his hands and everything seemed intact, including his sense of touch. He sat up, though in this strange void he couldn't tell if it was his head and shoulders, or his legs that actually moved.

"What the hell's happening to me?" he whispered into the darkness. The words were flat and perfectly audible.

He reached down and pressed the light on his digital watch.

He could see the milky green glow of the watch's face. It read one-fifteen. Beyond where the glow touched his hands and wrist, the world was darkness.

From out of the void came a voice. Deep and wet, the tone was ugly and disturbing, unclean in a way that Nate couldn't name.

"Azrael. It is time."

CHAPTER THREE

IT WAS THE first time that Nate had ever heard anyone call him by that name. It made his bowels shrink and become water.

"Who are you?" Nate yelled into the darkness at the voice. The sound seemed to die as it left his mouth, to vanish without an echo.

Something had changed in the darkness around him. It wasn't a void any longer, there was a thick sense of presence around him, as if he might reach out a hand and feel slick skin and undulating flesh. He felt as if any moment something heavy and damp might wrap around his throat, strangling him.

"Which road?" The words were heavy, cloying, and came from organs that were not meant for human speech.

They're coming for Azrael. Take the road when it is offered.

The darkness resolved into something. Two somethings. Nate started to have a sense of direction again, of up and down, left and right. Behind him, he could dimly see a corridor in the classroom building. In front of him was what might have been a hill or a lawn, backed with blue sky. Both views seemed incredibly distant. At the same time they felt intense enough that he need only reach out to one or the other to touch it.

"Choose."

The sense of alien presence was overwhelming on

all sides, as if cascades of rippling flesh were about to engulf him.

A searing anger gripped Nate. This *thing,* this invisible alien meat, it had to be @. This *thing* whether it was real, or some brain-damage induced distortion of what was really out there, was the source of the e-mails. *Take the road when it is offered. . . .*

It *was* blackmail.

The corridor swelled in his peripheral vision, and when he looked directly at it, it seemed to grow, as if he was falling toward it. *Don't buy into it. It's pushing you. Go back. Take the evil you know.*

"Choose."

The presence was upon him with a sense of imminent suffocation. Nate's pulse was racing again, thoughts firing a mile a minute. He had to take some concrete action *now* or this thing around him would envelop him, absorb him, take him apart from the mind outward.

"Choose."

All he had to do was reach out and touch. He knew his hand would touch cold linoleum. He would be back where things made sense . . .

. . . and where cops waited to put him away for ten or twenty years.

"CHOOSE!"

Nate reached out, but in the impulsive way he acted when panicked, he put his hand backward, away from the corridor—

It touched grass.

Sunlight blinded him as a sense of normalcy returned to the space around him. There was ground beneath him, and sky above him. He lay on his back, his arm thrown backward above his head.

He sank his fingers into the dirt, and stared up at the clouds above him.

"Some sort of stressed-out nightmare," he whispered to himself. He thought of several possible scenarios. Making his escape outside, and being so strung out that he fainted. The blackness, and the alien presence, just some paranoid dream—one intense enough that it wiped out the memory of him collapsing here in the grass.

Maybe the e-mail, and the cop outside his classroom, were part of that same dream. That would be a relief, though Nate thought *that* might be too good to be true. . . .

Of course, that left open the question, where was he?

He sucked in deep breaths, calming himself, staring at the clouds sliding over the intense blue above him. There were no sounds of traffic or people, just the wind rustling the grass around him, and the sound of water nearby. His peripheral vision was blocked on his left by the slope of the ground, and on his right by an old black stump covered in shelf fungus.

Somewhere a bird let out a piercing call.

This wasn't anywhere on the Case campus by University Circle.

Did I drive myself somewhere in the Metroparks and forget about it? Did I get mugged in the Cultural Gardens?

The initial relief of finding himself in this quiet spot, not surrounded by Feds, gave way to unease. The idea that he traveled here with no memory was almost as disturbing as the thought that the alien presence in the darkness was real.

He stood up and felt a cold, salty wind bite into him. When he looked down at his feet, he froze.

Less than three feet away from him, the ground fell away. If he bent over, he found himself looking down a cliff of black rock that descended a hundred feet, maybe more. At the foot of the cliff, gray-green surf crashed against boulders the size of small houses.

"My God," Nate whispered, taking a step back.

He looked to where the water met the horizon. It didn't seem like Lake Erie. No sailboats, no buoys, and the waves crashing on the rocks carried no more than seaweed and driftwood. Not so much as a single floating beer can.

Nate stared at the water a long time. He had been to the East Coast twice, and he could smell the salt—almost taste it. Wrong. He had to be wrong. He was hundreds of miles from the ocean.

The surf crashed with enough force to send spray as high as he was. Nate stumbled back from the precipice, looking behind himself to keep from tumbling over the stump.

Behind him were mossy hills resembling a crumpled sheet of paper that wouldn't lie quite flat. The occasional twisted tree clung to the rocks, only gathering into something that could be called woods in the far distance.

Beyond that, mountains hovered over the landscape. They were far enough away, and rose high enough into the sky, that the snow on their flanks took on the bluish cast of unmoving clouds.

"What the hell happened?" Nate couldn't dismiss what had happened as a nightmare—if he ever believed that explanation in the first place.

"Where am I?"

He stared at the mountains facing him.

He had never experienced blackouts or hallucinations before. But he didn't know what to believe. Moments ago, he was thousands of miles away from any terrain like this. And the mountains were undoubtedly there, like the salt spray sticking to his skin.

Am I hallucinating now?

Nate felt his skull, prodding for the head wound that would explain his blackout and the landscape in front of him. His scalp was untouched and the only pain in his head was the cognitive whiplash of finding himself in a place so far removed from where he had been.

Nate looked at his watch. Etched into the LCD display was the time. One-fifteen. The display was odd, cracked, and he noticed that it wasn't flashing anymore. He tried the button for the date, and nothing happened.

The plastic case was warm, and the metal buttons were actually hot.

"Christ, the time is *burned* in."

His watch was dead, victim to what looked like a massive power surge.

"Holy Fuck!" Nate pulled his PDA out of the pocket of his jacket. He dropped it immediately. The case was too hot to touch. It fell screen up on the ground in front of him. The screen was a burned rainbow, and a wisp of smoke trailed up from it.

Nate knelt, shaking his head. The damn thing had been top of the line, close to five hundred dollars. His gigabyte, Internet-enabled, custom-hacked operating system PDA had been rendered a static art object. All his contacts, class lists, MP3s . . .

It took a moment before reason set in. *My man, you have worse problems than a dead PDA.*

Nate checked his cell phone, and it was dead, too, and it smelled funny. He looked up, realizing how isolated he was. He couldn't remember the last time he wasn't in reach of a cell phone, a text pager, or e-mail. He had no way of telling anyone where he was. Though his equipment all seemed dead, he stowed the PDA and cell phone back in his pockets.

I still don't know where here *actually is.*

Nate looked around for signs of civilization.

He found them.

He saw an old multilevel bridge spanning some deep wrinkles in the terrain; a huge brick and stone arch that supported a series of smaller arches above it. Nate started walking in that direction and realized that there was something wrong with the bridge.

First, it was too narrow to support any traffic. And the ends of the bridge didn't feed into a roadway that Nate could see. Instead, it fed into a half buried brick tube that resembled a turn-of-the-century sewer that hadn't been completely covered.

"An aqueduct," Nate whispered.

No, I can't be looking at a Roman artifact. That would mean I'm somewhere in Europe. That can't be right. No way.

The aqueduct ran in an almost straight line from the mountain range, past him about a mile and a half away, toward what looked to be a coastal city a few more miles away.

Nate's relief at seeing civilization ended when he climbed up a hill that gave him an unobstructed view of the aqueduct's destination.

"Oh, shit, I *am* hallucinating."

The city wasn't *on* the coast. It was actually *beyond* the coast.

The aqueduct launched itself off of the mainland from a cliff as tall and sheer—if not taller—as the one by Nate. It arched over the surf with a spidery grace that seemed impossible with stone and brick. The terminus of the aqueduct was a promontory crag, a gigantic stone three miles across, thrusting up from the surf a quarter mile from the mainland.

The city was on that rock.

No, the city is that rock.

Halfway up from the crashing surf, the sides of the rock smoothed to blend with brick and stone walls, fortresses and towers. Buildings of gray stone and white plaster almost spilled over each other, crowding for room.

The aqueduct fed into the city at a level that seemed to be the top of the rock, though the buildings covered it so densely that it wasn't possible to see where the original rock had ended.

The wind was getting colder, and he zipped up the front of his jacket. His breath fogged in the air before him. The air was bracing and smelled of sea and grass. For a moment he believed that he was looking at a ruin, some medieval city . . .

But he could see smoke rising from various places, and on balconies and roads he could see movement, the people so far away they were little more than specks.

The place was inhabited.

Nate had to stare a long time before he could figure out how to get to the city. Barely visible at this distance was a road carved in the flanks of the rock. It spiraled around the crag at least once, feeding into the city somewhere out of Nate's sight. At the base of the rock, the road unspiraled across a tiny peninsula connecting the rock to the mainland.

It appeared in constant danger of being swamped by the surf, but it was the only obvious destination he had.

"Look on the bright side," Nate said. "Maybe this place doesn't have any extradition treaties with the US."

Even as he said it, the reasonable part of his brain kicked in. He wasn't meant to be a fugitive. He didn't want to chuck everything to avoid Azrael's sordid history. Hell, the only crime he had ever committed as an adult was that panicked escape from the Fed. He could probably plead that if he accepted the charges on Azrael.

Realistically, what could they do? He'd been a juvenile, and the current law wasn't even in effect back then. Hell, if he'd been smart, he would have turned himself in when he got the first of @'s messages. Now he had an assault and resisting arrest rap, and God only knew where he was.

Mom must be worried sick.

Damn @ for pushing his buttons, Nate was smarter than this.

He looked at his watch again. Still 1:15. *Well, we know that I was out for a lot longer than fifteen minutes. . . .*

Don't we?

As he walked toward the aqueduct, he saw more signs of human habitation. Long, low stone walls broke up parts of the wrinkled terrain around him. He cleared one rise and had to climb over one. The wall was a pile of black and gray stones, stacked without mortar. The soil was rocky around here, the evidence of the walls said that it was, at one time, much worse.

On the other side of the wall he faced a tangled

mat of vines. At first he thought it was some rampant weed, but after walking a few feet he could see that the vines emerged from the black soil at regular intervals. The vines also bore some sort of fruit, a green fleshy thing shaped like an eggplant but ribbed like a pumpkin. He bent and rapped his knuckle on one. It made a solid thump.

Some sort of squash, Nate thought.

He walked through the vine patch, and saw a number of other types of plants, none familiar.

The aqueduct was larger and farther away than he first thought. He made his way across two more stone walls and three more fields of obscure vegetation before he reached its side.

Here the aqueduct itself was at ground level. It faced him as a brick wall, slowly curving away from him to reach its apex about twenty feet above his head. He could hear the water within as a nearly subliminal rumble. He placed his hand on the wall. The stone was cool and damp.

A few feet down, toward the city, Nate saw a plaque. He walked up, hoping for some clue to where he was. He was hoping that he'd at least be able to recognize the language.

The words—if that was what they were—were completely alien to him. There was some resemblance to Arabic, the way the "letters" seemed to flow into each other, but the strokes of each character were orthogonal in a way that resembled Hebrew, and there were flourishes that joined distant characters to each other that didn't resemble any language that Nate had ever seen.

He stared at the plaque. Bronze gone to green, attached to the wall with four square-headed bolts. The embossed text covered its surface in lines not quite wider than Nate's thumb. He traced the text with his fingers.

Indian maybe? Some other Asian language? South and Southeast Asia had hundreds, if not thousands, of languages with alphabets to match. The only one he'd have a hope of identifying by sight would be Chinese.

"Great." The whisper came out in fog that left a ghost of condensation on the surface of the metal plaque. However he'd gotten here, "here" was looking to be a bit farther away than he'd ever choose to run.

There was a narrow gravel pathway that hugged the side of the aqueduct. Ahead of him, he saw the path dip down one of the folds in the ground. The aqueduct bridged the small valley with a single stone arch. Nate headed for it, the closest route past the aqueduct.

The path cut into the hillside diagonally away from the aqueduct, joining a broad road that cut between the two hills, snaking under the arch of the bridge like a river of gray stone. As he walked out onto the main path, he stepped in a pile of brown manure.

"Ugh." Nate scraped his boot on one of the larger stones that marked the edges of the roadway. What he thought was mud or dirt on the path turned out to be a minefield of horse droppings. He also saw hoofprints scuffing the gravel surface.

At this point he would have felt more comfortable seeing tire tracks.

As he stood there, scraping horseshit off his boot, the magnitude of his problems were starting to sink in. If he was really stranded in some faraway foreign country, communication was just the first of his problems. What if the local gendarmes decided to object to his lack of a passport? What if he was stuck somewhere *really* nasty—like North Korea? Even China wouldn't be too hot for a US citizen without a visa. There was a laundry list of countries who'd make a tour with the Feds look as unpleasant as a boring undergrad calc class.

It wasn't a pretty picture.

That thought was almost enough to make him retrace his steps, steal a squash, and head directly away from the city.

"Get a grip, if they don't have an American embassy, they might have a Canadian one, or a British one—"

Nate trailed off. He heard hoofbeats approaching.

Chapter Four

Π ATE TURNED toward the sound. He couldn't see the approaching horse yet. The path in that direction curved around the hillside under the aqueduct. He stood still, pulse racing in his neck. He wasn't ready to meet the locals.

He had less than a second, not enough time to decide to run for cover. Barely enough time to step to the side before the brown head of a draft horse appeared around the curve. The animal was taller than Nate's head at the shoulders. Its eyes looked down from a height of seven feet.

A black, complicated-looking harness wrapped around the animal's neck, connecting to a flatbed wagon with high wood walls. Between the horse and the body of the wagon, an old man sat on a spartan bench, gripping the reins.

The horse saw him before the driver did. It slowed and veered away from Nate. Then the old man noticed him, and the wagon came to a stop.

Welcome to Butt-Fuck Egypt, Nate thought.

Nate and Grandpa stared at each other for what seemed to be a long time. Grandpa's appearance seemed to confirm that Nate was in some part of Asia. His eyes, at least, were almond-shaped. His skin, however, was very dark. East Indian or African dark. He was bald, and had full gray facial hair that fell down to his chest.

After a moment, Nate decided that it was up to him

to break the ice. He smiled, raised his hands, and said, "Hello? You wouldn't happen to speak English, would you?"

Grandpa shouted something in a harsh, guttural language that reminded Nate of German, or Arabic, though he doubted it was either. Whatever the guy said, it didn't sound friendly.

If at first you don't succeed. "Look, I'm lost here—" Nate kept talking, even though the guy wasn't understanding a word. He hoped his tone of voice and his body language would calm Grandpa down, maybe convince him to help the stranger out. "I don't know where I am. I'm an American. I need food, lodging, maybe a telephone?"

Grandpa started repeating himself. He sounded agitated.

Nate raised his hands and took a few steps toward the wagon.

That proved to be a mistake.

Grandpa's shouting became shrill and he turned in his seat and started slamming his fist up against the wall of the wagon behind him. The man seemed to be on the verge of panic.

Nate lowered his hands and backed away, but it was too late to try to do anything to calm down the situation. The reins cracked and the horse almost leaped over Nate as it shot ahead faster than something that size should be able to go. Nate stumbled back out of its way and watched the wagon pass him.

There was a gate hanging open, banging against the rear of the wagon. The back was half loaded with bushels of green and red vegetable matter, some of which was tumbling out of the back.

Great first impression.

He turned to continue on the way he'd been going, and stopped.

Three very young, very large men were blocking his path. They all must have come off of the back of the wagon. The trio were all shirtless and wore black, mud-spattered, canvas pants. They all resembled the old man, dark skin, semi-Asian features, and straight—in their case black—hair.

Most immediately important, they all held long poles tipped with wicked-looking metal blades and looked at Nate with expressions showing that they didn't like what they saw.

"Hold on," Nate said. "If I'm trespassing, I can leave . . ."

They started moving forward.

"Look I'm sure we can come to some sort of under— Fuck it." Nate turned and ran.

Suddenly it was very apparent, to his body at least, that it had not been very long since he'd left the corridors at Case. His muscles objected to the sudden exertion, and his side cramped badly. He heard a shout from behind him, in that same guttural language, and before he had an opportunity to trip and fall on his own, something large and heavy fell across the back of his head.

Nate never quite lost consciousness, but the blow stunned him. He slammed into the ground, the impact taking the breath out of him. More blows landed on his back and kidneys, forcing him into a fetal position.

They pulled his arms out behind him, painfully bent backward, and thrust a wooden stick between his body and his elbows. They tied his wrists behind him with a rough hemp rope. They pulled the rope between his legs and tied it around his neck so he couldn't straighten his back.

He lay there for what seemed like hours, feeling the blood rush through his skull and feeling the burning throb from his kidneys and the bruises across his back. Occasionally a muscle spasm would cause him to straighten himself, and the rope around his neck would attempt to strangle him.

After some time, he heard the wagon return. They tied the stick to the back of the wagon and force marched him back toward the city. Nate had to concentrate on staying upright, keeping his view confined to a narrow strip of road in front of his feet.

Every few minutes he would wonder, *Why are they doing this to me?* But the question fell to the necessity of placing one foot in front of the other quickly enough that the wagon wouldn't pull him over.

The nightmare seemed to last forever. He kept time by muttering profanities. His captors ignored them. His curses became more and more elaborate as time went on.

Nate was in the middle of calling the quartet a bunch of "inbred, shit-kicking, pig-fucking Tibetan hillbillies" when the wagon stopped.

For a few panicked moments Nate thought he must have discovered a few English words these assholes actually knew. But after they stopped, Nate began to hear an unfamiliar voice. He raised his head slightly— not enough to have the rope tighten on his neck—and stared through the strands of sweat-matted hair that had fallen over his forehead.

Grandpa had come down from his perch on the wagon. He faced someone who belonged more at a Renaissance faire than some Third World Asian plateau. The new man was dressed in black, with a doublet that fit tightly to the chest and gut, closed by brass buttons the size of quarters. A scarlet cape was draped over his shoulders, held in place by a heavy brass chain connecting a pair of medallions embossed with an intricate pattern. On his head he wore a brimless hat that was little more than a tapered black cylinder adorned with feathers.

The clothing ended all of Nate's speculation about where he might be. He couldn't make that outfit fit into any reasonable scenario.

Grandpa was acting deferential to him, and the three younger men stood back, silent, not looking at the bizarrely-dressed gentleman. It took a moment for it to sink in—

Grandpa is acting like the cops just pulled him over.

Nate looked at the new guy more closely. He was armed. While he talked to the old man, one gloved hand rested on a sword that hung from a broad belt that rested on his hips. Nate also noticed a pair of tasseled cords that hung from his left shoulder across the left side of his chest. One was silver, the other gold. It looked like some indication of rank.

Grandpa made a few gestures in Nate's direction, and it became obvious that Nate was the topic of conversation.

Nate tried to imagine what it was they were saying to each other.

"It's like this Officer . . ."

"Uh-huh."

"This nut jumped out of the bushes and attacked my wagon—"

"Attacked you, huh?"

"He's a madman!"

"Looks mighty fierce, Gramps."

"If it wasn't for Larry, Curly, and Moe here—"

"Yeah, yeah, you didn't have a choice."

Grandpa finally made a derisive sound and spat on the ground. The officer shook his head as if he couldn't believe the yokels. The quartet of farm folk stood back as the officer stepped toward Nate. The officer reached out a gloved hand and lifted Nate's chin so they were eye to eye. The rope cut into Nate's neck as the officer said something in his guttural language that might have been a question.

"I guess it would be too much to expect for you to understand English?" Nate asked back, his voice wheezing against the rope.

The officer stared at him. His features were of a kind with the farmer's. Dark skin, vaguely Asian features. In his case, however, his hair and beard were meticulously trimmed, and had some curl to it.

The officer said something else which gave Nate the opportunity to observe that the man's teeth were in a lot better shape than Grandpa's, or Larry's, Curly's and Moe's for that matter. The color was yellowish brown, but they all seemed to be there. The guy's breath was another story; it made Nate's eyes water.

The officer turned toward Grandpa and shouted

something to him. Gramps stared back, glaring at Nate, then said something to Larry, Curly, and Moe.

Moe walked up and untied the rope from the wagon.

Thank God, Nate thought. For about a minute Nate allowed himself to believe that this ordeal was over.

The officer walked back over to Grandpa and the two had a short, heated exchange, at the end of which the officer reached into a pouch hanging from his belt and withdrew a pair of coins. He handed them to Grandpa, who looked at the offering with the distaste of a man who was hoping for a lot more. Gramps said something short and monosyllabic and waved dismissively in Nate's direction.

The officer walked back up to Nate, and withdrew a dagger from a sheath that was hidden by the folds of his cape. He said something in his guttural language, pointed at Nate, then at himself, then rested his free hand on the sword at his side.

It was pretty clear. Nate was this guy's responsibility now, and he wasn't going to take any shit from him. *Christ, did this fucker just buy me?*

The officer grabbed the rope at his neck and cut it free with the dagger. Nate straightened up, and the pole between his back and elbows fell free to clatter on the gravel roadway.

Grandpa was trying to look stoic and unflappable, but the noise made him jump back a bit. The bastard was still scared of him. They really didn't like foreigners here.

Nate stretched. His neck muscles felt as if they were on fire. He wanted to rub his neck, but his wrists were still bound behind him, and the officer made no move to cut that rope. As Nate rotated his neck, he noticed something that he hadn't realized until now. He was the tallest one here. He was barely six feet even, but he could stare down on Grandpa's bald pate, and he could look the officer here straight in the hat. He had six inches on all these guys, even Larry, Curly, and

Moe—though that trio made up for it in biceps and necks as thick as their heads.

The officer put away the dagger and picked up the free end of the rope, the end that had been tied around his neck. The other end still bound Nate's wrists. The officer looked at him with a bemused expression.

Gramps and company boarded the wagon and did a long slow turn around, back the way they had come. It was the first time Nate had gotten a chance to look around at where he was.

They were only a mile or so from the city. If Nate looked toward the ocean, a full two thirds of the horizon was filled by the architecture of the city, piled high on its rock overlooking the mainland. They stood on a road paved with cobbles that, a few hundred yards away, fed downward into a man-made valley toward the narrow peninsula that joined the city to the mainland.

Far away, to the right, the bridge of the aqueduct made its graceful leap from the top of a coastal cliff to the side of the city's craggy walls. The sky here was filled with the shadows of sea birds orbiting the city.

The officer said something and tugged on the rope.

Nate sighed and followed the man's lead. "Okay, my man, I'm with you now."

The officer shook his head and headed him to a narrow dirt track that headed away before the main road made its abrupt descent to the sea.

"Thanks for saving me from Gramps and the Stooges back there." Nate shook his hands so the rope swung a little between them. "Any chance of you finishing the job and cutting me free?"

The officer turned and said a few incomprehensible words. However, his expression and the way he shook his head made Nate think that the guy understood the gist of his question and that the answer was "No."

CHAPTER FIVE

★ ★ "YOU HAVE a problem with me entering the country without a visa, right?"

It was the latest in a long series of unanswered questions. The officer ignored Nate as he led him over another wrinkled hill. When they crested the hill, Nate saw a trio of men, all dressed similarly to the first officer, with black doublets and shorts that belonged in some art book on fifteenth century Germany. Unlike the officer, these guys didn't wear cloaks, or have gold cords on their breasts.

The three new officers stood up to greet them, shouting questions at the officer, who shouted back at them. For a few moments he was surrounded by curious eyes and hands.

"None of you guys ever see an American before?"

Nate was beginning to worry about these guys. They seemed fascinated by his clothing. That wasn't right. There shouldn't be anyone on the planet outside some Stone Age tribes in the rain forest that wasn't familiar with T-shirts or denim.

"Come on, you guys must know some English, right? I mean the United States dominates the world. Any of you understand, George Bush? CNN? Baseball? Michael Jackson? Levis?"

They didn't give him a single sign that they understood.

The first officer held Nate still while one of his men searched him. Nate was still trying vainly to spark some sign of recognition. "Marilyn Monroe, Marilyn Manson, David Hasselhoff, *Baywatch*, *Dallas*, *X-Files*, CIA, hamburger, blue jeans . . ." He kept rattling stream of consciousness at them. He found it hard to believe that there was anyone on the planet who didn't know a single English word.

While he babbled, they took his keys, his dead PDA and wristwatch, his wallet, and all his change. Everything went into a little sack. The guy emptying Nate's pockets gave everything barely a passing glance, but he seemed fascinated by the photos in Nate's wallet. He flipped through them until the officer said something sharp, reprimanding him. After that, everything went straight into the bag.

When it was over, the officer grabbed the black bag and walked Nate briskly to the top of the hill, where the others had been. The guy seemed pissed now, and Nate wondered why.

The officer tied the end of Nate's rope to a stout tree about fifteen yards away from the remains of a campfire. He checked Nate's hands, then turned to face the others. His crew looked disgruntled as the officer laid into them with what had to be one hell of a dressing-down. He gestured with the little bag and pointed at Nate a few times.

Nate began to worry about what was going to happen to him.

After the outburst, the quartet finally sat down. After a while they started chatting quietly among themselves, passing a wineskin shaped like one of the squash, ignoring Nate.

"Any of you figure on just letting me go with a warning?" Only the officer looked in his direction, and his expression wasn't pleasant. "Like you've had a worse day than I'm having?" Nate asked.

The officer shook his head and turned back to the others.

"Great," Nate tugged at the rope, but beyond a foot or so of slack, it wouldn't budge. "What are you bastards planning to do with me?"

Nate tugged, but only managed to get his hands to fall asleep. He leaned back on the tree.

Fortunately, the officer had tied the rope close to the ground, so Nate wasn't forced to stand. Nate bent his knees and half sat, half fell, onto a flat white rock near the base of the tree.

Nate sighed with relief, even though a concavity in the rock had gathered enough stagnant water to soak through the left cheek of his jeans. It didn't matter. His leg muscles were so tight that they were vibrating and his body ached from the exertion and abuse he had suffered over the past few hours. It was a godsend just to sit and rest.

"At least tell me where the hell I am."

Even if they had been able to understand him, they were making a point of ignoring him now.

What the hell am I going to do? None of this is making any sense.

Nate stopped trying to get their attention and started looking around, trying to fit this place in his personal catalog of the known.

It didn't work.

He now had time to think about what was happening, and that wasn't really a good thing. He couldn't come up with an explanation for anything that had happened. Not a sane, reasonable one, anyway. And, as someone who lived a good part of his life in his head, he did not want to blame everything on hallucination.

But what the hell else was @? Did he really think that thing in the darkness might exist outside his own skull? He might just buy that the traveling Renaissance faire in front of him was really there, but @?

Someone was sending those messages. . . .

You just remember *that someone sent you those messages. . . .*

"That line of thought isn't going to get me anywhere."

Nate shook his head and looked around the campsite. The officer and his men had chosen to camp out on a hillside overlooking the road to the city. The hillside was littered with white stones like the one Nate was sitting on. The site was some sort of ruin.

The white stones were uncharacteristic of the terrain, and formed a near circular pattern on top of the hill. Beyond the innermost circle, the stones were more randomly distributed, as if a tower had fallen long ago.

Nate looked at the stone he rested on. Might be limestone. Water had pooled within the depressions of a bas-relief so worn that Nate hadn't recognized it as a carving at first. He slid aside so he could look at it.

Any fine detail was long gone. Nate could discern smooth humanoid forms striking flat, two-dimensional poses reminiscent of ancient Egyptian carvings. However, to Nate's eye, there was something wrong with the people carved here, the proportions seemed elongated and misshapen, the heads stretched and flattened, and the joints knobby and swollen.

The figures in the carving seemed to be facing— worshiping? fighting? making offerings to? Nate couldn't tell from the weathered stone—some central object. The object at the carving's focus was where most of the water had collected. Nate wished his hands were free so he could brush some of the algae and leaves away and get a better look.

The central carving had fared worse than the people. Not only had it suffered weathering, to Nate it looked as if it had, at one time, been purposely defaced.

Even with large parts of it obscured or broken away, Nate could tell that it had been something constructed with organic curves, almost plantlike. Unlike the people, it had been carved with an eye for depth. Part of it might even have risen above the surface of the stone before it had been defaced. The outline reminded Nate, from various angles, of a complex knot, an insect, a flower, and an octopus. Stone tendrils and leaflike objects fed into a central area where damage had rendered the whole as little more than a broken lump of stone.

The carving retained some of its original impact simply in the contrast between the flattened people, and the three-dimensional focus. It was as if someone had dropped a photo-realistic Renaissance etching in the middle of a tenth century woodcut. A sphere visiting flatland.

It was another thing that didn't coincide with any place he knew about. He had never seen anything like this in a museum. Though, from the remains of the building this stone had been a part of, the people who'd carved it had probably long since stopped being relevant.

● ● ●

It was late in the afternoon before anyone deigned to take notice of him again. The shadows of the great city had just overtaken the small camp, when the officer and his men stood up, looking down toward the road. Nate followed their gaze and saw four men leave the road to start up the hillside.

Changing of the guard, Nate thought. He wondered what they were guarding against, and why there wasn't a permanent structure here for them. *Perhaps a recent conflict, or a rise in the crime rate? Maybe they haven't had time to build a guardhouse.* Though, as far as defending the city went, there was little anyone could see here on the hillside that wasn't visible from one of the towers that rose from the plateau.

There was a lot of handshaking between the two groups of guardsmen. They were all dressed similarly, but with slight variations to each outfit that suggested that the clothes were all handmade at different times by different people. The leader of the new group sported the double cord of Nate's own officer, though his were both silver.

The two leaders met by grasping each other's forearms, pulling together and quickly breaking away, almost a macho hug. Then Nate's officer faced the remaining three newcomers and slapped his left shoulder. It seemed to be a salute. The three men repeated the gesture.

Then the new guy looked toward Nate's tree and started asking questions. The conversation lasted quite a while.

At the end of it, the new officer took a good look at Nate, but didn't approach. He waved his hand, seeming to take in all the scattered white stones on the hillside, saying something that made everyone nod sagely, as if great wisdom had been spoken.

Nate's officer came toward him with dagger drawn while his men picked up various pieces of gear. It took a lot of effort for Nate not to cringe as the blade approached, and he still closed his eyes as the officer bent over him. Intellectually, Nate knew that if this guy was out to slit his throat, he could have done it any time within the last four or five hours, but he still—in his gut—expected to feel the steel bite his neck.

What it bit was the rope binding him to the tree.

The officer said something to him and gestured upward with the dagger. Nate got unsteadily to his feet, staggering somewhat without his arms to help him. The officer didn't move to assist him.

"Couldn't you at least tie my hands in front—"

The officer had turned around and shouted something back at his men. There was some laughter. The officer had to repeat himself, and the man who had looked in Nate's wallet stepped forward wearing a sullen expression.

The man approached and slapped his shoulder in a salute. Then the officer handed the man the severed end of the rope that still bound Nate's hands. Nate's new escort gave him a look of pure disgust.

Nate looked him in the eye and said, "So what did I do to you?"

The man actually stepped back and put a hand on his sword.

Okay, maybe it's time to shut up.

The quartet marched down the path that their relief crew had walked up. Nate took up the rear with his unenthusiastic escort. They came down to the cobbled main road, and started heading in toward the plateau city.

Nate couldn't help but stare at their destination. It loomed over them, blocking out more and more of the sky as they approached. The details were endless. Even on the patches of rock that at first looked like unworked stone, a second look revealed details that had to have been carved, and weathered by wind and surf. A lump of stone suddenly made itself appear as a column. A crack in the rock became a weathered alcove, a boulder resting in the surf actually was a gigantic stone block fallen from some ancient wall.

Nate looked down at his feet and saw that the cobbles that made up the road they walked upon contained fragments of old carving. The stone under his feet matched the ruins up on the hill.

They walked across the peninsula joining the rock to the mainland. The air was a constant salt mist down here, and the surf crashed so loudly that Nate's guards couldn't talk to each other over the sound.

A wooden cart drawn by a pair of ratty-looking mules slowly passed them. Another farmer, who could have been Grandpa's long lost twin brother, was slowly drawing a load of chickens up toward the city.

Nate looked up at the man.

Grandpa's twin saw Nate, and his eyes widened. The man quickly looked away and muttered something to himself.

"What the . . ."

A gloved hand backhanded the side of Nate's face. He turned, spitting blood, to see his new escort staring at him. He shouted something incomprehensible at Nate and looked pissed.

Okay, we don't spook the locals. I get it.

Nate wished his hands were free to probe his jaw to see if anything was loose. The FBI or the Secret

Service would definitely have been the better alternative.

The wide road they were on started on an upward slope, edging toward the right side of the massive rock. They were now too close for Nate to see the whole city. Most of it was too high up to see anything from this steep an angle.

They walked on, starting the spiral that circled the rock. On the left wall, where the rock face shot almost straight up, some long-ago sculptor had carved statuary into the rock. They passed every type of scene imaginable, romantic to violent, single people to massive crowds of activity. All had details worn away by ages of surf spray. And all seemed to have the same distorted proportions as the figures Nate had seen in the stone up on the hillside.

Many had been likewise defaced.

It wasn't until nearly the end of the forty-five-minute hike up the spiral road that Nate realized that the distortions of the sculpture were not simply artistic license.

As they walked up, they passed the occasional wagon heading downward. Many seemed to be farmers returning home, wagons empty, goods sold. But there were a few that seemed to be taking trade in the other direction. Those wagons were towed by teams of fresh looking animals, driven by men with finer dress and thicker guts than the farmers Nate had seen. These vehicles were covered and richly painted.

Near their ultimate destination, Nate saw a wagon that didn't fit into either of the two categories. The wagon was black, covered by a few silver highlights. The single gray mare drawing it was driven by a cadaverous man wearing a brown-hooded cloak. The only details Nate saw of the driver were long-fingered hands bearing several rings on each finger. As it passed, Nate looked backward, and saw into the rear of the open cart.

"Holy shit," Nate whispered. He stood frozen, star-

ing, until his escort backhanded him again. He stumbled on, not seeing much of anything anymore.

He could no longer put this place anywhere on the Earth he knew. The passengers in the back of that wagon were not human.

Even if Nate could ignore the elongated skulls with their fixed expressions, the oversized joints, their purplish skin . . . he couldn't ignore the fact that their arms and fingers had extraneous joints.

What rode in the back of the black wagon was alien. Were aliens. Aliens with the same body type illustrated in the defaced carvings.

Chapter Six

AFTER CIRCLING the rock twice, the great road fed into the plateau city on the side opposite the shore. The road widened until it reached a huge flat area that jutted out from the side of the rock.

Two large towers flanked the road where it fed into this plateau. A bridge connected the towers, high above the road, and Nate could see signs of some sort of mechanism that was designed to fall across the road blocking any passage.

Nate saw armed guards watching from up near the tops of the towers. Like his escort, the preferred colors seemed to be scarlet and black.

Past the guardian towers, and on to the area beyond, Nate saw at least half a dozen ways into the city itself. The flat area was roughly circular, half of it looking over the open ocean and the last blood-red glimmer of sunset, the other half butting up against the side of the plateau and fifty-foot walls that were now obviously man-made.

There were six more towers on the plateau side, built into the massive walls. Between the towers were doorways and portals leading inside. The largest gate filled the whole space between the two rightmost towers. Looking beyond, it seemed that it was a continuation of the great spiral road, now carving gradually into the plateau rather than hugging its side. Instead of blank sculptured walls to the left, beyond the gate Nate could see structures that could be storefronts or houses, piled over each other in a crowd for space.

While the plateau area outside the gates could accommodate hundreds, the only people here other than Nate and his escort were those with six carts queued up for the large gate. From the droppings on the stone beneath him, Nate figured this place was a lot more crowded during the day.

He naturally gravitated toward the largest gate, but he was corrected by a sharp tug on the rope binding his hands. He turned and the guy with the rope looked as if he was preparing to hit him again.

Nate tried to look nonthreatening and they headed to the leftmost gate, little more than an iron door set into the wall next to the plateau-side tower they had just passed on the way up. The officer leading them pulled on a chain that hung from a small hole in the wall above the door. Nate heard a distant bell ring.

They waited.

As the stars came out above them, the gates around them began closing. It started with the first gate, between the towers flanking the spiral road. A giant iron portcullis slid down from above, blocking the way they had come. Then, on the opposite side of the circular clearing, wooden gates closed behind the last of the wagons entering the city.

Nate watched as the other gates into the city closed themselves against the night. Nate noticed that with each gate closing, the space out here grew darker.

Soon, they stood in blue-black twilight, the only illumination the flicker of the stars and of tiny windows too high above them.

After what seemed like hours, the door in front of them creaked open. The light from a torch spilled flickering upon them as a man in crimson and black dress stepped out.

After a short conversation with the lead officer, the man stepped aside and let the five of them enter. The door led into a hallway that had been carved out of the rock. The walls were solid stone, polished smooth as concrete. The floor was stone as well, but a depression was worn down its center, stained green in places where water had collected. The air was thick and smelled of damp.

After about a hundred feet, the walls opened up into more traditional masonry, and the air became a little fresher.

Nate couldn't follow where they went after that, or exactly what was happening. They moved through a warren of corridors, past several checkpoints manned by the scarlet and black guards. The passages were gray and utilitarian, with little to distinguish them except the occasional sign written in the alien script Nate had seen on the aqueduct.

After what seemed like miles of sameness, they led him to a narrow staircase. This was the third one, and—like all of them—it took them downward. At this point, Nate felt that they must have walked halfway back down to sea level.

The stairs led them through a Gothic archway, and into a long chamber whose arched ceiling was supported by squat columns that bore writing in a script even more alien than the writing Nate had already seen.

Light came from iron candelabra that bore up under decades' worth of wax drippings. Two flanked the entrance, two more flanked a rectangular stone object that could have been a desk, an altar, or a sarcophagus. Behind it, a man stood at a wooden podium on which a large leather-bound book rested in an open position.

Unlike everyone else they had met so far, this man wasn't wearing the scarlet and black that Nate associated with the guardsmen. This man wore a plain brown robe, with a hood resting on his shoulders. A blue cord was wrapped around his waist. He looked like the driver of the black wagon that had passed them on the way up the side of the plateau.

He was also different, because the officer in charge, the man with the two gold braids, did not approach him, or even speak. Every time up to now, this guy, the man who had bought Nate from Grandpa, had acted like the man in charge. Everyone had shown the guy some sort of deference. He spoke first, and told the people what to do.

Not here. Here, the officer waited for the robed man to acknowledge him.

After a few minutes, at least a full minute beyond the point where he knew he had visitors, the robed man took out an elaborately-embroidered ribbon and laid it across his book. With the bookmark placed, he closed the book and turned to face his visitors.

The man was old, with the same semi-Asian features as Nate's handlers. His skin was maybe a shade lighter. Like the man who drove the black wagon, this man wore a multitude of rings. Also, his face was scarred. The scarred flesh looked as if it was intentional. The scars resembled the patterns on the columns surrounding them. Nate didn't get a good look because the man lifted his hood up. He did it quickly, shadowing his face as if he was trying to hide his disfigurement.

Only then did the man speak, and he didn't sound happy at being interrupted.

The officer responded, saying something and pointing at Nate.

The two of them went back and forth with some sort of Q & A.

While they talked, Scarface walked up to Nate. The new guy was tall, Nate only had about an inch on him. He grabbed Nate's chin and pulled his face so he could look in Nate's eyes. Nate winced since the rings dug in where he'd been backhanded.

There were scars on the guy's hands as well. The scars were based on a grid pattern that reminded Nate of pictures he had seen of the I Ching. The guy's face was still too shadowed for Nate to get a look.

Suddenly, the man let go and shook his hands as if they'd been soiled. He barked something at the officer and held out his hand. The officer produced the pouch that had held all the things they had taken from Nate.

Scarface didn't even look in the pouch. He just walked over and placed it on the altar/sarcophagus. Then he turned around and pointed at Nate, barking something at the guards.

There was a quiet pause, and the robed figure shook his head as if *he* couldn't believe the locals. He barked again, and this time he sounded pissed. Nate understood nothing he said, but the impression he got was, *Listen to me, you bastards, or there's going to be trouble.*

Nate's officer didn't want trouble. He shouted orders to the rest of his crew, and Nate was suddenly surrounded by a trio of naked swords, all pointing at him.

The lead officer took out his dagger and stood behind him. Nate felt the ropes cut free from his wrists. Nate stood there a moment, not quite sure what he should do. Pins and needles raced across his palms as blood rushed back into his hands.

Very slowly, he brought his hands forward and started rubbing the feeling into them.

The swords still pointed at him.

"What?" Nate asked.

In answer to his question, a brown robe was tossed at his feet. Nate stared at it until he felt a sword poke his side. Nate looked at the guard who'd poked him— big surprise, it was the same guy who had backhanded him—who said something, gesturing with his sword, first at Nate, then at the robe.

"You're kidding . . ."

They weren't.

They made it very clear that they now considered his clothing as much contraband as the stuff they'd emptied from his pockets. After repeated sword pokes, Nate had to strip off everything from his bomber jacket down to his jockeys.

They didn't even let him keep his socks.

Standing naked in the still, cold air made Nate realize just how much of an alien he was in this place. His tall angular body, pale skin, and auburn hair was completely at odds with the appearance of the folks surrounding him. He got more than a few stares from the guardsmen, and he suspected they'd be chattering away if it wasn't for the presence of Scarface.

Nate saw, uncomfortably, that the swords had dropped to point below his waist. It made him wonder if circumcision was practiced here.

He picked up the robe. It was damp and smelled of piss and mildew. He would have preferred going naked, despite the stares, but he doubted that he could convince his hosts.

The rough-woven fabric itched against his skin, and after thirty seconds, Nate was convinced that the fabric was host to some insect colony that found him rather tasty.

Scarface picked up everything Nate had worn, and piled it next to the pouch the officer had given him. Then he walked around the sarcophagus/altar and bent down. When he straightened up, he held a red mask in his hands. Facing away from them, Scarface lowered the hood of his robe and placed the mask on his face.

Scarface had white hair that was thinning enough that Nate could see the rectilinear patterns carved into the skin of his scalp as well as his face. The mask had its own hood of black fabric that covered the back of Scarface's head, so Nate only had a glimpse.

Scarface turned around and faced them.

The mask was blood red and decorated with inlaid gold and ivory. It had bulging eyes and a gaping, fanged mouth. The nose was long and hooked, the chin pointed. Nate noticed a change in the room when the mask was on. The guards around him, straightened somewhat. Scarface's posture was more formal, his body language lost the characteristics of annoyance and disgust—and if anything, the loss of those human characteristics made Scarface seem much more intimidating.

Scarface spoke something in a language that Nate swore was not the tongue he had heard everyone speak until now. Scarface didn't speak above a conversational tone, but something in the words made Nate feel sick. The liquid vowels reminded him too much of the thing that had occupied the darkness between the Case campus and the world he was in now.

As Scarface spoke, Nate saw him gesture with his hands. The motions were almost too quick to see, made, arms lowered, with the first three fingers of each hand. Almost typing in the air.

The words themselves were odd, monosyllabic, spoken with no emphasis or inflection. As if someone was sounding out a random string of letters, or chanting from memory.

Scarface spoke that way for less than ten seconds, but the words seemed to add a physical weight to the air around Nate. Nate looked around and saw that the guards had backed all the way to the entrance to the chamber.

This can't be good. . . .

Nate didn't want to be left with Scarface. With the guards he at least had some clue as to what was going on. Scarface was frightening and alien. . . .

Nate saw lights flicker in the rear of the long chamber, on the other side of the columns. The lights soon resolved into torches carried by other robed, masked figures. In a few minutes Nate was faced by a semicircle of brown-robed men and women. All wore masks, though none as elaborate as Scarface's. Their masks were blocked out in basic primary colors, mostly red and yellow. All had prominent noses and chins, some had fangs, some had beards, some had long tongues. All variants on the devil face that Scarface wore.

"Okay, guys," Nate whispered, "If we're doing a virgin sacrifice, I have bad news for you. . . ."

Scarface barked something. Unlike before, his tone wasn't bitchy and irritated. The tone was one of command. Nate turned to see the guards back away, closing a set of massive doors behind them. When the doors slammed home, Nate felt the impact in his chest.

Oh, fuck. . . .

He considered running, but there was the problem of where, exactly he'd run to. The masked congregation might not be carrying obvious weapons, but there were a dozen of them, half with torches. He couldn't outrun *all* of them, and he didn't think it would be fun being beaten with a flaming club.

Two of Scarface's followers carried in a heavy wooden trunk where they placed Nate's possessions. Scarface shut the box solemnly. They closed it with an elaborately carved padlock. Nate could see hints of the patterns that he had seen carved in Scarface's skin.

They really got happy with that motif.

Scarface spoke some more of that other language when he closed the padlock. To Nate's eyes, the lock closed seamlessly and had no obvious keyhole. He tried to get a better look at it, but when he took a step, the people surrounding him pressed together and held their torches in his direction.

Once Scarface was finished with the trunk and his cronies had hauled it away, he walked around the parameter of the crowd that now completely encircled Nate. He started talking in the speech Nate was beginning to think of as the "common tongue" to distinguish it from the disturbing liquid monotone that Scarface had used earlier.

Scarface walked around, talking to the gathering as if he was a professor giving a lecture, or a staff sergeant telling the troops how to use a bayonet. Nate knew that Scarface was talking about him, because, while Scarface never made a motion in his direction, his audience studied Nate with every word.

After about ten minutes, class was over, and about two thirds of the audience filed away. A pair of them grabbed Nate's upper arms and faced Scarface as their leader gave a few more instructions. The pair holding Nate nodded sagely, the noses on their masks bobbing in a manner Nate would have found comical if it wasn't so obvious that he was in deep shit.

"You guys don't speak English either, do you?"

They ignored him.

A torch-bearing trio took the lead, while the pair holding Nate brought up the rear. They walked toward the back of the long chamber, where there were six doorways leading off in various directions. Of course, they led Nate down the darkest, dankest looking corridor.

The air was damp and smelled of mold. The floor was slimy under Nate's bare feet and every part of his body was starting to itch.

This was the point where any action hero worth his salt would overpower his guards and escape. Nate ran through a number of movie scenarios. None seemed particularly doable at the moment. In his head he took the pair holding his arms, and swung them together so their skulls collided, rendering them conveniently unconscious. Then he'd grab one of the torchbearers and head butt him insensible and throw the limp form at the remaining guy—

Of course, even in the fantasy, this was when the last guy brought the torch down on Nate's head.

When it came down to it, Nate wasn't Arnold Schwarzenegger. He only had one take, and the fight choreographer didn't know who was supposed to win. So Nate was the model prisoner all the way down. He chatted up his new guards, but the conversation was completely one-sided.

They took him down one stone corridor after another. The torches were the only light. After the third set of stairs going down, they came to a hallway lined with large wooden doors. They stopped and one of the torchbearers pulled a door open.

"Oh, shit, guys. You aren't going to put me in there?"

The room was eight feet square, with no furniture.

The floor was covered with straw that looked black and green in the torchlight. Nate could see rats scurrying away from the light.

"No, you fuckers, I'm not—" Nate surprised himself at how suddenly the action hero option seemed viable. Probably because he'd been docile up to this point, he caught his captors by surprise. He managed to tear his right arm free to slug the guy on his left. He felt the mask crack as the parts of it sliced open a knuckle.

The one on the right grabbed at him, and Nate elbowed him in the forehead. The move actually dropped the guy.

Nate was free of his handlers for all of two seconds. Then a burning weight slammed across the back of his neck, something kicked him in the face, and three sets of hands were tossing him into the fetid straw of the cell.

Nate scrambled to his feet as the door shut out the light. Nate fell onto the door, pounding on it with his fists.

"You motherfuckers. I didn't do shit to you. You can't leave me in here."

He pounded against the unyielding wood. *"You can't leave me in here!"*

Of course, they could.

Chapter Seven

CHIEF ARMSMAN Ravig Kalish held his scarlet cape around himself. He stood in one of the tiny open gardens of Manhome, a struggling patch of green that nestled in the plateau of the city like a spot of lichen. The ocean spread below him, reflecting the many lights of the city in imitation of the nighttime sky above.

The chills he felt were deeper and stronger than the sea wind that blew against him. Ravig had always been a practical man. A guardsman had to be. Myths and angels were the province of those poor souls who entered the College. Ravig would happily live his entire life without once considering anything except the law and the world beneath his feet.

But what was a practical man supposed to do when the College's angels walked the same earth he did?

"Armsman Ravig?"

Ravig turned to face the Armsmaster of Manhome. "Master Ehrid."

Ehrid Kharyn walked to the stone railing that separated the garden from a sheer drop to a cobbled street below. "You've served well Manhome and the Monarch today, my friend."

"Your praise is welcome, but unearned. A farmer found the wretched beast, not I. And the College is not pleased with me."

"I know." Master Ehrid shook his head and stared out at the water. "Their scholars believe that any contact with your 'wretched beast' is too dangerous. They want trials and hearings and executions."

"We only did what they asked of us."

"A point repeatedly made." Ehrid sighed. "Fortunately, I think they may realize that we are as essential to them as their ghadi. They only want one example."

Ravig's cloak suddenly did nothing to relieve the cold. "One example?"

"You understand who."

"No. It was a single slip, a moment of curiosity. I've already reprimanded him."

"It was a breach of the law, and it was insubordinate." Ehrid turned to look at Ravig. "I find it a cruel fate, as you do. But the College is within its rights."

Ravig shook his head. In his mind he was replaying the incident over and over. How his youngest guardsman, Alogas, looked through the items—stared at them—when they took the possessions from the babbling creature they had captured. Such things were taboo, not to be studied except by the eyes inside the College of Man. Ravig had hoped the breach was too minor to notice. "What has Alogas done that my other men have not?"

"Be thankful that the College makes a distinction." Ehrid's voice was cold and distant. "They have already taken him."

"What?" Ravig's head swam. "They've taken— Not even a plea on his behalf?" He grabbed Ehrid and pulled him around. Touching the Armsmaster of Manhome in such a manner was worthy of his own execution, but Ravig was angry past caring. "Did you call me here only to prevent me from intervening? From defending Alogas?"

Ehrid looked down at Ravig. "To prevent you from being lost to the College. I need you. The Monarch needs you."

Ravig let go. "A Monarch who cannot even defend the men who serve Him."

"Mind yourself." Ehrid smoothed his cloak where

Ravig had gripped it. "I know your pain right now, but you've exhausted the license it gives you."

Ravig backed up a step, straightened, and gave a stiff salute. "I await the Armsmaster's pleasure, and that of the Monarch."

"Good. Then please relate exactly the events you were a party to." Ehrid turned back toward the ocean. "Especially what the scholars of the College might have said in your presence once you delivered to them the creature they sought."

• • •

Dawn broke over Manhome, burning off the mists that hugged the base of the plateau and bringing the call of sea birds feeding off the waste of the city. Ehrid stood on his balcony, looking into the ocean. Something about the water both terrified and fascinated him. Like fate or history, it was something whose depth and breadth was unimpressed by any one man. Something vast and implacable to which all men, from Monarch to beggar, were little more than grains of sand.

He had yet to sleep. Ravig had told him things that disturbed him greatly. The College itself seemed worried. In what Ravig had said there were hints that the scholars weren't as sanguine as they would like to appear. Ehrid had some cause to believe that what the College might be worried about was not an angel striding from the mythic shadow, but something closer to Ehrid's mundane reality.

"What words have you for me?" came a familiar voice from behind him.

Ehrid turned to face the acolyte with the plain mask. He looked into the featureless white face, attempting to discern something beyond the black eyeholes that were the only break in its surface. This anonymous scholar from the College of Man had come to him with the sanction of the Monarch himself. However, Ehrid now wondered if it was the plots germinating behind that white mask that had the College nervous.

Did they know how close they were to a contest for their power?

"I have many words," Ehrid spoke finally. "I would like some in return."

"I serve at the Armsmaster's pleasure." There was an irritating tinge of amusement in the way he said it. Ehrid ignored it.

"What is this pale creature to the College?"

"A stranger. A trespasser from beyond the realm of our ken. Something to be kept from public knowledge and examination. Something to be interrogated and destroyed before any harm is done."

"There is more."

"There is always more."

"The College acts in a manner to suggest that it fears something. Is it this creature, or do they intuit your machinations?"

The acolyte laughed.

"I do not share your amusement."

A bow toward Ehrid. "Forgive me. You have not lived in the College, so you do not know its mind. Suffice it to say that the only emotion permitted by doctrine is fear. The College itself is fear personified, and views plots and omens in the shapes of clouds and the entrails of slain ghadi."

Ehrid frowned. "The Venrable Master Scholar himself displayed nervousness and uncertainty enough for my Armsman Ravig to comment on it. Whatever state of mind is normal within the College, it is not normal for them to allow outsiders to see it."

"A different thing, I am sure. However, what Armsman Ravig might have seen was none of my doing, to answer your question. The distress they display is solely of their own making."

"Meaning the stranger?"

"Meaning what they have convinced themselves the stranger might be."

"What then?"

"Have you read the legends of the Angel of Death?"

CHAPTER EIGHT

AFTER THE FIRST hour, Nate's hands were too sore to pound on the door. After the third hour, his voice died. After the fifth hour, fatigue won out and he had to sit down.

Nate paced around, probing the ground with his feet, kicking aside things that felt too squishy. He sat down, back to the wall, wondering if he had gone completely insane.

The complete darkness made it too easy to imagine that he had never left the blackout he had fallen into, running down the halls of Case. The thought was almost comforting, until he realized that he hadn't been wearing lice-infested burlap then, and *that* darkness didn't smell like mold and shit.

Perhaps worst of all right now was the fact that he had beaten his hands too sore to scratch himself.

A masochistic voice in his brain started a list of things that he would do just about anything for now. A ticket home was top on the list, even if it was to a life sentence in a Federal Supermax prison. Food was high on the list, along with some water. He would kill for some clean jockeys.

What's going on at home? Does everyone think I'm dead? Has it made the news?

Nate thought of Mom and Sis being surrounded by reporters asking about the fugitive hacker Nate Black. Nate pictured a CNN reporter shoving a mike into

Mom's face and shouting, *"Did you know your son was a criminal wanted by the FBI?"*

That was when Nate finally started to cry.

● ● ●

They didn't kill you, so they'll be back. . . .

The thought kept returning. When they came back, Nate knew that somehow, despite the language barrier, he could make a deal. There had to be something he could do to convince them to let him go, or at least put him in a clean cell with clean clothes.

At least some air, and some food. He had a craving for sausage stuffing, which made him think of Mom again. . . .

I'm making myself crazy. . . .

Nate tried to put his mind somewhere else.

He closed his eyes, and tried to force himself to forget about the smell, the filth, and the itching. To give himself something to focus on, he started composing C++ code in his head. Every time he felt distracted, he punished himself by starting over from the first line.

It worked, and soon he was deep inside his own head, putting together a simple bubble-sort algorithm.

When he was satisfied with the algorithm, he translated the C++ code to Perl, then he translated it into AZ, a programming language he had invented when he was fourteen.

When he traced the code in his head, it showed up a bug in the way AZ worked. He fell asleep mentally rewriting the code for AZ to properly handle recursive subroutines.

● ● ●

Light woke him up.

For a few moments he didn't know where he was or what had happened to him. But the memories came back too quickly as he blinked in the sudden torchlight.

Boy, am I fucked.

As his eyesight cleared, Nate got to see one of the aliens close-up for the first time.

Its face was elongated and tilted back, the mouth wide and rubbery, the brow smooth and hairless above round eyes with no whites and irises the same purple-black as its skin. The arms had an extra elbow, and the fingers had an extra joint, and it had a gait showing legs with the same design.

It wore a dirty-white toga, bound with a rope at a waistline that would be even with the sternum in a normal anatomy. The torso was way too small for the spidery legs and arms. Nate couldn't guess gender.

It stood in the doorway, carrying a bucket.

Nate slowly pushed himself upright, thinking he might push past this thing. Then he saw the masked men with the torches, out in the hallway.

The alien set the bucket down on the floor and backed away. The door shut behind it. Everything was dark again.

Nate felt for the bucket and found it. Inside it was a bowl filled with a lumpy broth and half a loaf of some hard, flat bread. However plain the food was, it awoke Nate's hunger. He hadn't eaten in at least twenty-four hours, if not longer.

It took only a few moments to realize what the bucket itself was for. It was a bit of a trick relieving himself while holding his meal. But he didn't have much choice, it would be unthinkable to eat anything that came in contact with any surface of his cell.

Fortunately, the bucket was wooden with a fairly thick rim, so he could raise his robe and sit on it without much discomfort.

He ate his first meal sitting on the piss bucket, soaking the bread in the broth so he could manage to chew it.

• • •

He woke up in the middle of the "night" chilled and sweaty, and threw up that first meal into the half-full bucket.

• • •

The alien came with a new bucket and took the old one.

Nate didn't move from the corner. He was shivering and weak, and it felt as if his insides were melting away.

He tried to eat, but he threw up again. When he managed to pull himself up on the bucket, he had diarrhea as thin as his urine.

Not good, Nate thought.

• • •

He couldn't stand up to get the next meal. He dragged himself across the floor without paying much mind to what lived in the straw. He felt around for the broth, and fearing he'd vomit again, left the hard bread. He sucked the broth through his teeth leaving the solids in the bowl.

That he managed to keep down.

• • •

His time was spent mostly in semiconscious darkness. He was so weak that sometimes he didn't reach the bucket. When the alien came and saw this, it responded by fetching more straw and shoveling away the most solid part of the mess.

He tried to play with code in his head, but the fever had scrambled the focus of his mind.

He would wake up, shouting into the blackness. . . .

"Is this what you want? @, you fucker? Why? What the hell is the point? I'm going to rot away here and not even know where the fuck I am. If you wanted something out of me, you bastard, boy, did you blow it. . . ."

"I'm sorry, Mom, I didn't mean to do this to you. But tell those CNN bastards to back off. . . ."

"You 'Mission Impossible' bastards did it, I admit it. I'm Azrael, I'll sign anything, you can all stop the act now. . . ."

"Microsoft will *always* have security holes, they have a business cycle that's based on a two-year product turnaround no matter what shape the software's in. If it wasn't for folks like me, testing the holes, you think they'd even code the patches?"

"You know, I don't think I'm going to make Thanksgiving dinner."

"For Christ's sake, it's not like I killed anyone . . ."

"Who the fuck else would you want running your network security?"

"Please, God, don't let me die down here."

• • •

When they came for him, Nate was lucid enough to know what was happening, to know how bad off he was. He was suffering from some filth-borne disease. Dysentery, cholera, or some other infection was dehydrating him. The diarrhea wouldn't stop, and he could barely keep the broth down. He could feel his own ribs, and under a scraggly beard it felt as if his cheekbones might slice open his face.

When the robed figures gripped his arms, it was more to hold him upright than it was to restrain him.

The walk was exhausting, but Nate didn't have a choice, they forced him to go on. A few times Nate stumbled and nearly collapsed, but they held on, dragging his feet behind him.

• • •

They pulled him through corridors, and up stairs, until Nate could smell the sea air again. It was a shock to be suddenly reminded that there was, in fact, a world beyond the stone walls that had imprisoned him.

They took him through a plain wooden door that opened into a massive arcade. Unlike the dungeons that they'd been in up to now, this long gallery was wide, well-lit, and clean. Huge tapestries hung from the walls and light shone in from small windows set near the top of the vaulted ceiling. Statues flanked the tapestries, showing figures that were unquestionably human, and of the same breed as his captors. The tapestries carried scenes of warfare, showing cities burning and people being slaughtered. Nate saw that the battles all seemed to be between the humans and alien creatures like the one that had brought him his daily bucket.

One of the last tapestries showed a *thing*. Nate couldn't name it, but it had the same insect-tentacle-plantlike characteristics as the defaced sculpture he had seen on the hillside what seemed like a millennium ago. It hovered over a blasted landscape, piled with smoldering bodies.

They didn't stop to allow Nate a better look. They were headed for the massive doors at one end of the huge gallery.

They entered a great circular chamber and dragged him to a high chair set in the center of the room. He faced a tall U-shaped desk that half circled him. Ten masked figures looked down at him from behind that desk. Their masks were all equally elaborate, with shining highlights of silver, gold, ivory, and precious stones. All were different. Nate saw Scarface's red devil mask, but he also saw a clown, a cat, some sort of bird, an abstract pattern with no nose or mouth, and a frowning face that was very realistically human.

Nate saw the box that held his clothes sitting off to the right. The padlock was gone and it was guarded by a pair of Scarface's cronies with the red-yellow devil masks.

After setting Nate down, the pair who had carried him walked up to the desk and conferred with Scarface. Nate looked around. His skin felt flushed and his neck felt rubbery. He knew he was too weak to make a run for it, even though the doors were still open behind him.

As he watched, two of the toga-clad aliens closed the doors.

Nate looked back at the desk facing him and realized that he was the focus of attention. He called out, "What do you want? Just let me go and you've got it."

No one responded. At this point he didn't expect them to.

Another pair of cronies left Scarface's side, taking a small box, and walked over to Nate. They set the plain-looking box down at the foot of the chair Nate sat in, almost under his feet.

One of them opened the box to reveal a metallic sphere about the size of a softball. It sat, cushioned by black velvet. Nate stared at it and realized that it was the most elaborately engraved thing he had seen here. Like the cuts in Scarface's skin, the sphere's engravings were repeated square rectilinear symbols. Only, in the sphere's case, the individual characters—Nate was becoming convinced that these symbols represented a language of some sort—were vanishingly tiny, little more than a few millimeters across, wrapping the metal ball in a tight spiral.

Scarface chanted something in that liquid second language.

Everyone around the desk repeated the words, if that's what they were.

At his feet, the sphere was vibrating. Nate could hear a high-frequency hum coming from it. The two masked characters next to him backed away.

Nate pushed himself upright and muttered, "This is getting fucking weird."

The sphere resonated with his voice. It almost seemed to speak in the strange common language these people spoke.

Scarface said something.

With a tone rather like overstressed metal and fingernails across a blackboard, Nate heard the sphere speak.

"UNDERSTANDCOMPREHEND YOUUSME."

Nate looked up at the masked people and whispered, "Holy shit."

Chapter Nine

ΠATE STARED at the sphere as he heard its vibrations resonate in the guttural tones of his captors. *What a wonderful impression that's going to make. How's that going to translate?*

Scarface barked something, and Nate could tell that he didn't like what had come through his end of the sphere. "ANSWERRESPOND YOUUSME."

Nate looked up. The sphere was weak in carrying tone, inflection, or emotion, but Nate had heard Scarface speak and the words out of his mouth, incomprehensible as they were, sounded terse.

"Yes, I understand you, somewhat." Nate looked at all of them in turn. Who were these people? What was this place?

"NAMEIDENTITY TELLCOMMUNICATE YOUUSME." *Who are you?*

"My name's Nate Black. Look, I don't have anything against you people. Can we come up with—"

"QUESTIONSREQUESTS TELLCOMMUNICATE YOUUSME NOCANNOTBAD. QUESTIONSREQUESTS TELLCOMMUNICATE MEUSYOU YESWILLGOOD." *We are the ones asking questions here.*

Nate looked up at Scarface's mask and felt afraid in a way that made him ashamed at the same time. "Please, just tell me what you want from me." Nate's voice cracked, and he felt dizzy. It was a good thing that they set him in a chair, because the effort of speaking might have made him collapse.

Nate saw the masked figures deliberating in whispered tones. He wondered if what he said made any sense to them.

Scarface's voice was threatening even before the sphere got hold of it. When the words rang off the metal orb, they were dry-ice cold. "LIFEEXISTENCE YOUNATEBLACK HEREWORLDMANHOME VIOLATIONFORBIDDENDANGER. DESCISIONCONTROL LIFEEXISTENCE YOUNATEBLACK MINEOURS. DECISIONCONTROL PAINDEATH YOUNATEBLACK YOUYOURS."

Nate could tell a threat when he heard one. He also managed to glean one nugget of information, a name to call this place.

"HEREWORLDMANHOME"

Manhome.

"EVENTSSEQUENCEPROCESS ARRIVALENTRANCEINVASION YOUNATEBLACK TELLCOMMUNICATE YOUUSME."

"I'm not an invasion. I'm not a spy. I was just minding my own business—" *running from the cops,* "—everything blacks out, and I end up here. I don't want to do anything to you guys. I can cooperate, but I'm sick. I need medical attention."

It was probably too much to hope for. They conferred a while, probably deciphering his compound sentences. Then Scarface yielded the floor. The new speaker had a feminine voice and wore a mask with a very human face—though it was a face frozen in the midst of screaming.

"EVENTSSEQUENCEPROCESS BLACKDARKNESSVOID YOUNATEBLACK TELLCOMMUNICATE YOUUSME."

Nate felt a little uneasy about the question. He didn't want to tell anything about the alien presence in the void. Not only did he have a bad feeling about the thing, @, itself, but he had a gut sense that the folks here might react badly to it.

"I don't remember exactly what happened."

"EVENTSSEQUENCEPROCESS BLACKDARKNESSVOID

YOUNATEBLACK TELLCOMMUNICATE YOUUSME. HIDE-
LIEFALSIFY FACTSMEMORYHISTORY VIOLATIONFORBID-
DENDANGER CAUSERESULT PAINDEATH YOUNATE-
BLACK."

No shit.

Well, if anything, these guys would be the last ones
to accuse him of being nuts. Nate shook his head. "I'll
tell you anything you want—" Nate started coughing.
His voice wasn't up to a speech. The coughs shook
his ribs until they ached. When it was over, he wiped
his mouth and saw traces of blood. "But you're killing
me right now, holding me in that cesspit." Nate shook
his head. He was feeling a little light-headed and
wasn't exactly sure what he was saying. "I was a bad
boy in high school, guys. Caused enough server problems to give me a nice long stretch in the Federal
pen—which compares real well with this place, so if
you have extradition to the United States please use
it—you guys really have no idea what I'm talking
about. . . ."

"CONTINUERESUME TELLCOMMUNICATE YOUUSME."

"Sure," Nate coughed into his hand again. "I re-
formed, put on a white hat. MS in Comp Sci and a
60K job running net security. That was the plan. Then
this @ guy—whose handle would take too long to explain to computer illiterates—starts threatening to
blow Azrael's cover. A Fed shows up, I book, and fall
into this spaceless black that doesn't have anything in
it but me and this *alien* whatsis. Tells me to choose.
One side was the Fed, so I went the other way. My
mistake, sorry."

Nate broke off with another coughing fit. The more
he spoke, the worse it was getting. When he was
through trying to hack a lung up his throat, he hyper-
ventilated and decided that he would stick to one-
sentence answers for the rest of the interview.

Fortunately, he had a reprieve as the masked contingent conferred over his latest revelation.

Nate put his head in his hands. The dizziness was
getting worse, and he didn't want to pass out. The fact

was, he relished every moment he was out of that hole they were keeping him in. He was actually more afraid of going back to that pit than he was of them killing him.

Hang on to the slim hope that when they understand what happened to you that they won't treat you as a foreign trespasser or a spy. It's not your fault you're here.

"IDENTITYNATURE NAMEAZRAEL TELLCOMMUNICATE YOUUSME." This speaker wore one of the animal masks. It was something like an Egyptian jackal head.

"It's the alias I used when I was doing the black-hat hacking, viruses, back doors, that sort of thing . . ." Nate wondered if any of this was translating at all. These guys looked as if their only concept of a server was the guy who brought the wine to your table. It certainly looked as if he'd confused them. Their conferring lasted almost as long as it had the last time.

"IDENTITYEQUIVALENCE NAMEAZRAEL YOUNATE-BLACK."

Nate nodded weakly. "Yeah, you got it." Parsing their questions was almost as fatiguing as answering them.

"IDENTITYNATURE BLACKDARKNESSVOID TELLCOM-MUNICATE YOUUSME."

Huh? "I don't understand."

"IDENTITYNATURE BLACKDARKNESSVOID TELLCOM-MUNICATE YOUUSME. HIDELIEFALSIFY FACTSMEMORY-HISTORY VIOLATIONFORBIDDENDANGER CAUSERESULT PAINDEATH YOUNATEBLACK."

Nate straightened up. "I told you, I don't understand what you're asking."

"IDENTITYNATURE BLACKDARKNESSVOID TELLCOM-MUNICATE YOUUSME. HIDELIEFALSIFY FACTSMEMORY-HISTORY VIOLATIONFORBIDDENDANGER CAUSERESULT PAINDEATH THISINSTANTNOW YOUNATEBLACK."

The pair of robed men who had dragged him from his cell were approaching him again.

"I'm cooperating! What do you want? I don't know what the name of the blackness was. I don't know the

name of the thing that lived in it. All it did was tell
me it was time to choose a road."

Scarface gestured and the pair stopped approaching Nate.

"WORDSLANGUAGECOMMUNICATION BLACKDARK-
NESSVOID TELLCOMMUNICATE YOUUSME."

Nate shook his head. He was having trouble thinking. The panic hadn't helped his equilibrium. "What?"

"WORDSLANGUAGECOMMUNICATION BLACKDARK-
NESSVOID TELLCOMMUNICATE YOUUSME."

Scarface was nice enough to leave off the threat of
execution. Nate guessed at this point it went without
saying. . . .

What did it say?

"Oh, yeah. It called me Azrael. It said 'Azrael, it is
time. Choose. Choose which road.' That was basically it."

"DECISIONSELECTION YOUNATEBLACK HEREWORLD-
MANHOME."

"I didn't know what I was doing."

"DECISIONSELECTION YOUNATEBLACK HEREWORLD-
MANHOME."

Nate sighed. "Yes, I chose this place. It was a snap
decision, a mistake."

More conferencing. Nate wished he had some clue
what he was on trial for here. If he had some idea
what these freaks wanted . . .

Nate looked down at the sphere and wondered exactly what it was and how it worked. The translation
was bizarre, unlike any translation software he had
ever seen. Almost as if the thing was translating
context-sensitive meanings—and if they knew English
that well, then why couldn't they get a better
translation?

Why couldn't they get someone who *spoke* English?

If they could program something that sophisticated,
then why hadn't Nate seen anything electric since he
had arrived here? Why did they react so oddly to his
clothes? To him?

He kept coming back to the conclusion that he was

not on the same planet anymore. However, if that was the case, then what the hell were human beings doing on it? And how was this metal ball speaking English?

Most important, how the hell did *he* get here?

"WORDSLANGUAGECOMMUNICATION YOUNATEBLACK YOUOTHERS HEREWORLDMANHOME TELLCOMMUNICATE YOUUSME." The new questioner wore a mask that was an abstract pattern that flowed across his face reminiscent of a Dali painting.

The question made Nate's head hurt. "If you're asking what I've told people since I got here, I don't speak the language. What could I tell anyone?"

Someone somewhere chuckled.

Score one for the prisoner.

Nate realized the gibe was not a good idea. His head was messed up with fever. It kept him from thinking clearly.

"IDENTITYNATURE MEETCONTACT YOUOTHERS HERE-WORLDMANHOME TELLCOMMUNICATE YOUUSME." Scarface clarified the previous question.

"That's different," Nate said. He sucked in a breath and went down the list slowly, starting with Grandpa and the Stooges, through the guards who bought him from Grandpa to Scarface.

"WORDSLANGUAGECOMMUNICATION YOUNATEBLACK COMPLETETOTALALL."

"That's everyone except the folks we passed on the way up here."

Strangely, the reaction from the gallery seemed to be one of relief. *Why? Why do they look so relieved I haven't had contact with anyone . . . ?*

"Oh, shit," Nate whispered as the implication began sinking in. These bastards didn't want Nate in contact with anyone outside their little circle. That meant that they must have no intention of letting him go.

"Hey, I'm sure we can work something out. Come to some sort of understanding. Just don't throw me back in that hole."

"IDENTITYNATURE OBJECTTHING TELLCOMMUNICATE YOUUSME." Clown mask this time.

"Please, just say you'll work something out. Keep me prisoner if you want, just give me a bed, some light—"

The masked gallery was passing his wallet around, looking at it. Scarface decided to emphasize Clown's question.

"IDENTITYNATURE OBJECTTHING TELLCOMMUNICATE YOUUSME."

"I don't want to die down there."

"ANSWERRESPOND YOUUSME."

"It's a wallet. Money, ID, credit cards, and you can't even pretend you're understanding what I'm saying."

Scarface flipped it open and showed it to Nate, it was open to one of the photographs he carried.

"It's a picture of my ex-girlfriend, Sarah Green. *What do you want?*"

"OBSERVEPERCEIVE OBJECTTHING OTHERS IDENTITYNATURE TELLCOMMUNICATE YOUUSME."

Who else saw this?

"The guard who kept hitting me. Come on, I'm helping you out. You don't have to stick me back—"

"OBSERVELEARN YOUNATEBLACK."

Scarface's pair of masked goons flanked Nate and grabbed his arms. Nate tried to struggle, but he didn't have the strength to stand, much less fight off these guys.

Scarface stood and said something that was untranslated. *What? It only works when they're talking to me?* It seemed so. Up to now Nate had thought it hadn't picked up the whispered conferences in the gallery because they weren't spoken loud enough.

Two more masked men walked into the chamber, dragging a man between them. The clothes were ragged and torn, but still Nate could see the scarlet and black under the filth. The new prisoner cast a look of pure hate back toward Nate.

It was the guard who had been too fascinated by Nate's wallet. The one who had backhanded him repeatedly. Now he looked as malnourished and sickly as Nate felt.

Scarface started talking, a long speech. The sphere

didn't pick up a word. However, Nate could sense the gist by the way Scarface gestured, displayed the wallet, and pointed at Nate and then at the guard.

The gist was, *You shouldn't have looked in the wallet.* VIOLATIONFORBIDDENDANGER.

Scarface addressed his comrades in the gallery, apparently asking a question. Then he turned to each member in turn, looking for a response.

From Clown, a monosyllabic *"Jin."*

Dali, *"Jin."*

Screamer, *"Jin."*

To the apparent growing dismay of the ex-guardsman, the verdict was a unanimous, *"Jin."* From the reaction, Nate figured he had learned the meaning of his first word in their language.

"Jin," meant "fry the bastard."

With great ceremony, Scarface descended to the floor of the chamber, to stand in front of the ex-guardsman. More of his goons emerged from the shadows to help hold the prisoner down. Another masked goon tore open the guardsman's shirt as Scarface removed a dagger from his robe.

Nate didn't want to see, but he couldn't turn away from the scene.

Scarface carefully, with a delicate hand, started to cut the skin of the guardsman's chest. Five other men were holding the man down as he bucked against their grip. Scarface's hand was steady, despite the movement. He sliced lines into the man's chest. The same kind of glyphs that Nate had seen cut into Scarface's flesh. . . .

What is he doing?

Scarface carved about two handbreadths' worth of glyphs across the guardsman's pectorals. And the instant Scarface finished, the guardsman screamed. It was a piercing, almost feminine wail of agony. The bucking of his body wasn't a struggle to escape anymore, it was a full-blown seizure.

Scarface backed away and gestured his goons to do likewise.

The guardsman dropped to the stone floor, his back arched above the stone so only his heels and shoulder blades touched the ground. His eyes rolled back in his head, and his mouth opened in a scream so wide that it took up half his face. He flopped and jerked, slamming his head repeatedly into the floor so hard that blood began marking where it hit the stones.

The agonized wail died for lack of air.

The air became sour with the smell of something burning, and wisps of smoke emerged from the guardsman's mouth and nostrils. The thrashing became more frantic as the skin began to blister and turn dark.

The extremities caught first, hands and feet erupting in a sickly green flame. The flame snaked up the body in branching patterns that seemed to follow the paths of the major arteries. When the flames met across the chest, where Scarface's glyphs were carved above the heart, the body froze, erupting in a pillar of foul green fire.

Nate looked across to Scarface, who was busy putting his dagger away.

"What did you do?"

"CLEANSEPURIFYREPAIR," the sphere responded.

CHAPTER TEN

ΠATE WAS shaking when they threw him back in the hole. It wasn't from the fever.

Nothing had prepared him for what happened to the guardsman. He had never seen a man die before. He couldn't stop thinking of the flame, and the smell of charred flesh so thick he could taste it.

These were the choices they were giving him—darkness, or the fire. Perhaps Nate would be lucky, and the dehydration would kill him before they were through.

• • •

He dreamed of going home for Thanksgiving dinner. Mom asked how his midterms went and he couldn't speak. When the turkey erupted into screaming green fire, she spoke in the sphere's voice.

"CLEANSEPURIFYREPAIR."

• • •

The interviews repeated. The same questions. Who was he? Why was he here? What is the thing in the darkness?

In Nate's mind, his answers were becoming less comprehensible with each iteration. Sometimes, in his fevered state, he would parrot back the pidgin that the sphere spoke to him. Other times he babbled pleas for a lawyer, or a bottle of Mountain Dew, or a clean pair of jockeys.

He lost count of the times they interviewed him.

• • •

Sometimes he would disassemble the events of his life in his mind, string them together like pseudocode, and try to debug it.

• • •

Nate felt someone slap his face and he blinked his eyes into consciousness. He sat in the interview chamber, on the chair, without knowing how he got there.

The only one here this time was Scarface. The light came from only a single candelabrum. He was the one who had smacked him awake. In his hand he held the translation sphere.

"OBSERVEPERCEIVE OBJECTTHING OTHERS IDENTI-TYNATURE TELLCOMMUNICATE YOUME."

"What?" Nate slurred.

That earned him another blow.

"OBSERVEPERCEIVE OBJECTTHING OTHERS IDENTI-TYNATURE TELLCOMMUNICATE YOUME."

Scarface stared at Nate, and Nate realized that this was the first time he had seen the man maskless since he'd been brought here. The guy was seriously pissed.

"OBSERVEPERCEIVE OBJECTTHING OTHERS IDENTI-TYNATURE TELLCOMMUNICATE YOUME," he repeated, adding, "TELLCOMMUNICATE IDENTITYNATURE OB-JECTTHING OTHERS IDENTITYNATURE TELLCOMMUNI-CATE YOUME."

"Holy Christ, we've been through this. You know everyone who saw me, spoke to me—the only people on this planet who know me are you and your masked friends."

That earned a blow that knocked Nate clear off the chair. He fell to the stone floor with a choking gasp. Scarface stood over him, the candlelight picking out the lines carved in his face.

"TAKEREMOVESTEAL OTHERS OBJECTTHING IDENTI-TYNATURE TELLCOMMUNICATE YOUME."

Nate rolled over and grabbed the neck of his robe

and tore at it. "Do it. You want to cut me? Do it now! *Because I don't know what the fuck you're talking about!*"

Nate waited, certain that the end had come. But Scarface just stood there, looking at Nate, then at the sphere. After a few long moments, he turned away and called his goons to carry Nate back to the hole.

Nate lost consciousness before they got halfway back.

• • •

There was a lucid moment, in the darkness, when Nate realized what Scarface was trying to say.

TAKEREMOVESTEAL . . .

OBJECTTHING . . .

Someone must have taken Scarface's little chest of Nate's stuff.

• • •

Nate blinked the fuzz from his eyes and realized that the alien didn't have a bucket this time.

"What?"

The alien, as always, didn't speak or acknowledge Nate's words. Instead, it walked into the cell. Instead of Scarface's demon-masked acolytes, the torches out in the hall were borne by two more aliens.

Nate sat up, making his head swim.

"What the?"

The alien in the room with him was carrying something in lieu of a bucket—a rough burlap sack. It opened the bag as it approached, and Nate tried to scoot backward.

He held up his hands to ward the thing away. "Wait—"

His words were smothered as the bag came down over his head. He choked, mouth filled with the musty remnants of the bag's prior contents.

He grappled with the thing, and he felt inhuman joints wrap around him and lift him off the floor. The thing was stronger than its spindly-bendy arms and legs made it look. Not that it took much to over-power Nate.

Other hands, with fingers too long and too many, gripped Nate's wrists and ankles. Nate could feel rope binding him.

Nate tried to shout at the things, but every time he opened his mouth, he ended with a coughing fit. The last one was so violent, he passed out.

• • •

Fade in.

Alien hands supporting him under the armpits and by the ankles. He could hear a torch burn. He could feel his butt swinging over empty space. He smelled sewage, and heard footsteps walking through shallow water.

Fade out.

• • •

In.

Cold air. Damp, salty. Dripping. Still being carried. Out.

• • •

The bag is gone, he can breathe easier. Footsteps echo in a vast space around him, though he cannot summon the energy to open his eyes.

• • •

The robe is gone. His skin is damp. He feels a gentle hand drying him. His eyes are open, but a gauze cloth covers his face. He's forgotten what clean feels like.

• • •

"Who's there?"

Nate had been drifting in and out of semiconscious-ness. He was weak, and his insides burned as if some-one had scoured his body out with a wire brush. He blinked his eyes. The candlelight was too bright, mak-ing his eyes water.

While his eyes focused, Nate was able to harbor a slight hope that he was waking from a long hallucination. It didn't last. The first thing he saw was the face of the woman tending him. She was the same dark Asiatic race as everyone else he had seen so far. Her hair was straight, long, and tied in a braid.

Nate's initial guess at her age was early twenties, then he saw a streak of gray that wove in through her braid. When she leaned over him, Nate saw the wrinkles marking her eyes and mouth.

Then, abruptly, he felt her hand on his shoulder, and she rolled him on his side. Nate's body moved as if he didn't weigh any more than the bedding he lay on. He felt a damp cloth on his backside, and was too weak to move. All he could do was tremble in embarrassment.

He had borne it for so long he had ceased to notice it. But as the nurse washed the mess from him, Nate realized that the fetid stench that filled the air wasn't from his cell. It was from him.

Through some sleight of hand, after she had washed him, she somehow managed to change the bedding without removing Nate from the bed. She rolled him from side to side as she worked, as if he was an inconveniently placed sack of potatoes.

"This can't be fun for you, can it?" His voice was hoarse and whispery, and he could taste blood through his cracked lips.

She had been washing her hands off in a basin that was set up by Nate's bed. She turned around and looked at him, studying his face. She said something in the "common" language.

"Fuck if I know, sister."

She looked in his eyes. It took a moment, but Nate realized that she was trying to determine if his babbling meant anything.

She spoke again.

"The name's Nate Black. Pleased to meet you."

She walked up and pressed the back of her hand on his forehead. It was damp and cold from washing.

Nate was grateful for the touch. It was the first physical contact in ages that wasn't there to restrain him or do him injury.

"What's the prognosis—?" Nate started to ask. Then his voice broke up, coughing.

She backed up and let Nate's coughing fit subside. Then she walked over and placed a hand on his lips and gave him a look that was easily read as "shut up."

Then she washed her hands in the basin again.

At least she has some concept of sanitation.

Nate tried to elbow himself upright, but his arms didn't seem quite right. He couldn't get them under him.

She turned around and barked something at him that made him stop moving. She pointed at him with one hand, and passed the other over her face, closing her eyes.

Think I need sleep?

Nate had to admit that it was very easy to lie on the bed, unmoving. It was even easier to let his eyes close. . . .

Book Two

There was a slave whose child was sick unto death. She prayed unto Mankin, the god of her people, and was not heard. She prayed unto her master, the richest of all ghadi, and was not heard. At last she took her son's body and laid it on the white marble altar where offerings to Ghad were placed before being cast into the pit. There she prayed unto Ghad for her son's life.

The slave's son was spared, and his life given to service of the ghadi. His master was pleased with his service and gave him charge of all his slaves. In time his mother became too old to work for his master, and the duty to cast her into the offering pit fell to him.

She prayed unto her son to spare her life, and was not heard.

—The Book of Ghad and Man,
Volume I, Chapter 5

CHAPTER ELEVEN

"DO YOU NOT appreciate the severity of this?" The voice echoed off the high stone walls of the audience chamber. Two men sat at the great U-shaped table, both men robed and masked in a manner appropriate to their station. The speaker, the Venerable Master Scholar Jardan Syn, wore a red devil mask whose fierce expression seemed to mirror his mood precisely.

The other man, Scholar Uthar Vailen, wore a mask of a clown with two mouths, one frowning, one smiling. Uthar had known Jardan for many, many years. He had, in fact, been instrumental in the power struggles inside the College that made Jardan the Venerable Master Scholar. Uthar often served him as an adviser, and knew Jardan very well.

"I merely suggest that rash actions will not serve you or the College well," Uthar responded to his superior.

"We must take all resources to recover the creature before any more damage is done."

Uthar shook his head and tapped his fingers on the table. His elaborately carved rings glittered in a beam of sunlight streaming in from the high windows. The light picked out the sacred runes of the Gods' language carved in their surface.

"You say nothing?" asked Jardan.

"I defer to the Venerable Master in all things."

"Do not be false to me. What faults do you see?"

"How is it you plan to recover this creature? Send armsmen to the countryside? Search the site of every ghadi shrine? Question the populace?"

"These acts allowed us to find the creature once."

"My Master should consider two important facts. First, what you propose will inform everyone, far and wide, that we have lost control of this creature. Is it in the College's interest to admit such a humbling weakness? It may embolden the Monarch and his civil authorities to challenge our will elsewhere."

The Venerable Master Scholar dismissed that concern with a wave of his hand. "The College is supreme, and always has been. We have nothing to fear from men. The Monarch knows that to challenge the College would cost him his own power."

Uthar tapped the table again. The stones of his ring cast multicolored reflections on the walls of the meeting chamber.

"But you said two facts," Jardan said. "What other fear do you have?"

"Just this. This creature was near to death. If it could so easily escape on its own, it would have done so long before now. This means that the creature was stolen from us—as were its possessions. Therefore, we must ask, stolen by whom?"

"Perhaps you know?" Jardan asked.

"What people knew where this thing was imprisoned? The cellars of the College here are vast and unmapped, but the people who took this prize knew exactly where it was housed. Therefore, either it was plucked free by the hand of Ghad himself, or—"

"—or this was done by someone inside the College."

Uthar nodded. "Who else would know its value, or its danger?"

"I cannot believe such a thing."

"Why not? There are arguments every day in these halls about what knowledge is fit to be learned. There are many who believe that, in this age, man is supreme enough to know all of Ghad's mind."

"You know how we punish such heresy."

"When it is spoken, Master."

Uthar knew the Venerable Master Scholar well enough to know the seed had been planted. He could tell in the shift of Jardan's shoulders, and in how the nose of his mask tipped downward. Behind his own mask, Uthar smiled.

●　●　●

Yerith carefully brushed cobwebs and niter from her skirts before she emerged from behind an ancient tapestry. The heavy fabric hid a long unused doorway that led to several ancient cells. And while Yerith had a ready excuse for any acolyte who might see her emerge from this hidden passage—as keeper of the ghadi she needed to look for available storerooms and sleeping chambers to ease the overcrowding—she didn't want her appearance to raise any more questions than necessary.

She especially didn't want anyone to think she had gone beyond the dozen rooms immediately accessible from here, or to even think there were such passages beyond the last room.

She took several deep breaths and listened. Even with her story scripted before her, the ideal would be to avoid the questions entirely.

Fortunately, beyond the tapestry was only silence.

Yerith slipped out from behind the tapestry, releasing a cloud of dust that made her sneeze. She stood still, heart racing, feeling as if the sneeze had alerted every scholar in the College above her. The brief panic didn't keep the dust from making her sneeze again.

The gods must not have noticed her, because no one else seemed to.

Yerith replaced the tapestry so it was hanging as it had before her exit. She smiled to herself. She had done it, and for all the supposed omnipotence of the College, no one knew. No robed acolytes waited to take her into custody.

She walked down the corridor, doing her best to hide her feelings.

She was in the lowest level of the College. The air was heavy down here, and there were too few lamps. But she was not very far from her work. The College's ghadi were housed in a small set of chambers not quite removed from the cells where heretics were imprisoned.

Yerith made a point not to look at the iron doors she passed, because it would make her think of the desperate souls behind them. Doomed victims of the College who were not going to be spirited away. Victims who weren't important enough to . . .

Stop it.

She forced her mind away from defying the College, and on to doing her job. She had several ghadi that needed some sort of attention. Then there was the evening feeding.

Yerith stopped at another iron door that was larger and in better repair than the others, one that saw a lot more use. She pulled it open, and the warm smell of the ghadi rolled across her.

She stepped inside and did a quick inspection. The bedding in the open cells looked in good shape. That had been a major improvement ever since she trained the ghadi to change it themselves. When she had taken over down here, the ghadi had to rely on guardsmen on punishment detail to keep them from standing and sleeping in their own filth.

None of the ghadi standing in the common area, or in the stalls, seemed to require any immediate attention, so Yerith walked down the central aisle to the rear, where there were a few cells closed off.

She checked on the isolated ghadi. The pregnant ones seemed to be doing fine. The one with a broken arm seemed to be healing up nicely. But, when she checked on the cells where the more critical ghadi were, the cells were empty.

"What?"

Yerith looked around. The cells only opened from the outside, and the trained ghadi here had never shown any interest in opening the doors.

"I'm afraid they were taken."

Yerith turned to face an acolyte in a brown robe wearing a blank white mask. She knew him.

"Taken?" She had a sick feeling.

The acolyte nodded. "It was decided that those ghadi were a waste of your efforts and resources. They'll be used elsewhere."

"A waste?" Yerith shook her head. "I'm the ghadi master here. That was my decision." Her decision, but only at the pleasure of the Masters of the College. The ghadi here were nothing to them other than resources to be used up and discarded. Yerith had never officially disposed of a ghadi, because she knew all too well what that meant. Better to let the creature die of disease, or infection, or age.

She leaned against the door of one of the empty cells. "Why are you here, Arthiz?"

The acolyte stepped into the aisle and looked at the ghadi. The ghadi parted before him, casting wary glances at his mask and robe. "I wanted to compliment you on your efforts."

Yerith felt nervous talking about it here, in the College. However, she knew enough about the acolyte calling himself Arthiz to know that he would not be here if there was any chance of the wrong person hearing the conversation. "You've never told me why," she said.

"This is a dangerous game. I am necessarily cautious."

"Maybe. But your creature is freed, and hidden. Is it too much to ask why I used my ghadi to save this deformed half-human monstrosity, and not one of the hundreds of men, women, or children that the College keeps here?"

Arthiz shook his head. "Not too much to ask, no. Just too much to answer."

"I deserve something."

"All I can say is that your act has had the intended effect, and this pleases me."

Yerith closed her eyes. She shouldn't trust this man,

even if he showed the seal of the Monarch and claimed to have the end of the College in his mind. For all she knew, this was part of some elaborate game the College itself was playing.

However, all the doubts in the world would not change what she had already done. She had to keep to the course she'd set for herself, and hope that it was going in the right direction.

"What do I do now?"

"Treat it with the same care as one of your ghadi charges. It must remain hidden until it can be moved, and moved without notice."

"You realize this thing is chalk-white and as tall as a ghadi. How can it escape notice?"

Arthiz chuckled. "There is more than one way out of Manhome, my lady."

Chapter Twelve

NATE'S LUCID moments were getting longer.

Still, it was a while before he had the energy to do more than daydream about greasy hamburgers, Chinese takeout, and deep-dish pizza. When it became undeniable that there was a world outside his own head, and it wasn't going anywhere, he took stock of himself.

Upon his self-examination, Nate decided that he probably should have been dead. He had always been skinny, but his body now was skeletal. There didn't seem to be any muscle mass left at all. He could see the details of every joint, every bone, through sickly-pale skin.

Sores dotted his body, scabbed over for the most part, but a few were actively discharging.

The reason he didn't feel his insect companions anymore was because someone, probably his nurse, had shaved him bald. Not just beard and the hair on top of his head, but also his eyebrows, his armpits, and his pubic hair. It was all just now growing back.

His groin itched so badly with the hair growing in that he would have scratched it until it bled if he was up to that kind of exertion.

His new home had walls of yellowing plaster, revealing carved stone underneath a few major cracks. Light came from a brass oil lamp that hung from a wrought-iron hook by the door. Soot from the lamp had cast permanent shadows on the wall behind it and the high-arched ceiling above. The bed was long and narrow, and still seemed to fill more than half the width of the room.

He was not yet strong enough to get up and try the massive iron door and see if it was locked.

Where am I?

The question had worn such a deep groove in his psyche that it was nearly meaningless. The words were little more than an arcane incantation that might have been chanted by Scarface behind his demonic red mask.

A forever ago Nate had decided that he had permanently left what he had known as the real world. The place he occupied was no more a part of the planet Earth of the twenty-first century than was the land of Oz. The darkness he had fallen through had been some sort of rift, some portal or transition between his world and someplace else.

A few times Nate tried to decide exactly how "real" this world was, but ended up tying himself in the kind of solipsistic knots that had made him drop the one philosophy course he had tried to take in college.

He had no end of theories that could deny the reality around him; he could postulate his own hallucinatory madness; he could invent some entity trying to manipulate his perceptions; he could even pretend that he was embedded in the ultimate virtual reality roleplaying game. The problem with all of that was the fact that he had nearly died in that black pit where they had kept him. Reality itched. Reality made him smell his own shit. Reality was a painful bite of hunger burrowing in his nonexistent stomach.

Pretty much, reality sucked.

In a way, it was even worse here than in the pit he'd been rescued from. Up until now he'd been too sick and delirious to really contemplate what was happening. Now he was well enough to think, and to brood.

He wondered how long he had been here. He wondered what was happening to his family. He wondered if Thanksgiving had come and gone yet. And he wondered if all his speculation meant anything when he had so clearly and completely left his own reality.

If there was anything open to question, it was the world he had come from. The only proof he had that his memory of another world had any validity at all was his physical appearance. Racially, he was so different from the people who lived here, he *had* to come from somewhere else.

● ● ●

His nursemaid came in twice a "day." She would examine him, and feed him a bowl of thick, bland broth. When Nate seemed to have regained his senses, if not his strength, she left him a chamber pot.

Each time, Nate would ask her, "Who are you?"

Each time she'd mutter something in her incomprehensible language and get down to her business.

On the eighth visit after Nate regained the ability to count, she did something new. After helping him eat, she took his left leg and bent the knee upward. She held it there and gave Nate a meaningful look.

Nate stared back.

She put his leg down and repeated the motion. Nate could feel unused muscles tightening in his thighs. She looked at him again, and appeared frustrated that Nate didn't get it right away.

She sighed and started doing it repeatedly, chanting, *"Phi. Ghno. Ka. Lek. Dho. Shin."*

It took a moment, but Nate got the idea. Physical therapy. He had been sick and immobile for so long that he probably would have to exercise at least as long to get back to where he had been. Maybe longer.

"Okay, sister. I get it."

Nate shook his leg free and did the bending motion himself, raising the knee above the bed. It was harder than it looked, and he couldn't hold it up as far as she'd been raising it, but he managed.

Keeping time, he imitated her. *"Phi. Ghno. Ka. Lek. Dho. Shin."*

She stared at him as he dropped the first leg and started on the other. *"Phi. Ghno. Ka. Lek. Dho. Shin."*

By the end, he was covered in sweat. "Okay, how many reps am I supposed to do before I lose consciousness?"

She still stared at him, a look of fascination on her face.

"What?"

She held up a finger and said tentatively, *"Phi."*

Nate held up his left index finger and repeated, *"Phi."*

The look of surprise on her face was comical, as if she had just run across a Shetland pony that quoted Shakespeare. She held up a second finger and said, *"Ghno."*

Nate repeated it with his own finger.

"Ghno." Nate smiled at her reaction. "You like that? You'll love this." Nate went through the fingers of that hand. *"Ka. Lek. Dho."*

"Ka. Lek. Dho," she repeated.

Nate held up the thumb on his right hand, *"Shin."*

She laughed. He liked her laugh.

He held up his right index finger and wagged it, arching his eyebrows in what he hoped was a quizzical expression.

"Phishin," she told him.

"Phishin," Nate repeated. *Phi Shin? A base six counting system? Why not, it's as weird as anything else here.*

Nate held up his right middle finger and, before she could prompt him, he said, *"Ghnoshin?"* Looking quizzical again.

Her eyes widened and she said, *"Ghnoshin"* as if she was correcting him. As far as Nate could tell, it was the same word.

"Ghnoshin," Nate repeated.

She clapped her hands together and laughed again. Nate used up the rest of his fingers on *"Kashin,"* and *"Lekshin."*

Conan goes to Sesame Street, Nate thought.

His keeper was mighty pleased with him. It was as if the possibility he might pick up on part of her language never occurred to her. Nate was happy he managed to correct that idea, because if he was going to survive once he left this bed, he had better be able to understand the natives.

"Let's see just how far your mathematics has gotten," Nate told her. He held up both hands toward her, and started lowering fingers, the reverse of what they'd been doing. He counted backward, stumbling a little when he confused *"Ka"* and *"Lek."*

"Ka," Three.

"Ghno," Two.

"Phi," One.

With both his hands curled into fists, Nate gave her the quizzical expression again. Her face looked blank, so Nate repeated counting down, *"Ka, Ghno, Phi . . ."* This time she slapped her forehead and said, *"Tga."* She held out her hand and counted down the last three fingers, *"Ka, Ghno, Phi, Tga."*

Zero.

Nate tried to pronounce it, but *"Tga"* seemed more phlegm than word. It came out sounding more like *"Ka"* than anything else, which amused his nurse.

"Yeah," Nate said to her, laughing himself. "Let me see what your learning curve in C++ is, huh?"

She shook her head and came over and, businesslike, started showing him exercises for his arms.

"Phi. Ghno. Ka. Lek. Dho. Shin."

Though, for practice, and out of a perverse hacker's sense of humor, when he counted the reps he started with *"Tga."*

• • •

Over the days, as Nate recovered, he thanked God for the diversion of his exercises and the task of learning a new language. Deep in his soul Nate was a problem solver, and having something to keep his mind occupied held at bay the slow rot of depression.

During visit *"Dhoshin"* Nate discovered his nurse's name was Yerith. He was also able to get across his own name, Nate. While she was obviously fascinated and pleased that Nate was picking up words in her language, her ability to teach was strained by time. Nate could have kept her at his side for hours, pulling words into his vocabulary, but she was obviously worried about staying too long.

Nate tried to be gallant about it, but it was frustrating when she could only stay fifteen minutes or so, though now that he could feed and clean himself, most of that time was devoted to language and keeping tabs on how well his recovery was going.

During the time between visits, Nate would push his body as far as he could manage, while chanting foreign words to himself, trying to make sense of things. He had a goal of being able to speak a complete sentence by the time he was ambulatory.

His recuperative powers exceeded his linguistic ability.

By the middle of his second week of lucidity he managed to struggle out of bed, but he was barely at the "Me Tarzan, You Jane," stage.

Again, he seemed to have surprised his angel of mercy. They both startled each other when she pushed in the door while he was pacing next to the bed, supporting himself on the wall. He fell on his ass on the bed, and she spilled his dinner—which by this point consisted of pieces identifiable as meat, bread, and a tankard of some weak beverage that in a previous life might have been warm beer.

"I walk." Nate said, using what parts of the alien tongue he had learned so far. He felt as if it still sounded as if he was trying to cough up a hairball. He knew his accent was absolutely horrible.

Yerith understood him. "I see," she responded in kind. She knelt to retrieve the items she had dropped. The floor was piled with threadbare carpets, and the broth along with about half the grog had soaked into them. She managed to save the bread, and a hunk of meat. She looked at him and he saw concern in her face. She pointed to the door and said, "No."

It wasn't harsh, the way she said it, and her eyes looked at him to see that he understood.

Nate understood, and he wished he had the ability to explain it to her. He wanted to leave, but he also knew that on the other side of that door lived a group of men with masks who seemed bent on making him disappear. The most he could manage at his level of comprehension was, "I hear you."

He smiled and hoped she knew what he meant. He was okay staying here until . . .

Until we can communicate enough so you can explain to me why I shouldn't. Until you can explain why I'm here in the first place.

He didn't try to explain that he had already tested her goodwill. Of course he had tried the door. While it was latched, he could see a dark corridor beyond the small barred window. He had stared out there for a long time, reminding himself that there was a world beyond the four walls he saw every day.

Yerith did appear relieved as she set what was left of his dinner on the table. Then she sat down, waiting for Nate to start the lesson.

Probably because Yerith wasn't trained to be a teacher, she let Nate lead. That was okay. Of anyone, Nate was the best judge of how quickly he was picking things up. He still wished that she could give him some guidance. He was certain that he didn't know what questions he should ask.

He decided that, now that he was upright, he would attack a subject that had been a pet peeve since he had gained consciousness down here. While he had long outgrown any shyness—he couldn't really feel embarrassed being naked in front of a woman who had wiped diarrhea from his ass and who'd shaved his lice-infested pubic hair—being naked 24/7 was getting kind of old.

He started by reaching over and taking her sleeve. Her clothes were a little more normal-looking to Nate as far as style went. Probably because they were more utilitarian. She had a blouse and a bodice that fit close at the waist and then fell into a skirt. The colors were somber. It was only rarely that he'd see a hint of color peek out from the grays and browns.

Today there was a little color. She had a patterned blue scarf around her neck.

He rubbed the fabric of her sleeve and said, "You have." Then he slapped the skin of his arm. "No have."

Sometimes she looked at him like he was spouting gibberish. This was one of those times. He repeated himself with a number of different items of clothing until she got it.

She responded with one word that she repeated until he could make a shot at pronouncing it.

"Clothes," Nate repeated his newest noun.

"Yes," she said.

Nate pointed at the table and said, "You bring food."

"Yes."

"You bring drink."

"Yes."

Nate pointed at himself. "You bring clothes."

She got it the first time, Nate could see it in her eyes. However, it took her a long time to respond.

Long pause. Then, "Yes. I will bring you clothes."

Chapter Thirteen

YERITH COULD not stop thinking about the stranger.

Long ago, when she had agreed to become part of Arthiz's conspiracy, she had never thought she would be in such intimate contact with something so alien. His long pale body, hollow face, and bizarre atonal gibbering dominated her mind even as she walked the market.

Around her, life went on, completely unaware of the secret that preoccupied her. Farmers stood in front of their carts, calling at her to just look and see that this was the largest eggfruit, the finest blood-melon, the most aromatic herbs from the most pampered of gardens, the rarest of spices. . . .

Every farmer acted as if he knew her. They probably did. She walked through the market twice a sixday, buying food for the College's ghadi. The fact that she represented the College and, more importantly, spent large sums of the College's money, made her a person of some notoriety.

Several times, she stopped and purchased grains or vegetables to maintain the College's stock of ghadi.

More than usual, she felt the weight of her dual allegiance. In her heart she had hated the College of Man ever since the death of her father. However, here she was keeping enslaved ghadi of the Manhome College healthy and fed. Ghadi for the scholars of the

College to consume like rats feeding on an overripe eggfruit.

It was hard to keep her ambivalence out of her voice as she haggled over the price of salt beans. Even so, she did her job.

The market itself seemed endless. The merchants were spread over three of Manhome's widest boulevards in an ever-changing chaos. Not just food, but cloth, jewelry, livestock, and—in the public square where all three boulevards met—ghadi.

Yerith passed by the ghadi auction and stopped. The ghadi stood, long-limbed and mute, as their keeper pulled them to the stage, one by one. The interested buyers were encouraged to approach the stage and examine the ghadi in question.

He is tall as a ghadi. As thin as one.

But he spoke. He even named himself. Yerith couldn't understand that. Speech, language, that was part of the mind. There was the language of Man, and the language of the Gods.

But the gibberish her charge spoke was neither. And, somehow, like an infant, he was learning the language of Man. How could this thing do that, and not be a man himself? No ghadi could ever speak, or even understand, human words, no matter what was spoken in their presence. At best, Yerith could train them to understand hand signals and whistled commands. Something as basic as a name was beyond their comprehension.

But they were more than brute animals. Yerith knew that, and in the end, that was what made her dangerous to the College, and that was why she was valuable to Arthiz, the Monarch's pet acolyte. The ghadi were invisible to the scholars of the College, mute and interchangeable.

In other words, they were perfect spies.

The third ghadi was brought to the stage. A male whose skin was a faded rose-violet. The lower knee on either leg was swollen, as was the second elbow, the first stages of arthritis. Yerith saw the callused hands and feet and shook her head. This ghadi was trained for heavy labor, but was probably only a year or two away from being crippled. She hoped his new owner would use him for domestic tasks, maybe make things easier for him.

A vain hope. Those rich enough to have domestic servants didn't buy ghadi at a street auction. The people bidding here were merchants and farmers who needed laborers, or acolytes who needed blood and power. In either case, this ghadi did not have long to live, and the life wouldn't amount to much.

"So, can you offer an opinion of the goods they're selling?"

Yerith turned to see Arthiz, his blank mask a blazing white in the midday sun. She felt a slight relief at seeing him. She hadn't seen him since the day she had brought his creature down to the secret chambers under Manhome.

"You're late." She spoke quietly.

Arthiz made an act of studying the ghadi onstage, then looking down at her. "There is a place where we can talk, down the Avenue of Gods. There is a temple with a red door beyond the end of the marketplace. Go there after they've sold two more ghadi."

Before Yerith could respond, he slipped back into the auction crowd.

●   ●   ●

As the name would suggest, the Avenue of the Gods was once a place for temples and altars and offering houses. That time had passed centuries ago. The current crowded street now bore little resemblance to the broad avenue that showed in some old paintings and tapestries that Yerith had seen. There were no public altars, or marble statues lining the street. The buildings pressed to the edge of the avenue now—boardinghouses, inns, residences, shops.

Several centuries of construction had built over and around Arthiz's ancient temple, so that it was completely absorbed into the stone flesh of the city. Even the cobbled avenue itself passed above it, so Yerith only spotted the red doors because she was looking for them.

The doors had once been part of a grand entrance. Yerith could see signs of a great arch and a broad stairway, both ending as they met newer walls. The elaborately carved doors themselves had been cut, now ending midway up, truncated by the first floor of an alehouse.

Yerith climbed the makeshift stairway down to the doors and saw that they were still half again as tall as she was.

The doors weren't locked or barred, so she walked inside.

"Arthiz?" Beyond the doors was a large room that was dark and smelled of damp.

"Here." Inside, Arthiz lit a lamp, illuminating a small area of the old temple. It felt as if they were between worlds here, the floor was smooth marble, the ceiling rough-hewn timbers supporting the alehouse above. One side of the room was dominated by truncated stone columns, the other by black wooden casks that were just as wide.

"Why did we leave the auction?" Yerith asked. She was nervous about deviating from the pattern they had established. The only places that Yerith was free to mingle with acolytes from the College and not arouse interest or suspicion was either at the market auction or inside the College itself. She might be employed by the College, but she was still an outsider who was only permitted contact with actual members of the College within very strict limits.

Exchanging words at the auction might be passed over as a chance meeting. If anyone became aware that she was here with an acolyte, alone, she could easily find herself in one of the cells under the College.

"There is growing suspicion within the College itself. We need to meet in places unobserved."

"What has happened?"

"Nothing that was not anticipated. How is the creature?"

Yerith shook his head. "The thing talks."

"Talks?"

"Barely a sixday passed and it spoke words to me. It counts. It has a name. This is no strange ghadi. I am thinking it may be human."

Arthiz was quiet for a long time before he spoke. "It learns the Language of Man?" He spoke quietly, mostly to himself. He looked up and nodded at Yerith. "You are right, of course. He is human. A stranger so removed from us that he does not even know the Language of Man. His name was given as Nateblack." Arthiz twisted the odd syllables with his tongue, but it was recognizably the words spoken by the creature.

"Nate Black." Yerith corrected in a neutral tone, placing the pause in the appropriate place. "You told me none of this."

"You did not need to know this to keep him alive and hidden."

"What else have I not been told?"

"Yerith, you are valuable to me and the Monarch. The more I tell you, the more danger you are in."

"And if the College discovers me now, who will my ignorance protect?" Yerith looked at Arthiz. "It, he, wants to learn. Am I wrong to teach him?"

"No. Though I wonder what this implies."

"He wants clothing."

"What?"

"He has told me he wants clothing. Shall I get him some?"

"No," Arthiz said. "I will bring his clothes to you. There are things I must do."

Yerith nodded. "Is there anything else you would have me or my ghadi do?"

"This is your sole duty now. After our next meeting I will travel to confer with the Monarch. You will keep Nate Black well and safe in my absence. I am trusting to your discretion."

"Thank you."

"Do not thank me." Arthiz extinguished the lamp. "Talking to this thing is the most dangerous act anyone could ask you to do."

Chapter Fourteen

THE CLOTHES she brought him were the same ones that he had worn here. That raised a whole host of questions that Nate didn't have the linguistic skill to express yet. They also raised a sickening wave of emotion that Nate wasn't prepared for.

In the days he had spent here, recovering, his method of coping with the loss of his world, his family, real food, his stupid cat, was denial. He had managed to half convince himself that his life before captivity had been some sort of delusion. He never directly questioned his own perception of reality, but seeing his leather bomber jacket, jeans, even his old cotton jockeys, shattered some protective illusions that Nate didn't even know he was building.

He held the old concert T-shirt, and his hands shook. *Is this it? Is this the only fragment of my life I have left?*

He'd never even liked that band.

It wasn't until Yerith started talking in a rapid panic that Nate realized he was crying. He didn't understand her, but her gist seemed to be, "What's wrong?"

"I'm a fucking prisoner. What do you think?" Nate looked up at her and saw from her expression that she might not get his English, but she seemed to read his expression well enough.

Nate sighed. "Shouldn't blame you, should I? You did what I asked."

He didn't have the local word for "thanks," so he

just held up the shirt and did his best to smile. "You bring," he told her.

She looked at him uncertainly and replied, "I bring."

Aren't we the witty conversationalists?

Nate looked back down at his T-shirt. The language barrier was rising on his list of frustrations. Every new word he learned almost seemed to make the communication barrier worse. Every time he looked at Yerith, a tidal wave of questions tried to smash through his thirty-word vocabulary.

Who the hell are you?

Where the hell am I?

Who the hell were the people behind those masks?

If I told you what Cleveland was, could you point me in the right direction?

At least she seemed more interested in keeping him comfortable than Scarface and company had been.

Nate got dressed, impressing himself by being strong enough to stand up and pull on his pants without help.

She does seem to be as interested in talking to me as I am in talking to her.

"Let's see," Nate muttered to himself, "how committed we are to the learning process." If he was going to progress at anything approaching a reasonable pace, he needed more than a couple of fifteen minute visits a day.

He didn't have the words he needed, but he used the concert T-shirt to help get his point across. He laid the shirt on the bed between them, the back of it facing up. The back didn't have any pictures, just a list of bars and gig dates.

He grabbed a spoon from his last meal and squatted over the shirt, tracing the letters with the tip of the spoon.

Nate looked up at her and said, "You bring . . ." He waved the spoon at the unknown word. She looked at him, then down at the shirt. He could tell he had surprised her again.

She traced the lines of text with her fingers.

He tried to figure out a way of telling her that these were words in his own language. The best he could come up with was, "Clothes speak to eye." He moved the spoon and traced the letters. "Hand speaks to clothes."

She looked at him, eyes wide, and said, "You can . . ." The word that followed, almost certainly meant, "Read."

Yeah. I am just full of surprises.

"You can read," she repeated.

"I can read," Nate said, doing his best to pronounce the new verb.

Yerith started pacing. She shook her head and chattered in her language too fast for Nate to pick up on the words he did know. She seemed to be debating something with herself. After a few moments, she looked at him, then at the shirt. She looked as if she had come to a decision.

"I bring," she said.

•   •   •

Yerith did bring.

And she brought a lot.

First, she brought a worn wooden case three inches wide and about a foot long. Inside it were a pair of brushes and a small black oval that had a depression worn in the center. The set was very well used and completely unadorned.

Then she brought him a journal. It was a foot square, with a cracked leather binding, and had about a hundred pages. Except for handwritten notes on the first two pages, the rest of it was blank. The paper was thick and brown, but still seemed flexible enough that Nate wasn't afraid to turn the pages.

Finally, she brought him books. So many books that for the first time Nate saw one of the aliens helping her with her burden. The creature didn't enter the room, it just stood there holding the volumes in its arms as Yerith started piling books into the room.

There must have been twenty volumes of various sizes.

"I bring, you can read," she announced.

• • •

Nate started keeping notes in the journal. Diary entries mixed with notes on the language mixed with speculations concrete and theoretical. He came up with a rough estimate that it had been between two and three months since he had arrived in this world. He was pretty certain that he was into his second month under Yerith's charge.

Yerith's schedule was regular for the most part. A "morning" visit and an "evening" visit. She brought him food, linens, water, took away the used chamber pots, and helped him with his language.

He occupied his days, outside the half hour or so that Yerith spent with him, continuing to exercise— running in place, doing sit-ups, chinning himself with the chains holding the lamps.

When his body was worn out, he would take the journal and one of the books, and try to read. The attempt was taxing. Trying to figure out the written language was worse, in some sense, than the physical exercise. But, unlike the spoken lessons with Yerith, his time with the text was unlimited.

He was fortunate in that the written language was phonetic, not ideographic. That meant he could tinker with it and get some idea what a novel word might sound like. Armed with that information, he could have a list of questions ready for Yerith when she came, which made the process go much more efficiently. Instead of getting one or two words a day, Nate was picking up maybe half a dozen.

He also learned that the language was tonal. The way you said a word—rising, falling, the accent— changed the word's meaning. That was the reason behind all the strange flourishes he saw connecting distant characters in the written text. They were guides that showed how to intone the basic syllable, word, sentence, or paragraph.

Fortunately for Nate's learning curve, the language wasn't like Asian languages where a different tone on a syllable could give a word a completely different meaning. This language used tone to indicate the tense of a statement—which explained a number of misunderstandings he had had with Yerith. Whenever he had been asking a question, the rising tone at the end—which meant a question in English—placed the whole sentence in the historical past tense.

That was going to be a hard habit to break.

By the middle of his third month as Yerith's charge, Nate could honestly say, "I can read." Even if it only meant one sentence every five to fifteen minutes while referring to his growing crib sheets on Yerith's language. He had, so far, bulled through a quarter of the first of Yerith's books, a gardening textbook.

That was also the point where he started seriously examining the latch on the door that kept him prisoner.

● ● ●

When Nate felt adept enough, he asked, "Why am I kept here?"

"We keep you safe," Yerith said. "You are not safe out there," Yerith pointed toward the door.

"How long?" Being sequestered here was fine enough while he was recovering, but he was back to normal physically. In fact, since he had kept up with the physical regimen, he was probably in better shape now than when he had come here.

"I am waiting," she said.

And I am the one in the fucking hole.

"You wait for what?" Every sentence was a struggle. He could come so close to what was in his mind, and still have to dance around it.

"A man."

"Who?"

"His name is Arthiz." *Godot by any other name.*

"Why do you wait for him?"

"He . . ." Nate watched her struggle for a common word, before she came up with, "He leads."

Just following orders, huh?

Nate frowned. In reality the only thing that made his current captivity tolerable was how it fared in comparison with the bastards who got their paws on him first. He was still a prisoner, and objectively, if it hadn't been for his horrific initial experience, he wouldn't be nearly as sanguine about being kept here.

However, he was becoming less inclined to wait for Yerith's leader to come to some decision about him.

"Why do I wait for him?" Nate asked.

Yerith took a long time to respond.

"He needs you," she finally said.

How nice. "Why do I need him?"

She looked at him in a way that made him realize he had sacrificed a bit of mutual goodwill with that question. Nate couldn't help it. He was stir-crazy. He needed to see the sky, smell the air.

Have a cheeseburger.

Yerith obviously had the same frustrating time with language that Nate was having. Whatever she wanted to say couldn't be easily put in their common vocabulary. She finally repeated, "You are not safe out there."

It wasn't a very satisfying answer, and she knew it. She looked at his face, then she stood up and grabbed one of the volumes that still sat by the foot of Nate's bed.

"Read this," she said.

• • •

That day, Nate switched from the gardening textbook to the volume that Yerith had handed him. That day, he also figured how to jimmy the door latch from the inside.

CHAPTER FIFTEEN

THE BOOK WAS local mythology, at least that's
how Nate interpreted it . . .

• • •

*Thousands of years ago, a race called the ghadi ruled
the world. They worshiped a demon named Ghad.
Ghad gave the ghadi race the Language of the Gods,
the language of creation. With it, they could write words
to change the world, create or destroy, and form the
earth itself to their liking. The Ghadikan nation had
lived and prospered for uncounted aeons.*

*There were other demons, brothers to Ghad. Ghad
would show them the Ghadikan and say, "Look how
prosperous. Look how powerful and happy my ghadi
are."*

*Mankin, one of Ghad's brothers, rebuked Ghad for
his unseemly pride. Ghad laughed and said, "No race
could do better than my Ghadikan."*

*Mankin then wagered with Ghad that he could place
his own race in the world, naked and helpless, and in
twelve hundred years they would surpass the Ghadikan's prowess.*

Ghad, in his pride, allowed it to be done.

And Mankind appeared in the world.

• • •

Yerith was obviously not an experienced jailer. Either that, or she never examined his clothing very closely.

The mechanism of the door was very simple, just a hinged iron bar that fell across the front of the door. The belt from his jeans provided Nate with the means to lift it from the inside. He just needed to loop the end of the belt and dangle it out the small window in the doorway. It took a toss or two, but he could catch the end of the bar and lift it out of its cradle.

If anything—once he decided that it wasn't time to cut and run just yet—the mechanics of closing the thing from the inside were more difficult.

However, he managed.

After one dry run, opening and closing the door, he waited for Yerith to notice something amiss. She didn't.

After that, he timed his explorations carefully.

He left the room at "night" a few hours after her second visit. While there was some variation in the times she came during the day, she never came before Nate woke up in the "morning," so Nate was sure of something like ten or twelve hours by himself.

After she would leave in the evening, Nate would study for long enough that he was certain that Yerith was no longer in the vicinity, then he would unhook the oil lamp and open the door.

The first few times sent his pulse racing, as if masked acolytes waited in the shadows to pounce on him. It was nerve-racking enough that he confined his first travels to the corridor in the immediate area.

The corridor was stone, with a peaked arch for a roof about fifteen feet above him. Doors like the one to his room were spaced at irregular intervals, though all had been rusted shut. Nate noticed that the face of his door looked no different. When shut, it would appear, at first glance, as frozen and immobile as the rest.

Not far down the hall from his room, Nate discovered what this place was.

Between sets of doors were low, long niches set into

the walls. Nate held the oil lamp close and saw a pile of bones.

Catacombs, Nate thought, *they're hiding me in a place of the dead.*

The bones weren't human. He saw the extra joint in their limbs.

Are these the ghadi?

• • •

First the ghadi thought the new creatures brute animals. They kept them as slaves and pets, which amused Ghad. For six hundred years, they used Mankind as slaves, to bear the work that no Ghadi should do. Ghad was pleased with this; he saw it right that his creation should do no mean labor.

"See," Ghad told Mankin, "Your race is fit for nothing but slaves to my beautiful ghadi."

However, because the Ghadikan kept Mankind so close, Mankind learned. Mankind learned to speak, to use tools. They learned writing and science. Some were also able to learn the Language of the Gods.

One day the Ghadikan woke up to find their servants had gone. Their food was left uncooked, their crops left unharvested, their palaces left unfinished. So long had they relied on Mankind's labor that the whole Ghadikan nation ceased to function.

Overnight, it seemed to the Ghadikan, Mankind had raised their own city far from the ghadi, halfway around the great crescent of the world from the farthest ghadi outpost.

This displeased Ghad, and Mankin said, "Why should you fret? Our wager's half done and your wondrous Ghadikan still rules all the world—except this small bit."

Ghad knew that Mankin taunted him. So he ordered the Ghadikan to prepare for war.

• • •

After the first few days of exploring, Nate realized that it was a good thing he was cautious in his explora-

tion. It was a maze down here. Seemingly endless
stone corridors, walls piled with bone, and iron
doors—all the same.

One time he passed a door that had frozen partway
open, and Nate got a look at what his little cell must
have looked like, originally. This room had the same
long narrow footprint, but occupying the center of the
floor was a marble sarcophagus.

Great, Nate thought, *I've been living in someone's
crypt for the past three months. Damn good thing I'm
not superstitious.*

Not long after that, he had to take his journal along
with him so he could map out the passages to keep
himself from getting lost.

On the page, lines grew from the small box representing his cell, spreading out like a spiderweb. It was
clear that there were miles of these passages that
twisted and turned in on themselves.

Nate began to think that the only way he'd ever find
his way to the surface would be to follow Yerith there.

• • •

*In the six hundred years that Mankind were slaves,
the Ghadikan had grown soft. It took them many years
to prepare their war against Man. While the Ghadikan
prepared for war, Mankind studied, learning of the
world, and of the Language of the Gods.*

*When Ghad sent his Ghadikan against Man, he was
prideful and confident. "See," he told Mankin, "What
a glorious army. Surely nothing could stand before it."*

*"Indeed," Mankin said, "Nothing in the world can
stop such a force."*

*But Ghad feared, because he knew Mankin taunted
him again.*

*True to Mankin's word, nothing in the world stopped
the mighty army of the Ghadikan. The men of the city,
seeing the force upon them, turned to the College of
Man who spoke the Gods' Language.*

"Deliver us from this threat," they pleaded.

The men of the College said, "Long have we studied

*the Language of the Gods. We have learned much.
There are words in it too terrible to be spoken."*

*"Please," said the men of the city, "speak them so
we shall be delivered."*

*The men of the College, seeing their plight, chose to
speak those terrible words.*

*The Ghadikan did not know that Mankind could
speak words of such power. When the great army heard
them, it trembled, for those words called stones to fall
from the sky. Great boulders, as large as mountains,
fell and slew the whole Ghadikan army. The fires of
their destruction were so great that the smoke blocked
out the sun for sixty years.*

● ● ●

One foray, one of the farthest from his cell, brought
him into a chamber that was different from any of the
others he had seen so far in this labyrinth. It was
nearly a half-hour's walk in a nearly, straight line from
his cell. In terms of his map, his cell was near the
center of the page, while this place was over the edge
of the neighboring page.

It was the terminus of one of the corridors, the first
place he had come to that dead-ended rather than
looping back on itself, or branching into two or
more corridors.

The hall emptied into a cylindrical chamber with a
peaked ceiling twice as high as the corridor itself.
Stone chairs were carved into the walls, and seated on
them were skeletal remains that seemed to be held in
place by elaborate suits of armor. The bodies were
the alien race, that Nate had now mentally named
"ghadi" from the mythos he was reading.

Unlike the living ghadi Nate had seen, these Nate
could picture taking part in a great army. As long
dead as these ghadi were, they still bore a great
fierceness that showed through their expressionless
skulls and corroded armor.

Standing, central to the chamber, was an oversized
sculpture of a ghadi, resting its gauntleted hands on a

massive sword. One foot stood on its helmet as its bare face looked upward—

Waiting for the asteroid to hit? Looking for Ghad? Expecting rain?

At the base of the statue was a plaque. Nate looked at it, hoping for an inscription in the common language that he could try to translate. Instead he saw a rectilinear scratching that was all too familiar.

The same symbols that Nate had seen marking Scarface's flesh, marking the sphere that had spoken, that Scarface had carved into the doomed guardsman's chest.

For some reason he couldn't fathom, the presence of these runes frightened Nate.

"Just symbols," Nate whispered, trying to talk himself out of the inexplicable reaction. "Just words . . ."

Just another language.

The language of the ghadi, perhaps?

The Language of the Gods?

Nate sat down and took his brush to copy down the symbols so he could study them back in his cell.

For such simple symbols, Nate found it very hard to copy them accurately. It seemed to take all of his concentration to copy each mark. The symbols were all composed of some combination of three horizontal and three vertical lines and half lines. The combinations varied from a single hash mark to something that looked like the Microsoft Windows logo.

Even so, it took all of Nate's concentration to copy them. The simple transcribing was worse than any of his efforts to translate the common language. By the time he was done, he was covered with sweat and his hand was shaking.

He had a feeling that he had spent far too long here.

He ran back, even though fatigue coursed through his body and his legs felt rubbery.

Nate was back in his cell less than ten minutes when Yerith arrived for her morning visit. When she stared at him, panting and tired, he explained that he had been exercising. If she noticed the fresh ink on his hands, she said nothing about it.

• • •

Ghad was not pleased.

Mankin believed that Ghad had suffered enough for his boastfulness. He said, "Let us end this wager now. Look at what we have wrought on this world. Let us not let pride destroy what you have created."

Ghad cursed his brother. "You have not yet won. Your time is three quarters gone, and your manlings have only one city. They have wrought what destruction they can, but my Ghadikan are still strong. They shall repay your manlings sixtyfold."

That, the Ghadikan did. No more did they build great cities, or tend the fields. Each ghadi studied the Language of the Gods to learn the words that had delivered such a blow. They learned this and more. They called such plague and destruction on Mankind that those that didn't die were scattered throughout the countryside.

Mankind, seeing themselves scattered, turned to the College of Man who spoke the Gods' Language.

"Deliver us from this threat," they pleaded.

The men of the College said, "Long have we studied the Language of the Gods. We have learned much. There are words in it too terrible to be spoken."

"Please," said the survivors of the city of men, "speak them so we shall be delivered."

The men of the College, seeing their plight, chose to speak those terrible words.

Within the Ghadikan cities, the matter of the very stones rebelled upon hearing the words of the College of Man. The stones tore themselves apart with such violence that the cities and all who were in them were enveloped by fire, and the fires of their destruction darkened the sun for sixty years.

• • •

There were six more cylindrical chambers. Nate didn't have to do any more transcription, by inspecting the inscriptions on each of the statues, he saw that the markings were the same. That seemed odd for some sort of memorial, but he wouldn't be able to explain it until he knew exactly what those markings meant.

The map was filling out.

The chambers with the statues and the seated warriors were laid out in a circle as far as Nate could tell, with his cell roughly in the center. The pose of each statue was slightly different, but each faced the entrance to the room, meaning they all faced the center of the "circle."

Each time he looked at the inscriptions, he felt an odd sensation, a pressure in his brain. It was as if he almost knew what it said, the meaning on the tip of his tongue. . . .

Of course, that wasn't possible.

● ● ●

The wager had less than sixty years to run out. Both Mankind and Ghadikan hid from the world, in barrows and caves. The land was thick with smoke, and the sun would not deign to shine on the broken crescent of the earth.

Mankin looked down on the slaughter, a world where more dead lay on the ground than living walked upon it, and mourned the destruction. He turned to his brother and said, "Ghad, you see here the result of your pride. Say the wager ends now and this will be over."

"The wager is not yet over. My Ghadikan yet number more than your manlings."

Mankind itself was dying, as was the Ghadikan race. Mankind, seeing the doom the war with the ghadi was bringing upon them, turned to the College of Man who spoke the Gods' Language.

"Deliver us from this threat," they pleaded.

The men of the College said, "Long have we studied

the Language of the Gods. We have learned much. There are words in it too terrible to be spoken."

"Please," said Mankind, as one, "speak them so we shall be delivered."

The men of the College, seeing their own doom approaching, chose to speak the most terrible of those words.

Upon hearing those words, the bodies of the ghadi, and their seed, went deaf to the Gods' Language. The Ghadikan could no longer speak, and their writing became as dust, mute and meaningless. They became no more than the brutes they had once taken men to be.

Mankind took the ghadi as their servants, to rebuild their cities and till their fields. Ghad finally saw that his pride had lost him the world, and he walked away, never to speak to his brothers again.

• • •

Of course, his last exploration of the catacombs ended with him being caught.

Nate was walking down one of the corridors, and taking the last corner to return to his cell. He was paying more attention to his hand-drawn map than he was to where he was going and he walked right into one of the alien/ghadi. He dropped the journal and upset the oil lamp so it went out.

Without a word, the thing enveloped him in its too-long arms and lifted him off of the ground. This time Nate dropped the oil lamp as well. He could smell the oil as it spilled on the floor.

He struggled, but the thing was too strong.

The thing holding him let out a high-pitched whistle. Nate couldn't see much, but there was enough light coming from somewhere for him to spot sudden movements filling the corridor around him.

There were only three or four ghadi, but the length of their limbs and the insectile way they moved made it seem as if there were many more of them. The only sound they made as they moved was the rustle of their feet across stone.

The one holding him let him go as one of the newcomers wrapped its hand around Nate's upper arm. Another alien took hold of Nate's other arm, and they marched him back toward his cell.

The door was wide open, spilling light into the corridor.

Well, this was bound to happen, eventually.

The ghadi pushed Nate into the room, where Yerith stood, staring at him. A lamp burned on the table.

"Hi, honey, I'm home," he said in English.

It was probably a good thing she couldn't understand him. She looked to be in no mood for sarcasm. Her eyes were red, she was on the verge of hyperventilating, and the cache of books that had sat neatly by the foot of the bed were scattered everywhere. One had its spine broken in half and was shedding pages on the bed.

"Liar," she yelled at him, throwing the book she held at him. *"You evil . . . !"*

Nate held up his arms to ward off the missile. The book must have weighed ten pounds and bruised his forearms with the impact. "Yerith, I was coming ba—"

She grabbed the edges of his jacket and shook him. "He trusted me. How can you . . . need me and you go . . . not safe out in . . ."

The way her words wove in and out of comprehensibility made Nate's head hurt. He balled his hands into fists and yelled at her, *"Stop it!"*

She stopped shaking him.

"I am not your—" *Slave? Property?* Damn the gaps in his vocabulary. "You do not own me. I cannot live in this room all day. Every day. I am losing my mind in here." The idiom sounded very strange in Yerith's language but it seemed to get the meaning across.

Yerith pushed him away. "You have no mind to lose, Nate. I told you to read this."

She picked up the book of myth Nate had been working his way through.

"I have been reading it. It does not explain why you keep me here."

Yerith threw the book at him with an exasperated curse Nate couldn't translate. He caught it. "You can read, but can you think?" She slapped the book in his hands. "The College are the ones behind the masks. In their minds, anything from another place, a new thought, a new race, it all must be . . . destroyed, so the College does not suffer the fate of the Ghadikan."

"I was only—"

"You do not come from here. Anyone who looks at you knows that. If you leave our protection, you will die."

She pushed past him to the door and paused. "I came to tell you that Arthiz is coming here to meet with you."

"You came down here just to tell me?"

"I knew you would want to know." She turned around and said, "Thank you for coming back."

Nate was feeling like an asshole again, though he didn't have a reason to. "I am sorry."

"We can't let you go."

When the door closed behind her, Nate heard the bolt slam home. After a few moments he heard the screech of metal, and a rusted barrier fell across the small barred window.

Nate knew if he tried to open it, it wouldn't budge.

He stood there a long time before he started gathering up books.

Chapter Sixteen

ATE ONLY endured confinement for three more days before she took him to meet Arthiz. She came with her ghadi escort and had him put his hands in front of him so she could bind them together.

Even so, while the way he left his cell echoed his first day here, binding his wrists seemed more formality than restraint. As if she wanted a concrete reminder of what their relationship actually was.

She took him down a corridor that ended in one of the cylindrical chambers where a ghadi statue looked over the fallen. A man waited for them there. Yerith's and Nate's ghadi escort stopped in front of the man.

At first, Nate thought it was the long awaited Arthiz.

He spoke in a very clipped manner, "All is well?"

"As well as the demons dwelling between the worlds."

The man nodded and took an old, tarnished dagger out from under his cloak. Nate briefly saw a blade engraved with the same rectilinear symbols that adorned the statue's pedestal before the man walked up and inserted the dagger into a sheath worn by one of the long-dead ghadi.

Nate felt something, like a static charge in the air, then he heard stones grinding together. The massive carved stone chair, where the dead ghadi sat, slowly withdrew into the wall. The armored skeleton disappeared into the darkness, out of range of their lamps. When the grinding stopped, they faced a dark opening in the wall.

Nate wondered if all the entrances to the catacombs were similarly hidden.

Yerith led Nate through the opening, with her ghadi attendants following. The man who had guarded the secret passage came out last, walked up to the ghadi skeleton and, carefully standing to the side, withdrew the dagger.

Nate felt the same static potential in the air, and heard stone grinding again.

Yerith didn't wait long enough for him to see the dead ghadi return home. They headed downward, along a series of wide stone steps. There was a breeze down here, the air cooler and fresher than the stagnant atmosphere in the catacombs. As they descended, Nate could smell salt and began hearing the crash of surf.

At the end of their climb they were greeted by another man standing guard over a narrow crack in the rock ahead of them. Yerith exchanged the same greetings with him as she had with the guard by the secret passage.

They emerged single file from a fissure in the base of a sheer rock wall that rose impossibly high above them. Nate had to squint because, for the first time in months, he could see daylight.

The ground was sand and gravel that sloped toward a lagoon that might have been several hundred feet across. The rock cliffs circled the lagoon almost completely, only leaving a narrow gap to Nate's left that, at this distance, looked barely large enough for one man to walk through.

Waves crashed at the base of the gap, sending white spray up twenty feet or more. Nate could feel the mist from the waves as a cold breeze on his skin, even this far from the surf.

Above the waves, through the gap between the cliffs, Nate saw the bluest strip of sky he had ever seen—as if the world itself had cracked open to let some unearthly light seep in.

Nate kept looking up. Hundreds of feet above their heads, the sheer rock walls leaned together to meet.

"Where is this?" Nate asked.

"We are at the foot of Manhome," Yerith said. She touched Nate's shoulder and pointed. "That is where we are going."

Nate looked in that direction and saw a boat sitting a few feet away from the farthest edge of the lagoon. Nate stared at it, wondering how it could have navigated that pounding surf and eased through a passage that small.

She led him around the beach, toward the boat. It was larger than it appeared at first, thirty or forty feet long, and had a mast that seemed to loom upward at least as far. It seemed to sit shallow in the water, narrow-bodied with a knifelike bow.

The boat was moored to a stone pier that emerged from the sand to extend halfway toward the center of the lagoon. The blocks that made the pier were five feet on a side, and must have weighed tons. They had been here long enough for the water to polish their edges smooth. The aisle down the center had been worn concave by long use.

A trio of grizzled, nasty-looking characters sat on the deck, watching them approach. They were bare chested and wore black canvas pants. Their hair was long and gathered into dozens of tight braids. Unlike Scarface's ritual mutilations, the scars these guys wore were neither intentional nor followed any intellectual design.

One of them looked Nate up and down, staring at the alien clothes, and spat over the side of the boat, into the water. One spoke to Yerith. "All is well?"

"As well as the demons dwelling between the worlds," she repeated.

The third one, who was missing the last two fingers of his left hand said, probably unnecessarily, "This is the stranger?"

"Yes," Nate answered for Yerith. It probably wasn't a good idea to surprise these guys, but Nate did get some amusement at how shocked they looked when he spoke.

The last one waved Nate forward with his mutilated hand, "Come then."

• • •

Arthiz met Nate in a cramped room down below, in the back of the boat.

The room held a narrow bed that folded against the wall, allowing just enough room to seat one man at a desk that was little more than a ledge on the opposite wall. Nate stood, crouched in the doorway, until someone brought him a stool to sit on.

"I understand I did not need to bring this," his host said, once Nate was seated. Arthiz turned toward Nate, and in his hand was a softball-sized sphere that shone metallic in the lamplight.

"You are one of them," Nate said when he saw the white, featureless mask covering Arthiz's face.

"You are an intelligent man, by Yerith's account. But you suffer from incautious thinking." Arthiz set down the sphere and patted a book that lay on the desk. Nate recognized the journal Yerith had given him. The one he had dropped when the ghadi had grabbed him in the catacombs.

"Do not think in haste. Do not talk in haste. Do not act in haste. Haste is the father of error, and error is the father of all misfortune."

"Why am I here?"

"If I knew that, I would surely be a wise man." Arthiz looked down at Nate's journal. "What I know is that your presence frightens the College, and what frightens the College is of interest to me."

Nate frowned. He wished he could think of a way to say, *Quit the metaphysical bullshit.* Instead, he told Arthiz, "You are an intelligent man. You know what I was asking."

"You have an interesting manner of speech, Nate

Black." He flipped a page. His fingers were long and jeweled, and Nate could see engravings on the rings, as well as the gems mounted within them. "You are a stranger here, and all you've known of this world is violence, disease, and captivity. It must seem an awful place." Arthiz made no concession to Nate's linguistic skills, Nate had to concentrate to follow him, even though he wasn't speaking particularly fast.

"I would rather be imprisoned in the country of my birth."

"This world could be better," Arthiz said.

"I would like to return to where I came from."

Arthiz laughed. It wasn't quite what Nate expected. Arthiz said, "And is it in your mind that such a thing is possible? The College of Man, the most powerful—" He used a word Nate did not know. "—in the world, the keepers of all of Mankind's knowledge since we first trod the stones of Manhome, they want nothing less than to erase your existence from the face of their world. If such was possible, they would have granted you that wish out of their own fear." He shook his head. "Again, you think in haste."

Arthiz turned to face Nate, closing the journal.

"Why did you take me here?" Nate rubbed his temples. "What do you want from me?"

"I brought you here so I would know what you are. Do you know what the College of Man is?"

The name was familiar from the myth in Yerith's book, but Arthiz went on before Nate could form a response. "They—" Arthiz picked up the sphere. "*We* bear the knowledge of the Gods' Language. No one outside the College may write these glyphs or speak their names. These are words of power, of creation, of destruction. They remake the world to their pattern."

"Meaning?"

Arthiz handed it to Nate. "This is an ancient artifact, engraved by many, many artisans."

Nate saw the tiny inscription spiraling around the entire object.

"A single unbroken line, carved continuously over weeks."

"I am impressed." Nate hefted the thing, and to his surprise, it was hollow. There was no weight to it at all.

There was a hole in one end and Nate looked inside and saw no mechanism, just an inner shell where the engraving continued. He stared at the sphere in his cupped hands and said, "This spoke." *How could this thing make any noise at all?*

"Yes, it did."

"How?"

Arthiz spoke some words in the alien tongue that Nate had heard Scarface speak. Like Scarface, Arthiz also gestured with the first three fingers of either hand. This time Nate realized that the gestures traced the rectilinear glyphs in the air.

Arthiz spoke—

As did the sphere in Nate's hand.

"LANGUAGEALPHABETSYMBOL INCANTATIONPOWER CAUSERESULT MEARTHIZ TELLCOMMUNICATE YOUNATEBLACK."

It wasn't metaphor. Words of power meant, *words of power.*

Nate stared at the hollow sphere and his mind filled with the image of Scarface and the guardsman—the glyphs carved into the man's chest, the green flames, the grotesque smell of charred meat. Somehow, he had allowed that memory to hide. He had pretended to himself that it was a fevered vision of a time when he had been too sick to be lucid.

So we can quit pretending we're anywhere near Kansas, Toto.

Arthiz spoke and the sphere stopped vibrating.

• • •

Arthiz stayed several hours with Nate. Much of it was spent describing the College of Man, to which Arthiz admitted being a member.

The College was only nominally an organization of learning. It was actually dedicated to the *control* of knowledge. Its origins were ancient, dating back to the great war between Mankind and Ghadikan.

Because it was the sole repository of the Gods' Language, the College could hold itself above any law, even the rule of the Monarch, who supposedly reigned over the Nation of Men. The scholars of the College could command anything of anyone, without fear of question. In the great city of Manhome, there wasn't even a pretense of an independent civil authority. There were the guardsmen, and there was the College.

The acolytes of the College were required for much of the social infrastructure—medicine, public works, manufacturing, communication.

The College ran the educational system, a centralized network of primary and secondary schools with professional educators and a standardized curriculum, with universal and compulsory attendance.

A system that existed because of the College's universal control over what subjects could be taught, and which subjects were forbidden. A control so absolute that deviation from the accepted path meant death or imprisonment for both teacher and students. A system that was used to fill the College's own ranks.

Acolytes of the College of Man did not choose their fate. It was chosen for them. Anyone who had a demonstrable ability in areas the College deemed restricted was taken into the College with no chance of appeal.

And joining the College was a life sentence, an acolyte forbidden to leave except by death. They lost all contact with the rest of humanity, and their public face became, literally, a mask. Their family never saw them again, and no one would be informed even if the College's draconian rules resulted in the acolyte's execution.

For their small taste of power, the vast majority of the College lived a life of discipline and servitude. They endured ritual scarification that permanently separated them from the rest of humanity. They could not fraternize with people outside the College. They could not appear in public without wearing a mask. They could not even identify themselves as individuals. Bearing a name was a privilege only allowed to the most senior scholars.

To most members of the College, the miraculous Language of the Gods was composed of meaningless symbols, memorized by rote, with no context or explanation. It was taboo to deviate in execution, to change any of the set incantations.

Nate, of course, asked how anyone would discover a new effect, a new "spell," if no one could change the rote incantations.

The answer was, no one did. The point of the prohibition was to *prevent* any such thing from happening. Change was the enemy. Too much knowledge about the nature of the Gods' Language was evil and dangerous.

Of course, given the College's totalitarian outlook, any stranger that came in contact with their regimented society had to be removed before the people became contaminated with alien concepts.

It seemed, however, that Arthiz didn't share the worldview of the College.

"What the ghadi is to Man, Mankind is to the College. I would see this grip broken."

"Why tell me?"

"So you will help us."

"How can I do anything to help you?"

"There is a game of stones we play. It is called siege. A man can spend a lifetime learning mastery of the game. However, a master who plays the same opponents over and over can be undone by an unexpected move. Even a foolish move by a novice." Arthiz leaned forward. "The College cannot think outside the walls of the rules they have imposed upon themselves."

Arthiz picked a blade up from the desk, took Nate's hand, and cut the bindings on his wrists. The move was unexpected, and it left Nate speachless, rubbing his wrists.

Perhaps Arthiz could afford to be a little more generous with Nate's freedom. Even if Nate slipped away from him, the picture Arthiz painted of the College did not lead Nate to believe he could escape them for long. In a choice between Arthiz and the College, Arthiz won hands down.

Arthiz turned back to Nate's journal. "Your arrival here was not simple chance." He hefted it. "You were chosen."

"What is it you want from me?"

He handed the journal back to Nate. "I am sending you somewhere where the Monarch rules alone, not the College."

Nate looked at the journal in his hands. "Why do you believe I can help you?"

"You can, and you will. But, for now, knowing that you are being kept safe from the College should be enough."

Nate stared at Arthiz, then at the sphere. "You were there when they questioned me."

Arthiz steepled his fingers. "Do not think in haste. Do not talk in haste. Do not act in haste. Remember that creed. It will save you much grief."

Chapter Seventeen

"THIS IS YOUR sole duty now," Arthiz had said. The implications were slow to sink in, but Yerith began to realize that she had cast her fate with something much larger than she was.

Up until Arthiz reappeared this morning, she had a very definite view of her place in the world. Her life, the person that everyone saw, was Yerith, the ghadi keeper for the College of Manhome. Somehow, she had come to see that person as being real. She did her job well, cared for the ghadi in her charge, and did what was in her power to make their lives comfortable.

The secrets she kept, her relationship with Arthiz, the thing—the man—called Nate Black; all of this was hidden, not really a part of her identity. She did it out of a desire to serve the Monarch, and a desire to punish the College that had erased her family so thoroughly that she didn't even dare use her birth name. But it didn't seem real, it was almost a game she was playing, removed from the world she actually lived in.

She had discovered it was more than a game.

"Leaving?" Yerith had told Arthiz when he had appeared unannounced this morning. She had spoken the word as if it was some bizarre syllable in Nate Black's language.

Arthiz's robes and white mask had been waiting for her when she had gone down to feed the ghadi. He

stood in the center of the aisle, the mere presence of
his masked and robed figure intimidating the ghadi.

"You cannot stay here. You will accompany Nate
Black to Zorion. It is the Monarch's city. We cannot
leave you here."

"You need me here," Yerith waved at the ghadi.
"You cannot lose everything we've worked for. My
ghadi obey me, they walk freely through the College
of Man. How can you abandon—"

"These are the words of the Monarch himself," Arthiz snapped at her. "You do not choose how your
service is used."

"But—"

"Nate Black is more important than your service
here. It is too much of a risk to take him, and leave
you here with the knowledge of what has happened
to the College's demon. You must both leave."

"What about the ghadi?"

"The ghadi are not our present concern."

In an instant, the careful life she had pieced together here at Manhome was wiped away. As she took
Nate Black through the secret ways down to where
Arthiz was waiting, she found herself wishing that this
creature had escaped. What faced her now? She was
abandoning everything she knew for the second time
in her life, and she didn't even know why.

No, that was a lie. She might not know Arthiz's
mind, or why Nate Black was so important to the
Monarch, but she knew why she led the unworldly
creature down to the hidden cove where the Monarch's men waited. She did it for her father.

She stayed on deck while the men took Nate Black
downstairs to meet Arthiz. She studied their reactions
to her charge, perhaps to find some clue to Nate
Black's importance. It was unenlightening. The sailors,
who probably knew what to expect, looked at Nate
Black with suspicion. They spat into the water, and
were reluctant to touch him, as if his strangeness was
some sort of contagion.

When the men returned, without Nate Black, they

looked at her with almost the same suspicion. Perhaps it *was* contagious. Yerith stared into the water and tried to be beneath their notice. Two spoke, making no effort to hide their conversation from Yerith, or include her in it.

"I do not like this thing."

"I know. We're paid to avoid the notice of men, not the Gods."

"A true demon, you think? Not just some malformed ghadi?"

"Would the Monarch pay as well, just for a ghadi?"

"What use could it be?"

"What use are any of the broken acolytes we ferry for the Monarch? I swear he is building an army of the crippled and the dead."

The third sailor walked up to them. "Perhaps both of you can prepare for departure? The tides do not wait on your pleasure."

"Yes, sir."

"Sir, aren't you concerned about this creature we're taking on board?"

"Son, if you are fretting about the cargo, you are in the wrong line of work."

The sailors started work and Yerith kept thinking about their words.

An army of the crippled and the dead.

Chapter Eighteen

ARTHIZ LEFT Nate with Yerith and the trio of tough-looking sailors.

He wasn't allowed on the deck, but Nate could stand in a doorway and watch their progress. The sailors untied the boat and let it float free to the center of the lagoon. Nate wasn't sure how they were to proceed. There seemed to be no wind to fill the sails in this sheltered area, and no one seemed in a hurry to grab an oar.

Beyond the breakers Nate saw the sliver of sky visible to them, purple and shining with a wealth of stars. The cavern around them was lost in blackness, the boat itself only illuminated by a dim lantern that shone through smoky red glass.

He wanted to ask Yerith questions, but she had passed him and closed herself inside the lone private cabin.

So Nate watched the sailors. For an hour or two, the sailors did inscrutable things with rope and canvas. None of which made any particular sense to Nate. They scrambled up and down the boat, half visible and ghostlike in the ruddy light. They shouted to each other with words that Nate didn't understand.

After a time, Nate realized that, despite the calm surface, there was a current in the water, drawing them toward the great crack in the rock, the sky, and the breakers.

Tides, Nate thought, *this place was engineered to be accessible only at high tide.* What was happening around him was that the sailors were scrambling to steer the craft out of the lagoon as the tide slid out.

The progress was slow, the crack in front of them gradually opening up to unfold the sky in front and above them. The sound of the breakers grew louder, and Nate could feel salt mist in his face.

Gradually, their progress speeded until the great rock walls of the lagoon shot forward to embrace them. They were in a sudden channel barely wide enough for the boat that carried them. Either side, seemingly close enough for Nate to touch, slick rock shot up into the sky.

Under the boat, the water became quick and violent, sending spray up between the hull and the rock. The sailors' shouts became louder and more urgent, as somehow they kept the boat to the center of the rushing channel.

Suddenly, above them, sky. The rock walls no longer shot upward without limit. They now broke off into rocky outcrops two or three times a man's height above them. As Nate looked up, one of the massive ocean breakers struck those rocks from the opposite side. The wave towered over him, briefly, then collapsed into a white foamy rain that slammed across the rock above him, and the deck in front of him.

The boat made a turn that Nate would have thought impossible in the confined space, and suddenly they were paralleling the great plateau. The sheer side of the rock rose above them to the right, a black wall blocking out the stars. To the left was a broken jumble of rocks that seemed barely enough protection from the breakers.

Slowly the channel widened as the rocky barrier peeled away from the plateau. There was an element of navigational prestidigitation that Nate couldn't quite follow, and they were suddenly rocking on the waves of the open ocean. It wasn't until they furled the sails completely and made a wide turn, that Nate could see the great plateau city of Manhome, blocking out the stars, and receding in the distance.

•   •   •

Within a few hours, to the great amusement of the crew, Nate was bedridden again. He had never been on a boat for any extended period of time, and he had never been on a craft this small. At some point, as he watched the shadow of Manhome recede against the night sky, some part of his brain realized that the motion wasn't going to stop.

The only bright spot was that he had been to enough serious parties to recognize the signs before it had been too late to make it to the rail, and he had run to the leeward side of the boat so the wind didn't throw his rejected dinner back up onto his pants.

To his horror, Nate discovered that this was the first time in his life when throwing up didn't at least make him feel better. It, in fact, made the rocking nausea even worse. Even after he stumbled into one of the bunks that formed the majority of the common area belowdecks, the sickness didn't ease.

This was worse than the illness that afflicted him in the College's dungeon. Here, there was no fever softening the edges of his mind. Every lurch of his bowel, every acidic belch, every ripple inside his abdomen, he felt with the crystal clarity of someone in complete command of his senses.

After the first few hours, he decided that permanent confinement within the ghadi catacombs would be preferable.

Nate curled up in the bunk, staring at the rough weave of the sheet underneath him. It seemed to be the only thing he could focus on without making things worse. Looking at anything else in the cabin seemed to amplify the sense of motion.

At some point the next day—Nate could tell it was day because the quality of light changed on the bit of fabric that filled his field of vision—Yerith came out of the master cabin and stood by him.

"They tell me you're sick."

"No, I actually enjoy trying to squeeze my insides out through every hole in my body."

Yerith didn't react, probably because it was hard for Nate to be ironic in a language where he barely made sense in the first place.

Nate squeezed his gut and closed his eyes. "I only want it to stop moving. Just a moment."

"This is a fast boat," she said. "We have caught the current. Our journey should only last a sixday."

Nate groaned. "You're not saying that to make me feel better, are you?"

"You talk strangely, Nate Black."

"By all accounts I am strange."

Nate felt the back of her hand on his face, as if checking for fever. "Don't worry," Nate said, "I am only sick with the moving."

She kept examining him. Nate decided he was thankful. He didn't really want one of those sailors to be in charge of his well-being. After a few moments, she said, "You will live."

Thanks for the good news.

• • •

Six days went by as slowly as the three months Nate had spent buried in a hole under Manhome. He made one or two attempts to study, but his physical state made it impossible to concentrate. So what time he spent not dwelling on his seasickness he spent talking to Yerith.

Fortunately for his state of mind, if Yerith was still upset over his attempted escape, she didn't show it. Also, his linguistic skills had finally progressed to the point where he could hold a conversation with someone who comprehended his accent.

"Tell me about the place you come from," Yerith asked him. "What did you do? Where did you live?"

"There is a lot to explain. It is very different, so much that I still don't have enough words—" Nate shook his head. If she was trying to get his mind off his illness, she'd picked the right topic. Any mention of home still brought a tidal wave of memories and emotions. "At the moment I am a student. I *was* a student—"

Nate spent several hours describing the contemporary United States to her. It wasn't as difficult as he thought it would be. For all the technology that didn't translate, he could describe it as a machine that did such-and-so. It came out in a rush, an endless stream of description. As if telling someone else about it, even in the alien language, validated it. Made it real.

The hardest things to explain were cultural differences. The fact that the university where he studied was not an arm of the government, really, even though the Feds did spring for a loan or two. It was, in fact, alien to her how little the government did control things. Nate did explain that the US was an exception, and went on a tangent explaining Europe, colonialism, the American revolution, and constitutional government.

"How many nations does your world have?" she asked after a while.

"I don't really know. A lot. Over a hundred."

"How many people?"

Nate spent five minutes with her going through the orders of magnitude of the number system before he could tell her, "About six or seven billion."

That, she couldn't grasp. It was clear to Nate that the population here was much less, more like a few million.

What she found even harder to comprehend was the idea of a democratic government. Not only did the logistics of a popular vote among three hundred million people stretch her imagination, she couldn't understand why those in power would accept a change in government every four years.

"We sometimes wonder about it ourselves."

She asked him what he studied, and that *was* hard to explain. He told her about machines that followed instructions, as long as you could speak to them in their language. Nate understood several of those languages, and was studying how to professionally tell them what to do. He had Yerith open his journal and he pointed out a few pages where he had been jotting down code just to amuse himself. The lines of formal symbols stood out from the rest of the haphazard note taking.

She looked at it and said, in a rather hushed tone, "Like the scholars of the College."

"From what I understand, there's a similarity or two. But the languages spoken by our machines were invented by man."

"But you would speak it and these machines would do your bidding?"

"Yes."

"Are they alive?"

"No, they aren't . . ." *Like Arthiz's sphere.*

For good or ill, Yerith's comment got Nate thinking.

• • •

Of course, in return, Nate questioned her about her world, and herself. Especially how she came to be his baby-sitter.

Yerith came from a distant town that had been ruled by a powerful family for a few hundred years. Yerith's family. Her father was head of the local government, a popular and well-loved leader according to her. Nate mentally translated the title as "baron."

The baron had been too creative for his own good. He was tired of sending the College money and resources for every little thing, so he encouraged, or at the least allowed, the local citizens to work around the requirements of the College in local commerce.

For example, one butcher found that he could preserve his meat by packing it in salt rather than by paying a hooded mage to scrawl glyphs on a carcass. A smith could heat iron just as well without the incantations of an acolyte. Fishermen could fill their nets and farmers could sow their seeds without aid from the College.

None of this was strictly against the rules of the College, so they did nothing. Not until a teacher in one of the apprentice schools said that it was not necessary to have a mage present when slaughtering meat.

That single deviation was enough pretext for the College of Man to declare Yerith's family, and the city, a rogue regime.

The College came in force and not only imprisoned Yerith's family, but burned the farms, the fisheries, the smithies, any place that had engaged in heretical practices. Her father had saved her by sending her away to friends of his who lived far away, before the College came to take them away.

To stay safe from the College, she had to change her name and live as someone else's child. Her family—mother, father, brothers, everyone—had been put to death by the College. If they discovered her and her parentage, she would be executed as well, simply for being the child of a man who defied them.

In her village, her family name had been erased. Speaking their name, or referring to their history was forbidden. The College had even gone so far as to take the Stalinesque step of renaming the village. According to Yerith, the practice was not uncommon. Enemies of the College didn't just disappear, their whole existence was erased.

Nate asked her about Arthiz, but she didn't reveal anything more than he already knew. Arthiz was a man from within the College who worked for the Monarch. Apparently, he was the point man in a brewing civil war between secular civil society and the rigid theocracy of the College of Man. Even with that sort of backing, the opposition was very circumspect, the College seemed more than powerful enough to replace the Monarch himself.

Nate asked her about the ghadi. She told him about her favorite ghadi, how they were trained and how you commanded them. She talked about them the way people talked about dogs or horses. A smart animal that could be trained to do some useful tasks.

Nate asked her about the ghadi statues, and the catacombs, obviously made by an intelligent and sophisticated species—

All of which—she pointed out—were created a long

time ago. Before the great cataclysm. The ghadi that cleaned the streets today were only the dimmest shadow of that past, they couldn't even speak anymore.

She then went on at great lengths about how proud she was of the ghadi that had taken him from the hole where the College had imprisoned him. The College and its masters made extensive use of ghadi servants since they could do all the menial chores without risking the betrayal of any secrets. The ghadi who had rescued Nate had been, long past, servants to Yerith's father. To the College, the ghadi were simply property to be disposed of. Property that was seized by the College.

But Yerith's ghadi had been well trained and were loyal. Even after many years, when she found them, she could command them and they would treat her as their mistress. In serving Arthiz and the Monarch, the ghadi became a great asset in slipping things in and out of sealed College enclaves.

While Yerith obviously saw the ghadi as little more than trained animals, she did care about them. She talked about what her ghadi had done with pride, but Nate saw that she was on the verge of tears. When he asked why she seemed upset . . .

"I am afraid for them. They are such gentle creatures, but if anyone at the College discovers their disobedience . . ." She sucked in a breath. "They will be made *ghadon*."

Nate didn't understand the word, so he asked her to explain.

The College consumed ghadi, and not just as servants. To write or speak the Gods' Language required energy. Not just physical energy, but energy from the mind and soul of the person casting the incantation. Also, once started, the incantation could not stop. Even something as elaborate as the language sphere had to be engraved as a single unending spell. Casting words of such permanence could fatigue, age, and even kill the one investing the effort.

But the masters in the College didn't need to expend their own energy. The ghadi, as a race, had much deeper reserves of such energy, even though they couldn't use the Gods' Language themselves. To inscribe such a spell, the caster could suck the required energy from a nearby ghadi.

The ghadi that were used for such purposes were called *ghadon*. They were usually those no longer useful for anything else, too old, sickly, infirm. . . .

• • •

"It destroys them from the inside out. They are in such pain before they finally die. They don't even know what is happening to them. All so the College can be carefree in flaunting their power." She shuddered. "I once saw a ghadi die so one of them could light a fire. The chamber was cold, but rather than taking a brand to the kindling already in the fireplace, the acolyte wanted to impress my father. He waved and spoke a word, and the logs erupted into flame. I was spying on the adults from the corridor, and I saw that, when the acolyte spoke his spell, one of his ghadi servants shuddered and collapsed. I was too frightened to scream. I watched as the acolyte's other ghadi servants picked up the body and carried it out of the house."

Yerith shook her head. "Such cruelty. When he left, the man didn't even question where his servant had gone."

"I hope that doesn't happen to your friends," Nate said.

She shook her head. "It happens to all of them. I only hope it doesn't happen now, because of what I've done. They deserve a longer life."

Chapter Nineteen

WHEN THEY arrived at their destination, Zo-rion, Yerith told Nate to come up on deck.

He had expected them to come in under the cover of darkness. He certainly wasn't inconspicuous. However, he walked out into full sunlight for the first time in months.

Above him, the sky was so blue it hurt, and below, diamond daggers of light lit the water as if someone had scattered broken glass. The deck only moved slightly as Nate blinked at the glare. It took several minutes for his vision to adjust enough for him to see Zorion.

Blinking tears from his eyes, it became clear why no one was overly worried about being seen. The ship had lowered sail and set anchor about three or four miles down a marshy coast from the city. South of them, dominating a massive bay, squatted a city as imposing as Manhome. Black stone walls held in buildings that piled around the shoulders of a single massive ziggurat like an architectural landslide.

At this distance, and half blinded by sunlight, Nate had no decent sense of scale until he realized the black specks of flotsam he saw bobbing in the waters of the bay were ships five to ten times the size of the vessel he stood on.

The central building had to approach four or five hundred feet high. A pyramid of steps and pillars as large as anything Nate's world had produced. Maybe larger.

They were more than far enough away from the city to escape notice. Even someone on top of that massive building would need pretty good optics, and would have to know where to look, to see their little smuggling party.

While Nate studied Zorion, the sailors were busy lowering bags and boxes over the side. They were anchored next to a low stone pier that resembled the one they'd moored against by the catacombs. This one looked more weathered, and was missing sections along its length. Where gaps occurred, makeshift bridges of logs crossed the water.

The pier didn't lead anywhere obvious. It went deeper into the marsh, and was quickly overtaken by dense tropical foliage. Nate couldn't see any obvious sign that there was a way to pass farther inland.

Above them, a sea bird screeched.

Nate didn't hesitate when Yerith asked him to leave the ship. He would have gotten off on the wrong side of the River Styx, if it meant his feet would be on solid ground.

The rope ladder they used, as well as the stones, was wet and slippery. That, combined with vertigo from nearly a week of seasickness, meant that Nate almost fell on his ass several times as he climbed down. And when he had both feet on solid ground, the world lurched and he had to sit on one of the boxes that the sailors had already off-loaded.

Nate leaned back and stared up at the sky. It was deeper and wider than he remembered.

Yerith joined him, leaving the boat with considerably more grace.

"I think I could stay here forever," Nate muttered in English.

"What?"

"I am happy to get off that boat," Nate told her. He tried to shake the feeling of the ocean out of his head as he looked around. Sitting on the low-lying pier, he lost sight of the city. The pier and its make-shift repairs became the only man-made object in sight, outside of the boat itself.

The sailors didn't waste much time. Once Yerith had disembarked, the ladder came up, followed by the anchor.

They raised the sail and the boat pulled away.

Nate suddenly felt like a contestant on a Fox Network reality game show.

"Where are we?" Nate asked. He closed his eyes and turned his face to the sun. It had been a long time since he had felt sunlight on his skin. He was surprised at how much he had missed it.

Yerith didn't answer immediately.

Nate stretched and sucked in a deep breath. Along with the sunlight, it was the first real taste of being outside in quite a while. The air was free of the smell of mildew, of sweat, of his own old clothes. The air was cool and salty, and carried a rich collage of plant smells.

She still hadn't answered him.

He opened his eyes, his brain feeling clearer than it had in weeks. "What do we do now?" Nate asked her.

She stood, slightly removed from him, at the edge of the cargo the sailors had unloaded. Her arms were folded, and she faced the dense tangle of jungle that was all they could see of the coast. The end of her long pigtail bobbed over the small of her back as her head moved, very slightly, side to side.

"Yerith?"

"Where are they?"

Nate yawned.

She spun around to face him. "Why are you so calm?"

"I can see the sun. I can breathe the air. After everything, I might be happy spending the rest of my life sitting on this crate, on this rock." Nate looked back at the ocean, at the boat shrinking in the distance. "And I will be happy never to set foot off of solid ground again."

She made a frustrated sound and turned back to face the jungle.

You're out of your element, aren't you? She was acting nervous, and that should be scaring him. He looked at her and tried to decide if she was a draftee or a volunteer. She had spoken to him about Arthiz and her own past as if she was a true believer, but she acted as if standing here, with Nate, was not something she had planned to be doing.

In fact, for once, Nate was looking at someone who seemed as out of place as he was.

Nate understood Arthiz's reasoning. Yerith wasn't a bodyguard, a guide, or a warden. She was here with him because she knew about Nate. Nate couldn't make much sense of what was happening to him, but he did know that something about him made him important to the College of Man, if only because he frightened them.

If Arthiz wanted to keep Nate out of the hands of the College—a goal Nate supported—the fewer people who knew of Nate and what happened to him, the better. Yerith knew too much to hang around the College safely. If Nate was Arthiz, he'd send her into hiding, too. If there was one thing he understood from his days as Azrael, it was paranoia and covering your own tracks.

Nate just wished he knew *why* he was so important and so threatening to these people.

All he had was a partial explanation of why the College of Man wanted him imprisoned; he just had the bad luck to walk into a culture with a taboo on foreigners so draconian that it made fifteenth century China look welcoming. But there had to be more to it than that if Arthiz's intervention was to make any sense. The man wasn't in a position to be altruistic.

The man wanted Nate to "help" his cause, and while Nate could sympathize with people fighting a totalitarian regime—and until he found a way back to the world he knew, it made no sense to cast his lot with anyone else—Nate couldn't see what Arthiz got out of the deal. He simply didn't buy Arthiz's vague references to games. A person in Arthiz's position had to be pragmatic. Nate doubted that what he added to Arthiz's side of the equation was purely hypothetical. He had to mean something specific to Arthiz.

None of which informed Nate what he was bringing to the table, or what he meant to any of these people. He was an alien here, and the rules were so different that it could be anything.

Nate's thoughts were interrupted by the sound of rustling foliage. He looked at where the pier met the jungle, and for a long time didn't see anything. Then, some tropical bird exploded from the bush, propelled by a flutter of primary colors.

Nate stared at where the bird had come from and saw a shadow in the midst of the leaves. The shadow seemed to have eyes.

He kept looking and decided that the shadow also held a wicked-looking crossbow pointed at them.

"I think your friends are here," Nate said.

Now that he was looking, he could make out half a dozen people hidden just inside the tree line, attention focused on Nate and Yerith. Yerith was still looking around, as if she didn't notice the men in the woods. Maybe she didn't.

Nate was surprised at exactly how calm he felt. This kind of episode would have easily fired off his panic reflexes pre-"@." *Guess I lost that particular reflex, along with everything else.*

After a few more long moments where Yerith became visibly more tense, someone pushed aside the foliage where the stone pier met solid land, about sixty or seventy feet away from them. The man who walked out carried a long machete. His skin was as dark as anyone's Nate had seen in this world, which made the scars that marked his skin all the more apparent.

Unlike Scarface, this man was young, and the detailed ritualistic inscriptions did not cover every inch of skin. Words rolled across his forehead, and down his cheeks, but the skin of his arms, neck, and the visible portions of his chest were unmarked.

He wore sandals and the baggy black canvas pants that seemed to be the universal peasant garb here. Over it he wore a short robe that made him look like a refugee from a martial arts movie. As the guy strode down the pier to meet them, Nate realized that their welcoming committee had waited until the boat had completely vanished in the distance.

The man stopped about ten feet from them, and looked Nate up and down. For the first time in quite a while, Nate was self-conscious about his appearance. His hair and beard had grown out the past three months or so, and were both at about the same length. And both probably looked like hell. His skin was an awful, dead-looking, pasty white. The only touches of color were ropy blue veins under the skin on the back of his hands. Not to mention clothes that hadn't been washed in how long?

"So this is his stranger?" The man asked Yerith.

"You are Bhodan?"

The man snorted. "Bhodan is too important to waste on frivolities like this. I am Osif. I am to guide you and our prize back to the mountain." Nate wasn't quite adept at reading subtext in the new language, they didn't use tone to carry emotion, but Nate received the distinct impression of sarcasm.

Yeah, kid, like I want to be here, too.

Yerith said. "I was told—"

"I am sure that you were told many things," Osif interrupted. "We were told to fetch this dubious creature." Osif sighed. "Does it take instruction?"

Yerith opened her mouth, and it was all Nate could do to keep from laughing. The bastard had no clue. Nate stood and walked up to Yerith, who was busy watching Osif as he looked at all the cargo the ship had off-loaded.

Osif shook his head. "Well?" He looked up. "How well behaved is this thing?"

"What do you—" Yerith looked at Nate, who hadn't said anything up until now. He gave Yerith a look that said, *Let him think I'm a deformed ghadi.*

Yerith sucked in a breath and said, "We should move on while there's daylight."

CHAPTER TWENTY

GHADI IN LOINCLOTHS carried most of the cargo. Nate, at Osif's insistence, carried one of the bags himself. He was the only human who carried anything that wasn't a weapon. Nate didn't mind all that much. The time he had spent working out in the catacombs had left him more fit than he had been when he came to this place, he was just a little wobbly from the sea voyage.

Nate kept within earshot of Yerith and Osif, listening to the Sandanista-lite bitching about being pulled from his important studies to escort Nate to the mountain. For this guy, Arthiz had been too long away from the Monarch's people in the jungle, and he didn't understand what things were like here. He was out of touch.

What they needed here were new recruits, fresh mages to learn the skills needed to fight the College. They didn't need pale novelties. Now they had to spend their own resources on studying this stranger when it would have been better to let the College keep the misbegotten thing, and let Arthiz's intelligence within the College gather what information on it they found.

After all, what possible use could this creature be to anyone?

Nate listened to about two hours of this guy before he suspected that they were reaching their destination. The signs were old stonework—first, in the path they followed, where ancient pavestones peeked from the earth, then in mounds that formed unnatural geometric patterns in the jungle floor, marking the sites of long crumbled buildings.

They walked toward the sound of water, and about ten minutes after first hearing it, they stepped out from under the jungle canopy, to face a cliff towering about three or four hundred feet straight up before the face fell back into an eroded bluff.

At its base surged violent rapids that filled the air with a gray mist and the sound of rushing water.

The cliff face itself was carved over its entire surface area, except for a few places where the river had claimed a portion of it. Paths switchbacked across the face of the cliff, stairs were carved into the stone, man-sized holes peppered the surface accessing some interior structure.

Stone vines and leaves competed with the real thing. Columns reached up fifty, a hundred feet, some even taller. Balconies and terraces jutted from the face of the cliff. And, everywhere, statues.

Ghadi statues.

A stone skyscraper. A whole city carved into the valley wall. An *old* city. But it was only a ruin at first glance. After more than a casual observation, Nate could tell that the clearing that he followed Osif into was not a natural occurrence. Looking back and forth, the ground had been cleared and exposed from the river to about a hundred yards back. No one could approach here from the south without being completely exposed to the inhabitants of the cliff face.

There was a single bridge crossing the river, a rope and wood construction that was placed about fifty feet downstream from the remains of a stone bridge—the rubble was obviously the result of recent demolition. The rope bridge was over one of the more violent parts of the rapids, and was so narrow that people would have to cross single file.

A single torch there could stop the advance of an army.

Admittedly, most of what Nate knew about strategy
came from computer gaming, but to him at least, it
looked as if the people here were serious about defending themselves.

Osif led them across the rope bridge, which was
more stable than it looked, and up one of the ramps
that hugged the cliff face. It reminded Nate a lot of
the road that spiraled up the plateau of Manhome.
The construction was the same, as was the artwork.

He glanced back at the ghadi porters, wordlessly
carrying their burdens for their human masters. Nate
wondered how they could go from point A to point
B. The artwork alone made it clear that the same
creatures built this place.

*Could they really have completely lost their
language?*

Osif led them into one of the holes in the cliff wall.
Nate's feelings of being watched were confirmed
when, once inside the cliff, a quartet of men stopped
Osif and double-checked everyone. They gave Nate
the once-over half a dozen times, muttering to
themselves.

"—This is what they've been talking about—"

"—what is that it's wearing?"

"—ever seen skin that white? Is it alive?"

"Ugly, isn't it?"

Osif turned to Yerith and said, "Have him put that
down. I have to present you to Bhodan."

Nate dropped the crate he was carrying before Osif
had finished his sentence. Osif was a little too self-
involved to notice, but the four guards did a double
take, and Nate made it a point to smile at them as
Osif led him and Yerith deeper into the cliff face.

Bhodan was deep inside a warren of caverns. They
reminded Nate of the catacombs under Manhome, except these were larger and better lit. The occasional
tapestry hung on the wall, half disintegrated. The carving was finer and more precise, giving Nate the feel
that this was carved for living space.

At the end of a long maze of corridors, they walked

through an unornamented door into a darkened chamber. Nate felt a wave of claustrophobia, as if he was going to be locked up in a dungeon again. He felt his heart race, and was prepared to rush the door if it started to close.

Instead, a raspy voice called out, "Osif, my son?"

"I've come back with Arthiz's gift to us."

"Let me provide you some light." Something sparked a few times, on the far side of the room, and eventually an oil lamp was burning.

Yerith gasped.

Nate sucked in a breath, too. The man by the lamp looked as if he shouldn't be alive. His face was a twisted mass of scar tissue, ragged cuts following the lines of the typical College writing. The man's eyes were gone, in their place more sunken scar tissue filling the orbits of his skull. He didn't have hands, his arms ended in two leather cups where a complex set of blunted hooks emerged.

The man smiled, the expression rendering his face even more skull-like. Nate could understand why this man wouldn't come to meet them himself.

"Welcome guests. I am Bhodan, and this is *my* College."

Osif started to say, "Master, this is the stranger that—"

Nate stepped forward and said, "My name is Nate Black. Thank you for meeting with us."

Osif's expression was worth the price of admission. He turned to face Nate and said, "You can speak," as if it was an accusation.

Nate smiled at him. "Yes, I can."

"Slowly," Bhodan said. "Your words are spoken strange."

Osif turned on Yerith. "Why did you hide this from me?"

Because you're an asshole. Nate answered Osif. "She answered every question you addressed to her." Nate turned to face Bhodan. "Why was I sent here?"

Bhodan got to his feet with a slight limp. "Arthiz

said he had a special student for us. He believes that
you might cause the College of Man much distress."

Osif grunted, causing Bhodan to laugh. "Osif
doesn't share Arthiz's opinion."

"Even if he can be trained at all, what use is he?
Even in an acolyte's robe and mask, he could not walk
among men without being known. He couldn't leave
here, so what use is that?"

Bhodan kept chuckling. He pointed a hook at Osif
and said, "I cannot leave this refuge, so you say I
am useless?"

"No—I— Master, you are a great teacher, a great
leader. We cannot say the same about this interloper."

"You judge too quickly." Bhodan faced Nate and
asked, "Why did you not speak to my student, Osif?"

Nate looked across at Osif, who looked pissed. A
long time ago, Nate hadn't cared about making social
enemies. There were other things to worry about in
life rather than whether people liked you or not. Either he, or the situation, was different enough now for
Nate to realize that he had made a diplomatic misstep.

One consolation—the guy was an asshole who probably wouldn't have been on Nate's side anyway.

"I learned more about him by remaining silent,"
Nate said.

Bhodan seemed to find that amusing.

"Do you actually believe that he is who Arthiz
thinks—" Osif began to say.

Bhodan whipped around and snapped at him, "This
is not the time. Raise such questions to me, alone."

"Master—"

"Go now, make sure there are rooms for our guests.
We will speak of this later."

Osif opened his mouth, but Bhodan made a violent
gesture with his hook, and Osif grimaced, glared at
Nate, and left.

"I apologize. At most times Osif is not like this."

"Why am I here?" Nate asked. "Who does Arthiz
think I am?"

"You are here because Arthiz thinks you might aid our cause."

Why do I think you're not completely forthcoming?

"How?" Nate said. "From what I have seen, the only reason I am here is because I would probably be killed if I was anywhere else."

Bhodan nodded. "You are here now."

"How do you think I can help you?"

"Perhaps you cannot, perhaps Osif is correct. Perhaps you are a harmless animal, the way the ghadi believed the first men were." Bhodan frowned. "But when the gods play their games, the result is always severe. If you have a purpose here, it is the Monarch's preference that it serve us and not the College of Man."

Uh-huh.

"What is it you want from me?"

"To be an acolyte. A soldier in the coming war."

Nate unconsciously touched his face and thought of the scarring that these people went through. *Like hell, old man. You're not cutting anything in my skin.*

"What if I don't want to be part of your little army?"

Yerith touched his arm. "Please—"

Nate shook off her attention. "Do I not get a choice in all of this?"

Bhodan gave him his skull-like smile. "Yes, you do. If you insist, we will keep you in a safe place as long as the Monarch believes you may be of use."

"Like my cell back in Manhome?" Nate looked over at Yerith.

"I suppose," Bhodan said. "Is this what you want?"

"What I want is to be sent back home."

"Only the gods can walk between worlds."

"What's the alternative?"

"We will teach you as an acolyte, until we find something you cannot learn."

"Can you do that without cutting my skin?"

Bhodan actually seemed surprised at the request. "Do you understand what I am offering?"

"Maybe not. But I do not want to be scarred. Is that necessary for me to learn what you want to teach?"

"No." The vibe from Bhodan was odd. To Nate it seemed as if it was perfectly reasonable not to want his skin cut up. However, even Yerith looked at him with some surprise. *They're almost acting as if the scarring was a fringe benefit.* . . .

Maybe that's how they saw it. They did act as if he walked into a job interview and said, "I'll take the position, but please don't pay me anything."

Bhodan shook his head. "If you do not wish to pass through the . . ." He used a word Nate had never heard before. "It will be your decision. So you will train here?"

"Teach me whatever you want."

"Good. I will show you to your room." Bhodan walked toward the door.

Nate looked at Yerith, who looked even more lost than she had on the pier. "What about Yerith?"

"We have ghadi here that need to be cared for." He addressed Yerith. "When Osif returns, he will take you to them."

Bhodan walked out the door and waited in the hallway for him. Nate took a last look at Yerith, then he followed the blind man.

BOOK THREE

A ruler of men once became jealous of the College of Man. He saw the wise men of the College say what was true, and what was not. What was right, and what was not. When the wisest scholar of the College came to him and told him what power he held, and what he did not, he responded by saying, "You will see what power I have."

The ruler closed the places of learning, and banished the scholars of the College of Man to the countryside outside his domain.

"Tell the trees what is true," he told them. "Tell the river what is right. Tell the sky what power it has."

Even as the ruler told the scholars this, Ghad walked the streets of the city and told the people what was not true, what was not right, and told them of power. . . .

—*The Book of Ghad and Man,*
Volume III, Chapter 23

Chapter Twenty-One

B HODAN TOOK him to a room even less inviting than the one that he had left to come here. It was little more than an unadorned stone box, lacking even a door for privacy. There were only two pieces of furniture; a rough cot, and at its foot, a large chest about twice the size of a footlocker.

When Nate opened the chest, half of it was filled with the books that Yerith had given him. For some reason, that made him feel better about being here. His journal sat on top of everything.

Next to the books was clothing similar to that Osif had worn to meet them. Sandals, canvas pants, a robe with a vaguely Oriental cut, and a long sashlike belt. All of which was probably a good thing, given the state of filth his current clothes were in.

"You are a student here," Bhodan said, "You will live as a student here."

It took a little while for what that meant to sink in. Nate had his own idea of what a student's life was like. His mental image of higher learning was so ingrained it even influenced his mental translation of the word "College." However, to Nate, this College bore more resemblance to a military training base or a Soviet reeducation camp.

Let's hope these are the good guys.

Shortly after Bhodan left him, a man with a long, carved staff walked down the corridor and stopped in his doorway. He stared at Nate and said, "You are a student here."

"That's what I have been told."

The man slammed the bottom of the staff on the ground. The sound was like a whip cracking in the enclosed space. "You were not asked a question."

Nate backed off a step.

"You will wear the clothes of a student." He pointed at Nate with the staff. "Remove those rags."

Nate's immediate impulse was to mouth off to this guy. But trying to communicate in a different language gave his brain enough pause so he didn't pop off the first thing that came into his head. Which, in this case was, *How'd you like to wear that stick, big boy?*

Nate erred on the side of discretion and stripped, peeling the fabric off his body. Rings of gray marked him where the elastic of his T-shirt or jockeys had touched his skin.

Big-stick stared at Nate while he stripped, and if he had known the words, Nate would have mentioned something about the homoerotic overtones of what was happening.

Big-stick instructed him to fold his old clothes and place them in the chest, and take out his new uniform. Nate started to put the new clothes on, but was interrupted by another whiplike crack of the man's staff. The metal-shod tip came uncomfortably close to Nate's foot.

"I did not tell you to dress."

Nate stood there, waiting.

"It is time for the baths."

• • •

Big-stick wasn't kidding when he said it was time for the baths. Not only were the baths communal, *every* student bathed at the same time. Nate placed his clothes on a stone bench at the edge of a steaming pool of water as more and more people filed by him. No one spoke as they filed into the room, though every single one of them, men and women, stared at him as they passed. Each of them took their clothes and placed them on the bench set into the perimeter of the cylindrical room.

The only folks who didn't strip were a trio of men bearing staffs who clustered by the entrance. The only difference between them and the students was age—the students were all younger than Nate, the guards perhaps slightly older—and the color of the belt at their waist. The students, Nate included, all had plain black belts while the guards wore embroidered blue belts with silver and gold highlights.

Nate watched the others for what he was supposed to do. He had already screwed up enough first impressions to last him the rest of his life. The last thing he needed was a dozen new people to be pissed at him because he ruined their bathing ceremony.

Fortunately, as far as Nate could tell, there was no particular protocol involved. Other than the general silence, and a slight segregation of gender—men on one side of the pool, women on the other—everyone seemed to be free to proceed as they thought appropriate. All slipping in the pool in a semi-haphazard fashion.

Nate decided that he must have had the modesty beaten out of him, because he was slipping into the warm pool of the bath before he realized that he was more uncomfortable about how filthy he was in front of all these strangers than he was about being naked.

Even that discomfort faded when he slipped into the pool. It reminded him of how he missed showers, and indoor plumbing. His body slipped into the warm water and suddenly every muscle in his body tried to relax, dropping him so that he was only head and shoulders above the surface. He rested there for a few moments, floating. It was the most luxury he'd been afforded since coming to this world.

It was a few minutes before some order was imposed on the proceedings. Once all the students were in the water, one of the guards walked along the perimeter, using a hooked tool to drag lids off of cylin-

drical pits that ringed the edge of the pool. Once he
had completed this task, everyone edged to the pit
nearest them and withdrew a white cloth. Nate followed everyone's lead, noticing that the holes ringing
the pool were filled with water about twenty degrees
warmer than the water in the pool itself.

Still unsure if he was engaged in something whose
primary focus was ritualistic, social, or hygienic, he
picked one guy out of the crowd and decided to follow
his actions, dunking his head, and wiping each part of
his body with the cloth.

For Nate's part, it didn't seem that he screwed anything up. At least no one came and hit him with a
stick. Everyone washed in silence, and the stares he
got were covert.

Nate returned the stares, a little less covertly.

Everyone here, it seemed, had been touched by the
knife of the College. Nate wore the lone unscarred
body. Men and women had, at the least, their faces
marked. That made an evil sort of sense. If the College wanted to isolate you, keep you behind their
mask, that would be the first place they marked.

Only in a few cases did the scars extend much beyond the head. Nate realized that he was seeing the
neophytes, the people who did the scut work for the
College. He also started to understand why Bhodan
seemed surprised that Nate wished to stay unscarred.

The extent of the carvings was a measure of rank,
it defined your place among the scholars and acolytes.
Essentially, he had told Bhodan that he didn't want
any status at all.

• • •

When he was clean and back up in his little room
he began wondering if he'd see Yerith again. That
took his thoughts through a downward spiral, itemiz-
ing a long list of things he probably would never see
again; Mom, Tux, indoor plumbing, stand-up comedy,
ice cream.

Nate sat on the edge of his bed and tried to tune

out the crowd noises around him. Unlike when Bhodan had first brought him down to this corridor of alcoves, the place was now thick with people. Rooms up and down this particular corridor were home to about a dozen other male students, and gave the place a feel somewhere between a dorm and a barracks.

Outside the baths, they didn't try to hide the fact that they were staring at him. Nate tried to understand their whisperings, but it only frustrated him. He was still too new to the language to understand anything that wasn't spoken directly and clearly. A quickly whispered conversation was no more intelligible to Nate than a coughing fit.

Nate was wrapped up in composing a mental list of his favorite restaurants, when someone decided to walk up and confront the stranger who had been dropped in their midst.

"So what, exactly, are you?"

Nate looked up at the speaker. The man had sharp features, and the scars on his face looped around his brow and down the edge of his nose like a large question mark.

Several responses occurred to Nate. As with the guard, the language barrier gave him enough pause not to use any of them.

"My name is Nate Black," he said.

"Nateblack?" It was strange the way a foreign mouth chewed up the name. Nate doubted he would have recognized his name spoken by this guy if he didn't know something of the language. "What kind of name is that?"

"A common name where I come from."

"Where do you come from?"

Nate thought for a few long moments and said finally, "Not here."

Question-mark looked back behind him, as if there was a group, out of Nate's view, that was egging him on. "We want to know if you're a—" Unknown word. Mutated? Deformed? Gifted? "—ghadi."

"I'm speaking to you." Nate shook his head. "I am

as much man as you. As your friends. Where I come from, I am not strange."

"You are a strange ghadi."

I guess I would be. Nate knew he was being insulted. He considered telling Question-mark what an asshole he was, but Nate decided that wasn't the greatest idea right now. Feeding this guy some of his own rotten teeth might make Nate feel better, but he doubted it would make life in the immediate future any easier.

Instead, Nate shook his head and said, "In your sight, perhaps."

It was hard to tell if his visitor was pleased or disappointed at Nate's failure to rise to the bait.

"Why did you come here?"

"I was brought here." Nate looked at Question-mark and asked, "Why did *you* come here?" Nate still had trouble with tone, and his question came out with English intonation which put stress on the pronoun and raised the tone on the end.

"You speak oddly, ghadi."

"My name is Nate Black."

Question-mark chuckled. "There are no names here. Only students and teachers."

"And ghadi," Nate said.

Question-mark shook his head and muttered something inscrutable too low for Nate to make out the words. He turned and left Nate alone in his doorless alcove.

See you in class, Nate thought. Which made him wonder what "class" would be like.

•   •   •

During the night, hedging against depression, Nate made a conscious effort to itemize the things he needed to be thankful for. He was definitely in a better situation than the one he had started out in, and, for whatever reason, the locals on Arthiz's side of things seemed to think Nate was useful, or at the very least, tolerable.

He wasn't in a fetid hole, he wasn't sick anymore,

and he was being given a chance to at least establish some sort of status beyond that of an untouchable.

When it came down to it, at this moment he was probably better off than at least half of the population of the world he remembered. He was healthy, had a roof over his head, and was not in immediate danger of being killed.

Of course, the irony was that the improvement in his physical state actually made it easier to indulge in self-pity. He kept thinking of home, and he couldn't shake it. He tried to sleep, and his mind kept fixating on random memories—the smell of pizza, his sister's slightly nasal voice, the feel of a keyboard, a paperback book.

You're alive.

You're alive and no one has proved that going back is impossible.

It was probably a vain hope, but somehow @, the thing in the darkness, had opened a doorway between Nate's world and this one. There was no reason to assume that travel was strictly one way. At least, telling himself that helped him sleep.

Chapter Twenty-Two

IN THE MORNING, Nate was ready for class, or whatever passed for it here. Understanding how this place worked was going to be a necessary step on the long road back to planet Earth, and Nate was willing to learn whatever these people were ready to teach him.

The blue-belted guards woke them and called the acolytes forward. Nate walked with them down a long stone corridor. They walked two abreast, and filed into a large open room filled with ranks of high tables with slightly angled tops. At each table burned a thick black candle and a thinner white candle.

Nate filed in with the group. They kept the order imposed by the location of their beds, and when Nate followed his line, he found himself standing next to one of the tables. At the table was a pen and brush set, and a sheet of parchment.

Glancing around, Nate decided that it had to be "his" desk, because it had been raised about four inches higher than anyone else's.

This was the point where Nate's expectations diverged from reality. For about five minutes, he stood there, waiting for someone who looked like an instructor to begin whatever the lesson was supposed to be. When no one entered the room to take on that role, it began to sink in that this "class" wasn't going to be that straightforward.

Arthiz had dropped Nate into the middle of a situation that resembled something more akin to a medieval devotional ritual. So much so, that Nate began second-guessing the exact meaning of words that, until now, he'd thought he understood in the language.

I told Yerith I was a student. Maybe that word doesn't mean quite what it does in English? Maybe they're assuming I know what to do.

"Great," Nate muttered in English. Several people shot him sharp looks, including two of the blue-belts by the door.

Okay, silence, I get it.

Nate looked at his desk, trying to get a feel for what they wanted out of him.

The two candles were obviously different in more than size and color. The white one looked merely utilitarian, and dripped wax over a small brass holder as it gave off a fair bit of light. It looked as if it had been freshly placed here.

The black candle looked ancient. It burned dim and slow, and wouldn't give off enough light to write by. It was as thick around as Nate's forearm, and had a line of rectilinear symbols carved near its bottom. The same language that was carved in the skin of the people around him, that had been carved in the base of the ghadi statue.

Okay, a ritual candle of some sort . . .

There was a small ledge at the top of the desk, between the two candles. Resting on the ledge was a rectangular length of inlaid wood. It was about the proportions of a wood ruler, but about five times as thick. The inlay, which seemed to be mother-of-pearl, was a long inscription in more of the rectilinear language.

The inscription took effort to look at. It was as if studying the symbols themselves required physical exertion. Nate remembered the strain of copying the inscription off of the statue.

He scanned the inlay across once and blinked his eyes.

The black candle had guttered out.

Nate looked around, hoping he hadn't broken some bizarre rule by letting the ritual fire burn out. No one seemed to be paying attention to him. His fellow students were bent over their desks, writing with their brushes. The blue-belts were walking the aisles between the desks, glancing at the progress of the student's work.

From what Nate could see, everyone was making much better progress than he was. The papers he could see were all covered with writing. His was still blank.

Looking around, though, he did see another student whose candle burned out. The guy took the white candle and used it to reignite the black one. Nate followed suit, thankful he hadn't trod on another taboo.

Okay, what are we writing?

Nate's neighbor happened to be Question-mark. Looking at the guy's page, Nate saw more of the rectilinear writing. There was also the same kind of inlaid block of wood at the top of Question-mark's desk.

Nate frowned.

It was obvious now what they wanted from him. And it seemed like so much bullshit. What possibly could be taught to anyone by repeatedly copying one line of text, over and over again? Especially when no one told him what the words he copied actually meant?

Well, at least I'll get to compare it with what I saw on the statue.

Nate picked up the brush and started copying.

It was harder to do than it appeared. Just to hold the figures in mind as he drew them took a serious mental effort. There was something about this language that was different. It tried to hook itself inside his skull, burning itself there. When he finished the last stroke of the brush, he sighed in relief. Like when he copied the inscription on the base of the statue, at the end of the line he was sweating and his hand shook.

He glanced up.

The black candle had guttered out again.

Wait a minute . . .

Nate looked at the inscription on the base of the candle and at the lines he had just transcribed. There was a chunk of the inscription that matched what was written on the candle. Nate looked around and saw a few other students relighting their own candles. Once they did, they bent over their paper and started copying again.

Is this what I think?

Nate relit his black candle and started the copying again. It didn't get easier the second time. It still was fatiguing to hold the symbols in his head as he drew them, and his hand painted the lines as if he moved the brush through thickening cement.

Before he finished the last symbol of the inscription, Nate glanced up at the black candle. The wick still burned. He completed the last character without looking at the paper. He watched the candle as his brush completed the last stroke.

When the brush left the paper, the flame dimmed, flickered, and winked out.

Could the act of writing these words be enough to do that?

He'd been told about the Gods' Language, and read about words that could alter the world around them through their own power. For some reason, though, Nate had always kept in the back of his mind the thought that there must be some other element involved. He had expected there to be some aspect of meditation, mental discipline, some actual material aspect to what was described to him. . . .

He had expected that someone should know what the words actually meant. At the very least, how to pronounce them.

Nate relit the candle.

Up to now, it may have been some sort of coincidence.

He very deliberately copied the inscription a third time, keeping an eye on the black candle.

Again, once the alien words had been written on the page, the flame faded and winked out.

It sank in to him what he'd been told about this language, and the College. No one *needed* to know what these words meant. Rote memorization and repetition was all a mage required. The College itself seemed to discourage any deeper understanding.

Is there any deeper understanding?

How long would someone have to do this before they achieved anything useful?

The "class" lasted for a couple of hours. Nate wasn't exactly sure, but the timing coincided with the melting of the white candle. The guards began collecting the students' parchment once the white candle had diminished to about an inch in height. The whole episode felt surreal, as if he had walked into the final exam by accident. He also got the feeling that he didn't pass. Where most of the students had filled their pages with writing, some continuing on the other side, Nate had barely covered half of his sheet of parchment.

One of the guards pulled the sheet away from him as he was studying his own handiwork.

The point is? Aren't we supposed to study this?

Nate looked at the model on the inlaid block of wood. What did it *mean*? What was the significance of these symbols that were so hard to transcribe, so hard even to visualize?

Nate needed time to think about what he was looking at.

The guards didn't give that to him. As soon as they collected the last page from the students, the lead blue-belt brought the butt of his staff down on the stone floor with a resonating crack. Everyone took a sideways step to the left, into the aisles between the desks. Nate followed a half beat after everyone else.

In the moments before they filed out of the room, Nate took the opportunity to look at the model inscription on the desk in front of his own.

The same symbols, it seemed. The same—except for

one series of characters. Where Nate's inscription quoted the string of symbols marking the bottom of his black candle, the guy in front of him had a different sequence. They started moving before Nate could get a glimpse of what was carved in that guy's candle.

Even so, he had a pretty good idea.

• • •

Breakfast was after devotions—Nate had mentally stopped calling it a class. From their morning devotions, the acolytes were led into a large hall set with long wooden tables. They sat on long benches in roughly the same order they had stood for their transcriptions.

For Nate, it was just a relief to get off of his feet. He caught a whiff of something cooking, and he felt his stomach tighten. He had worked up one hell of an appetite during the morning.

Once everyone was seated, tall ghadi in togalike outfits walked in, bearing large platters. Each table received one on each end. The platters were metal ovals nearly four feet long, piled indiscriminately with stewed fruits, well-done meats, and starchy vegetables mashed into a lumpy paste. Beside the pile of food were stacks of thick, flat bread.

At first, Nate was at a loss due to the lack of utensils, until it became obvious that the bread was the utensil. He watched as the people next to him used one flat piece as a plate and another to scoop food from the massive platter. People tore at the bread, used chunks of it as a spoon, or used their hands. Nate watched the others eat and didn't gather his own food until he was certain what the rules were.

The lack of silverware was strange to him, but after the brain-deadening exercise this morning, it was probably a good thing that the students weren't given anything that could be used as a weapon.

While they ate, more ghadi came by and set down tankards by each student. When Nate tasted his, it was some sort of dark fruity wine that had been warmed slightly above room temperature. Nate didn't care for it, but he needed to drink something.

At the tables around him, the students all babbled at each other. In the mass of overlapping words, it was very hard for Nate to make anything out. That was fine, since no one seemed to be talking to him. His entire table seemed to be making a point of ignoring him.

The new kid, Nate thought. He wondered if everyone got this treatment, or if his appearance inspired a special effort. The people at other tables didn't make any effort to hide their stares, and several pointed at him while they talked.

Nate looked down at his hands.

He had always been something of a loner. He had spent way too much time on the computer, and inside his own head. This certainly wasn't the first time he had sat in a room full of strangers with whom he had no connection. It *was* the first time he had felt so alone.

As far as they know, I'm not even the same species . . .

. . . as far as I know, they're right.

Chapter Twenty-Three

THE HIGHEST scholars of the College of Man filled the audience chamber at the heart of the College's home in the city of Manhome. Most sat behind the U-shaped table that dominated the center of the room, and all of them wore their most intricate masks and robes.

All but one.

One of their number wore no mask at all. Polan Ostiz had once been as high in the College as anyone aside from the Venerable Master Scholar himself. Now Polan was stripped of his jeweled mask and robes, blindfolded, sitting bound upon the interview chair. Guards held blades at Polan's throat, lest he attempt to speak any words of power.

Between the seated scholars of the College, and the bruised, scarred and half naked form of Polan Ostiz, strode Scholar Uthar Vailen. When Uthar talked, he had the habit of facing the smiling half of his clown mask at Polan, the frowning half toward the scholars in the audience.

"Are you a loyal servant of the College of Man, Polan Ostiz?"

"Y–yes."

Uthar nodded. "You are sworn to live a life with a single duty."

"Yes."

"State that duty for us."

There was a long pause while Polan swallowed and

licked his lips. The prisoner's voice was raspy and his lips scabbed and bloody from the studded leather gag that had filled his mouth for much of the week since his capture.

"A scholar of the College lives only to protect Mankind from the secrets he possesses, known and unknown."

Uthar picked up a leather-bound book from the desk where it rested in front of the Venerable Master Scholar Jardan Syn. "And you chose to deny that duty."

"No."

"Lies only compound your sins, and will only prolong an already unpleasant process."

"I have done nothing."

Uthar opened the journal and read, " *'It seems apparent that the Gods' Language itself must, in fact, have grammar and meaning within itself. Each rune within a sequence we utter must own its own meaning, contributing to the whole in an unknown, but not unknowable manner,'* These are your words?"

"Y–yes, but—"

"And you wrote, *'We could divine meaning within the Gods' Language by taking a simple invocation, such as used for an acolyte's initiation, and changing a rune therein. If done in a methodical manner, with the results of the acolyte's devotion carefully observed, one could begin to understand the structure of the invocation as well as the runes themselves.'* "

"I did nothing but write down—"

"Enough," Uthar slammed the journal shut. "You protest you have done nothing, but you do not even attempt to deny writing such heresies. *'Unknown, but not unknowable?'* You presume that we can know the mind of the gods. More, you suppose that we should!"

Polan shook his head, ignoring the blades at his throat even when his motion caused them to draw thin lines of blood. "Please understand. I only wrote down ideas on how the College could proceed."

"The College?" Uthar said. "Is it in your mind that

this is how the College of Man should perform its duty? Shouting random runes at the gods and hoping they grant us more power rather than destroy us? Would you risk all of Mankind for your own vain desires? What is the knowledge you seek worth?"

"I have done nothing."

"If you have done nothing, where then is the stranger that the hand of Ghad inflicted upon us?"

"I don't know . . ."

"Lies will not serve you well. We found a decade's worth of your writing. You documented well your obsessive curiosity. You even wrote of what we might hope to learn from this creature, what insights there might be from questioning Ghad's Angel himself."

"We were questioning him."

"But it would have suited you better to have him for yourself," Uthar looked up at the scholars watching the questioning. "Only one of us could have taken the stranger as well as its possessions. If not you, then tell us who did."

"I don't know . . ."

Uthar remained facing away from Polan. "Not even a suspicion? You protest your innocence, but you cannot even suggest someone with a fraction of the desire you had for such a prize?"

"I do not know anything of it. Nothing."

Uthar nodded. "I will yield to the Master Scholar now. I have contributed all I can."

• • •

The scholars' deconstruction of Polan Ostiz lasted several hours. Uthar watched as the seeds he planted in the fertile soil of the College's paranoia grew, flowered, and bore their poison fruit. Right now, truth was beside the point. The College needed a sacrifice for the loss of the stranger. Nate Black. Ghad's Angel of Death.

Polan could have been anyone. He just happened to be convenient to Uthar. Uthar had long known about the man's heretical thoughts, the volume of which made the man an easy distraction for the scholars of the College.

For the living fossils that sat at the table with the Venerable Master Scholar, it was obvious that the traitor responsible for the theft of Nate Black would be a heretic. Polan was just enough of one to draw the full force of the scholars' attack, despite the fact that no evidence aside from his unconventional thoughts was forthcoming.

Uthar knew none would be. None was necessary.

After the scholars were finished with the wreck that was Polan Ostiz, Uthar had an audience alone with the Venerable Master Scholar himself. Uthar spent some time reassuring his master that eventually the questioning of Polan would reveal the fate of the missing Nate Black, or, at the very least, reveal the threat of other heretics within the body of the College.

The threat of the spread of heresy within the walls of the College was enough to make the Venerable Master Scholar forget about the stranger, the nominal reason for the imprisonment of Polan Ostiz.

Uthar left his audience with a feeling of satisfaction.

After leaving the Venerable Master Scholar, Uthar walked down through the corridors of the College of Man. He descended below the barracks where the acolytes slept, below the cells where Polan Ostiz was imprisoned, below the chambers where the ghadi were kept.

He slid behind a dusty tapestry that was of an age with the stone corridor around him, through the rooms hidden behind it, and into a passage that few people still knew about.

Uthar walked deep into the ancient ghadi corridors, the way lit by an incantation that gave the air around him a deep green glow. He stopped in front of a stone panel that appeared to have rested in place for millennia.

The appearance was deceiving.

Uthar spoke the incantation that moved the grinding stone aside. With the way open, he walked through into a wide chamber dominated by a single stone chair. On the chair lay a brown robe and a plain white mask. He dismissed the green light that had followed him as the stones above him began to glow.

Uthar waited for the door to grind shut behind him before he walked to the chair and traded Arthiz's mask for his own.

● ● ●

"Why can I not see him?" Yerith stood in front of the Scholar Osif. He shook his head. His expression seemed to say that coming down to the ghadi quarters was not a good idea.

Osif stepped around her, and continued walking down the corridor, looking in the rooms. *As if he was actually concerned with the living conditions of the ghadi down here.*

"I deserve an answer," she continued.

Osif stopped in front of the birthing room, empty at the moment. Empty and not really necessary. They were close enough to the wild ghadi population here that Yerith doubted that there was any intentional breeding here.

Osif stared into the empty chamber. "Your service to the Monarch does not give you the right to question us here."

"The workings of the College are not open to question." Yerith spat at Osif's feet.

Osif turned to look at her with an expression of shock.

"All you have done is take off the mask," Yerith told him. "You could be the Venerable Master Scholar himself."

She turned and started walking away from him.

This is your sole duty now, Arthiz had said. The words rang weak and hollow. What was the point of fighting the hold of the College of Man, when the scholars here showed the same arrogance, the same absolutism as the scholars in the College itself?

"You don't understand," Osif told her.

"What's to understand?" Yerith turned around and glared at him. "Nate Black was placed in my charge by the Monarch himself. By Arthiz. But apparently the words of the Monarch mean as little here as they do within the College of Manhome."

"You question my loyalty."

"Scholars are only loyal to each other."

Osif shook his head and looked down at the straw bedding in the birthing room. "We both serve the Monarch," he said finally. "But Nate Black is a dangerous creature."

"I've been told."

"You have no idea how many heresies we commit simply by housing him here, much less allowing him in with the students."

"But I cannot see him."

"If Arthiz wishes him as an acolyte, we must treat him as an acolyte," Osif said. "Their isolation is not without reason. Until a student's concentration is developed, until they can read the Gods' Language empty of thought or meaning, any distraction is a danger. You would endanger him as well as yourself."

Yerith shook her head, dissatisfied.

"That is the only answer I can provide you," Osif said.

As he walked away he turned and told her, "You keep the ghadi well."

What else do I have to do?

Chapter Twenty-Four

AFTER A FEW days, Nate was desperate for anything approaching an actual class.

Nate wanted an instructor, a lecture, a textbook, a syllabus, something that gave him some sort of guidance to what they were trying to accomplish. His days were filled with activity that seemed more appropriate to a monastery than a college. They copied their model text, then after a meal they spent as much time chanting and gesturing the same string of—

Nate didn't even know if "words" was the appropriate term. What they had them memorize was so divorced from context that it could have been language, mathematical symbols, or machine code.

The day would end with all of them standing in a large amphitheater that was open to the sky. The first time Nate had the vain hope that they were going to get their lecture, finally. But after about twenty minutes of sitting in silence with his other classmates, Nate realized that wasn't going to happen.

He looked at the others and saw that most had their eyes closed, and a few moved their lips as if they were chanting silently. Nate shook his head and rubbed his temples. He wasn't looking at an institute of learning, he was looking at a place of worship.

By day three, Nate knew two things.

First, he didn't have the patience for this, and unless these guys radically altered the agenda in the next couple of days, he would probably go nuts.

Second, he still had to go through the motions.

Nate racked his brain trying to think of some way to reconcile those two facts. He needed something to keep the oppressive routine from making him crazy.

If only there was some way to figure out what the "words" they're studying actually mean. If they aren't just a string of arbitrary symbols . . .

• • •

Day three ended the same as the first two, with another ritual bath. That marked the end of the regimented part of the day. Nate walked back into what he thought of as the "dorm" with most of his classmates. A few people wandered off toward other areas after the baths.

Nate was tempted to wander off himself, but he deferred his curiosity for when he had a better mental picture of the floor plan here. At the very least, getting lost would be embarrassing. And, with the blue-belted chaperones everywhere, Nate suspected that there were places they didn't want him to go.

Back in the dorm, Nate stood facing his alcove, mentally exhausted and still trying to figure out what was expected of him. He didn't see the point of dropping him in here without any instruction at all. Right now he wanted to question Arthiz. Or Bhodan. Or Yerith. Or even Osif, if the guy would lower himself to answer him.

He needed to talk to someone, anyone, at this point.

Nate looked around, and saw Question-mark sitting on the chest at the foot of his own bed. It looked as if he was sewing something.

Nate walked over to Question-mark's alcove. When he approached, Nate saw that the sewing project was an elaborate mask. It was half complete, the outside a mass of twisted wire forming some sort of superstructure, the inside a layer of quilted padding that Question-mark was busy sewing into place.

"Shall I talk to you?" Nate asked. His language

skills still gave him trouble, and the question didn't come out exactly right.

Question-mark looked up from his mask and looked at Nate with an expression that had become too familiar to Nate—

Yeah, the creature talks, get over it.

"You wish to talk to me?"

"I wish to talk to someone." Nate looked around. "You are here. You talked to me before."

"I did," he answered, looking as if he regretted the decision. He looked down at his project and said. "Then talk to me, ghadi."

"You know my name."

"There are no names here."

"Then what name do you not have?"

He glanced up at Nate, hesitated a moment, then told him, "Solis. But it would not be proper to address me by it."

"Why not?"

"Do you know where you are?"

"That may be the only thing I do know." Nate knelt down and looked at Solis. "I am a stranger here. Not just to this place. To everything. I don't know why I was taken here. I don't know what I am expected to do here. I don't know the meaning of anything I have done here."

Solis stared at him.

"Help me," Nate said.

The silence was uneasy. For a few long moments, Solis stared at him. Nate was afraid that his fumbling efforts had been pointless.

Finally Solis spoke, his voice a little above a whisper. "If the gods brought you from Outside, the College should have destroyed you. An alien is—" Solis used an unfamiliar word.

"They almost did," Nate said. "But they seemed to want to question me first."

"And you have nothing of our ways?"

"When I came here, I didn't even have the language."

Solis stood, setting the mask on his bed. "Perhaps we should take a walk."

• • •

Solis led him through several corridors, until they reached open air. They walked through overgrown vines and bushes into a small clearing, and at first Nate thought they had left the underground city completely. However, around the edges of the clearing, Nate could still see stone walls rising above the foliage on every side and they walked past piles of overgrown mossy stone, the remains of an ancient cave-in.

Solis sat on a broken column and looked up at the emerging stars. The clearing was silent except for the sound of insects chirping.

After a long time, Solis said, "Do you know what you are?"

"Just a man," Nate said, hoping they weren't going into the deformed ghadi nonsense again.

"You are a stranger." The way Solis said it, the word carried more sinister connotations. "The College of Man will not abide a stranger. You are a tool of the gods."

"I could be a tool of your god."

Solis stared at him. "You are very strange if you think a man can possess a god. Stranger still if you think I am such a man."

Nate shook his head in frustration. "No, that's not what I meant—" He was about to add, *"and you know it,"* when he realized that maybe Solis didn't.

"What else could you possibly mean?"

"Maybe I don't understand. I come from a different place. A different language. I know what the gods are there. What are the gods here?"

Solis still looked as if he was trying to get his head around the concept.

"How would you explain it to a child?" Nate asked, hoping to glean some information.

Solis nodded. "The world is the gods' siege-board and we are the stones they play with. They dwell between the worlds, playing their games. Mere men are fortunate if they never attract their attention, or worse, become part of their game."

"No temples or offerings? No one worships any gods here?"

"No one sane. Long ago, men made offerings to the gods. Longer still, before the—" Solis used a word that Nate couldn't immediately translate. It was familiar though, from the book of the local mythos that Yerith had given him. It seemed to refer back to the war between the Ghadikhan and Mankind. "—then the ghadi ancestors worshiped such a god. All believed that they might receive some measure of favor."

"Did they?"

"Any fortune brought by the gods brings sixfold of misfortune with it. Including you, I suspect."

"Arthiz does not seem to believe I am a misfortune."

"He may believe that your misfortunes will plague our enemies rather than ourselves."

What an optimistic thought.

"What happened to the men who worshiped the gods?"

"The College of Man," Solis said.

"What do you believe, Solis? Why are you here?" Nate walked over to a large stone block and sat down himself.

"The College was founded to protect Mankind from the whims of the gods, and the power of the Gods' Language. It is corrupt now, more interested in serving its own power."

"And Arthiz would replace it?"

"The Monarch would."

Nate nodded. For all his hope at progressive reform, it was probably too much to ask for a fundamental revolution spontaneously erupting in a totalitarian dictatorship. Without war or an economic collapse, a factional war was probably all anyone was going to get.

"Can you tell me what we are doing here?" Nate asked.

"You do not know?"

"I was told that I would be taught."

"That is so."

"This is . . ." Damn his vocabulary. "This is how we are taught?"

"This is how you become a scholar. This is how you receive the . . ." He used an unfamiliar word, though Nate gathered it was something like "mysteries."

"Just by repeating things over and over, without guidance?"

"The effect on the world is enough guidance." Solis touched his forehead where the line of symbols carved its arch above his eye. "To use the Gods' Language, it must be carved in your mind, and your heart."

"And skin?"

"So it cannot be taken from you."

Nate looked at Solis' face. Darkness had fallen and only a small amount of moonlight leaked through the branches. The scars carved into Solis' skin raised shadows that made a third of his face an abstract collage of light and dark.

"How does it help you? You can't read the . . . marks."

"The marks have their own power, by themselves. If you know its name," Solis traced the carving on his face with his finger. "You can invoke the whole—" another unfamiliar word, *Series? Sentence? Spell?* "—by calling on its name."

It sounded more and more like a computer language to Nate. Code a function, then you just have to call it with some parameters to run it. But, instead of residing in some computer memory somewhere, this "language" was physically represented somewhere. Written on paper, inlaid into wood, or carved into someone's skin.

There actually was a practical reason for the scarification.

"What does that do?" Nate asked.

Solis lowered his fingers. "It is an old spell to purify water. Invoked on the foulest swamp, all disease, poison, and filth sink to the bottom, leaving the clean water on top."

"Sounds useful."

Solis frowned. "All the salt in Manhome comes from seawater the College mages purify to irrigate crops."

"That was what they had in mind for you?"

"That is what I did for them." Solis shook his head and touched the unblemished part of his face. "You thought me unfinished?"

"Well, I—"

"The College thought me finished."

Nate didn't know what to say. He had gotten the guy talking and now Nate was paranoid that somehow he had insulted him. Especially since Solis had gotten Nate's first impression right on the nose. Nate had thought the guy *was* a work in progress.

"Did they—" Nate started, halting on his imperfect language.

"Did they what?"

"Is that all they wanted from you?"

"All they ever want," Solis said. "Their acolytes don't serve to preserve the sacred language, or to honor the mysteries, or to protect Mankind. Their servants are taught just enough to be used. I was recruited into the great College of Man, had this carved in my face, and I was shown how to invoke it. That was all."

Nate looked back at the now darkened walls that surrounded them. "The College doesn't do this?" Nate waved back where they had come from.

"Only for those destined to lead the College one day."

"I see."

"A strange honor to bestow upon someone such as you," Solis said. "Appreciate what you are being taught."

Chapter Twenty-Five

NATE MANAGED to keep his sanity for the full week before they offered him any break in the routine.

Nate woke and dressed for the morning devotion. He started to follow the rest of the acolytes, but he was stopped by one of the blue-belted chaperones.

The man took Nate's arm and pulled him out of line. "Stay with me."

Nate had learned enough at this point not to speak to the guards. They were very touchy about novices knowing their place.

He stood with the guard as everyone filed out of the dorm area. Several of his peers cast furtive glances in his direction, while the majority stoically ignored him. Nate didn't need anyone to say anything for him to pick up the vibe—

Being singled out for anything was not a good thing.

Bad or not, the break in monotony was welcome, as long as no one threw him back into a cell.

"We go this way." Blue-belt took Nate down a side corridor, away from the dorm and where the devotions were held. They walked through stone corridors that gradually became more familiar.

Back toward Bhodan, Nate thought.

They didn't return to exactly where Nate had come into the complex, but they were close enough that Nate knew that they were in the same general area.

If he listened hard, he could hear the river that passed the facade of the old ghadi city.

Also, if he listened hard, he could hear an argument raging ahead of them. More precisely, he heard half an argument.

If Nate concentrated, he could make out some of the words.

"—an insult. This place is not Arthiz's personal kingdom—"

Pause.

"—I know what you believe. That does not mean we disrupt our—"

Pause.

"—How can it not be disruptive? Anyone who looks at him knows he is a—" The speaker used an unfamiliar word. "—they will think of him more than their studies."

As they approached, Nate could make out another, calmer, voice. That speaker's words were too low for him to catch.

"—then do it away from our students. We risk too much—"

Nate recognized the speaker now. *Osif.*

"I guess the bastard really doesn't like me," Nate muttered to himself in English.

Blue-belt glared at Nate, and Nate smiled back at him.

They stopped by a massive wooden door held together by black iron bands and square nails with heads the size of Nate's fist. The voices came from behind it.

"Wait," said Blue-belt.

Like I have much choice at this point.

Blue-belt knocked on the door, interrupting the argument on the other side. After a moment, the door swung aside.

Osif looked at Nate and waved him in. Blue-belt didn't follow.

The room was a high-arched chamber with faded frescoes on the wall. The paintings were of ghadi, pastoral scenes showing what the city had once looked like. The rough wood table and benches looked odd contrasted against the graceful old columns—like Archie Bunker's chair in a Frank Lloyd Wright house.

Bhodan was seated at the head of the table, his damaged face looking toward a spot about three feet to the left of the entrance.

"Our stranger has arrived. Good."

Nate stood in front of the table, looking from Bhodan to Osif and back again. Again, communicating in an alien language gave him the pause to think about what he was going to say.

He looked over at Osif and asked, "Have I done something wrong?"

Osif ignored him and walked to the side of the room where he retrieved a small carved chest from a niche set in the wall. Bhodan answered Nate, still talking to the phantom spot to the left of the entrance. "No, Nate Black, that isn't why you are here."

"Why am I here?"

"A test," Bhodan said. "We wish to see what kind of progress you are making."

Osif set the carved chest on the table, casting a look at him as if Nate was a vile insect floating in his bowl of favorite porridge.

"I have only been here seven days." Nate said.

Osif spoke. "If you have any capacity, we will see results."

And this is your idea, isn't it?

Osif opened the chest and Nate saw a familiar-looking black candle. As Osif took the candle out of the chest and placed it on the table Nate asked, "Do you do this with all your students?"

"Only some," Bhodan said. "When there is a question of their ability to absorb the mysteries."

Osif set a sheet of parchment and a brush on the table before Nate. Then he walked over and lit the candle. "After seven days, there is a question about me?"

"You are a stranger," Osif almost spat. "If you—"

Bhodan raised a hook to silence Osif. He smiled, his face becoming skull-like in the process. "You are a special case, Nate Black. I think you know that. You, we must observe most closely." He waved toward the parchment. "Please compose yourself and show what you have learned."

Damn, they could at least warn you the midterm is coming. . . .

Fortunately, he had memorized the sequence they were studying. He was beginning to see it in his sleep.

He took the brush in his hand and began the laborious process of transcription. Without a model, the effort was even more taxing. He had to force himself to visualize the symbols, and holding them in his mind was almost as difficult as committing them to paper.

He sweated through the line of mystical script without pausing. He could feel, in the back of his skull, the pressure of the incantation building. He knew that, if he hesitated in his writing, that energy would break loose prematurely. He could feel it.

When he finished the transcription, he felt the wave break and sighed with relief as he set the brush down. The characters filled the first line in the page. He knew that he had done it correctly because of the way it felt to look at what he'd written. It took effort to study the characters, more than it should have. . . .

His smile lasted until he looked up at the candle.

It still burned.

What the—?

He had followed the script down to the last line. Nate knew that he had written an exact copy of what he was writing every day.

He glanced at Osif, who looked way too pleased with himself.

Nate looked back at the candle.

The inscription on the candle was different.

"You sneaky little bastard," Nate whispered in English. "You're setting me up."

"Are you finished?" Bhodan asked.

Am I?

Nate decided that he shouldn't play it cagey, since he didn't know what they'd do with him if they decided he wasn't getting anything out of their lesson plan. Besides, he didn't like Osif's shit-eating grin. It would be just too galling for Nate to let Osif believe he'd outsmarted him.

"No," Nate said, "I made a mistake. I need to do it over."

He picked up the brush again. Before he started, he saw Osif's expression waver, then he was too absorbed in the spell.

Hopefully it was just a matter of replacing the candle's label in the script. That's what Nate did, retaining the remainder of the characters as is. It was actually easier, now that he had a line of text to use as a model.

This time, upon completion, the candle obediently snuffed itself out.

Nate looked up, smiling. "I suppose that was an easy mistake for a novice."

Osif looked at the candle. His expression told Nate all he needed to know. It *had* been a set up. Whatever ability Nate might have picked up in the last couple of days, Osif hadn't expected him to get the idea that the ritual candles were individually labeled.

Probably part of the advanced course . . .

"Does he perform satisfactorily?" Bhodan asked.

"He completed the task."

"Then send him back." Bhodan waved toward the door with a hook. "You may test him again next sixday."

Osif clapped his hands, and the door to the chamber opened, letting in the blue-belted guard who had escorted Nate here.

That's it?

Nate turned back toward Bhodan and said, "Can I ask a question—"

"We did not speak to you," Osif snapped. "If you are to be an acolyte, do not forget your place."

Nate glanced at Bhodan, who he had thought had

been on his side. The damaged old man said nothing, his empty sockets staring somewhere else. Nate felt a wave of frustration. "No one has told me my place."

Osif's skin turned a shade darker, deepening the contrast of his facial scars. He clenched his hand into a fist, and when he talked, his voice was cold.

"You will not address your betters unless you are asked a question. Any future break in discipline will be punished. If we must have you as an acolyte, you will behave as one."

But no one has told me the rules. . . . Nate thought better of saying that out loud.

Osif waved at the guard, and Blue-belt took Nate's arm and led him away from the room.

Chapter Twenty-Six

NATE'S "TRAINING" went on.

Devotions and rote memorization—no context, no explanation, and very few obvious principles to follow. You inscribe this set of symbols, you invoke it, this happens. The ability of an acolyte was measured in how many strings of arbitrary symbols could be remembered accurately.

It was as if he had descended into a medieval monastery where the liturgy was taught, but no one knew Latin or cared to learn.

Worse, every time he broached the subject to Solis, one of the few acolytes he could actually talk to, he seemed to be running into some sort of taboo. At the very least, some sort of conceptual barrier. When Nate asked why they couldn't be told the *meaning* of these symbols, the answer was along the lines of, "One cannot know the mind of the gods, and hope that speaking their words does not drive you mad."

Worse, it appeared that some *were* driven mad. In the first two weeks, Nate saw three people collapse, and one who, one day, stayed in his alcove in the dorm, staring at the wall, and had to be carried away by the blue-belted guards.

There was obviously a real danger in what they did.

Nate could only imagine what a mistranscription might do. Like a typo in an English sentence, nine times out of ten a random error would be gibberish. But who knew what the tenth error might produce?

Instead of snuffing a candle, it could snuff something in your own skull.

If that was the case, doing random experiments was a bad idea.

However, that didn't mean Nate wasn't going to experiment.

How in the hell could he avoid it? It wasn't as if he could turn off his brain and stop thinking about it. Even if he wanted to, that would have been hopeless. What he needed was a discreet and safe way to, at the very least, think about what he was learning in some structured manner. Not only did he want to make some sense out of the symbols he was memorizing, but he needed to engage his mind in *something* or he was going to go nuts.

But that wasn't easy. Not only did the daily ritual devotions take most of Nate's time, but there were difficulties in even the basic process of taking notes. In the case of the Gods' Language, the map *was* the territory. If you transcribed a symbol, you transcribed a spell. Not only did it require concentration and an unbroken effort to do so, but writing down symbols in isolation or in differing orders would have some sort of effect and would be, in essence, the sort of random experiment that Nate was trying to avoid.

Nate had need of something that was *just* a map. He needed to refer to the symbols in his notes without actually using them. At first it daunted him, because there were more potential symbols in the Gods' Language than in any written tongue he knew of. It was daunting to come up with a means of representing them. It was laid out so simply;

But each one of the twelve lines could be on or off,

like the lines in the numbers on an old-fashioned LED
calculator. Twelve lines, which meant there were thousands of possible characters.

It took an embarrassingly long time for it to occur
to him how to transcribe the symbols. It was a full
two days before he realized that each symbol was a
representation of a twelve-digit binary number. When
that finally occurred to him, it made him want to turn
in his hacker hat.

Even more embarrassing was the fact that the
way the runes were pronounced observed the same
sort of concept, breaking the symbol into parts that
represented different syllables. Not that anyone
went out of their way to tell Nate that this line
was named "H–" and when it was half there, it
was "Hö," but the pattern was fairly obvious. Obvious enough that after a week of exposure, explanation or not, pronouncing a new rune wasn't any more
difficult than pronouncing a new word in any phonetic language.

Once the code warrior inside him was duly chastised, he calculated exactly how many symbols there
were. There were $2^{12}-1$ symbols in the Gods' Language. When considered as single indivisible objects,
it was a staggering number to memorize, worse than
any ideographic language that Nate had heard of.

But considered in the proper organizational frame-
work, it was no harder to conceptualize than the numbers between 0 and 4095, or the subset of English
words of six letters or less. That made it simple to
come up with a mapping scheme that gave each symbol a unique label that Nate could understand almost
instantly, but had none of the side effects of using the
actual characters.

He started transcribing spells in his notebook in
hexadecimal notation, lining the pages with columns
of three-digit hex numbers that mapped to the twelve
"digit" "numbers" of the Gods' Language.

•   •   •

He stole what time he could. He began smuggling his own paper into the morning devotion, sliding it under the parchment they gave him for practice.

Then he could spend half the time copying the model, and the other half jotting down the hex equivalent of the spell, as well as the fragments of spells he saw carved into the skin of his comrades.

Making his own copy was a nerve-racking process, since everyone was so closely observed by the bluebelts. He only risked one number, sometimes only one digit, at a time. However, time was on Nate's side here, since they spent several days on one string of symbols.

Into the fifth week, they had just begun Nate's fourth spell.

So far, they had snuffed out a ritual candle, lit it again, and caused a pebble to rise to the surface in a glass of water. Also, with clockwork regularity, two days into the new study, he would be pulled aside to demonstrate to Osif and Bhodan that he was, in fact, absorbing the lesson.

Now they were returning to the candle-snuffing ritual. Nate had to suppress a groan, until he realized that the model he was working on was different from the first.

He copied the model dutifully on the parchment, as did the other acolytes, but he noticed that the spell was, in fact, several characters longer than the first spell they had taught here. It started with some minor variations, then copied the first spell almost exactly, then ended with a brand new sequence.

Then Nate noticed something about the new sequence.

In five weeks of surreptitious study, the single breakthrough Nate had managed in understanding the Gods' Language was a small grasp of syntax, the idea that some of the runes existed for the purpose of punctuation.

The first punctuation symbols he found were from looking at what was inscribed on the candles, and the

way that it was copied into the spells affecting that
particular candle. On *all* the candles, Nate saw the
same pair of symbols beginning and ending the candle's "name." To Nate, those symbols appeared to set
off a string of symbols as a label, an identifier rather
than part of a spell.

The second set of punctuation Nate found, after
he had seen more than one spell, was a pair of symbols that seemed to mark the beginning and end of
an entire spell, distinct from the symbols marking
a label.

By week five, Nate had already modified his notation so that instead of the three-digit hex code, he was
writing these two types of opening and closing symbols
as square and curly brackets.

So, when he was near the end of marking up his
own surreptitious copy of the spell, he saw himself
writing a sequence: . . . *A32 05F B10* } { *1FF CD7* . . .

If he was right in his assumptions about how this
language was punctuated, the sequence "}{" should
never appear inside a spell. "{" was the opening character and "}" was a closing character.

Unless these are two separate spells.

There was a simple, quick way to test it, and he
could do it without alerting the blue-belts. The nature
of these spells was that, in order to work, they must
be written in a continuous act. If there was a pause
in the writing, the energies built up by the act would
dissipate.

On his next copy of the model, Nate painted the
symbols up until the first "}" symbol. There he
stopped, and waited.

What he had just written was very similar to the
first spell he had learned. The only differences were
some additional symbols beginning the line. Whatever
the difference was, it prevented this spell from behav-
ing like its cousin. The candle snuffed itself immediately upon Nate finishing the effort of writing spell
number one. Here, he went through the same mental

effort transcribing these symbols, and nothing happened.

Nate counted silently a full sixty seconds.

Then he commenced copying the remainder of the model on a new line.

This part of the spell was only a few characters long, enclosed in its own set of "{}" symbols. Much of it, in fact, seemed similar to the additions at the beginning of the spell.

As soon as Nate completed the last brush stroke for the "}" symbol, the candle snuffed itself.

Nate relit the candle and looked at the guards. None appeared to be paying special attention to him.

Telling himself that it wasn't random experimentation, Nate started a new line of transcription. This time, however, he only copied what appeared to be the second spell in the model.

He copied the short sequence of symbols, and the candle snuffed itself again.

"The marks have their own power, by themselves. If you know its name," Solis had said, *"you can invoke the whole by calling on its name."*

What do you know?

• • •

Late in the evening, during the short amount of free time he was allowed, Nate left the dorms and found a quiet spot where he could jot down notes in his journal. He had transcribed enough of the hex translation of these spells that he was able to see definite patterns.

There was a syntax to it, a grammar. He was just beginning to see something of the underlying structure, laid out by the punctuation marks he was unearthing.

He was so engrossed in divining the naming convention that was used when today's spells invoked each other, that he didn't notice Solis approach until the man spoke.

"What is it you do?" he asked.

Nate looked up, startled. "I am—" He didn't have the words for "taking notes." He thought a moment before he said, "I am studying."

"It is not the time for study. You need rest, or tomorrow's study will be lost on you."

Nate set down his brush. "I am surprised you care how a stranger does here."

Solis frowned. "What you learn is a—" another unfamiliar word. "I care that respect is given to it."

"You believe I do not respect it?"

"I see you and think you do not respect the traditions."

Nate didn't say anything immediately. He couldn't see any way to honestly contradict the guy. Nate *didn't* respect the traditions that Solis was talking about. Nate was beginning to understand that the way he was translating the common tongue might not be strictly correct.

"The College" might just as easily be read as "the Church."

"I come from a different place," Nate said. "If I am to learn, there are ways I need to think, things I need to think about, and thoughts I need to write."

"You do not write the sacred tongue . . ."

"No. I do not wish to invoke anything. I write about the sacred tongue."

"About?" Solis looked puzzled. "You write about our devotions?"

"I write about what we are writing."

"You are talking in circles."

"No one is willing to explain what the symbols in the sacred tongue mean—"

"Why do you ask senseless questions? Does the air need explanation? The earth?"

"—so I need to discover them myself."

Solis stared at Nate, then down at the journal in Nate's lap. "What are you doing?"

"Learning the Gods' Language."

Solis actually looked afraid, as if Nate and his journal might burst into flame at any moment. "Do you know where you tread?" Solis whispered.

"If someone would tell me—" Nate started to say, but Solis had already left. There was little doubt that he was breaking some sort of taboo here by examining the spells too closely.

I shouldn't have tried to explain myself.

Nate didn't know what to do. He was trying to work and play nice with others, but he couldn't imagine going through this sort of training and *not* trying to decipher what he was being "taught."

Nate picked up his brush and resumed taking notes.

• • •

Nate knew that it couldn't last.

The sensible thing would have been to let them go through the whole training until he went through whatever graduation/promotion/rite of passage happened at the other end, and do it without drawing attention to himself. Occasionally, he would let it dawn on him that if he pissed off these guys, that would be it. Even if all they did was cut him loose, he was in a world where foreigners were taboo and there was no way he could look like a native, much less talk like one.

Not that they'd ever cut him loose. He knew way too many details of Arthiz and the anti-College. No one here could risk what he might tell the actual College before the masked scholars killed him.

Thinking that way, Nate would go a day or two without note taking. But he couldn't turn off his mind. He needed to work on it. He needed to understand it. . . .

He needed to hack the damn language.

If anything, the taboo, the risk, made it *more* necessary for him to understand what it meant. It wasn't just knowing. It was knowing what someone didn't want you to know. For most of Nate's life that had been his lifeblood—Azrael's lifeblood.

So it wasn't a complete surprise when the blue-belts

walked into the transcription class one morning, and grabbed Nate, his "official" parchment, and the page he had smuggled into class, and marched him off without a word.

Chapter Twenty-Seven

THE BLUE-BELTS took Nate into the room where Osif and Bhodan had been testing him. As before, they were waiting for him. This time, however, there were no tests.

Instead, on the table in front of Bhodan, Nate saw a handful of the crib sheets he had been smuggling in and out of class.

He also had Nate's journal.

Nate wanted to shout something about invasion of privacy, but he doubted that privacy meant much in an environment where they didn't put doors on the dorm rooms.

Bhodan bent over the pages, appearing like a twisted gargoyle. His eyeless face hovered over the pages as if he could actually see what was written on them.

The guards sat Nate down and he realized that this was the first time he hadn't heard Osif and Bhodan arguing before he arrived. That couldn't be a good sign.

Osif placed his fingers on a loose sheet of paper and said, "This is your work?"

It would be pretty useless denying it. Nate could see a surreptitiously transcribed spell, as well as his hexadecimal notation on the page under Osif's fingers. "Yes, it is."

Osif touched another page, "And this?"

Nate sighed. "Yes." Before Osif moved to the next

document, Nate said, "Shall we save time? I don't deny writing any of those papers. You took them out of my trunk. They are mine."

"All of them?" Osif asked.

"Yes."

Bhodan spoke without raising his face. "For what purpose?"

"I am trying to understand what you are teaching me."

They both nodded, as if they had expected his answer. "Do you know the path you tread?" Bhodan tapped the pages with one of his hooks. "Well trod, by the mad and the dead."

Nate looked from one to the other, and the expression on both their faces was grave. The fact that Osif didn't even look satisfied at Nate's predicament made the atmosphere even more ominous.

"What is it I've done? I am supposed to be learning here, that's how I learn . . ."

Osif tapped the desk. "A single step into the mysteries as an acolyte and you've indulged in the most dangerous of heresies." Nate's mental translation of heresy was a guess.

"How am I to know what is a heresy—" Nate stumbled over the word, "—and what is not? I was a student, but what you have here is more worship than learning."

Bhodan leaned back and faced the ceiling. "I wonder sometimes if our patron Arthiz is much wiser or much more foolish than we."

"Will you at least explain what I did wrong?" Nate asked.

"The College of Man had a purpose once," Osif said. "Its law was meant to defend man from the mind of the gods."

"Originally," Bhodan said. "Much of that law now exists only to serve the College and the scholars within it."

Osif shook his head. "Staring too deeply into the mysteries will destroy a man and those around him."

Nate got the vibe. He had screwed up and alienated the only folks on this planet who seemed willing to cut him a break. For all the excuses he might make about no one telling him the rules, he knew it was so much bullshit. *If you thought it was okay, why did you try and hide your notes, huh?*

"What do you want me to do?" Nate asked.

"That is our question," Bhodan said. He pointed a hook at the remains of his face. "This you see before you was payment for a much more minor heresy— valuing the acolytes I taught as more than human ghadi."

Nate swallowed. "What are you going to do with me?"

"You cannot remain with the acolytes," Osif said. "Your influence is disruptive to their study. You would encourage them to gain just enough understanding to destroy themselves. What is it you think our acolytes learn here?"

"I thought—"

"They learn discipline. Self-control. The skill to stay on the path in front of them without losing themselves."

"However," Bhodan said, "I cannot be unsure that this is not what Arthiz and the Monarch expected from you."

"What?"

"We are all heretics here, Nate Black. The existance of this Shadow College is a heresy. You are here not because this—" Bhodan tapped the papers, "violates the laws of the College of Man. You are here because this is dangerous. I suspect you have little idea how dangerous."

"I have been careful."

Osif laughed.

"You do not understand." Bhodan said. "Even a careless thought about the mysteries you have here can kill."

"I have not been careless."

Bhodan nodded and waved a hook at Osif. Osif

called to the guard by the door, "Bring in the other one."

Other one?

Nate turned around to face the doorway and saw a pair of blue-belts walking Solis into the room.

What?

"Why is he here?"

"We cannot be careless either," Bhodan said. "Arthiz may want to see what your curiosity gains. Perhaps he wants a fool to bear the consequences of his own curiosity—but those consequences will begin and end with you. And him."

Nate shook his head. "Why Solis? He didn't do anything."

Osif walked around the edge of the desk. "He saw. He talked to you."

Solis looked at Nate with fear in his eyes.

"You shouldn't punish him for something that isn't his fault."

"This isn't punishment," Osif said, "we are protecting our students from the consequences of your actions."

● ● ●

A pair of blue-belted guards escorted Nate and a very subdued Solis to a twin of what Nate had been thinking of as the dorm. It was deeper, and aside from being empty, the only major difference between this place and where they housed the students was the presence of a heavy, barred iron door.

When the guards brought them in, a quartet of ghadi was just finishing placing lamps, cots and the few possessions Nate and Solis had been allowed in their dorm rooms.

"Could be worse," Nate muttered to himself in English as the guards left them alone in the room with the ghadi.

Solis stared at Nate. The look was a dangerous mix of fear and anger. *Guess you have a right to be pissed.*

"I didn't intend for you to be caught up in this."

"Do not talk to me," Solis said coldly. He walked over and sat on the cot in the alcove where the ghadi had placed his chest and clothing. He picked up the unfinished mask from one of the piles and threw it against the wall.

"Solis—"

"Begone, demon!" Solis shouted at him. "Just by talking you've tainted me. I do not want to hear anything more from the Angel of Death."

"What?"

Solis refued to respond, or even look in his direction.

Nate wasn't even sure he was translating what Solis had said correctly. Given what little he'd already found out about gods and such, the word Angel could mean Demon or Devil. . . .

Now that Nate thought about it, the word could apply to anything from another world. The more he thought, the more the implications began to sink in. . . .

No, there's no way . . .

"Solis, look at me." Nate stepped up, grabbed Solis' shoulder and turned the man around. "Why did you call me that?"

The fact was, Nate's old hacker handle, Azrael, wasn't just a name picked out of a hat or made up at random. The name was specifically a Judaic name for the Angel of Death.

"Don't touch me!" Solis cringed and struck out in such desperation that it might have been comical if the blow didn't lay Nate out on his ass in the aisle.

Solis looked down at Nate and the anger seemed to have won out over the fear. "Arthiz might be willing to take the council of Ghad's own demon. Not me."

Nate shook his head. It had to be some sort of superstitious nonsense. *Yeah, but why the sudden change of mood—*

Unless he had heard something from Osif or Bhodan.

You're being paranoid.

Even as he tried to second-guess himself, he remembered an exchange from when he had arrived here:

Osif: *"Do you actually believe that he is who Arthiz thinks—"*

Bhodan: *"This is not the time. Raise such questions to me, alone."*

Who, exactly did Arthiz think Nate was?

When the College had imprisoned him, he had told them his handle, Azrael. But they wouldn't know anything about what the name meant.

No, I told the sphere. . . .

What if that golden sphere had "translated" Azrael?

Nate pushed himself up. Solis had turned away again, and Nate decided that pushing him any further wouldn't be productive. The man was going to be his roommate for who knew how long. If he was lucky things might cool down enough for them to be on speaking terms again.

Nate stood up and brushed stone dust off his robe.

The ghadi, finished with their work, filed by him. When the door opened to let them out, Nate saw a familiar face.

"Yerith!"

•   •   •

"Osif finally agreed to allow me to see you." Yerith sat on Nate's cot while he sorted through the items the ghadi had brought him. Solis was a dark silence on the other side of the hall, by the iron door. "It seems that I won't disrupt the students' studies now that you are here."

Nate shook his head. "From one cell to another. It's all beginning to look the same to me."

"I'm supposed to take care of you," Yerith said. "Just let me know and we can arrange to go outside. They just want to keep you from interacting with the students."

Nate opened his mouth, but he decided it would take too long to explain why supervised, guarded excursions did not exactly make it feel less like a prison. Besides, belief systems aside, the powers that be did have a point. Given Solis' reaction to him, his isolation might serve his own safety more than the students'. Nate decided to change the subject. "They have you keeping the ghadi here?"

Yerith nodded. "This is a small enclave, made entirely of scholars and acolytes. They have the ghadi to do most of the labor, but they only had acolytes to tend the ghadi. They might be wise in many ways, but they knew little about caring for them."

"I guess it worked out for you."

"Your phrases are still strange, Nate Black."

"I am strange," Nate said, putting away the last book—the myths that Yerith had given him. "Can you tell me something?"

"What?"

"Do you know any stories about something called 'The Angel of Death'?"

Chapter Twenty-Eight

FOR CENTURIES after the great war between Mankind and Ghadikan, men worked to rebuild the broken crescent of the world. The College of Man who spoke the Gods' Language, seeing what had been wrought, closed the tomes that held the most terrible words so that no person who walked the earth might speak them again.

Ghad walked alone between the worlds.

He watched his ghadi enslaved and mute for six centuries. He saw his people broken under the weight of their labor. He felt their bodies consumed by the College of Man who spoke the Gods' Language.

Ghad saw all this and thought, "How cruel is man to curse a race so, when one word could heal these wounds." After thinking this, Ghad sat down in the darkness in the center of the world.

He watched as men forced armies of ghadi to dismantle the great temples that once proclaimed Ghad's glory. He saw the great cities rebuilt to house manlings. He felt man cut forests that Ghad meant to be uncut and move rivers that Ghad meant to be eternal.

Ghad saw all this and thought, "How wasteful is man to destroy such beauty, when one word could serve their needs." After thinking this, Ghad closed his eyes.

For six centuries more, Ghad listened to man spread across the face of the world as the Ghadikan slowly died. The ghadi could not even give voice to their pain, and this hardened Ghad's heart with rage.

Ghad thought, "How proud is man to come to this world as a stranger and live now as my ghadi had?"

Ghad decided that man needed to learn humility as Ghad himself had. Ghad wrapped himself in the skin of an old man and walked before the College of Man who spoke the Gods' Language.

The men of the College trembled because they knew that it was no old man who addressed them.

"How foolish is man?" Ghad asked.

The men of the College trembled and said, "We bow to your power, Ghad of old. We know much, but we cannot answer your question."

Ghad opened his hand and revealed a book that was not a sixth of the size of the great tomes where the College of Man had written the Gods' Language. "I created the language you study. I have seen you struggle where one word could ease your labors. Take this gift."

One wise man asked, "We know your name and who you are. Why should we trust your gift?"

Ghad laughed. "All I offer is knowledge."

And the men of the College accepted Ghad's gift.

The words within were indeed more powerful than any man had spoken before. At first, the College of Man reveled in their new power, the youngest among them forgetting the lessons of the war with the ghadi. For, though a word could raise a mountain from which an acolyte could view the world, somewhere else a chasm would open and swallow an innocent town. The College would call forth the rains with a word to make their land fertile, and elsewhere a desert would spread. They could call up a city out of the earth itself, and the ground beneath it, bled of its stone, would swallow it up into mud again.

To the wise men of the College it was clear that Ghad's gift was no gift, but other men of the College did not wish to give up such power.

"You cannot take this book away, for with it we can be like gods ourselves."

But the wise men of the College saw the destruction these men wrought. As did Ghad, who was amused.

Ghad wrapped himself in the skin of a young woman and walked before the College of Man who spoke the Gods' Language.

The men of the College trembled because they knew that it was no young woman who addressed them.

"How greedy is man?" Ghad asked.

The men of the college trembled and said, "We bow to your power, Ghad of old. We know much, but we cannot answer your question."

Ghad opened his hand and revealed a single sheet of paper whereon a single word of power was written. "I created the language you study. I have seen you struggle where one word could ease your labors. Take this gift."

One wise man asked, "We have seen what your gifts have wrought. Why should we trust this gift?"

Ghad laughed. "All I offer is knowledge."

And the men of the College accepted Ghad's gift.

And Ghad's gift was the word that could destroy Ghad's book and all that it had wrought. It was one word that could tear the knowledge itself from men's minds. The wise men of the College tried to speak it, but the men who wanted the power of Ghad's book fought them, speaking words of great and terrible power. Five-sixths of the College died, and a sixth of all men died in flood, fire, and storm before the wise men could speak the word.

And when Ghad's last word was spoken, the book burned, and all that had read it fell as mute as the ghadi.

Only one wise man was left in the College of Man who spoke the Gods' Language. Ghad wrapped himself in the skin of a child and walked before the man who spoke the God's Language.

The wise man trembled because he knew that it was no child who addressed him.

"How doomed is man?" Ghad asked.

The wise man of the College trembled and said, "I bow to your power, Ghad of old. I know much, but I cannot answer your question."

Ghad opened his hand and revealed a man who was not a man, strange and pale in form. "I created the language you study. I have seen you struggle where one word could ease your labors. Take this gift."

The wise man looked at Ghad, and at the Angel Ghad held in his hands. "Your gifts bring nothing but disaster. Destroy me if you must, but I will not take this from your hand."

Ghad giggled. "All I offer is knowledge. My Angel can teach you more of my language than any man has ever known."

The wise man said, "Your gifts are death. Your Angel is death. Take it away, or I will destroy it myself."

Ghad smiled and closed his hands. "How ungrateful is man?"

The wise man did not answer.

"No more riddles," *Ghad said.* "I see you have no use for knowledge anymore. But I am old, and I am patient, and I know that some manling yet unborn will beg me for the knowledge my Angel can give mankind."

"No man will beg for your Angel of Death."

Ghad smiled and left the wise man alone.

● ● ●

Nate sat on his cot and shook his head.

Yerith said, "The appearance of the Angel of Death foretells the end of Mankind."

"Bullshit." Nate said in English. "I am not this world's fucking Antichrist."

Chapter Twenty-Nine

THE TRAVEL from Manhome to Zorion took two sixdays. The Scholar Uthar Vailen traveled as an anonymous acolyte with a plain robe and an unadorned white mask. Those outside the College didn't question him, and those from inside the College were satisfied with a few words that referred to the Venerable Master Scholar of Manhome.

As far as the College of Man was concerned, the Scholar Uthar Vailen was on an overland journey toward some provinces north of Manhome. Those who cared to watch him would be satisfied to see Uthar's mask and robes on the northbound wagon. So much of the College relied on forms and ceremony that it would not occur to observers that the man behind the mask was not Uthar Vailen—not any more than it would occur to the servants of the College of Man that the rankless acolyte facing them was perhaps the second most powerful man among the scholars of Manhome.

Even so, this kind of travel was a risk not to be taken lightly. Years of effort had gone into creating Arthiz. The conspirator that Uthar had manufactured was meant only to appear briefly, then evaporate back into the College. That was a trivial exercise in Manhome, where the College was everything and acolytes were thick on the ground.

In Zorion, seat of the Monarch himself, the College was less conspicuous, which made Arthiz more so.

However, it was unavoidable. Uthar's long years of effort were close to completion, and when the events he planned began to unfold, he could not be anywhere near Manhome or the main force of the College.

So, the white-masked Arthiz strode through the nighttime streets of Zorion with the arrogance that even the lowest member of the College of Man was trained to display before outsiders. Even here, at the opposite pole of power from Manhome, the people deferred to his mask. No guard challenged him, and even the beggars shied from his path.

He walked a crooked route to the ancient ziggurat that was the center of the Monarch's rule. Most of the entrances were well-guarded and even an acolyte of the College might face challenge upon entry. However, the ziggurat was ancient when the first man strode the earth here, and there were many ways inside.

Uthar walked down a hole that led under the old streets several buildings away from the massive structure. He followed the damp tunnels until he was deep under the ziggurat. From there, he followed hidden stairways and passages up toward the chambers of the Monarch himself.

He was expected.

Uthar emerged from behind a false pillar and into a great room dominated by frescoes and a vaulted ceiling. A throne carved from a single stone sat on a dais overlooking the massive chamber.

Facing Uthar upon his entrance were about twenty guardsmen, weapons drawn. Uthar froze, and was glad that his mask hid any displays of shock or emotion. His first animal urge was to retreat, however fruitless that effort might be. Instead, he stepped fully into the room and stood facing the guards, consciously feigning confidence as he mentally searched for an incantation that would extract him from the situation.

"Arthiz?" called a youthful voice from behind the guardsmen.

"Yes," Uthar managed to say with as much dignity as possible.

The guardsmen parted to reveal a young man in a rich set of robes. The Monarch was barely a man, smooth-cheeked and weak-looking, but there was a hardness in his eyes that was much older than he was. Arthiz was in the presence of the one man who had enough temporal power to challenge the College on any level. The Venerable Master Scholar might be disdainful of this callow youth, but Uthar knew better.

"My apologies for the display of force," said the Monarch. "Many rumors spread, and prudence seems to be in order."

"I am here for my Master's service. I defer to your wisdom."

"So you do." The Monarch waved a bejeweled hand, motioning him forward. "We shall talk while my men assure themselves that you were not followed."

Behind his mask, Uthar smiled slightly. Fear drove the Monarch almost as much as the Venerable Master Scholar. Uthar liked fear. It was a useful emotion.

• • •

"Why is it that we wait?" asked the Monarch when they were safely inside an audience chamber. The room was more lavish than any in the College, with seats of carved woods and cushions made of exotic fabrics. To Uthar, it felt as if the Monarch compensated for the discrepancies in power by amassing wealth.

The Monarch sat on a heavily embroidered sofa while Uthar remained standing.

"I am awaiting your reasons," he prompted.

"I have long been your obedient servant and adviser. The College rots from within, slowly consumed by its own paranoia and corruption. When you move, the blow should be quick, decisive, and final."

"You have given good counsel, Arthiz. But only to a point. Wasn't it you who pointed out that the College's greatest weakness was its belief in its own invulnerability?"

"To this point, the Venerable Master Scholar believes that no earthly force can challenge them."

"We squander that advantage."

Uthar frowned behind his mask. "I do not see what you mean."

"My dear Arthiz, do you think that the Monarch of all Mankind has no mind for strategy, no eye for tactics?"

"Not at all . . ."

"I understand your own motives better than you think I do. Not that I begrudge you them, as long as they parallel my own. Reconstructing the College of Man with you as the Venerable Master Scholar, or the equivalent, isn't it?"

"I serve at the Monarch's pleasure," Arthiz said. The meeting wasn't going quite as he had planned. He had the unpleasant feeling of growing danger, that he walked a precipice that only now became visible.

"This is my problem, Arthiz. I have massed armies, trained and housed them within a sixday ride from Manhome itself. Every passing day is another day when the College might open its eyes and see a knife at its throat. At the same time, your masterful stroke of abducting their Angel of Death has begun the College cannibalizing itself, looking for you."

"The plan proceeds even more swiftly than anticipated."

"Much more swiftly, Arthiz. You know as well as anyone that a blow too late is as costly as a blow taken too soon. It is time."

"No!" Arthiz snapped before he could stop himself. "Please, may the Monarch forgive my outburst."

The Monarch waved his hand as if Arthiz's insubordination was beneath his notice. "I am aware how you feel."

"It will be another year at the soonest before your Shadow College is equipped to take over."

"Arthiz," the Monarch shook his head, and he no longer looked young. His expression was ageless and

cruel, like an old ghadi statue. "Your Shadow College
is a path, not a destination. It serves so I can break
the grip of Manhome and the College of Man. So it
will do so."

Arthiz shook his head. "I don't understand. No
scholar there is prepared to combat the College. We
only just captured the stranger, and we haven't yet
uncovered what advantage he can bring us."

The Monarch laughed.

Uthar stood there, completely dumbfounded.

"Oh, that was impolite." The Monarch's smile was
worthy of Ghad himself. "Arthiz, you are a genius in
planning, conspiracy, and the manipulation of events
to your own advantage. I think the vast intricacy of
your vision prevents you from seeing the simple, the
basic, and the obvious. Will it surprise you to know
that I can tell you precisely what advantage the Angel
of Death can bring me? How this thing will spell the
destruction of the College of Man?"

Uthar was silent a few moments before he quietly
asked, "How?"

"The death of the College will be in the fear they
place in this creature. The fact that they will move the
path of the sun itself to capture this strange being will
be in itself enough to undo them."

Uthar shook his head.

"I see you do not understand. Shall I recast it? Your
Shadow College will, you have said, be ready to take
on the scholars defending Manhome in a year's time.
Why should I wait if—at this very moment—they can
draw the main force of Manhome away from the College, leaving it nearly undefended?"

What the Monarch planned to do sank in. "You
cannot mean to waste years of work."

"If Manhome is taken, it is not a waste."

"But—"

"You understand now why I require your presence,
and why you will stay here."

"Please reconsider this path. You are casting aside

years of patient effort. You are casting away the Angel of Death itself before it has revealed anything to us."

"Arthiz, do not lower yourself with such pleas. You are more than that. You know how the powers move in the world. I will remember you as a good ally, and you may yet head whatever I put in place of the College of Man. But forces are moving as we speak, and your role has ended."

I gave you this, and you cast it away. No, my role has not ended.

"I serve at the pleasure of the Monarch."

"My guard will escort you to a set of apartments you should find comfortable." The Monarch waved his hand to dismiss him.

Uthar walked to the door.

"Remember, Uthar Vailen, you have chosen sides. You cannot go back."

Uthar heard his own name and swore that he would live to see the Monarch's death.

BOOK FOUR

A merchant once insulted an acolyte of the College of Man. The acolyte's Master in the College could not abide such disrespect. The Master searched the streets and the woods to find the merchant, and did not find him.

The Master, in his anger, said, "Will no one show me how to punish this man who does not respect the College?"

And Ghad appeared to him, "This I will show you; you need but ask."

Knowing Ghad to be false, the Master turned away.

The acolyte however, in his anger, spoke to Ghad. "Tell me, then, how do we find this man who shows such disrespect?"

Laughing, Ghad turned to the acolyte with the face of the merchant and said, "He has found you."

—The Book of Ghad and Man,
Volume IV, Chapter 15

Chapter Thirty

SIX DAYS later, in the middle of the night, Nate awoke to the sound of thunder.

He blinked his eyes open and tried to get his bearings in the semidarkness. The only light was that which leaked from a hooded lantern at the end of the hall. At first, Nate only saw various shadings of shadow.

Another roll of thunder came, loud enough to make Nate's chest ache.

What the . . . ?

Grit stung his eyes, and his lips tasted of sand. At about the same time, he realized that his alcove was filled with a cloud of dust and that he shouldn't be hearing thunder this deep underground.

Nate didn't know what it was, but it wasn't good.

"Solis?" he called out as he rolled out of his cot. The blankets and the robe he'd worn to bed were coated with dust and grit.

Nate heard coughing from down the hall, where Solis had made his room. Up by the light.

It came again. Nate grabbed the archway in front of his room, and felt the chamber shake around him, rumbling in response to the rolling resonant blast from somewhere above. Dust and powdered rock sprayed from gaps in stones that seemed much less permanent than they had when Nate had gone asleep.

It's like we're being bombed. . . .

When the floor stopped moving, Nate let go and ran to Solis' end of the corridor. *"Solis!"*

At first, all Nate could make out was a white mound of dust on the floor, but in a second, he saw the mound go into spasms with a racking cough. Nate reached down, found an arm, and pulled Solis up and out of the room.

Another blast, larger, throwing them both as if the whole chamber had been dropped from a height of about twenty feet.

"Are you all right?" Nate asked.

Solis pushed him away. "This is your doing!"

"What?"

"You. They're coming for you!"

Oh, God. They are *bombing us.*

Another blast. Nate could feel the stones shift around him. His pulse throbbed in his neck and his temples as he sucked in air, filtering the dust though his hand. He felt the panic envelop him like quicksand. The more he tried to think clearly and calmly, the more his heart raced, and the more he felt the weight of the stone above pressing down on him.

"Got to get out of here," he said in English. Even as he said it, he knew it made no sense. Whatever bombardment was happening, was happening on the surface. They were probably in the safest place they could be. The tons of rock between them and the explosions was the best protection they had. . . .

But Nate was more afraid of the tons of rock than he was of the explosions.

When he started slamming his shoulder into the metal door, he rationalized that he really wanted to go deeper, away from the blasts, away from the danger of a cave-in.

Another blast.

Spitting dust, Nate yelled at Solis, *"What are they doing?"*

"Cleansing," Solis told him.

Nate kept on slamming his shoulder into the door. The iron was as immobile as the stone wall that it was set in. All Nate managed to do was bruise himself and raise even more dust as rust particles mixed in the air with crushed stone.

Nate slammed into it, again, again, again . . .

It took him a moment to realize that the bombardment, or whatever it was, had stopped. He staggered back from the door, and realized that the air was still and quiet. The stone dust was settling in the hazy light from the lantern.

"They stopped . . ." Nate whispered.

"They will destroy this place looking for you."

Nate shook his head. "The College has enough reason to destroy this place without me."

Solis gave Nate a look that made it obvious what he thought of the College's reasons.

"You don't even know that it is the College."

"Who else could it be?"

Before Nate could gather his thoughts on how to react, the door began moving. The door scraped across the stone sounding like an opening sarcophagus.

Nate backed away, looking madly for something usable as a weapon. He grabbed a three-legged stool and brandished it over his head like a club. The inquisitors of the College weren't going to take him back without a fight.

Solis stood there with the same deadpan fatalism that he'd shown since Bhodan and company had locked him up with Nate.

The door opened outward into an inky darkness barely touched by the lamp. Nate squinted, trying to make out their visitor, or at least determine how many there were.

"Who's there?" Nate called out.

The door stopped moving.

For several long moments, the only sound Nate could hear was the sound of his own breathing. Then Nate heard footsteps, one person, limping. Nate backed up as a pale shadow emerged from the darkness beyond the door.

A ghadi?

The hunched alien form limped into the room. The creature looked thinner and paler than most of the ghadi Nate had seen. Its large eyes were clouded slightly gray, and violet blood dripped from a wound in the side of its torso.

It was bent forward, one long arm wrapped around itself, the other pressing against the iron door.

Solis backed away from it and Nate. "What is it doing here? What does it want?"

The ghadi had trouble moving forward. Its feet scraped along the floor, the joints on both legs seemed frozen. Nate took a step forward, and the ghadi seemed to finally see him. The large eyes blinked, and the rubbery, expressionless mouth silently opened as if the creature did have the power of speech.

It let go of the door and reached a long spindly arm toward Nate. Nate lowered the stool and looked into the thing's clouded eyes. He didn't know what it was he saw there.

Recognition?

Solis pushed Nate out of the way and tackled the ghadi. Nate stumbled back, dropping the stool. Nate knew the things were stronger than they looked, but as Solis fell on top of it, his body looked like a crushing weight on the spindly form.

"What are you doing?" Nate shouted. "It's hurt."

Solis was shouting too fast for Nate to translate. Nate stepped up and grabbed the other man's shoulders and pulled him off the unmoving ghadi. "What are you doing?"

As Nate pulled him away, he could understand the words, "It has a knife."

Nate looked down. The creature did have a blade, clasped in the hand that it had been holding close to its body. However, the ghadi made no move to threaten them with it.

The ghadi made no move at all.

The stones beneath the ghadi were slick with violet blood, and its skin was a pasty gray color. Nate swallowed as he knelt down next to the ghadi. He didn't see any sign of breathing, and the creature's eyes didn't move. Now that Nate saw the wound, he wondered how it could have been walking around.

The creature was past being a threat.

Nate tried his rudimentary first aid knowledge. But, even if the thing had a remotely human anatomy, the hole in its side was too massive. There was no way to stop the bleeding, and even if there was, the thing had bled into, and past, shock already.

"He's dead," Nate said, as he peeled the ghadi's fingers off of the dagger it had gripped. At first, he wondered if the massive wound was self-inflicted. Once he looked at the dagger, he realized that there was no way it could have caused the damage. Not only was the blade too small, it was also corroded and dull. In a fight, this weapon would probably be more of a hindrance than a help.

Nate looked into the dead gray face. "Did Yerith send you?"

Where was Yerith? He didn't even know where the ghadi were kept here. He had no idea how to find her, even if she had the bad sense to stay put when this place was under attack. . . .

With the door open, Nate began to smell smoke wafting in from the hallway. He could also hear echoes in the distance. People shouting, metal clashing, wood splintering . . .

"They're here," Solis whispered. "They're in the caves."

Nate turned the violet-stained dagger in his hands. He had seen something like it before. He stood up and held the blade over the hooded oil lamp. He smeared the ghadi's blood from the blade with his thumb. There were carvings in the blade and hilt, inlaid in gold and ivory.

The linear glyphs of the Gods' Language.

"He was trying to help us," Nate whispered.

"What?"

"The ghadi. He wanted to help us. This dagger isn't a weapon. It's a key."

"What are you talking about?"

"I saw something like this, in the catacombs under Manhome. One of Arthiz's men used a dagger like this to open a passage. A passage the Ghadikan had built."

Solis looked at Nate and the blade dumbly.

Nate picked up the lamp and said, "Come on."

"Where are we going?"

"Somewhere safer, I hope." Nate stepped though the doorway and into the hall beyond. The air hung heavy with a haze of dust and smoke. Nate looked in both directions.

Where to now?

The problem was, he had no idea where the door this dagger opened might be. The ghadi caverns honeycombed the cliffside and it would be very easy to get lost. Wandering around at random, with the lantern announcing their presence to all who cared to look, was little better than waiting in their cell for the bad guys.

Nate looked down and saw splatters of slick violet on the floor by the door. "Okay," Nate muttered in English. "Let's hope this guy pulled this from its normal resting place."

"What?"

"I'm going to follow the ghadi's trail," Nate told Solis. "Back to where he picked up the dagger." Nate started following the blood splatters on the floor.

"That's toward the fighting," Solis said, hanging back.

"You can stay here." Nate half hoped that Solis would stay with the dead ghadi. He kept following the blood trail, and Solis eventually jogged after him.

That was probably a good thing. Solis irritated Nate, but his presence helped rein in his own panic. The last thing he wanted to do was admit to Solis that he didn't know what he was doing. Nate felt the pulse in his neck, and every breath he took tasted of fear, but he kept moving to keep Solis from seeing it.

Nate only barely reined in his strides so Solis could

keep up. He followed the blood through several branchings, and up one short flight of stairs, before Solis grabbed his arm. "No!" Solis urged in a harsh whisper. "Up ahead!"

Nate looked up and saw another light, much brighter, shining out of a doorway down the stone hallway. It was about thirty yards down the arched corridor. When Nate hooded his lantern and squinted, he could make out splashes of violet on the flagstones in front of the open door.

Nate barely had a chance to hope that the light was from some unattended lamp or torch, when the air was cut through by an animal's scream. The sound cut through Nate like an ax blade, felt down deep behind his sternum.

"God . . ." Nate whispered, in English.

In response to that terrified, pain-filled wail, someone—several someones—laughed.

Chapter Thirty-One

NATE GRITTED his teeth, knelt, and set the lantern on the ground. He gripped the inlaid dagger like a weapon, even though it looked to have been dull and ceremonial when it was new. Slowly, he walked along the wall toward the door.

Solis whispered something desperate, but Nate didn't answer him. He wasn't thinking about what he was doing. He was only thinking about what was happening in the room up ahead.

Another wail, this one more agonized than the last.

Nate ran up to the edge of the light, losing his pretense at stealth. It didn't matter, the men inside the room weren't paying attention to him. They were more concerned with the ghadi.

The smell hit Nate and he had to suck in a breath and clench his teeth to keep his bile down.

And they think the ghadi are animals?

The floor was covered in straw bedding. The straw was a shiny violet under the torchlight, almost black. Two ghadi corpses had been dumped in a small alcove each with a massive hole in its torso. One ghadi lay on a table, its back arched, gasping for the breath to scream again, as a demon-masked human sank his arm into its chest. Another masked human held an uninjured ghadi facing the wall.

A third human in a similar mask stood guard, though he seemed to pay more attention to the torture in front of him than the door behind him.

Something bumped into Nate. Nate whipped around and grabbed Solis by the neck and slammed him into the wall before he realized who it was.

From inside the room came the words, "Did you hear something?"

"Yes, the last of this creature's power squeezed into my hand."

Nate backed up a step and placed his hand over Solis' mouth. He turned to face the doorway. Fortunately, he hadn't stumbled into the light and it seemed the guard couldn't see him from inside the brightly lit room.

"No, Thantis, something outside. Could that ghadi come back here?"

There was laughter from the one holding the remaining ghadi. "All that thing could do is find a place to curl up and die."

The one at the table, Thantis, rolled off the now-dead ghadi. The guard kicked the too light body into the corner with the other corpses. The one holding the last ghadi laughed and spun the creature toward the table. "Now I will enjoy this." This last one had lost his mask, and his scars were fully visible across his face and his shaved head. There were also a set of fresh scratches across his left cheek.

So the ghadi fight back?

Apparently, at least, this one did. The ghadi kicked and clawed, and it took all three men to restrain it.

Nate let go of Solis and gripped the dagger.

Think, you can't just charge in there. These aren't fumbling acolytes. They are scholars of the College and who knows what the hell they can cast just by naming a spell.

Naming a spell.

Naming.

Nate stared at the man without the mask. He knew the runes carved into the flesh, and he could see three spells.

The names of the spells.

Like the candles were named.

Nate concentrated and whispered the incantation, one of the three invocations he had memorized. Instead of naming a candle, however, he named one of the spells on the face of the man holding the ghadi.

Nate could feel the pull of energy, the potential force building in his words, released when he completed casting the simple beginner spell.

This time he wasn't lighting a candle.

The man screamed and clutched at his face as if someone had poured acid into his eyes. The runes in the man's skin were traced in fire, the spell branding the man's skin.

"God help me," Nate whispered. The one who had guarded the door had his back to Nate. Nate jumped him, stabbing with the dull ceremonial dagger.

Nate's subconscious suffered from a perverse sense of humor, only letting him realize the full implications of what he was doing when he had grabbed the masked man from behind.

What the fuck am I doing?

Nate jabbed the dagger into the man's back, above the kidney. It seemed to do little more than bruise his opponent. The dull blade couldn't pierce the man's robes, much less his skin.

The man reacted to Nate's attack by letting go of the ghadi and stumbling backward into Nate as they both slid on the blood-slick straw. Nate felt the man grabbing for his arm and Nate tried another blow with the dagger, under the arm this time where the clothing seemed thinner. The blade tore the fabric and might have gone in half an inch.

I'm in trouble.

The man threw himself backward, slamming Nate into the wall next to the doorway. The impact stunned Nate enough to loosen his grip on his opponent's neck. The man pulled away and spun around, reaching for a blade hanging from his own belt. As he moved, Nate could hear the unmistakable syllables of the Gods' Language emerging from behind the snarling demon mask that faced him.

That couldn't be good.

Nate clutched the handle of the dagger in his fist, and punched the demon as hard as he could in the center of its crooked nose. Nate's fist, weighted with the dagger, made a satisfying crunch against the mask. Satisfying enough that Nate barely noticed the skin on his knuckles splitting open.

The blow had the intended effect. Nate could feel the dissipating potential as the incantation was interrupted. Nate threw his fist again at the cracked demon face. The left cheek of the mask caved in and the man's head snapped back. He was still trying to pull his weapon.

Nate kicked him, low. As the man doubled over, Nate brought the pommel of the dagger down on the back of his skull. The demon mask came off as the man fell to his knees. He was about to hit the man again, when something slammed into the small of his back, sending him tumbling over his kneeling opponent.

"Shit . . ."

Nate rolled over on his back just in time to see the end of a staff hurtling toward his face. He jerked his head to the side just in time. The staff struck the floor next to him, close enough to burn his ear and deafen him with the sound of the impact.

Above him, Nate saw his attacker's snarling face. Freshly burned runes wept clear fluid over the man's cheek and shaven head. Nate tried to scramble to his feet, but he saw the next swing coming.

I'm dead.

Before the staff came down, someone jumped the man from behind. The swing went wild, giving Nate a chance to scramble upright. Nate saw his chance and ducked inside the staff's reach. He began slamming his weighted fist into the guy.

With the third blow, the man dropped the staff.

By six or seven, the guy was on the ground.

Nate turned to face the table, looking for the third man.

The last one lay on the table, still wearing his mask. A massive gash ran the length of his torso. Nate shook his head and turned back to the man he had just dropped.

"Thank you, you probably saved my life . . ." Nate trailed off. He had thought Solis had jumped the guy to help him out. But he wasn't talking to Solis.

Standing next to him was the last living ghadi, its arms stained red with blood. Nate stared at the blood-drenched ghadi.

"Kill it!" Solis yelled from the doorway.

Nate looked at him. "What?"

"It killed a man."

Yeah, and you watched. "Good for him," Nate said. "These—" He choked back the words because he didn't have the appropriate vindictiveness in this language. Now that the adrenaline was leeching away, he was thinking about Yerith. What had happened to her and the other ghadi? Looking at the straw bedding and the chambers off the main room, Nate thought that this place must be where the ghadi had been kept.

Where Yerith worked.

The rooms were small enough that he could just turn around and see the whole of it. There was no one left here, not Yerith, not any other ghadi.

Nate dropped into English.

"Bastards!" He kicked the unconscious man closest to him. He looked back at Solis, who still stood in the doorway, refusing to enter. "I'm not crying for them."

Solis was shaking his head "That thing isn't human. If it realizes it can hurt us—"

What a fucking revolutionary.

Nate walked up to the remaining ghadi. "The one that came to our cell. He was here." He talked as he approached, even though he knew the ghadi couldn't understand him. Nate hoped that a calm tone and body language would get his point across.

"What are you doing?"

"Shut up," Nate snapped at Solis. The coward made him nostalgic for Osif.

Nate didn't make any sudden moves. He didn't want to startle the ghadi. "A ghadi brought us this." Nate slowly held up the dagger. "Maybe you know why."

Solis sounded panicked. "You can't speak to these things. They don't conspire. They barely think. . . ."

Nate ignored him, and fortunately, so did the ghadi. The ghadi looked at Nate, then at the dagger. Like the other ghadi, Nate saw something akin to recognition in its eyes.

Maybe it does know me. Could I tell them apart? How could I tell if I met this one before?

It turned and walked toward the doorway. Solis almost fell on his face as he scrambled out of its way. The ghadi stopped in the doorway and motioned to Nate to follow him.

Nate was worried for a few moments that Solis might jump the creature, but it seemed that Solis didn't have it in him. He shrank back against the wall as first the ghadi, then Nate, passed by him.

Nate only paused long enough to gather the lantern.

"What are you doing?" Solis whispered now, as if he was afraid the ghadi might actually understand him.

"I'm following the ghadi," Nate said.

The ghadi walked back the way Nate and Solis had come. Nate walked after him, and after a few moments, Nate heard Solis' footsteps behind them.

• • •

Soon they were in another branch of the caverns. The ghadi led them into an unused area, and past a couple of partial cave-ins that made Nate feel nervous. Nate was starting to think that this ghadi wasn't leading them anywhere, when they stopped in a cylindrical chamber.

It was a dead end, and the ghadi stopped in the center of the room. They seemed to have left the sounds of fighting far behind them.

"What now?" Nate asked.

He looked at the dagger. There weren't any warriors lining the walls as he had seen under Manhome, so there was no conveniently empty sheath to fill. Even so, he was still convinced that he held a key to something. It was too much like the dagger that Arthiz's men had used. For all he knew, it could be the same dagger.

Nate held up the lamp and studied the walls. They were carved in bas-relief, an army of flattened ghadi staring out at Nate. These weren't warriors, and from the way they were dressed, Nate suspected that they had been ghadi of some status. They weren't armed.

Nate carried the lantern around the circumference of the room, looking at the walls. He heard Solis gasp when Nate illuminated the central focus of the carvings.

It was familiar, he had seen this before. . . .

No, that was wrong, he had only glimpsed a vague outline on a weathered stone that had been defaced. No one had gotten around to defacing this, the carving was as sharp and detailed as the day it was made.

Erupting out of the flat bas-relief was a plant-cloud-creature that extended parts of itself a full foot above the surface of the stone. There were plantlike tendrils, insectile feelers, organic floral shapes, and organs Nate had no name for.

"Ghad," Solis whispered.

This thing? Nate looked at the ghadi for some reaction. The ghadi did seem transfixed by the sight of the carving, but only for a moment. After a few seconds, the ghadi turned toward Nate and held out a hand.

Nate looked at the extended hand, with its extra joints and too-long fingers. It was still coated with blood.

The ghadi clenched its hand and opened it again, several times, insistently. *What do you want?*

Tentatively, Nate held up the dagger and the ghadi grabbed it so quickly that Nate worried that he might have misjudged the whole thing. Solis pulled away, stumbling back into the wall, as the ghadi gripped the dagger.

For a moment the ghadi faced both of them with

the dagger raised, then he turned and sank the dagger into one of the many orifices that were scattered around the Ghad carving.

Nate watched the dagger slide in to the hilt and he felt the same sense of electric potential that he had when he had last seen something like this done.

The sound of grinding stones filled the chamber as the relief sculptures moved, sliding along the wall. Solis sprang away from the wall, as if it burned him. In front of them, the Ghad sculpture seemed to unravel. It split in two around the dagger with the halves sliding open to reveal a doorway.

Behind them, the bas-relief walls met where the entrance had been, sealing the room off. The air from the new doorway was heavy and damp and smelled of age.

"Now we're trapped down here," Solis muttered.

Chapter Thirty-Two

ATE WALKED up to the part of the Ghad sculpture that still held the dagger. He pulled the dagger free. When he did so, there was a slight resistance, as if there was some suction or magnetic force holding it in place. The ghadi made no move to stop him.

The walls didn't slide shut. Instead, the newly revealed hallway started glowing. Nate blinked, because it seemed for a moment as if the air itself had become luminescent. The brightness hurt his eyes.

It took his eyes several long moments to adjust enough for him to realize that the light came from stones evenly spaced along the walls of the corridor. Bricks the size of Nate's fist cast full-spectrum light that seemed as intense as full sun.

The ghadi walked into the hallway, waving them forward.

Nate took a few steps to follow and saw Solis still standing in the entranceway.

"Come on," Nate said.

Solis hesitated, then started walking after Nate.

Nate touched one of the glowing rocks. The surface was as cold as the surrounding stone, and covered in familiar rectilinear runes. Nate noted the regular positioning of the stones and could see half a dozen that seemed dead. The dead ones all had suffered cracks that obliterated part of the inscription.

There were other, longer inscriptions on the walls

along the base and the top. The patterns reminded Nate of an Islamic mosaic, even though these were carved into the stone. Seeing the broken light bricks, Nate could understand why the stone was carved rather than painted or tiled. If these runes served a function, carving them into the rock was the most durable way to record them. Tile could break and fall apart, paint might flake away or fade, and metal could rust or corrode.

Carving into the rock would preserve it for thousands of years.

"How long has this been waiting?" Nate whispered.

Solis looked around and said, "This ghadi knew this was here?"

"It's easy to keep a secret when you can't talk." The ghadi weren't as completely docile and pliable as they had seemed. The lack of linguistic skills didn't mean they were only smart animals. There was a human-sized brain in that skull. . . .

Nate wondered what it was thinking.

The ghadi led them down the illuminated hallway and up a stairway to a vast octagonal room. Nate guessed the chamber must have been at least a hundred feet across. Inscribed pillars supported a large arched roof. Seven other corridors led away, one in each wall, though only three were lit.

In the center of the chamber was a series of concentric circles formed by two-foot-square white stone blocks. In the center was a dark pit. Nate looked at one of the white blocks and saw a slight depression worn in the top.

Nate guessed the place was some sort of temple, and Solis confirmed it by saying, "All places of Ghad should have been destroyed long ago."

Nate looked over at the ghadi, who had walked to the edge of the pit and had taken a seat on one of the blocks.

Nate walked up to the edge of the pit, next to the ghadi, and stood where he could look down. He shook his head and knelt.

Bodies. Dozens or hundreds. All ghadi, with their too-thin, too-jointed, humanoid forms. So many that no bottom could be seen in the pit. Most were long-dead and mummified.

A few though, were fresher.

Some *much* fresher.

"A graveyard." Nate muttered.

"What?"

"I don't know what this place was, but now the ghadi are using it to bury their dead."

Solis shook his head. "No . . . the ghadi don't bury their dead."

"Care to tell me who you think has been throwing ghadi corpses here for—" Nate looked down into the pit. "Several years at least."

Solis walked up and glanced down. "This is just some old burial ground. Ancient skeletons and mummies . . ."

"Some of those mummies are still bleeding."

Solis turned away from the pit. "Who cares about a pile of dead ghadi anyway?" He walked away, shaking his head and talking to himself. "What am I going to do? The College is going to hunt us down. . . ."

"You need to calm down before—" Nate looked up from the pit and whispered in English. *"Oh, shit."*

"What . . ." Solis turned around and his voice trailed off as he faced what Nate was looking at.

Ghadi, living ghadi, were filling the opposite end of the chamber. First three, then six, then a dozen, two dozen. They walked purposefully and sat down on the stone cubes, facing the pit. None paid Nate or Solis any attention.

"This can't be happening," Solis said.

Nate backed up. It had once seemed so self-evident that language was the basis for intelligence that Nate had been lulled into thinking that the ghadi were animals.

Sure, he had kept telling himself that these creatures could think, but deep down he had *known* that the species-wide aphasia had knocked them several steps down from a human-level intelligence. Looking at the scene before him he had twin realizations—first, he recognized he had made that unconscious assumption, and second, *that* assumption was wrong.

. He watched the silent procession with a growing sense of unease. It was impossible to read the emotions in the ghadi, as if facial expressions had also been wiped from their palette of communication.

When the seats were a third full, they started carrying in the bodies. The ritual was conducted in silence, giving Nate an eerie feeling of detachment, as if he was only a phantom that no one else could see— or the ghadi were.

Four ghadi carried in the first body. The ghadi pallbearers had duller, less flexible skin, and their coloring was faded and washed out. Nate suspected that meant they were older than all the spectators. Between them they carried the naked body of a dead ghadi.

The four ghadi walked in from one of the lighted hallways and approached the central pit. Once they reached the edge, they tossed the corpse into the pit. The ghadi made no sounds, they just stood at the edge of the pit for a few long moments. Then they turned and walked back the way they had come.

Nate thought that the ritual was over.

Then they brought in another body.

And another.

Nate kept a respectful silence. Solis was silent, too, though Nate supposed his silence was more of disbelief than anything else. Nate was a stranger, and hadn't been raised with this culture's prejudices, and *he* was finding this death ritual a complete surprise. To Solis, this had to be doing fatal violence to his worldview.

Nate finally thought he understood what was happening, when the ghadi suddenly changed the rules on him. In the next procession, between four pallbearers, the corpse they carried was definitely not a ghadi. It still wore the robes of an acolyte, and scars carved their way around its exposed skin.

"I know him . . ." Solis whispered.

It didn't end there. In a procession of agonizing slowness, the ghadi carried in body after body. Twelve in all. About half of them Nate recognized from Arthiz's Shadow College. These were the people who had been studying with Nate and Solis. All showed mortal wounds, burns, slashes, crushing blows.

"They're killing everyone up there," Solis whispered.

Nate nodded.

In front of them, the ghadi pallbearers spilt up and took seats in the midst of the spectating ghadi. All of them sat, as if waiting.

Why bring us here, to show us this?

Nate began walking toward the pit, the focus of the ritual.

"What are you doing?" Solis whispered.

I am really getting sick of that question.

"We were brought here for a reason," Nate said.

Solis shook his head. "No. Someone's directing them, controlling what they do—"

Who? Yerith?

"I don't think so."

Nate walked slowly to the pit, carefully, wary that he not disturb what the ghadi were doing. He was alert for any disturbance, any movement that might tell him that he was violating some sacred space. However, the ghadi ignored him as if he wasn't there at all. Their attention was focused on the pit, as if something was supposed to happen.

Nate reached the edge and looked down at the fresh additions. Then he looked around at the staring ghadi. Oddly, what had seemed like a massive crowd initially, when he wasn't expecting them, now seemed small. About thirty, including the now-seated pallbearers. The room they sat in could seat a hundred easily, probably more. Nate had been in bigger classes at Case.

"What do you want?" Nate asked them.

They continued watching the pit.

Maybe this is how they grieve?

Nate walked around the pit. The edge was finished in beveled black stone that set it apart from the flagstone floor. When Nate looked close enough, he wasn't terribly surprised to see that the black stones were covered in the runes of the Gods' Language.

So why bring us here? What can we do that they can't?

Nate followed the inscription until he found the bracketing symbols that marked the "name" of a spell. Nate crouched and wiped some dust and a few drops of violet blood away with his thumb. The symbols were all familiar to him now. He could feel the draw of power just by looking at them, by understanding them.

He looked up from the stone, and saw that every ghadi was looking at him now. It was as if they knew what he had found. Solis was on the opposite side of the pit from Nate, behind the outermost ghadi.

"What is that?" he called to Nate.

The ghadi stared at Nate, the eyes burning into him. Nate understood what they wanted now. It was only a question of whether he should do it. He looked around until he saw the ghadi who had brought them here. He could tell the ghadi by the human blood that still covered his arms.

They weren't animals. They were slaves. Slaves whose masters had been killed, and who were capable of vengeance. Nate could feel the pressure. Do as they wanted and stay above the pit, or don't, and possibly join the bodies within it.

Nate licked his lips and looked down at the stone. Five syllables. Very simple to cast. He began reading the syllables out loud.

"What are you doing?" Solis called to him. There was a hint of panic in his voice.

Nate ignored him. It took all his concentration to stay focused on the carving before him. Each symbol took more effort than the last. More than any other spell Nate had read to date, this one required a physical effort. Once he committed to reading it, his pulse began to throb in his neck and his temple. By the end of the second syllable, he was breathing hard and could feel sweat on the palms of his hands and the back of his neck. Even his muscles began to ache, as if he was sprinting up the side of a steep mountain.

As Nate chanted, the air filled with a terrible potential. The energy hung in the air around the pit, making the hair on Nate's arms stand on end. He could even smell it, metallic ozone. The threatened impulse was several orders of magnitude stronger than Nate had felt with the candle lighting.

He could feel the waves of energy feeding into him, and into the invisible, unformed almost-something he was casting. He could sense it in some way he couldn't quite name, a directional itch inside his head. An itch that he could taste. An itch he could almost give a color to, even though it was outside his field of vision in a direction he couldn't point at.

He knew that he was feeling the ghadi. The spectators, all watching the pit again, were feeding him the power to cast this spell. Power he needed. Nate knew that if he stumbled, hesitated, or misspoke, the results would probably be fatal. He could also feel that halfway through the alien phrase that named what he was casting, he was hitting the edge of what his body could take.

The muscles in his arms and torso were locked and trembling. His skin burned with a sudden fever. Sweat stung his eyes. His breath burned in his throat. His voice ached as if he had been screaming at the top of his lungs.

He couldn't focus on anything now but the blurry image of the runes before him. They seemed distant, as if he was falling away from them. His eyes watered, and he had to squint to keep the characters in focus. Each one was taking longer to pronounce, until each rune, each syllable, was a separate mountain to climb. He no longer could place where he was in the name of the spell. The territory was too vast. He barely had enough concentration to hold the rune he was speaking in focus, just enough determination to move on to the next one when that peak was crested.

Then, it was over.

After what seemed hours of chanting, Nate spoke the last rune, completing the name of the spell. The moment he stopped speaking, he could feel the awesome potential that had been building around the chamber suddenly find shape. He could sense it fall on the pit like a waterfall, flowing into the stones where the spell Nate had named was carved.

Nate was finally free to think, *If naming the spell was such an effort, what the hell is the spell itself like?*

The runes carved around the pit seemed to glow with the energy. And the lights in the chamber seemed to dim.

Nate pushed himself up to his feet as he began to realize that the lights had not dimmed. The air above the pit was becoming opaque.

"What have you done?"

Nate didn't have an answer for Solis. All he had was a sense of dread that, maybe, this hadn't been such a good idea.

He took a couple of steps back from the pit. His stomach lurched and he almost lost his balance because he had the uncanny sensation that the floor was tilting toward the pit. His view through the darkening air was becoming twisted and distorted, as if he was looking through a lens. A black spot distorted Nate's view beyond it, as if it pushed the light around itself.

The blackness grew, and with it the sense of something inside the blackness. Something alien.

Something familiar.

"Oh, shit . . ."

The blackness unfolded into a shadow of something else. The shape was indistinct and kept distorting, and changing, twisting inside itself. Nate sensed, rather than saw, branches, or tendrils reaching out of a mass that seemed partly botanic and partly insectile. In his mind's eye, Nate imagined an orchid from hell. . . .

From out of this black mass came a dark, wet voice.
"I come before you, Azrael, to receive your sacrifice."
It spoke English.

Chapter Thirty-three

NATE BACKED AWAY.

It was too much to absorb. Nate was still too much of his own world. Despite everything, an actual deity was beyond what Nate was prepared for. The reasoning part of his brain wanted to deny it, rationalize it.

Its presence couldn't be denied.

Nate felt power radiating out of the pulsating thing hovering above the pit—a blazing sun whose heat was felt deep in the core of his brain. The sight made his head ache, but he couldn't turn away. The ever-changing organic form seemed to move through spaces that were beyond the capacity of Nate to perceive, or even imagine.

No. @ is not Ghad. Can't be.

"You brought me here." Nate was surprised that he had the breath left to form a complete sentence, even a rhetorical one. The sweat on his skin had gone clammy, and his mouth was dry. His pulse raced in his neck.

Blackness enveloped Nate, trapping him in the same netherworld he had fallen into at Case. Feeling that, and remembering Ghad's first appearance, managed to snap his mind into focus.

Fighting the fear and disorientation, Nate shouted into the darkness, "You brought me here. Send me back!"

Around him he felt the sudden presence of an unseen, fleshy weight. As if something the mass of a small planet was slithering by him, just barely out of reach.

"Your purpose is not fulfilled."

It was all Nate could do to keep a grip on his own thoughts. Losing the ability to see the thing made its presence worse, more overwhelming. The undulating blackness was now the whole of existence outside of Nate himself.

Nate managed to whisper, "What purpose?"

"Do not ask for what you already know."

Nate swallowed. He felt as if the darkness itself was curling around him, trying to slither down his throat and smother him.

He could still think. Deep in the recess of his brain, where reason had retreated, a small voice said, *It needs you.*

Despite the crushing omnipotent weight moving around him, despite the hellish claustrophobia that gripped him, Nate tried to focus.

It needed him.

And Nate had called it here.

Nate spoke. "How do I get back?" The words were barely audible.

"Complete your task and you will have that choice."

Nate closed his eyes. Even though there was nothing to see, it helped him hold his wits together in the face of this thing. *It will not crush me, or drive me mad. It needs me. It needs me. It needs me.*

"Can. You. Help. Me?" Each word was an effort. He had to pull each word as if the structure of language itself was disintegrating in the face of this thing.

"I offer information."

"What. Information?"

"Ask." The force of command felt as if it ripped Nate's brain free of his body. He was transfixed, unable to move. He wasn't even sure if his question was spoken, or merely thought, "What are you?"

"I am."

Uncontrollable panic started tearing at Nate. He was being tested, and blowing it. It was playing some sort of game, and Nate didn't know what the rules were, or how he was being scored. And this thing's very.existence was eating into his consciousness.

And the words were now being torn from him without his volition. As if Ghad's tendrils were burrowing into his brain to pull half completed thoughts free.

"How can I survive this mess? I don't belong here."

"You belong. You will survive."

"How can I fight the College of Man?"

"Use what you already know to create what you do not know."

"Why? Why is it me? Why did you pick me?"

"You understand more than you know. You know more than others understand."

"What do I do?"

"Do what you have already done."

Nate felt the presence withdrawing. The blackness was sliding out of his brain, slithering away.

Nate opened his eyes saw the darkness lightening around the edges. The alien presence, the shadow around him, folded in on itself, a dark implosion above the pit.

The darkness collapsed inward, falling into the distorted view of the other side of the room without actually moving. Nate felt as if reality itself was moving, swirling to fill a hole above the pit like water toward a bathtub drain.

Then the blackness was gone.

Everyone looked at him. The expressions of the ghadi were as impassive and unreadable as ever, but Solis was wide-eyed. The dark skin of his face was ashen and the lines of his scars had become almost pure white.

"It talked to you," Solis accused him. "It knows you."

Nate took a few deep breaths. It was hard adjusting

to being suddenly back in light and gravity. His legs felt weak. He looked up at Solis and said, "It should. That thing brought me here."

Looking at the expression on Solis' face, that probably wasn't the right thing to say. The man looked as if he had just confirmed his worst fears. Nate couldn't work himself up to give a shit. After what had just happened, Solis couldn't even rate as a minor annoyance.

Nate looked around at the ghadi and wondered what it was they had seen. It must have made an impression, because they were all standing and staring at him.

How long have they been waiting for that ritual to be completed?

Nate looked over the edge of the pit.

The bodies were gone.

"Ghad brought you here?" Solis said. "You *are* the Angel of Death." He kept backing away from the pit.

"Give it a rest," Nate said. The English idiom didn't translate well, at all really, but at least the non sequitur caused Solis to stop talking. Nate crouched down and stared into the pit.

There was still something down there, but it was hard to see. Nate could barely see the floor, a radial mosaic that was nearly fifty feet down.

The pile of bodies was forty feet deep.

How long had it been accumulating? A hundred years? A thousand? How long before weight and age turned the lowermost bodies into dust? Had the ghadi here reached an equilibrium point where the sinking from decay matched the rate at which new bodies were added?

How morbid is that?

There was, however, something left down there. Darker than the floor, and rectangular. Nate was wondering how to get a better look at whatever it was when he noticed that there was a ramp of sorts carved in the side of the pit.

A path had been carved into the stone wall, providing a steep spiral ramp as the way down. Nate stepped onto the path.

Solis said something, but Nate was beyond caring what. He walked down toward the object Ghad had left in the pit.

Nate stepped out onto the floor of the pit, giving his eyes a few minutes to adjust to the gloom down here. Solis shouted something, but the acoustics down here were muffled and Nate couldn't make out the words.

He walked over to the object that had brought him down here. It was an elaborate chest about eight feet long and four feet wide. The surface was made of some black material, cold and smooth to the touch. It was hard to tell what the material was, it could have been wood, or metal—or plastic for all Nate could tell.

Nate looked for a means of opening the thing, but he couldn't find one. *Could this have been here, under all those bodies, all this time?*

Nate felt along the edges of the chest, and couldn't even find a seam. He looked at the markings etched into the chest, and couldn't find any runic carvings waiting to be invoked. The carvings themselves seemed out of character. Stylistically, they resembled the ghadi artwork he had seen off and on since he came here. But the composition was very different. The figures on the chest were trapped in poses that seemed to represent the dead and the dying. Nate was reminded of pictures he had seen of medieval European artwork during the black plague.

A sarcophagus?

That would make sense; this was a sacrificial spot. But if this was an offering, why wasn't it taken with the rest of the bodies?

Nate felt the relief carvings of dead and diseased ghadi until he came to something very disturbing on the top surface of the chest—a human being. The carving was unquestionably human; the proportions made that obvious. The human figure stood on a rise that overlooked a vast field of ghadi corpses. The ones closest to the human were still falling.

Or rising?

Nate couldn't get the imagery of the last judgment out of his head, medieval paintings showing tombs releasing their dead before a risen Christ.

On that panel, Nate found a hole about three inches long and an inch wide, above the man's head. The edges felt as if they tapered inward.

After a moment of hesitation, Nate pulled out the ghadi dagger and slid it into the hole. The fit was perfect, so perfect that it felt as if a magnetic force or a vacuum sucked the blade home the last quarter inch. Then the hilt was pulled out of his hand as the panel started moving.

Nate backed up as he heard a low hiss of rushing air. He felt a slight breeze as air fed into the crack that had appeared in the edge of the lid. Movement stopped as the pressure equalized, then the whole massive lid swung upward, away from Nate, on invisible hinges.

Nate could smell something slightly metallic in the air now. He couldn't see down into the sarcophagus from where he stood, but he could see glints of reflected light coming from inside it.

Nate walked up to the edge of the sarcophagus feeling a mixture of dread and anticipation. What, exactly, had the ancient ghadi buried here?

Nate leaned over and looked down. He sucked in a deep breath.

Gold. That was the first thing. The unmistakable reflection of gold shone off of every surface inside the sarcophagus. Even as the presence of that much precious metal began sinking in, Nate began realizing the true value of what was in here.

The sarcophagus was filled with oblong gold platters covered in the Gods' runic text—gold rectangles about the height, width, and thickness of a thin paperback book. Hundreds of them.

Nate reached in tentatively and removed one. It was heavy, solid metal. The carvings were etched deeply into its surface, on both sides. Without committing the mental resources to absorbing the whole text, Nate could see the symbols marking the beginnings and endings of at least three unique spells.

Maybe the language itself was some sort of sacrifice? Or maybe they saw the end coming and made a time capsule, just in case.

The people who constructed this thing knew what they did. Gold was a good archival medium. Nonreactive, and short of being melted down, it would last pretty much forever.

• • •

When Nate came up out of the pit, Solis was gone.

Chapter Thirty-Four

THE FIRST MOMENTS after the attack began were so frantic and disjointed that Yerith wasn't consciously aware of where she was running until after the initial explosions subsided. First, she ran through tunnels so opaque with dust and smoke that her lamp was all but useless. Then, somewhere, she lost the lantern and she was feeling her way through complete darkness. All she could do was move away from the sounds of fighting.

When she reached a light that wasn't something burning, she edged up carefully. It was a lantern abandoned in the acolytes' residence. The chambers were empty. She looked around and realized that the Monarch's Shadow College was doomed.

She was out of breath, and this was the first moment she had to think.

The College is attacking. They'll destroy everything here.

Arthiz's plans were over. The man she had trusted with her destiny was probably dead at the College's hands. Everything she thought she was working toward was crumbling around her. When the College found her . . .

Yerith grabbed the lantern with a shaking hand. The College wasn't going to find her. She couldn't even consider the possibility. She had survived before Arthiz, she could survive after him. She just had to get out of this warren before it became a tomb.

The sounds of fighting and burning were distant from here. Aside from a haze in the air, this place was momentarily untouched.

It gave time for the panic to recede.

Nate Black . . . The ghadi . . .

It sank in that Nate Black and the ghadi she was caring for were trapped behind locked doors.

She ran again, and this time she knew where she was going.

• • •

The ghadi chambers were a slaughterhouse. The College had been here. Yerith stood a long time in the doorway, trying to make sense of the scene.

The bodies of the ghadi had been slit open, their blood soaking into the straw bedding. Until now, she had only heard rumors of some of the College's more perverse rituals—how some scholars discovered that there were more gruesomely efficient ways to drain the power from their ghadi servants.

The bodies here were too few. They had dozens of ghadi housed here; most must have escaped or been taken.

A burning anger replaced the fear she had felt up to now. To do this to a creature that could not even defend itself. . . .

Someone groaned.

Yerith suddenly realized that some of the bodies here were human, and by the masks, scholars of the College. If it wasn't clear enough what they had been doing here, the ghadi blood on their hands told her.

One was alive and stirring.

By the time Yerith realized she had picked up a staff, the surviving scholar had stopped stirring. She pulled the end out of the man's face and dropped the staff. She couldn't quite believe what she had just done.

If they were here . . .

Nate Black was only a short distance away.

Yerith ran.

• • •

The Monarch had timed his betrayal with a precision worthy of the scholars he wished to displace. He had taken Uthar in at just the moment when it appeared impossible to moderate the damage. But as soon as Uthar was left alone in the Monarch's apartments, he tried to contact Bhodan.

When Uthar had been elevated to a full scholar of the College of Man, he had been given a choice of a phrase in the Gods' Language to become a permanent part of his body to commemorate the event. The far-speaking spell had been cut into the few remaining areas of unmarked flesh on his body. The only spell he had chosen himself.

Even then, before he had begun planning the overthrow of the College, he knew that communication was the most important tool of power.

Unfortunately, this time, it did him little good.

"We are under attack!" Bhodan's voice came from a spot on the floor in front of Uthar. The floor itself was smooth marble and spotless. The voice sounded far away, even though Bhodan was yelling as loud as he could. Under the voice, Uthar could hear sounds of fighting.

"Can you get out of there?"

"Only retreat is the jungle. They're between us and the City."

"The jungle, then!"

"Cave-ins. Half our people are cut off. We can't . . ." Bhodan was interrupted by a loud crashing noise. Suddenly Uthar was hearing several different muffled voices, and the sounds of something burning.

"Bhodan."

No answer, but Uthar heard a muffled scream.

"Bhodan."

Nothing but the sound of fire.

The situation was moving quickly there. Bhodan might just have retreated from the area that Uthar had contact with. The hope wasn't very likely. The

College's punishments had left the man incapable of defending himself. His only defense had been being deep inside the warrens where they had set up the Shadow College. If the College of Man was already that deep inside, there really was no hope of salvaging anything.

Over a hundred handpicked acolytes who would have been loyal against the College itself, gone. Years of work and training, gone in a single stroke.

Uthar sat down on an embroidered couch and held Arthiz's mask in his hands. The blank white face shook until he lifted it up and threw it at the marble floor.

The mask shattered.

Remember, Uthar Vailen, you have chosen sides. You cannot go back.

Uthar cursed the Monarch for a fool. There would be nothing left. Without a trained loyal cadre to take the College's place, a void would be left for Ghad only knew what kind of chaos. And when things went out of control, the only people who could restore order would be the displaced members of the College themselves. It would take years to create new scholars. . . .

It *had* taken years.

He looked down at the shattered white mask. *Nothing but the empty shell of the Monarch's agent, Arthiz. . . .*

•   •   •

Again, too late.

Yerith stood in front of the chambers where they had housed Nate Black. The strange man she was charged to protect, and his reluctant roommate, were both gone. The iron door hung open and the chambers were empty except for slowly settling dust.

And the corpse of another ghadi.

Yerith stared for long moments, trying to make sense of the body. It lay sprawled on the floor, gray from loss of blood, clutching a massive wound in its side.

Why would Nate kill a ghadi?

Yerith answered her own question. It was obvious that the ghadi hadn't bled to death in this room. From the amount of blood on the floor, it had obviously been near to death when it collapsed in here.

Yerith looked around the door and saw blood on the ground, leading back where she had come. Ghadi blood also covered the outside of the door. At first she thought that the wounded ghadi had just leaned against the door, but as she examined the door, she realized that there was a very distinct handprint on the latch.

The ghadi had opened the door. As a final act, it freed Nate Black.

She walked in and knelt down next to the ghadi. She recognized it as one of the ghadi who had been serving Nate Black and the other person here, Solis. It had been bringing food and water, emptying waste.

It knew they were in danger. It came here to save them.

Yerith had worked with ghadi most of her life. She knew how intelligent they could be when given the proper direction. Even so, she had never seen one show anything approaching this kind of sacrifice of its own volition. Until now, she wouldn't have believed they could.

She was so absorbed in the ghadi and its implications that she didn't realize anyone else was in here until she felt an arm wrap around her neck.

She dropped the lantern and started screaming and kicking as the man behind her lifted her up.

Then a familiar voice called, "Let her go, she isn't from the College!"

Her attacker let her go, and she collapsed, gasping, almost on top of the ghadi corpse. She looked at the doorway through watering eyes. "Osif?" she managed to croak.

"Yes, may the gods continue to ignore us." He turned to the acolyte who had grabbed her. "Help her up. We don't have time to waste."

Yerith managed to scramble to her feet without help.

"You wouldn't know where our stranger is?"

She rubbed her neck and shook her head.

Osif cursed.

"What is happening out there?" she asked.

"The end of the world," Osif said. "Come with us, we're retreating to the jungle."

She walked out into the hallway, where about a dozen men and women stood, tensely watching for any activity back toward the ghadi chambers. She started to ask where Bhodan was, or the rest of the acolytes. But she already knew the answer.

This was what was left.

"You take care of the three back there?" asked the acolyte who escorted her out of the room.

Yerith didn't know what to say, so she just shook her head.

Osif started leading them deeper into the tunnels.

• • •

Armsmaster Ehrid Kharyn knew that a catastrophe was brewing. Over the past two sixdays he had seen the College mass an unprecedented force, pressing Ehrid's most able-bodied guardsmen into service, forcing on them the circlet of direct bondage to the College. The better part of the civil guard in Manhome had departed with the better part of the College itself.

Ehrid had never seen the College mass such a force. They had never needed to. The threat from the mysteries they held was, in itself, enough to overwhelm any adversary. That they had gone to such lengths meant only one thing—

Someone had risen up in opposition to the College of Man.

Of course, Ehrid knew of only one place from where such opposition might come. And this was not how that opposition was supposed to reveal itself.

As small a part as he played in the Monarch's conspiracy, Ehrid knew the plan as Arthiz explained it did not call for large armies to clash outside of Manhome. Not now. The College was supposed to rot from inside, collapse almost before the first move was made against them.

Something had gone very wrong, and Ehrid was fearful that he and his men would suffer for his support of the Monarch. He stood on his balcony overlooking the sea and tried to consider options.

He didn't have any.

As he leaned on the stone rail and stared into the tumult of gray that beat at the base of Manhome, the wind spoke to him.

"Armsmaster."

It was a voice he hadn't heard for quite a while. Not since his men had seized the College's pale stranger. It was a voice that, at the moment, he cursed ever hearing in the first place.

"What calamity do you present me with now?" Ehrid whispered. He glanced back at the balcony, but the accursed white-masked acolyte wasn't there. Only his voice.

"The Monarch moves as we speak, as Manhome is left weakened."

"Now?" Ehrid frowned. "The College prepares for war as we speak, sending armies into the wilderness to battle."

"It is a feint." The disembodied voice sounded unconvinced. *"It has drawn the main force of the College away from the defense of Manhome."*

"You tell me now, why?"

"Events move quickly. The Monarch needs your force in reserve, not wasted in Manhome."

"But here we can aid in the siege, seize power—"

"The Monarch is decided in his strategy. Manhome will be emptied of all its fighting force. Nothing will remain to be pressed into service by the College."

Ehrid thought of the bulk of his men, wearing collars of servitude that made a mockery of a soldier's discipline. He would defer to the Monarch's wisdom in this instance. "How do I accomplish this without alerting the College of an imminent attack?"

"The Venerable Master Scholar is preoccupied with issues beyond the borders of Manhome. While he has been distracted, his servant Uthar Vailen has ordered all the remaining guard to support the Master Scholar's efforts. You will leave the city in support of their force, at their orders."

"And then?"

"And then, free of Manhome, you will follow the directions I specify, where you will arm, rest, and wait until the Monarch has need of your force."

Chapter Thirty-Five

SOLIS WASN'T in the big chamber. *Where would he go?*

Maybe he wanted to look around this hidden ghadi temple. Corridors lit and unlit snaked away from the pit chamber. There was certainly more to see.

Yeah, Solis has this real big streak of curiosity.

What did the bastard think he was doing?

Nate could answer his own question.

Ghad was the closest thing this culture had to Satan, and Azrael was what they had for an Antichrist. Nate had thought along these lines before, but he hadn't quite taken it seriously. In his mind, mythic stories were just that: *stories.* It just never really sank in that the people here might take such things as more than allegory.

What would Solis do?

Kill me . . .

No, there were ghadi everywhere, and Solis had seen a violent demonstration that the ghadi weren't passive animals. The safer course would be to slip away, and try to warn someone.

Try to warn the College.

Nate shook his head.

How many temples of Ghad had the College destroyed? The stones on the hill overlooking Manhome, the plateau city, must have come from a place like this. Not only had Solis seen the Angel of Death out of his myths, he had seen a manifestation of Ghad in an undesecrated temple.

"You stupid bastard."

Nate looked at the impassive ghadi. They were standing and filing away, and he began to wonder exactly what would happen to this place, the ghadi, and the trunk of golden tablets—not to mention himself—if Solis did run to the College.

I have to stop this guy.

As the ghadi had retreated to wherever the ghadi went, they left one behind. Nate could still see human blood on its arms.

My ghadi, Nate thought.

"You didn't see where he went, did you?" Nate asked rhetorically in English.

His ghadi, however, saw him looking around and actually seemed to get the gist of what Nate wanted. The ghadi gestured at him to follow. He didn't have any better options, so Nate followed the ghadi.

The ghadi led him out of the pit chamber and down a different corridor than the one the other ghadi were taking, stopping in front of a narrow doorway. Nate stepped inside and looked around.

"Solis, you bastard."

In the room was a tall narrow wall that was completely covered with deep cylindrical niches. In about a quarter of the niches, Nate could see the hilt of a dagger. After picking up three, Nate found one with an intact blade. Comparing it to the one hitched in his belt, Nate couldn't see a difference.

This was where it had come from.

Solis had come here, swiped a dagger key, and must have slipped out the way they had come. If he was lucky, he wouldn't be too far behind.

But when he returned to the entrance, he realized he had a problem. The door reacted as expected, there was a hole to receive a dagger key, and inserting and removing the blade opened the outer chamber so he could leave.

But Solis had taken the only lantern. The tunnels beyond the secret ghadi chamber were in complete darkness.

Nate stood in the circular antechamber, the only light coming from the glowing stones in the hallway he had come from. No convenient torches, and no way to light it if he had one. Nate walked back into the hallway, his ghadi pacing him and watching his every move.

Nate felt around one of the glowing bricks. There was no way to remove it from the wall.

He could, however, see the runes carved in the face of the brick.

Maybe?

It took a little bit of searching, but Nate was able to find a loose stone with a large flat surface on one side. Nate took it and a small, hard stone chip back to the hallway.

He intended to copy the spell inscribed on the glowing stone, but staring into the bright surface for very long wasn't going to work. Fortunately, there were a few broken light-stones where the runes had been chipped and the surface was dark. Nate found a pair of damaged ones where the cracks were in different locations, allowing him to see two halves of the spell. Nate knew enough—at least he hoped he knew enough—to tell what parts of the spell referred to a uniquely named stone.

Nate took the stone chip, and with very tiny strokes, began to etch the flat surface with the runes. With the first stroke, he could feel the energy flowing from the core of his being down to what he was writing. The feeling was more intense than any he had felt putting runes to paper. His hand felt as if it moved though thick mud. The stone chip pulled against him, pressing into the flesh of his fingers. It was becoming difficult to breathe. . . .

Nate felt something touch his shoulder. He was too absorbed in carving the spell to determine what it was.

Suddenly, his movements became easier, as if his

hand had broken through some membrane that had been dragging against him. Nate looked down at what he was scratching into the stone and saw tiny blue sparks where the stone chip wrote against the surface of the rock.

Almost unexpectedly, he was finished writing. He dropped the stone chip, which was now too hot for him to hold. The air smelled of smoke, heat, and electricity. The surface of the stone was etched with the runes and covered with a fine layer of dust.

Nate realized that the ghadi's hands were on his shoulders.

Somehow, the ghadi knew enough to donate some sort of energy to the process. Like at the pit. Nate looked at the alien creature.

"Thanks," Nate said, as if the ghadi could understand him.

Though, language or not, maybe in some way it could. Back home there were any number of animals that could communicate without a human language, and the ghadi here was more intelligent than any animal. . . .

Nate hefted his stone. "If you're going to stick around, I have to call you something besides, 'Hey, You.' " He stared into the alien face and thought for a moment, and then said, "You sort of look like a Dali portrait of Bill Gates. I'll call you Bill."

Nate shook his head, looked back at the stone, and spoke the words to invoke the runes he had just carved. It was much easer than scratching the spell in the first place.

His effort paid off. The stone in his hand started glowing with a cold white light, brighter than a hundred-watt bulb. It was almost too bright for what he wanted, the glare hurt his eyes. In order to obtain a measure of control over the light, Nate tore off a wad of fabric from his robe and wrapped the stone in it, leaving an opening to provide him with a flash-lightlike aperture.

"Come on, Bill, let's find our wayward acolyte."

• • •

Nate had thought he'd known what to expect. He had seen the College at work on his ghadi Bill. He knew that people would be dead. He knew that there would be remnants of some sort of battle.

Nate had been kidding himself. Nothing could have prepared him for what the College of Man had done.

The first sign was the smell.

As Nate carefully walked back toward the caverns that Bhodan's people had been using, the first sense of wrongness was the odor of smoke. A heavy, greasy smoke that held a sickening weight Nate could almost taste.

As he got closer to the inhabited caverns, he had to step over debris that had fallen from the walls and the ceiling. The claustrophobia was back, the weight of the rock above him pressing down on the back of his mind.

What if they caved in the whole tunnel system? What if we're trapped down here?

Nate ran into several dead ends that brought him to near panic as he looked at the piles of broken stone filling the corridors. Two things kept him from falling on the first pile of rock and trying to madly dig himself out of here.

First, the air was still moving, carrying the burned smell with it. So there had to be an opening to the surface somewhere.

Second, he hadn't caught up with Solis yet, and Nate was positive he had gone this way, back toward Arthiz's enclave—or what remained of it.

It took nearly an hour of backtracking and trying alternate routes, Bill dutifully following, before Nate found a passable corridor. Barely passable. At first it looked like another dead-end cave-in, but as Nate stood in front of the broken pile of rock, he could feel a slight breeze on his face.

Nate swallowed the growing feeling of pressure inside him as he walked up, close to the cave-in. His heart beat in his throat as he shone his glowing rock around every angle to see where the breeze came from. Nate found the source. Two flat rocks, each the size of a small car, had fallen nearly parallel, leaving a gap between them, cutting diagonally into the cave-in. At first, Nate thought that the gap was impassible. It didn't look as if a human being could slip through.

Then he saw the footprint.

A single footprint leading away from him, into the crevice.

No, I could get stuck in there.

Nate could feel sweat rolling down his back as he edged up to look down the crevice. The footprints in the stone dust were oneway. Whoever entered hadn't come back.

Solis made it through . . .

Or he's wedged somewhere ahead.

The crack wasn't straight. About ten or fifteen feet down, there was a sharp turn that took the exit, if any, out of Nate's line of sight.

What if there's another cave-in while I'm in there?

Nate's breathing had become rapid and shallow. He felt his pulse in the back of his throat. He turned sideways and took a step into the crack.

"Oh, fuck," Nate whispered.

The panic was barely controllable. His back was flat against an angled rock, and a slab of rock was less than an inch in front of his face. He barely had enough clearance to turn his head. He had to wave his arms as he moved, frantically trying to fight the feeling of being trapped.

Over and over he forced himself to think, *I have enough clearance to move. I'm not trapped. I can still back out.*

His body didn't believe him. He gasped for breath like he was drowning, and his heart raced so badly it was painful. His light source cast strange shadows in the confined space, and all he could see was rock or dead blackness.

It seemed he shuffled along the narrow passage for

miles, even though it couldn't have been more than twenty feet. He nearly panicked when his hand touched the wall where the crack abruptly turned left. For a few seconds he was convinced that the passage had dead-ended. It took a few long moments of convincing, telling himself that the footprints were one-way and that he still felt a breeze, before he could attempt to manage the turn.

Once he did, he was suddenly in a much larger space. He was still in the midst of a cave-in, but the rubble on this side was mostly confined to one side of the corridor. He had just emerged from behind the largest pile.

Nate leaned against the rock pile, closed his eyes, and started sucking in breaths as if he had just been saved from drowning. He stayed there for several minutes, relieved that there wasn't a giant rock half an inch from his face.

When something touched his shoulder, he jumped, dropping the glowing rock in his hand. He found himself facing Bill the ghadi, looking at him with what might have been a quizzical expression.

Nate suddenly felt a twinge of remorse.

"Oh, Christ, I'm sorry," Nate spoke English. "I left you in the dark." He looked back at the passage he had just emerged from. "Oh, boy, you went through that without any light? You're braver than I am."

Nate looked back at Bill's alien face. The eyes showed no whites, and had irises that were almost as dark as the pupils. As Nate looked at them, he realized that, while the exposed part of the ghadi eye covered proportionately the same amount of the face as the human variety, the eye sphere itself seemed to be half again as large.

Nate realized that the ghadi builders could have added their glowing stones anywhere, but they only bothered lighting the ritual space. Maybe they didn't *need* the light.

Nate turned around to pick up his own glowing rock. It had fallen out of its cloth binding, so it shone over the entire corridor. When Nate faced the passage ahead, he saw the first real signs of what had happened here.

Three bodies had been left here. All had been burned so badly that the only way to determine if they had been human or ghadi was to count the number of joints in the extremities. The realization that the greasy smoke smell came, in part, from the carbonized flesh that still barely clung to these blackened skeletons was too much for Nate. He turned around and emptied his violently churning stomach on to the rock pile.

When his body stopped objecting, he stood there for a few minutes, leaning against the rock pile and breathing from his mouth. "Bill, if I'm your messiah, you must really be impressed now."

Nate turned around and picked up the light-stone. Steeling himself, he looked at the bodies. Forcing it, as if in penance for embarrassing himself.

Human. From the position of the limbs, they had been bound.

Nate couldn't help thinking of the green fire burning through the guard's body after Scarface carved those runes in his chest.

How can a human being do that? Tie someone down and not just kill the poor bastard, but burn him alive? What point does it serve?

It was terror, pure and simple. This kind of atrocity had more to do with the people committing the act than those being killed. The people in control were demonstrating what happened to those in dissent.

"And Solis is frightened of me, Bill. *Me.*" Nate left the bodies and started to look for places Solis might have gone.

The College had been thorough in their destruction. They left burned bodies and broken furniture in their wake. They also defaced the ancient ghadi artwork, pulling down columns and ghadi sculpture. Some hallways were littered with piles of dismembered stone hands and heads, mixed with real ones.

To keep track of where he was, Nate had to pile loose stones at each intersection showing him where he had turned.

At least it seemed that the College storm troopers had retreated.

How much oil was left in that lantern? How long before you ended up feeling alone in the dark?

The thought of being trapped down here without a light source brought back feelings of claustrophobia, so Nate pushed it away.

It took a few hours before Nate and Bill made it to the entrance to the complex. By then, it was clear that the destruction was nearly complete. The College hadn't spared anything. Anything burnable had been burned, and what didn't burn had been smashed to pieces.

Nate saw daylight ahead and wrapped up his lightstone. He stepped over a fallen column and edged around a corner.

He stopped, facing a corridor that ended at a doorway framing a slice of orange dawn-tinted clouds. He could hear the rapids, and he could catch a whiff of air that wasn't heavy with smoke.

He held up a hand until Bill seemed to understand that he should stay put. Nate handed the ghadi his rock and crept up on the outside entrance.

He was emerging from higher up than where he first entered the complex. Close to the top of the bluff, Nate thought.

Nate had the feeling that something was wrong, even before he reached the end of the corridor. Halfway there, it seemed as if the floor and the walls ended too abruptly.

As he edged closer, his view of the sky was displaced by the green of the forest canopy. Then he saw the clearing across the river.

They were still here.

Nate caught a glimpse of movement at the edge of the clearing and fell down on his stomach. He crawled forward on his belly, hiding himself as much as possible.

Oh, God.

When Nate reached the end of the corridor, he saw why it seemed so wrong. It dead-ended in midair. He could look about seventy-five feet straight down. What had been the face of the bluff now formed a debris field that extended halfway into the river and was piled about thirty feet high.

The College's attack had peeled the face off the cliff, exposing the tunnels inside like termite holes in a piece of rotten wood.

This was the thunder. . . .

The river had been no defense at all. The rope bridge was long gone, buried under tons of stone, but there were half a dozen new wooden bridges laid across the frontier. Each could accommodate about five or six men across.

The river itself was a killing ground. Nate could see bodies, human and ghadi, piled half-submerged on its banks.

Beyond the river was a massive encampment. The attackers had even widened the clearing to fit the tents in. The trees they had cut down had been piled into a series of diagonal walls between them and the river—though it looked as if the threat from a counterattack was nonexistent.

Nate could see several men wearing black and red armor. Most of those had shiny circlets around their necks and wrists. The ones Nate saw stood at points around the perimeter of the encampment, holding weapons at attention. Among the tents, near the center of the encampment, a circle of masked and robed men surrounded the prone form of Solis.

Damn it, you stupid SOB.

Solis was staked down to the ground, encircled by men in gruesome and surreal masks. Nate couldn't hear what was being said down there, but he could see that Solis was talking to the men.

One of the men held a rune-carved dagger that was a twin of Nate's. The key that Solis had taken from the ghadi temple. The man turned it over with gloved hands, holding it before his gilded mask. The mask was a horned animal, probably a goat. The horns curled around to either side of this guy's face. It was the most elaborate mask in the crowd, which probably meant this guy was in charge.

Goat-face confirmed it by nodding and gesturing at the acolytes surrounding Solis. The others responded by moving to the four points of the compass, two men holding down each of Solis' limbs. One last guy knelt over one of Solis' legs holding a more utilitarian knife.

Goat-face's mask moved, nodding up and down, as he walked in a circle around Solis. To Nate it looked like an interrogation. If that was the case, whatever Solis might have said must have been unsatisfactory. Nate couldn't see what the kneeling acolyte did with the knife, but the result caused Solis to thrash as if he was having a seizure.

A sick feeling of helplessness started smothering Nate. Even if he could take on that whole encampment without getting himself killed, he had no way to get down there without jumping the seventy-five feet to the rocks below.

Solis had stopped moving. His left leg was covered in blood, tracing runes in his flesh. The acolyte with the knife stood and walked around to kneel down at the other leg. Nate could almost hear Solis yelling at them now. He could hear it as isolated high-pitched syllables disconnected from any words or grammar.

Goat-face wasn't impressed. He gestured to the acolyte, who began drawing in Solis' flesh with the knife.

This time Nate could hear Solis' screams clearly.

Nate closed his eyes. "You ruthless fucks."

He pushed himself away from the edge, but he froze when the floor of the broken corridor shifted. The damage that had sheared off the front of the cliff face had left the ground less stable than it looked. Nate's aborted movement had caused the ground to sink under his hands by a quarter inch. The floor groaned under his hands and Nate held his breath.

When everything stabilized and he could breathe again, Nate looked down at the encampment. No one seemed to have heard or noticed him. Very slowly, he started inching back from the edge. Every three inches or so, he stopped because of the ominous sounds coming from the rock around him.

He was three feet from the edge when the stress became too much. Something snapped, and the floor started making a prolonged grinding noise. Gravel and debris started falling down the outside, across the broken opening, making a sound like hard rain. For a few surreal moments, the opening to the sky moved downward, tilted, and rotated slightly. Then Nate was scrambling back as fast as he could as the rock in front of him caved in and slid downward in a roar of rock and dust.

Nate was quick enough to avoid getting caught up in the avalanche. He was standing, dust-covered and coughing, about a foot from the new edge when everything cleared.

When he blinked the grit out of his eyes, Nate realized he had the attention of everyone down in the College encampment.

Chapter Thirty-Six

"OH, SHIT," Nate whispered, spitting grit out of his mouth.

Down in the clearing, Goat-face was making gestures in Nate's direction. A dozen or two of the armored troops were crossing the new bridges back toward the cliff face.

Nate retreated back down the corridor, grabbing the light-stone from the ghadi.

"Come on, Bill, We've got to get out of here."

Bill put any doubts Nate had about the intellectual capacity of the ghadi to rest. Even with no language, Bill obviously grasped the salient points of their situation. The major two being: One, the College knew they were up here. Two, Solis had fallen into the hands of the College, meaning that retreating to the pit chamber was not an option.

When Nate tried to return the way they had come, Bill grabbed his arm and pulled him in an entirely new direction. Nate didn't argue. This ghadi was why he was still alive.

They passed through the remains of Arthiz's Shadow College rather quickly. It was obvious that the would-be dissidents had never occupied more than a small fraction of the ancient underground city. The doors that Bill led Nate through weren't hidden, strictly speaking. But while none barred passage like the secret pit chamber, they were heavy carved stone that age had blended with the walls so that they were easy to miss if you weren't expecting them.

Despite age, the stone doors opened easily at the ghadi's touch, swinging silently on some counterbalanced axis that had survived for millennia. Bill never slowed down, and Nate quickly lost track of where they were.

This is good, Bill, but they know I'm down here. If they believe the same things Solis does, they'll pick through this entire complex now.

Bill seemed to know that the caverns weren't safe. What remaining sense of direction Nate had, made him think their twisting passage through the tunnels was taking them directly away from the river and the cliff face. When they reached stairs, they traveled upward.

The air became fresher, and Nate felt a breeze that didn't smell of anything burning. The air was heavy with the smell of vegetation, and before Nate expected it, Bill pushed through a mat of vines and they walked outside.

The sky opened above them, tall trees to either side. The walls of the tunnel continued, but the tunnel itself had become an overgrown trench with a small stream flowing down the center. The walls became little more than overgrown heaps of rubble to either side of them.

They followed the trench into the jungle. Nate looked around as they emerged, and realized that they were in the aboveground portion of the ancient city. Ruins surrounded them, heaps of stone reclaimed by the jungle, humps of earth marking the foundation of some long-vanished structure, the surreal image of a ghadi statue half enveloped by a tree, appearing as if the stone was being born of the wood.

Eventually, Bill led him out of the trench and into the jungle. A few minutes later, Nate lost any hope of retracing his steps. He couldn't even find any visible sign of the path they were following.

All in all, that was probably a good thing. *If* Bill had some destination in mind.

Bill did.

•   •   •

Bill brought him through the jungle, a three-hour hike that felt like ten. Lack of food, water, and rest started catching up with Nate. His clothing also got in the way. The robe he had slept in was torn, covered in soot and blood, his skin was raw where the fabric rubbed against him, and his sandals weren't designed for this kind of travel. Nate was ready to call it quits long before Bill had reached where they were going.

Two things kept him going. The first was Bill's purposeful stride. The ghadi had been through everything Nate had, and more, and showed no sign of losing focus. Bill had led him through the labyrinth, which was probably why Nate wasn't being used as a runic scratch pad for some masked sadist right now. For that reason alone, he owed Bill enough to keep up.

The second, more pragmatic reason, was the fear that if he stopped, Bill might not. As bad as things were right now, Nate knew it would be worse if he lost his guide. Alone, lost in the jungle, Nate would probably make it a day or two at most. The closest he had ever come to living off the land was buying organic produce at the West Side Market.

When Bill found his objective, Nate shouldn't have been surprised.

Even though every ghadi Nate had seen to date had been under the control of human masters, simple logic would dictate that there would have to be ghadi living outside that control, in the wild.

According to the legends, and the evidence they left behind, the ghadi were once the dominant species. Even if the entire species suffered from a crippling aphasia, that wouldn't have precluded their survival. . . .

Still, Nate wasn't quite prepared for the village.

They had cleared a space under the jungle canopy, so

the entire community seemed housed within a gigantic green cathedral. Despite being woven from grass or reeds, the buildings were far from primitive. The walls were interlaced with sculptural patterns that were reminiscent of the bas-reliefs he had seen in ancient ghadi architecture.

There were dozens of buildings radiating in concentric circles around a central pit that mirrored what Nate had seen in the secret chamber in the old underground city. There were even stones circling the pit, like the seats inside the chamber.

Then there were the ghadi.

The number of them was overwhelming. There must have been close to a hundred of them dressed in rough loincloths and short robes that were obviously hand-woven. For the first time Nate saw ghadi with dull eyes and bones bent with age. Until now he had never seen an old ghadi, or a ghadi child.

Most disconcerting was the fact that they were completely silent.

The ghadi met Nate and Bill at the edge of the village, in a mass that slowly parted as Bill led Nate forward. All stared at him with their dark alien eyes.

They're staring at me as if they know me.

Nate still couldn't read ghadi expressions. What he saw in their faces could have been fear, or awe.

"This isn't happening. . . ."

The last ghadi stepped back, leaving the path open to the central pit, and Nate got his second surprise.

Standing on the other side of the pit were the two dozen ghadi from the pit chamber. Nate knew them because, like Bill and himself, they were covered with the dirt and soot from escaping the underground. These ghadi didn't just escape, they had looted the remains of the human settlement there. Nate saw books, weapons, clothing, masks, and central to it all, an elaborate black sarcophagus about eight feet long and four feet wide. The lid was open and Nate could see the gold glinting inside.

How the hell did they move that thing?

The exertion caught up with Nate and he sat down on one of the stones orbiting the pit. One of the ghadi handed him a carved husk that was filled with some aromatic liquid.

Nate drank the bitter liquid, and felt the fatigue pull his eyes shut.

• • •

When Nate woke up, he was lying in a hammock inside one of the woven buildings. His torn, bloody clothing was gone. He looked around, and saw Bill squatting in a corner of the one-room hut, staring at him.

"Who are you, Bill? My apostle?"

In response, Bill stood up and carried over a bluish, mango-looking fruit. Bill handed it to him and waited.

"Thanks, but maybe I can get dressed first?"

Nate sat up, and a wave of vertigo swamped him badly enough that he almost fell out of the hammock. The feeling surprised him, until he realized that he hadn't eaten in over a day, probably two. He had been surviving on panic and adrenaline.

The blue pseudo-mango started looking real good.

Trusting Bill to stop him if he tried to eat an inedible part of the fruit, Nate sank his teeth into it. The flesh was firm and stringy, like a cooked squash, and colored blood red in contrast to its bluish skin. The taste was a weird sweet-spicy flavor, almost like candied ginger.

At first it seemed seedless, but when Nate looked down into the fruit, the red flesh was shot through with tiny black specks. *Guess those are okay to eat, too.*

Nate was so hungry that it didn't occur to him until after the ginger-fruit was gone that the ghadi metabolism might be different enough that it could process food that was poisonous to humans.

Wouldn't that be ironic?

No sense worrying about it at this point. "Thanks, Bill. I needed that."

Nate got up and stood unsteadily on the dirt floor.

He wiped his mouth with the back of his hand as he looked for his clothing. It wasn't here, which didn't surprise Nate that much. What he'd been wearing when he'd come here had been in a pitiful state.

What was here was a pile of other human garments, up to and including a selection of masks. The neatly stacked and folded piles were placed on a low rectangular table as if they were an offering to the clothing god.

"Aren't you the thieves?" Nate looked over at Bill. "There's no way you managed to salvage all this while the College was attacking. You've been looting that place for how long? Months? Years?"

Nate shrugged. "Don't bother to answer."

The clothes fit him, after a fashion. Normal human clothing here was made for people shorter than he was. Fortunately, he was thin enough to get the stuff on, but a robe that was supposed to cover the whole body, ended mid-calf on him and he had to move the belt down about six inches.

Once he was dressed, Nate stood there a few long minutes.

"Now what?" he muttered.

Bill motioned him to come outside.

Nate followed Bill. From the light it was either early morning or early evening. In the center of the village, the entire population sat on the stones circling the central pit.

What?

As Bill walked forward, Nate shook his head. "No, I don't think you understand. I can't just summon Ghad. The other pit had inscriptions I could invoke, but I have no idea what the whole thing—"

Nate found himself standing in front of the mass of the ghadi, by the edge of the pit. He looked at their faces, and felt suddenly inadequate. "You can't even understand what I'm saying. I don't even know why I'm talking to you. You should know you got gypped on your messiah. I'm no savior. I'm just a fucking grad student, and I am sick of all this."

Nate looked down into the pit and saw the bones of dozens of dead ghadi. No miraculous visitation here to take all of them away. "You know, if I could figure out how to overthrow the College, I would. If I could fix you people, I would. But I'm just one person who doesn't belong here. *What can I do?*"

Nate shook his head and stared into the pit. After a long time, the ghadi got up by twos and threes, eventually leaving him alone with Bill.

Alone with Bill and the chest of golden tablets.

What can I do?

We don't really know that yet, do we?

Chapter Thirty-Seven

THE SECOND DAY out of Manhome, their column of about five hundred men had reached the foothills overlooking the coast. At dawn, Chief Armsman Ravig Kalish came for Ehrid.

Saying, "You must see this," he led Ehrid up to a bluff overlooking the way they had come. The high ground here gave an excellent view of the wrinkled landscape all the way to the coast. The gray sea was visible on the horizon. Even at this distance, Manhome itself was clearly visible, though it could be covered by Ehrid's thumb.

Manhome, however, wasn't the focus of Ravig's excitement.

Ehrid looked over the hills and farmland unfolded below him and muttered, "It has started."

The landscape below them was alive with movement. Three separate armies were in motion toward the rock of Manhome. Dawn sunlight glinted off the infantry's armor, as formations marched facing the sea.

"We need to return," Ravig told Ehrid.

Ehrid looked at Ravig. "We follow our orders."

"But—"

"Look down there, again. How many troops do you see?"

Ravig looked down at the force arrayed against Manhome. He didn't give an answer, so Ehrid provided one. "Just that left flank has at least three thousand men in formation, and they have twice as many cavalry down there as we have men. Half again as many archers. And that is only a third part of what we can see."

"Manhome is being attacked—"

"Your devotion is admirable," Ehrid said, "but do you know whose army you see?"

Ravig looked down at the force moving below them. It didn't take him long to see the colors of the Monarch's personal guard. Ravig stared for a long time, and Ehrid didn't interrupt the armsman's musings. Ravig wasn't aware of the maneuverings that Ehrid had been a party to; none of his guardsmen were. This sight was the first hint of civil war that Ravig had been given.

"Of course," Ravig said finally. "Who else could order such a force into the field?"

"Yes."

"You knew this was coming?"

"Yes."

There was a long silence. If Ehrid listened very closely, he could almost hear the troops marching. A distant sound like rustling leaves.

Ravig stared at him and Ehrid hoped the emotion clouding the man's eyes wasn't betrayal. Ehrid had unlimited authority over his men, and none had the right to question him. However, rule and custom were faint arguments against a deception so large.

"Why are we not in Manhome, sir?"

"We have our orders."

"Orders from the College. Our sworn duty is to the Monarch. With due respect, we should be opening the gate for his army."

Ehrid felt a tremendous wave of relief.

"Our orders are from the Monarch," Ehrid told him. "Half the guard of Manhome has already been pressed to serve the College in battle. Our leaving has denied them access to the other half."

"We should be down there, sir." It wasn't a challenge anymore, merely a statement of resignation.

"We serve at the Monarch's pleasure, and should be where he would have us."

Ravig nodded. "How long have you known?"

"Long enough." Ehrid clasped Ravig's shoulder. "Come, I should talk to the men. Then we should start moving while the daylight's young."

● ● ●

Even in myths, General Kavish Largan had never heard of a victory so sudden and so complete. Never an enemy that collapsed so cleanly and so completely without a single confrontation. He had led the Monarch's forces to Manhome prepared for months of siege, but the same day they had marched within sight of the city, his army was walking through the gates unopposed.

By the time the sun touched the western horizon, he had fully occupied the city of Manhome. His armies controlled the streets, and surrounded the walls of the College itself. His men were methodically searching through the endless tunnels that riddled the plateau. The advance into the city had happened so quickly that, if General Kavish hadn't given a belated order, there wouldn't be any of his forces on the ground outside the city, guarding against a counterattack.

The College he had been taught so long to fear was a cowardly phantom that vanished when confronted.

General Kavish made camp outside the main entrance of the College of Man. At sunset he sent a man inside, carrying a parchment bearing the seal of the Monarch, dictating the terms of surrender. Then he called his staff together to plan a victory feast for all of his men.

Midnight came before he became concerned over the man he sent inside with the terms of surrender. Before he could calculate the best response to his man's disappearance, a robed figure walked out of the main doors to the College. The man wore the mask of a scholar. The mask was a twisted red demon with a prominent hooked nose.

Armed men surrounded the figure, and General Kavish pushed himself through the crowd to face the College's representative. The mask faced him, frozen and expressionless. The general wanted to see what was hidden behind that facade.

"Do you accept the Monarch's terms?" he asked the scholar.

The scholar from the College of Man spoke quietly. "We have decided."

"Yes?"

"If you renounce the Monarch and have your army swear fealty to the College of Man, we will show you every mercy."

The general shook his head in disbelief. Within the ranks surrounding them, he heard some nervous laughter. "With respect, we occupy your city. Why would I surrender to you?"

"To save your men."

"The reign of the College is over."

"We protect the existence of Man. You cannot conceive of the powers we hold at bay. No temporal authority will remove us from that task. Those who do will taste that power."

General Kavish waved his men forward. He was tired of talking to this man. "Take him. Hold his arms, and if he utters something you don't understand, kill him."

The masked scholar took a step back, but he was surrounded before he got anywhere. Kavish's men grabbed his arms and the general walked up to him and grabbed the nose of the demon mask. "I want to look at one of you in the face."

Kavish took the mask. When he saw the scholar's face, he gasped. Realization swept through the troops restraining the man, and they let him go.

Standing there, facing Kavish, was the man he had sent inside to give the Monarch's terms. The face was bruised, and around his neck was a silver torc that was alive with the sacred writing of the College.

The voice that had spoken to Kavish said, "Since

you do not swear fealty to the College of Man, you are an enemy of Man."

The voice did not come from the beaten man in front of him.

The man's body jerked as all his muscles tensed. Wisps of smoke came from the torc around his neck, and Kavish began to smell burning flesh.

"Don't touch him," Kavish said, too late.

Three soldiers, seeing one of their own in trouble, reached out to grab him and calm the seizure. It was the last thing they did. Touching the affected body sent a jolt through the men, sending their bodies into spasms. After a moment, all of them collapsed.

The skin under the torc was completely black.

Victory no longer seemed as certain.

And, in the distance, Kavish began to hear the screaming of his men.

Chapter Thirty-Eight

MORE THAN ONCE Nate wanted to know exactly what the ghadi were thinking. In his more philosophical moments, he wondered *how* they were thinking. Language was such an intimate part of Nate's mindscape, he couldn't conceive of any sort of mental dialogue without it. Somehow, though, ghadi had managed to evolve communication, even a culture, without it.

Every evening Nate watched as the ghadi gathered by the pit of their dead. He had first thought that it was simply some meaningless ritual, a phantom pain from an amputated culture. But there was more to it. Each time, a ghadi or a set of ghadi would stand before the audience and dance.

The first time, Nate didn't pay attention until the sound startled him. He peeked out of the hut to see two dancers circling the pit, and the seated ghadi clapping out a beat. The sound of the beat was startling after seeing the ghadi as silent and ghostlike.

The dance was stylized, the movements exaggerated, the poses reminiscent of the bas-reliefs he had seen. The dancers moving together, then retreating without touching. It was clear that the dancers were acting out something. What, Nate wasn't sure. He had the feeling that he was looking at some sort of kinetic shorthand, where a single gesture stood in for a whole series of movements.

Perhaps the most disturbing element was the expressions the dancers wore. It was the first time Nate had seen a ghadi face showing an aspect more than shaded neutrality, and the passion they revealed was alien and frightening. One dancer's face was frozen in a grimace of pure fury, the other in a grin so cadaverous that it was worthy of death itself.

Nate noticed one member of the audience—Bill, it was becoming easier for Nate to tell individual ghadi apart—was doing more than clapping a beat. He was whistling and grunting, adding a surreal music to the performance.

Nate realized that the ghadi didn't lose language. They might have lost speech, and writing, and words. But looking at the performance, Nate knew that as much information was passing between the performers and the audience as did with any storyteller. These people communicated. They had a language.

They know themselves, they know their culture, they know their history.

• • •

The ghadi couldn't speak to him, but they were very accommodating. They brought him food, water, and strong tea. They would watch him, but carefully, at a distance, either trying to stay out of his way, or because they were afraid of him. The only ghadi who would come within a few feet of Nate was Bill. He was certainly the only ghadi willing to touch Nate.

Nate was grateful for the food and the place to sleep, but he knew that something was expected of him. And while he had some idea of the role he was supposed to fill for these people, he didn't have a clue about the specifics.

So he did what he could under the circumstances.

He studied the golden tablets of the Gods' Language and hoped that what else he was supposed to do would eventually become apparent.

The ghadi had a substantial supply of paper and books for him to use, all looted from humans at some point. More than enough for his notes. Unfortunately, he had to start from scratch, since his original notes were long gone.

The good news was that his notation scheme was simple enough that it was only a matter of a day's work to reconstruct the progress he had made before hell broke loose.

After he refreshed himself on what he had learned, he started on the tablets by selecting a spell to copy in his notation—knowing that he would then have to invoke what was etched on the tablet in order to understand what he copied.

The first invocation had to be a trial of faith, trusting the motives of the ghadi who made it, trusting that there were no traps or Trojan horses hidden in the runes.

He moderated the risk somewhat by choosing a short inscription to start, on the theory that the less complex the incantation, the less dangerous it might be. And while he had learned that one spell could invoke another, he thought he had learned enough to tell such a spell by inspection.

However logical he was about it, though, Nate couldn't avoid the fact that the first tablet he tried to invoke would be a massive leap into the unknown.

Okay, you have root access to the universe, and the next command you type into the console could be a directory listing, or it could format the server's hard drive. . . .

Nate sat cross-legged on the ground in front of the hut the ghadi had given him, his notes sprawled around him in a semicircle. Bill watched him from outside Nate's circle of paper, the ghadi's minimalist expression could have been fascination, amusement, or concern.

The tablet that Nate had chosen lay on the ground in front of him, polished and shining even after a millennium or two. The runes engraved in its surface were perfect, the lines straight and angles precise, as if it had been machine-made. The runes were large enough to be easily read at arm's length, larger than most of the other tablets. Even then, the runes covered only half the surface on this side.

Nate glanced up at Bill. The sun was just right, peeking through the canopy, to bounce metallic reflections off the tablet and onto Bill's face.

"I wish you could talk to me. Tell me what this means to you. Tell me what your myths and history are." Nate looked down at the tablet. "Tell me if this is going to blow up in my face."

Nate sucked in a breath.

Here goes. . . .

As far as his experience with the Gods' Language went, the runes inscribed here required little effort to read. As with any of the spells he had read, he felt some resistance, a force trying to stop him halfway through. But for this spell, that force was a mere token compared to what he had experienced before. Even the simple lighting of a candle required more effort from the caster.

So light was the effort that Nate wasn't particularly surprised that when he finished casting the spell, there seemed to be no effect whatsoever. No lights, no smoke, nothing bursting into flame. No sound, no movement.

Just Nate, and Bill, and his perimeter of notes rusting in a gentle breeze.

A gentle breeze . . .

Just as Nate noticed it, the soft wind died down, leaving the air as still as it was when he started. *Was that it?*

Nate repeated the casting, paying attention to the runes in case he had misread one. When he was finished, the breeze returned briefly.

Nate reached over and wrote down the effect next to his pseudocode copy of the runes. He smiled at Bill. "Well, good news, Bill. I cast this and the universe didn't implode."

Nate flipped the tablet over and copied the inscription that was on the back. After coding it in his notes, it became obvious the other side of this particular tablet carried an inscription that had about ninety percent of the same text as the one he had just cast. Except for a few symbols here or there, it was a line-for-line copy.

Nate highlighted the differences, underlining them in his notes.

Feeling a little pride at how well things were going with his first attempts, Nate cast the new spell. As he expected, since the spell was almost the same, the effect was almost the same.

Almost.

This one required more effort, and when the invocation was complete, Nate got a little more than a gentle breeze. A stiff wind spun a dust devil around him, picking up all his notes and spinning them around in a brief tornado.

Nate sat there and stared as the wind dropped his notes to the ground as it died.

Six symbols . . . Nate thought, *only six symbols changed. . . .*

Chapter Thirty-Nine

FOR THE FIRST time since he had set foot in this world, Nate felt as if he was back in his element. He was hacking code again. For hours at a time, he hunched over columns of symbols he transcribed, making notes, trying to perceive a pattern. Every time fatigue would set in, he would have some insight that would be just enough to keep him going.

He didn't have electricity or Mountain Dew, but he had the glowing rock he had taken from the tunnels, and he had the tea the ghadi brewed. So he was able to work long hours into the night.

Around him, the ghadi went on with their lives. They went out and gathered food, their children played, and they sat around the pit and danced their storied dances. Nate paid them little attention. If Bill didn't bring him fruits and the occasional small roast animal, Nate might not have eaten at all.

There was a nearly inevitable logic to the Gods' Language that slowly revealed itself to him. He already had notations to begin and end a block of "code" marked by "{" and "}." There was another pair of symbols, square brackets in Nate's notes, that enclosed what Nate thought of as labels, a string of symbols that named spells, among other things. Using a label, a spell could call another spell, just like a C++ routine calling another procedure. The spell itself could be called by invoking the label alone, as Nate

had done in the pit chamber, calling Ghad him/her/
itself.

Also, as with the code Nate was more familiar with,
those labels could be the target of some action. The
label could simply name an object, like a candle, and
the spell could do something *to* the named object
rather than trying to invoke it.

By studying the candle spell he had memorized long
ago, and the new spells, Nate discovered a difference
in notation that specified how such a label was used
in a spell. By itself, in isolation, the label was an invocation. Prefaced with another symbol, which Nate inscribed as a tilde in his notes, it became the target of
the calling spell.

Studying the difference in the two wind spells, Nate
became certain that he was looking at a primer designed by the ancient ghadi. There seemed no other
reason to place those two spells together other than to
highlight the meaning of the six elements that varied.

By some careful experimentation, Nate identified
each element. Each turned out to be the same kind
of data. They were three pairs, and each pair symbol-
ized a vector showing magnitude and direction. The
magnitude symbol was a raw value, apparently on a
logarithmic scale; the direction symbol gave two angular measurements, splitting the 12 bits into two sets of
6 to divide a circle into 2^6 segments between five and
six degrees wide. All were bracketed by yet another
pair of symbols that Nate wrote down as angle brackets, "< . . . >," in his notes.

The three vectors in the spell were simple enough.
The first gave the "location" of the target, the source
of the wind, the vector pointing from the location of
the spell, the angles measured based on the orienta-
tion of the spell itself—an interesting consequence
being that moving the tablet while he was casting it
actually changed the source of the wind.

The second vector was the velocity and direction of
the wind. The third was the magnitude and direction
of its acceleration. Of course, from what Nate knew

about basic physics, if the acceleration vector was not in line with the velocity vector, the accelerated object started going in circles—in the case of the wind spell, you got a whirlwind.

The other consequence, beyond discovering vector notation in the Gods' Language, was discovering that his hexadecimal notation was wrong. Wrong, at least insofar as it didn't follow the "natural" ordering the symbols had when representing actual numbers. Perhaps the largest error was the fact that Nate had mislabeled zero. In his notation, zero would have been a blank, which never appeared in his notation. In actuality, zero was the character where all the lines in the grid were "on";

Nate had the scheme reversed. *Removing* lines from this base added powers of two to a "number." After realizing this, Nate scrapped his original numbering scheme and adopted what the language actually seemed to follow. It took three days to revise all his notes, but it was comforting to discover that all his paired punctuation marks—"{ . . . },""[. . .],""< . . >"—turned out to be numbered consecutively in the new order.

• • •

During the second week, what he was doing seemed to become more interesting to the ghadi. Why was fairly obvious. The first week he had spent most of his time in transcription, taking notes and simply thinking about what he was trying to do with the Gods' Language. Not much of a show.

But while he had only concentrated on a single golden

tablet the first week, the second week he was averaging one a day. In some cases, the spells were something to watch.

Each tablet seemed to follow a set pattern, two—in some cases more, but always at least two—spells set together for the purpose of comparison, highlighting the differences between them, and showing what a variation in the spell construction actually did. Technically, it was a mother lode of information.

As performance art, it wasn't too shabby either.

The first tablet drew colored lights in the air. Nate was able to move them, change their color and their brightness. By the end of the day Nate had blue will-o'-the-wisp lights dancing all around the ghadi village, even sending one orbiting Bill's head.

The next day, the spell Nate tried moved pebbles across the ground. Then rocks. Then he levitated a large chunk of earth. Then, when he realized the similarity between this and the wind spell, Nate was able to set the dirt swirling into a dirty spiral galaxy hovering in midair between him and a ghadi audience.

After that came sounds. The spells on the next tablet pulled sounds out of midair. A police whistle down to a foghorn, a single tone that he could easily modify by origin, frequency, and volume. That spell was so short that the single tablet held a half dozen examples. By this time, he was familiar enough with the vector notation that targeted the spell that he was able to concentrate on aim. He could put a wolf whistle inside one of the huts, up in the trees, or in the midst of the watching ghadi.

He also felt the ghadi were helping him cast the spells. He could feel the energy flowing from them into the spells as he cast them. With all of them surrounding him, even the complicated incantations seemed almost effortless. Whatever resources the Gods' Language drew to power itself, the ghadi were closer to it. The runes that he invoked weren't meant to inhabit a human brain, be drawn by a human hand, or spoken by a human tongue.

Nate knew that without the ghadi, he would have plumbed the depths of his own reserves long ago. . . .

These ghadi were giving him freely what the mages of the College took by force. Yerith had told him how the mages of the College used the ghadi, used them until destruction, and the acolytes who had captured Bill had seemed to be indulging in some sort of ritual theft of that inherent power. Despite that, the ghadi opened themselves to him.

The potential almost scared him.

The day Nate read tablet number five, the potential became terrifying.

• • •

He began as usual, after eating the fruit Bill had left him during the night and drinking some of the powerful ghadi tea, which was really more kin to a thick herbal soup. Nate picked a golden tablet and walked over to his work space.

Nate's area was little more than a bare patch of ground about ten feet away from the hut they let him sleep in, but he already thought of it as his office. He had folded up a reed carpet to sit on, and had moved a half log with a near-flat surface next to it to act as a worktable. He had all his notes, brush and ink, and a small pile of stones to use as paperweights as he worked.

A selection of other tools had accumulated, some from the jungle, some from the ghadi cache of stolen human artifacts—all of which Nate used to take measurements and observe what it was he was doing. There was a straight staff that he used to take linear measurements, another pile of stones as equal as possible in mass, a length of rope that Nate attached to two sticks to make a crude compass, more sticks straight and strong enough to draw in the dirt, a wooden plate that he had appropriated—its edge now notched evenly around the edge, allowing Nate to use it to make angular measurements.

Nate sat down on his mat and positioned a golden

tablet on the split log in front of him. First off, as
always, he transcribed the runes into his notation.
After a fair bit of practice, that step only took about
half an hour. As usual, Bill came over and squatted
down to watch him. The other ghadi would come to
watch later, when he began to actually manipulate the
forces he was studying.

When Nate was done with the transcription, he set
down the brush and held up his work. He already
recognized some familiar patterns. He already saw
that there were what seemed to be another set of
bracketing characters. Nate recognized the pattern because it had appeared in every tablet spell he had
transcribed thus far. Four symbols, three of which
were the same in each spell. The first, Nate already
represented with a tilde, "~," the character that told
the spell that the label after it was the target of the
spell, not the name of another spell to be invoked.
The second and fourth characters seemed a new pair
of bracketing symbols, implied by the fact they were
consecutive in Nate's new numbering scheme.

So the pattern was "~(?)" where "?" was some individual rune. The interesting thing was that the "?"
was the same in the wind spell and the sound spell,
but different in the dirt spell and the one he was transcribing now. . . .

*If the ~ symbol is some sort of targeting word saying
"apply this spell to . . ." then what follows has to represent the target. If it isn't a specific label, then—*

"It's the air," Nate whispered to himself. That's
what the four symbols meant in the wind and sound
spells. It was telling the spell to target the atmosphere.
The wind spell set it into simple accelerated motion,
the sound spell set it into simple vibration. The major
difference between the wind spell and the earth spell
was just a matter of changing ~(air) to ~(dirt).

The sequence on the tablet wasn't either of those.
The "?" symbol was new, and wasn't even close to
the rune for "air" or "dirt."

"Water, maybe?" Nate wondered aloud. One out

of 4095 possibilities, and he couldn't have been more wrong.

Once he had the spell transcribed, and Nate had taken all the notes he could on the runes that made up the spell, it was time to see what it did. Now he had an audience, the ghadi encircling him at a respectful distance. They had learned his routine well enough that they knew that something interesting was going to happen.

Nate positioned the tablet and leaned over, staring at the linear runes etched in the golden surface. He could feel the potential building even before he invoked the first character of the invocation. Halfway into naming the spell, Nate could feel the hair standing on the back of his neck.

The vector targeted a spot of ground about six feet in front of Nate. Pretty much the center of the ghadi circle. Nate didn't even have a split second to look up as the spell resolved.

Out of a clear blue sky, a deafening thunderclap arced into the ground before Nate. The flash blinded him, and the force of it knocked him backward.

"Jesus fuck!"

Nate pushed himself to his feet. The air was rank with the smell of ozone and burning hair, the latter coming from him. His ears rang as he looked around. "Everybody all right?" He could barely hear his own words over the echoing thunderclap in his skull.

Fortunately, he was the closest to the impact, so the ghadi were stunned, but unharmed. Most were blinking, covering their eyes or shaking their heads.

Okay, testing this stuff in the middle of the village is probably a bad idea.

Nate walked over to where the lightning bolt hit, and he could feel the heat of the ground through his sandals. *What did I do? Did I just order all the electrons out of the vicinity?* Nate suddenly wished he had paid more attention in his high school physics classes.

Nate looked up, and realized that all the ghadi were staring at him. Then, one by one, they genuflected.

Their expressions were still difficult for Nate to read, but the broad gesture was unmistakable.

"Hell of a messiah," Nate whispered, "I don't even know what I'm doing. . . ."

BOOK FIVE

———

There was a time when men worshiped many gods. Even the men who served the College of Man would make offerings to the brothers of Ghad, the beings who walked between the worlds. Some men would even make offerings to Ghad himself, for it was Ghad who was most likely to answer.

It was a time of blood and war, for those who served one god would fight for power with those who served a different god. Those who served Ghad would fight against all.

The wisest scholar of the College of Man told those who served Ghad, "What does it gain you to be granted the greatest power, if you become a servant in the games between the gods?"

Much blood spilled on the ground before a half of those serving Ghad saw the wisdom of the scholar's words.

—The Book of Ghad and Man,
Volume III, Chapter 72

Chapter Forty

"THEY ARE COMING here, to Zorion." The Monarch stood in the doorway of the apartments he had granted Uthar Vailen and looked like a petulant child.

"Certainly a counterattack wasn't unexpected. Not with the bulk of the College's military force closer to here than to Manhome."

The Monarch shook his head. "It makes no sense. They should be returning, to defend Manhome."

"And Manhome should have surrendered."

The Monarch looked wounded.

"I serve at your pleasure, but I know the College. Their arrogance is without equal. But not without reason."

"I must organize a defense before the day is out."

Uthar rubbed his temples and cursed himself for ever considering allying with this fool. The dictators of the College at least earned their power and arrogance. This man was born into a position he was much too small to fill.

"What troops do you have?" Uthar asked. "What survivors from the attack on the Shadow College?"

"Two hundred guardsmen, and perhaps fifteen scholars from your Shadow College."

"Fifteen? Out of three hundred?"

The Monarch nodded.

"You give me less to defend this city than were

defending the Shadow College you sacrificed. Zorion
will fall."

"No. It cannot . . ."

"The College of Man has exactly the advantage you
sought in Manhome."

The Monarch shook his head. "What can I do?"

*Die, you pathetic little man. Slit your own throat and
allow your betters to salvage what can be salvaged.*

"Zorion itself is only important because of you, sir."

"Of course."

"If you wish to save the city, and yourself, you and
what force you can command, must retreat."

"You say I should show weakness before the
College?"

You are weak. "I cannot lead fifteen acolytes to
defeat the College's main force, but I can use them
to hide a withdrawal so you can regroup at a place of
our choosing." *A place of my choosing, where I may
yet have guardsmen ready to serve you.*

Uthar looked at the frightened child the Monarch
had become. "You show wisdom," the Monarch told
him. "Tell me of your plans." Uthar saw in the Monarch's face that he was no longer demanding, but
pleading for advice to salvage himself and his power.

No, Uthar thought, correcting himself. *Not serve
you. Serve the idea of you. The little man you are is
beside the point.*

"You should have an escort. Take only those close
to you who can be trusted, can wield a weapon, and
can move with speed. Have your advisers escape in
parties of two dozen or so, give them the lesser of
your guard and what servants can be armed. Send
them away from our route."

"How many am I to sacrifice?"

How many did you sacrifice of my College?

"You are giving them a chance to flee the College
of Man. You know that any of your household, all
those that serve you, would have their lives forfeit
should they stay here. Sending them away now gives

them some chance, as well as camouflaging our own escape."

"I will organize this at once. What of you?"

"Have me meet with the survivors of the Shadow College to form a plan to defend our escape."

• • •

Yerith had never felt such a sense of doom. Even when the College arrested her father and started putting his servants to death, even then there was some feeling of hope. Even during the frantic retreat through the tunnels, Osif had managed to keep his handful of acolytes calm and quiet as he led them through tunnels deep into the ancient ghadi ruin, long past any signs of the invasion.

However, by the time they had flanked the College's army and arrived at Zorion, the mood had become bleak. There had been almost infinite routes of escape from the old ghadi caverns, but despite planning for the possibility, the College had been too swift and too precise in their attack. They had finished two thirds of the Shadow College in the first five minutes.

Osif and his group were the only ones to escape.

That was a bad enough blow to the small group of outsiders, but even that realization wasn't the worst of it. All of them had held hope that the Monarch, the personification of all power outside the College of Man, might be massing armies, preparing to deal some miraculous counterblow to the College and its forces.

Their arrival in the city put an end to that hope.

Even before they reached the gates, they saw the signs. Farms had been abandoned. Livestock roamed the fields at will. What people they saw would see their robes and unmasked faces and flee long before they were close enough to even shout a reassurance.

Close to the city they were met by a unit of guardsmen that seemed to expect them. The guards were a pathetic sight, clad in ill-fitting uniforms, old and hastily donned. The men who wore them were

too young or too old. Some looked to be farmers and
shopkeepers who barely knew what end of their weapons to point at the enemy. They seemed to have been
without sleep for too long.

If anything, Zorion itself seemed less defended than
the Shadow College had been. And while no one had
explicitly said so, the eyes of every guardsman told
Yerith that the College's Army was on its way here.

*The Monarch would fall, and the College would se-
lect a puppet of their choosing to replace him. Or,
worse, the College would dispense with the pretense of
secular authority and declare themselves the sole rulers
of men.*

What little hope was left to Osif and his people was
gone by the time they reached the ziggurat, center of
the Monarch's waning power. The Monarch's guard
led them to an audience chamber deep inside the ziggurat. No one made any attempt to hide the situation.
They passed guards and bureaucrats madly racing
from room to room carrying boxes of the Monarch's
wealth. Yerith saw a trio of boys rush past them to
remove ceremonial swords and armor that had probably decorated the hall here for the past six centuries.

It is over, Yerith thought.

She hoped that, somehow, Nate Black and some of
the ghadi might have escaped.

The guards left them in a chamber that had been
stripped bare of all signs of wealth and luxury. For
hours they waited. Long enough to worry that the
Monarch might have forgotten them, abandoning the
seat of his power and leaving them to fight the College's invasion.

Nearly twelve hours after they had arrived in Zorion, Yerith heard a familiar voice.

"Things have changed."

It was Arthiz.

She turned to see the man responsible for her presence here, and it was obvious that things *had* changed.
Arthiz no longer wore the blank white mask of an
anonymous acolyte. His face was bare and his skin

twisted with runic scars. Yerith knew little about status inside the College of Man, but she did know that the more glyphs of the Gods' Language were cut into the skin, the higher the status of the scholar.

Yerith suspected that Arthiz must have been a high scholar in the College, just to have the temerity to fight the institution. But the evidence on his skin was a different thing entirely. Even his eyelids were marked.

As he studied the remnants of his College, Osif stepped forward. "Master Arthiz?"

"Yes."

"Are there any others?"

The expression on Arthiz's face said everything. They were all that was left. Someone muttered, "What do we do now?"

"There is a small force at an enclave north of Manhome. I plan to get you there before the College descends on this city."

"Then what?" Osif asked.

"For the next sixday or two, survival is the only strategy of any importance. We can plan for the future once we secure one."

Chapter Forty-One

Π ATE KNEW that there had to be a point where he would have to decide what he was going to do. He couldn't study runes forever, and, at some point, all the crap he was hiding from would catch up to him. Nate told himself that he would come up with a plan, once he understood what it was he had to work with.

Apparently, time was too much to ask.

Less than three days after he had managed to call down a thunderbolt from a cloudless sky, a new ghadi came to the village. Nate was hunched over his notes in a new clearing farther away from the main village. He didn't realize something was happening until he noticed that all the villagers who weren't out gathering food were running toward one end of the village. Even Bill, who seemed to make it a personal mission to baby-sit Nate, joined the others.

Nate put down the brush and stood up, trying to determine what the commotion was. He walked over to the mass of ghadi, which parted for him, allowing him to face a ghadi he had never seen before.

The new ghadi was female and filthy. She was covered with dirt, soot, and blood. What remained of her clothing was a knot of rags around her waist.

Nate knew she wasn't a villager when she looked at him. Facing Nate, her face lost all natural reserve. She stared at him with an expression of terror and seemed about to bolt back into the woods from which she came. Before she could, several villagers, male and female, came forward and touched her in what was, apparently, a reassuring manner.

Nate backed away from the new ghadi. Whatever she had just been through, the last thing she needed was him looming over her.

• • •

It turned out, though, Nate was exactly what she wanted.

Once she was cleaned, fed, and had her wounds tended to, Bill led Nate to the pit, where the villagers were waiting with the new ghadi. Nate couldn't get nuances from the ghadi gesticulating, but her story was painfully clear. Humans had attacked her and her village.

Nate hadn't speculated on how so many ghadi ended up in human captivity. But they had to come from somewhere.

After she had danced and gestured her story, all the ghadi villagers, including Bill, including her, stared at Nate.

So what are you going to do?

Nate stepped forward. "Take me to where this happened." His words received blank stares, but he got his point across with his clumsy human gestures, pointing at her, pointing at himself, and pointing back the way she had come.

• • •

Her village wasn't far away. Less than a day's walk starting the next morning. It was close enough for Nate to worry about possible attacks on "his" village. It also made him wonder how densely populated the jungle here was.

The expedition consisted of Jane Doe, Bill, and two other male ghadi from the village who Nate named Steve Jobs and Steve Wozniack. Jane still seemed to regard Nate with suspicion, but from what Nate had learned about ghadi body language, Bill and the

Steves seemed a lot more tense about what might be ahead of them than they were about Nate.

Nate wasn't sure about this himself. For all the impressive effects he had called forth from the gold tablets, he still barely knew what he was doing. And he also couldn't carry the tablets with him; the best he could do was take some of his notes folded inside his robe. Even with the long, silent trek through the jungle, he couldn't come to grips with a coherent strategy.

What if he came across a group of College slave traders? How could he deal with them? Every spell he had took time to cast, and while he could cast transcriptions by their names, what they did in an unmodified state wouldn't be terribly useful in a confrontation—except the lighting bolt, which sort of abandoned any pretense of stealth.

Nate was still pondering his options when they reached the village. Once they saw it, Nate stopped worrying about strategy and found himself wishing the bastards were still here.

It was a smaller village than Bill's, just a handful of huts around a central pit. All of them had been burned to the ground. The ghadi the invaders had killed were left to rot where they had fallen. Any ghadi that were above a certain age had been slaughtered. The College apparently wanted their ghadi young.

One old ghadi had been crawling toward the pit when he finally died. He had crawled about fifteen feet with his belly slit open down to his spine.

The site was silent, and smelled of smoke and blood. Jane sat down by the pit and closed her eyes. Nate didn't blame her.

After a few moments in a hopeless search for survivors, Nate helped Bill and the Steves to dispose of the dead. To Nate it seemed undignified and callous to throw bodies into a mass grave. However, it was clear that this was how the ghadi honored their dead. If nothing else, the old ghadi whose last act was to attempt to crawl into the pit with his ancestors told him that.

It was obvious where the ghadi had been taken. The attackers had no need to cover their tracks. They had left a trail ten feet wide, with cart tracks, horse droppings, trampled foliage and the purple blood of the ghadi.

Even if they could talk, Nate wouldn't have argued the decision to follow.

• • •

They must have been two or three days behind the attackers when they started. But they began catching up almost immediately. A party that was so large must have had to take a fair bit of time to set up and break camp. Nate's group had no camp to speak of, and it took Bill only a few minutes to forage something for them to eat when they did rest.

Every day it rained, but it wasn't enough to erase the swath cut through the forest. Even if the trail completely washed away, they could follow the bodies.

Every day they passed two or three ghadi who hadn't made it. Some were barely infants.

At each corpse, the ghadi set up a cluster of branches, marking the site. Nate guessed it was for other ghadi, to find the bodies and carry them to the appropriate place.

• • •

They had followed for three days, and it seemed that they were within hours of catching up with the stolen ghadi. At the last camp they had found, the ashes were still warm.

Then they found the road.

Nate walked out of the jungle, onto a dirt track that was roughly perpendicular to the direction they were going. It was no wildlife trail. There were ruts from wagon wheels, and Nate saw places where brush had been cleared, and fallen trees had been sawed into pieces to clear the way. The road wasn't straight, so Nate lost sight of it about a hundred yards before and behind.

However, its message was clear enough. They were back in human territory. It was also clear that the party they were following had taken this road. There was a light rain, and the road was just muddy enough to hold tracks, and little used enough to make it obvious which way they had gone.

Nate looked back into the jungle. The ghadi were so far back that they were barely visible. Nate could just see enough of them to realize that he was the center of attention again. No words, but it was clear that it was Nate's decision whether they should go on or not.

It would have made sense to turn back at this point. They had walked right into enemy territory, and the gods—or Ghad—only knew how many people they would face at the other end of this road. Nate knew that the people who built this road would not be kindly disposed toward wild ghadi, much less toward Nate, the taboo alien, or Azrael, the instrument of Ghad's wrath. . . .

"Fuck it," Nate muttered, waving the ghadi to follow him down the road.

• • •

They followed the road, paralleling it about ten yards inside the jungle. The foliage was dense enough to keep them out of sight of the road, while they could still follow it by keeping track of the break in the canopy above it. That worked until they ran out of jungle.

They reached the edge of a clearing in sight of where the stolen ghadi had been taken. To Nate, it looked like something out of the Wild West, a town made up of a dozen low wooden buildings. Beyond the town, Nate saw the ocean, and sitting in a natural bay was a large ship at anchor. The ship had four masts, and looked as if it might actually be larger than the town in front of them.

If there was any question in Nate's mind that this was where the trail had led them, it didn't last. Even in the fading evening light, he could see the ghadi from Jane's village.

The building was next to a stable. In front of the stable was a fenced-in clearing where a few bedraggled horses hung their heads trying to pull grass from the muddy soup in which they stood. Behind that clearing was a structure that seemed to be another stable, with the same tiny windows and same compartmental structure. But when Nate watched for a while, he could see ghadi inside. These weren't the blank impassive servants Nate had seen serving the College. With these, the wounds were still fresh. Nate could still see the bruises, and the fear in their eyes, even from his spot back in the jungle.

From what Nate could tell, there was only one guard by the ghadi barracks. One bored guy in a long cloak who looked as if he'd rather be inside one of the other buildings.

Okay, we can do this. . . .

The stable and the slave house were offset from the other buildings. Nate supposed that the residents here didn't want to be too close to the animals. That would be an advantage. If they were quiet, there would be less of a chance of an alarm being raised. All they had to do was subdue the one guard.

Nate spent about an hour of gesturing to the others before he was confident that they understood his plan, such as it was.

They would wait until after dark, sneak up to the slave house, free the ghadi, and escape. Nate would take care of the guard.

Nate *hoped* he would take care of the guard.

The problem was to disable him without alerting anyone. There were a lot of things he could do, all of which would be noisy and obvious. However, there was one thing he thought might do it.

The last breakthrough he had in his study was a realization—such as it was—of how the first spell he

had learned, the candle-snuffing spell, worked. It had
a good deal in common with the wind spells on the
tablets. There were just a few more lines whose net
effect was to cause air to move away uniformly from
a single point.

Centered on a candle, the small instant vacuum
snuffed it out.

But it didn't need to be small.

•   •   •

About an hour after nightfall, Nate led his ghadi
down toward the slave house. The single guard was
still there, paying more attention to his prisoners than
anything else. Nate was able to get down to within
fifty feet of the guy before he ran out of fence, and
cover.

A horse wandered over and snorted at Nate and
the ghadi on the other side of his fence, the only creature to notice them.

Here goes.

Nate quietly spoke the runes of the spell, changing
a few of the runes that referred to targeting and magnitude. And a sphere of vacuum ten yards in diameter
opened across the field, centered on the spot of
ground where the one guard stood. Nate could feel a
stiff breeze on his face from the displaced air.

The guard reacted instantaneously, and silently.
Eyes wide, he started gasping for breath. He was
choking and coughing, the sounds unable to leave his
body without air to transmit them. He grabbed his
throat and shook his head. For several seconds, the
man tried to force himself to breathe, but there was
nothing to breathe.

He started to stagger toward the other buildings,
but he was already disoriented, and he tripped. He
managed to get to his feet and walk another ten feet
before he passed out.

It sounded like a quick rush of water when the air
raced to fill in the shrinking vacuum.

Nate hunched over and darted toward the guard's

post, which was by an entrance to the slave house. Bill and the Steves followed Nate, Jane went toward the fallen guardsman. When Nate got to the door and realized he only had three ghadi with him, he looked back in time to see Jane holding a knife, crouched over the fallen man. The blade was dark and glistened in the firelight leaking from the other houses.

Nate swallowed.

I didn't want to kill anyone. . . .

That wasn't only bullshit, it was dangerous bullshit. But seeing her crouch over a corpse made Nate feel a little sick.

Nate turned his attention to the door. It was held shut with a heavy latch from the outside, but there wasn't any lock. Nate lifted the latch and opened the door.

The smell hit him first. The fetid odor rolled out of the open door in a cloud so strong it was almost visible. Filth and shit and death. Blinking through watering eyes, Nate saw the outlines of dozens of naked ghadi packed together in the gloom. More than could have come from Jane's village, the people here had been collecting ghadi for a while.

The ghadi all stared at him.

Nate stepped back and let Bill and the Steves enter. They didn't show shock, or disgust, or much of anything. They just took the arms of the prisoners and led them outside.

Nate was relegated to watching as his ghadi somehow indicated to the prisoners that they were to sneak back to the cover of the jungle. In a few moments there was a ragged file of naked ghadi making a crouching retreat toward the trees. There were more of them than Nate imagined. Easily over a hundred. The slave house was long and seemingly endless.

For about ten minutes, it seemed as if they were going to get to slip away without anyone noticing them. Then, with about two thirds of the prisoners out of the slave house, a magnesium glow filled the sky above them. The entire town was suddenly lit brighter than daylight, carving Nate's shadow as black as the void in the clearing.

Nate turned toward the other buildings and saw about a dozen armed men, centered around a robed figure wearing the mask of a red, howling skull. The masked figure had his arms raised, and his companions did not look happy.

Chapter Forty-two

R ED SKULL SHOUTED something, and the men started running toward the escaping ghadi. Then Skull started gesturing in what must have been another spell.

Things were happening too fast; the armed men were already circling around, blocking the ghadi's exit toward the jungle. When Skull finished his invocation, Nate felt the footing go soft beneath his feet. Between him and the advancing men, the escaping ghadi fell down as the clearing they ran through became a swamp of mud.

Skull had hit some sort of stride; he was already onto something else, just as Nate gathered his wits enough to respond. Skull had to go, and there was no time to reach the bastard, especially now that he stood calf-deep in mud. No time to pull out his notes. That left the spells he had actually memorized. The candle-snuffing spell would take too long, and only worked at all because of the element of surprise.

But the candle-lighting spell . . .

He hadn't tried using a vector as a target with this one, but if it worked for the snuffing spell—

Nate didn't have time to debate with himself. As soon as he had the concept in mind, he launched into the spell. Instead of naming a target, he slipped in a vector pointing from him to Skull.

Skull finished his incantation first, and Nate could feel the mud around his ankles freeze solid. They were all immobilized in front of their attackers. The men had reached the first ghadi and started clubbing them.

Nate finished his spell.

Not only did the spell respond in a logical manner to Nate's impromptu hacking, his aim was dead-on. Red Skull's robes caught fire. There was a sudden, keening scream that cut through the chaos. The attackers turned to see Skull trying to bat out the flames with his voluminous sleeves. All that did was ignite the sleeves.

Nate aimed a similar spell down toward his own feet. No flame, but there was a small puff of steam, and the ice weakened enough for him to pull his feet free.

At this point the human attackers realized that one of the ghadi wasn't actually a ghadi. They ignored the immobile escapees and started heading straight for Nate. Nate took the only escape route he could think of, and darted into the slave house.

That turned out to be a tactical blunder. Nate tripped in the muck that lined the bottom of the slave house and rolled into the wall. He had a brief view of the score of ghadi who still remained before his pursuers slammed the door shut and latched it.

"Fuck!" Nate pushed himself up and ran to one of the tiny barred windows. He reached it in time to see one of the men club Jane to the ground. He kept clubbing her. She couldn't fall over completely, because her legs were still frozen in the ground.

Okay, you bastards, you want it?

Nate pulled out his glowing rock and the notes he had taken with him. On top was the wind spell.

Magnitude seems to be on a logarithmic scale, let's see how high the fucker can go.

Nate chanted, pointing the largest acceleration vector he could manage, from the jungle, through the men, right at the town. Again, he felt the surrounding ghadi feeding him the strength to speak the runes. He needed the strength because the modified spell seemed harder to slog through than summoning Ghad

had been. The air itself filled with an awful anticipation as he chanted. It was as if he had to drag his brain through the icy mud outside.

Then he was finished.

The slave house shook. Outside the air roared like a freight train.

Was this a good idea?

Out the small barred window, Nate saw foliage and parts of trees tear by in the sudden wind. One of the men tried grabbing a fence post, but lost his grip, tumbling down toward the other buildings. One of the doors from the stable tore free and sailed by the window.

The violence was momentary, and Nate already knew what he needed to do next. He stuck his fingers in the muck of the floor, and smeared a runic name on the door of the slave house.

He found the sound spell and replaced the air symbol with the name he had given the door. Then he chanted up the most violent high-frequency vibration he could manage.

The door vibrated, shaking loose dust and splinters. Nails shook themselves free, and the hinges whined as if they were in pain. A cloud of dirt billowed up from the ground. After a moment, the vibration subsided. Nate walked up and pushed.

The door fell into several fragments on the ground in front of him. Nate stepped outside. The ghadi had all collapsed on the ground as well as they could with legs frozen into the ground. With their extra leg joint they managed it better than a human could. The humans, most of them anyway, were getting to their feet about a hundred feet away. Debris and foliage was everywhere.

Nate walked out, between the ghadi and the men, and called out, "Drop your weapons and leave this place!" Nate hoped that his grasp of the language was still good enough to get his point across.

One of them shouted up at Nate, "That is the property of the College!"

"Let the College take them, then!" Nate unfolded the page with the lightning spell on it. "Leave or be destroyed."

Nate could tell that they were debating it. These guys were just grunts. The only person who probably had a deep investment in the captive ghadi was Skull, and the last Nate had seen of that guy, he was on fire and running toward the shoreline.

Nate decided to make a show of force. He cast a lightning bolt about two thirds of the way toward the men. The blast knocked the men down again, and it still dazzled and half deafened Nate, even though he was expecting it.

That had the desired effect. The men ran for it.

• • •

Nate escorted a hundred and twenty-five ghadi back into the jungle. Nate followed at the rear of the migration, to provide some sort of defense if they were followed. They weren't, at least not closely enough for Nate to see any pursuit.

A hundred and twenty-five. That didn't include Jane, one of the Steves, and about ten other ghadi who had been killed in the fight. To Nate's relief, Bill was one of the survivors.

He let Bill lead the ghadi, since Nate had only the vaguest idea of how to get back to the village. Fortunately, Nate was the only one who didn't know how to live off of the jungle. Everyone they had freed had lived out here all their lives. They were also a lot better about not leaving an obvious trail than their human counterparts.

I wish I could talk to them. . . .

It was disturbing, being in the midst of such a crowd and not being able to have a conversation. The isolation was made worse because all of them seemed to look at him as a religious icon, not a human being.

Though it probably was a good thing not to be seen as a human being with this crowd.

It seemed to take a lot longer on the way back.

Nate understood. Not only did they have a lot more people, but Bill was trying to take them by a less direct route, in case they were being tracked.

When they finally reached the village, it felt as if Nate had been gone for years. It was a triumphant homecoming. He walked into the village, and the ghadi genuflected. Even the ghadi he had rescued, seeing the reaction of the villagers, did likewise.

Nate walked slowly up to the pit and turned around. He looked at the ghadi and sighed. "I'm going to figure out something to lift that language block, just so I can tell you to cut it out."

As Nate stood there, wondering what to do, Bill came from the crowd and stood in front of him. Bill moved from side to side, bobbing and moving his arms, and it wasn't until he stomped his feet and clapped in a gesture that recalled a thunderclap that it sank in that Bill had taken on the job of disciple. Bill was preaching the good word to the masses.

Another reason he needed to overcome this linguistic barrier.

• • •

The village was now three times its original size. About half the new ghadi were working on building new huts for the expanded population. Nate found himself back in his office, finding a new urgency in his studies. He knew it was only a matter of time before the College caught up with him now. He needed to be ready.

The ghadi needed to be ready.

He didn't know how he would manage it, but he knew that the answer was in the tablets. He sped through them now. Transcribing two or three a day, desperately wrapping his mind around the shapes of the runes. Picking apart pieces of the Gods' Language.

He discovered measures that specified time; he found symbols that represented living objects and—to all appearances—elemental matter; he found symbols that were analogous to control structures in the computer languages Nate knew; he found loops, and branches and comparisons that could form decision trees. So there were spells that could react differently depending on what type of matter they were targeted at.

He found segments of spell code that could "read" other parts of other spells, and parts that could actually "write" the Gods' Language—or anything else. It took a couple of hours before the significance of that began to sink in.

Holy shit . . . !

At its heart, you only needed three things for a completely functional computer language. You needed to be able to call other programs from within the main process—call them subroutines, system calls, user functions, classes, or objects. You needed a control structure that could make a simple decision to do one thing if a condition was true, and another if a condition was false. Lastly, the program needed some way to store and retrieve data, be it a register, a variable, or a file system. . . .

The Gods' Language had all the necessary elements.

It wasn't *like* a computer language, it *was* a computer language. The only difference was the hardware. He was looking at the code that was running on the universe. . . .

For a few minutes he had a brief sophistic panic that everything he was going through here was actually some sort of sadistically realistic computer game.

But if it was, did it matter? If you created something indistinguishable from reality—wasn't that just a way of saying you created a new reality? What if what Ghad did was create some universe-making machine, and allowed his creations access to the source code?

To create something as "there" as the world around him, to create a world where the wind bit his cheek, where he could smell the woodsmoke of the ghadi cook fires, where he could touch the damp moss under his hand, had to actually be "there." The only thing that had as much bandwidth as reality *was* reality.

Nate sat in the little clearing of his office and looked at the sky. Blue shone through a few openings in the canopy. The dense foliage rustled in the wind, and he could hear a few hooting birds in the distance.

"Worrying that the world is some cosmic video game makes as much sense here as it did back home."

Maybe that was all life was; God's own first-person-shooter. Accepting or denying the proposition made absolutely zero difference.

Nate looked down and took out a fresh piece of note paper and started working on some of the more practical consequences of unraveling the Gods' Programming Language.

Chapter Forty-Three

NATE HAD RENAMED the Gods' Language "MED." MED stood for Mechanica Ex Deus, which was probably butchered Latin but got the sense of it. Somehow he felt more at home working on something that was an acronym. And, even with a still limited knowledge of MED, after a few days of intense twenty-hour shifts, Nate authored the first completely new spell that had been written in millennia.

The logic of it was simple, though the execution covered several pages. He authored it first in his hexadecimal pseudocode, and spent two days mentally debugging it, running it through every permutation he could think of. When he was satisfied, he wrote the actual runes, which was akin to running a marathon, pushing through the inscription, rune after rune.

When it was done, he had a spell five pages long, consisting only of elements he had learned so far. The vocabulary was a crippled subset of MED, consisting only of around three hundred symbols, but people had programmed entire operating systems on eight-bit machines with less to work with.

When Nate looked up from the freshly written spell, the light had gone from the sky and he was alone. The only light came from his miraculously glowing rock. Fatigue sank into Nate's bones after writing so much of the language at once. His body could collapse and sleep for a week right where he sat.

He couldn't do that yet.

He took a sip of tea. All that was left was ice-cold dregs. He swallowed them and set down the new spell.

He had to test it.

He stood up. The long muscles in his legs ached and his left foot had fallen asleep. He limped around the clearing gathering the two things he needed. One of the golden tablets he had transcribed before; he chose the wind spell as fairly innocuous. He also found a blank sheet of paper. On the paper, Nate brushed in, very small, a runic name to allow it as a target. The spell on the tablet was already named.

Nate weighted down the blank paper and set the tablet next to it. Then he pulled out his five-page spell and proceeded to cast it. Fortunately, in his fatigued state, he didn't have to cast all five pages of the spell. It was designed to be cast by its name by another spell. The other spell was very simple, only a couple of lines long, and all it did was feed the names of the spell and the paper to the long five-page spell. It was short enough that Nate could change the targets on the fly.

It was still difficult to cast. It made Nate realize how much support the ghadi were, how much energy they provided just by being present. Fortunately, long and complicated as the new spell was, what it did was a fairly low-energy process. It wasn't beyond his ability to cast.

When he was done, he looked down at the paper.

"Yes!"

He was Azrael again, right after hacking root access to the Social Security Administration's web server. . . .

The spell did exactly what it was supposed to do. As Nate watched, hexadecimal code wrote itself across the surface of the page. In a few moments he had a perfect pseudo code translation of the wind spell.

Nate held up the paper and laughed. Not only had he just come up with a way to copy all the gold tablet source code he had access to, in a fraction of the time, but with the spell he had just written, he could reverse the process. The five pages of runes he had just com-

pleted would be the last time he had to write MED
by hand.

• • •

The next day, Nate discovered that what he had
created had broader uses. The I/O of the spell was
infinitely more flexible than any computer language.
Just by changing the target for the "translation," he
could have it transcribed into a rock, a tree, or in
midair. The source could be anything, not just the
name of the spell. In many cases he discovered he
could use it to unearth the "name" of something. Nate
used vectors to point it at a tree, a stone, the air, a
blank piece of paper.

In each case he got a string of symbols he could use
to target that tree, that stone, that piece of paper.

When he used it to read from Bill, he got one hell
of a surprise.

Instead of a runic "name" that could refer to Bill
the ghadi, Nate got a seemingly endless stream of figures. Writing to the air in front of Nate, pages and
pages of pseudocode shot by in front of him.

What the . . . ?

How did the ghadi fall in the first place?

*The men of the College said, "Long have we studied
the Language of the Gods. We have learned much.
There are words in it too terrible to be spoken."*

*"Please," said the men of Manhome, "speak them
so we shall be delivered."*

*The men of the College, seeing their own doom ap-
proaching, chose to speak the most terrible of those
words.*

*Upon hearing those words, the bodies of the ghadi,
and their seed, went deaf to the Gods' Language.*

Somehow, an aeon ago, the College cursed the ghadi
with some form of aphasia. A curse that propagated
through generations. Nate had assumed, if the story was
true, that the ancient College of Man had inflicted some
sort of congenital brain damage on the ghadi.

But what if what caused it was the spell itself? Some constant, self-replicating bit of code in MED . . .
Then it could be reversible.

• • •

That was the day the College caught up with him.

The warning came from a trio of ghadi running in from the surrounding jungle. For a culture without a spoken language, they got their message across within seconds. By the time Nate realized that there was something going on, ghadi were already evacuating the village.

Nate picked up his papers, and retreated to the edge of the village, finding cover in the surrounding jungle. He found a place behind the mossy root system of a massive tree and watched. He didn't have long to wait.

Nate heard them coming ten minutes before he saw the first soldier. The soldier he saw was dressed like the ones he had seen outside Arthiz's Shadow College. In fact, it could have been the same guys.

Unhurried and deliberate, the soldiers marched into the village. With them came over a dozen masked, robed acolytes.

Shit . . .

They lost no time. Once they had walked into the village, the huts began to explode. Nate didn't know what the mages were doing, but it was blowing the carefully woven huts apart in clouds of reeds and splinters. When some slow-moving ghadi were flushed out by a hut's disintegration, archers in the small army cut them down.

It was clear that this group of men weren't interested in prisoners.

Nate scrambled, looking through the notes he had with him. He had the transcription spell he had been experimenting with, and nothing else actually functional.

Christ, this was why they carved the spells in their

skin; otherwise someone could catch them with their pants down.

Another three huts exploded, and three more elderly ghadi fell with arrows through their chests. Half the village was gone.

Carved into the skin . . .

With one simple change, Nate suddenly realized he could copy a spell without any "translation" at all. And if he could copy a spell—

Nate cast the translator to read from the mage that seemed to be doing the most damage. The rest of the village was being blown to pieces, but the acolytes were fortunately fairly stationary, allowing Nate to point a vector right at the mage he wanted.

Above him, runes carved themselves into the body of the tree. Lines snaked around the bark as if they were a living thing. Nate watched, as all the spells carved into the mage's body were copied in wooden flesh. Nate stared into the remains of the village, trying to gather a clue to the spell from the mage's gestures. The tracing of the runes in air showed what the spell was named.

Nate couldn't see much at this distance, but he did see a stroke of three parallel downward lines.

Nate quickly tried to find that character in the name of one of these spells. He found it, just as the last building fell to pieces.

With the village in ruins around them, the soldiers started marching outward, in a ring toward the surrounding jungle. The mages started casting other spells, and Nate could see the ground cover wither, and the canopy disintegrate. The mages were deconstructing the jungle, taking away the ghadi's hiding places.

Not to mention Nate's. His tree was only about twenty feet in from the edge, and the plants were turning brown and yellow around him. The soldiers were only ten or fifteen yards away and heading straight for him.

By the time he saw how the spell was targeted, he

was already casting it at the center of the group of mages.

There was a satisfying explosion, throwing mages everywhere. The soldiers stopped their advance and Nate cast the spell at the soldier immediately in front of him.

The man's chest burst open, through his breastplate, and he collapsed with a puzzled expression on his face.

As if they'd been waiting for a cue, the jungle suddenly vomited a hundred pissed-off ghadi. The soldiers were caught completely off-guard. The ghadi were armed only with clubs and stones to the humans' bows and swords, but the humans were outnumbered three to one.

Within the first ten seconds that ratio was five to one.

Nate concentrated on keeping the mages from being a factor. Two more explosions, and none of them were moving.

In five minutes, he was the only human standing.

CHAPTER FORTY-FOUR

THE GHADI LOOTED the bodies and took to the jungle. Human armor and weapons looked odd on their elongated forms, but Nate could see the echoes of ancient ghadi warriors in them. For once, Nate could see that the same blood flowed in these veins, that these ghadi were ready to take their place next to the ghadi elders in the tombs under Manhome.

They left the gold tablets, as Nate had found them, in a chest, buried in the pit under the ghadi dead. He didn't need them anymore. The ancient ghadi primers had been etched into the pages of an old book, replacing the mundane text that had once graced its pages. Also in the book were copies of what the mages had carried on their own bodies.

The human bodies ended up in a ravine.

Many times, Nate wanted to talk, to devise some sort of strategy. But all he had was the ability to do broad gestures to get very simple things across. It seemed, at times, that the ghadi weren't quite in the same world that Nate was in. So he did what he could, and followed.

The ghadi, at least, seemed to have some clue what they were doing. When this human expedition was missed, there would be more. The College wouldn't allow what amounted to a ghadi insurrection.

Nate stayed with Bill and the cadre of ghadi who had salvaged the soldiers' armor and weapons. The other ghadi dispersed, fading into the jungle in all directions.

For the best, Nate thought. *We shouldn't drag everyone into a war. Especially when the College is probably looking for me.*

Bill's commandos marched north, toward the mountains. Away from the ocean and, Nate suspected, away from the bulk of humanity. They moved fast, and Nate hoped that he wasn't slowing them down. The pace was hard and, when they stopped, Nate only had the energy to eat what food Bill gave him, and sleep.

In his sleep, Nate dreamed of empty blackness, filled with a slithering alien thing. The thing was everywhere, and it was laughing.

As they moved north, the jungle fell away. The land became drier, the nights became colder, and the plant life became more temperate. By the time Nate saw patches of snow between the trees, they had reached their destination.

A tower of white stone emerged from the ground. Cylindrical and slightly tapered, it spiraled up about a hundred feet. The top was jagged and broken, and the visible mountainside was scattered with white stone, showing that the ruin had once been much taller.

Bill walked around the perimeter of the structure, which was almost as wide as it was tall, until he came to a large stone panel. He stopped and waved Nate over.

The slab was covered in the runes of the Gods' Language.

"Let me guess. You locked your keys inside."

Bill looked at Nate, waiting.

"Sure, sure . . ." He gestured at Bill. "I'll think of something."

Bill seemed satisfied and walked over to the other ghadi, gesturing more elaborately. Soon the contingent had broken up into small groups to gather food, firewood, and water.

Nate studied the door. The first thing he did was cast the translation spell to copy a pseudocode version of the spell on a nearby rock so he could study it without getting a headache or casting something by accident.

It was good that he didn't just try casting it. While he didn't understand all the spell code, he could decipher enough to see that if someone didn't invoke this with the correct password, something bad would happen involving a lot of heat. He also saw something that appeared to be some sort of delayed conditional clause.

If he understood it right, the same bad thing was supposed to happen if someone tried to physically move this doorway, either by force or by another spell. Like a booby trap or a trip wire. This was his first hint that a spell could have a persistent effect like that.

Then again, while he had transcribed all the ghadi primer tablets, he had only studied the first dozen or so. This concept was probably buried somewhere in the advanced tutorials.

The important thing was he needed the password to open this door.

Nate looked at the door and smiled, "I've hacked into better secured sites than this."

The password protection was actually so simple, Nate wondered that the builders of this thing could possibly imagine it was adequate. The password wasn't hard-coded into the spell itself—that would be almost as weak as leaving the door open. However, what the builders used wasn't much better. The spell referred back to a name carved inside the tower somewhere. And since the spell contained the reference to the place where the password was stored, it was easy for Nate to use his translator spell to pull a transcription of the password.

After parsing the code mentally a few times to make sure he didn't miss anything, Nate cast the spell, password and all.

The slab door slid aside reluctantly, as if chastised at being so easily circumvented.

Bill walked up, looked at the open door, then turned to Nate and gave a bow that was almost a genuflection.

"Yeah, right. So what is this place?"

Bill led him inside.

•   •   •

Walking inside, Bill seemed subdued, even for a ghadi. Even the air was still and quiet, and very cold. It seemed if the atmosphere in this place was fifteen or twenty degrees colder than it was outside in the sun. Nate's breath fogged in front of him.

The air tasted of something very old.

The room they entered first was obviously not the main entrance. It was small and oddly proportioned, barely ten feet square and twice that high. The ceiling wasn't flat, but had an uneven shadowed surface as if he was looking up into the base of a flying buttress. There wasn't much more to see in the light that came in from the doorway. Just two corridors hugging the walls to the left and right, curving into shadow. Bill gestured to the corridor to the right.

"Whatever you say." Nate pulled his glowing stone from the pouch where he carried it and walked toward the corridor, unwrapping it. The light revealed an arched hallway that followed the outer wall of the tower, sloping gently upward.

Nate walked up the corridor, passing columns and ghadi statuary. The ruin was eerily intact. There seemed to be very little damage from whatever disaster had blown the top off this tower. He stopped and studied one of the walls.

Embedded in it, he found a stone carved with an inscription similar to the one borne on the stone he carried. Bill waited patiently while Nate deciphered the code. It was clear that somewhere there was a trigger, but like the entrance, it was a simple enough bit of code that Nate felt comfortable hacking it. He spoke an impromptu incantation, and when he was done, whispered, "Let there be light."

All up and down the corridor, stones set into the wall released their light. If Nate startled Bill, the ghadi gave no sign of it.

Nate wrapped his own stone and replaced it in its pouch.

Ironically, in the light, the corridor was even more eerie. Despite a layer of dust, and a few cracked stones, it looked *too* perfect. It looked as if the builders had just left and would return at any moment.

Ahead, beyond the curve, Nate could see the light get brighter, whiter. He gestured to Bill and resumed the trek upward.

The brightness came from the exit, where the corridor opened out into a balcony inside the building. Nate stepped out onto it and had to catch his breath.

Above them, for fifty or seventy-five feet, buttresses came from the walls to meet in the center of a domed ceiling that was nearly the diameter of the tower that contained it. Each stone that formed the ceiling glowed with its own light, shining down onto a gallery of stone benches. The benches formed concentric circles around a central dais dominated by a large altar or podium. The walls carried frescoes thirty feet high, bearing ghadi figures that dwarfed the two of them.

"What is this place?" Nate asked in a puff of fog.

The balcony where Nate stood was even with the highest rank of benches, and he walked around until he found the steps down to the dais floor. He walked down to the dais, and when he looked back, he saw that several other ghadi had followed him and Bill into the building.

Nate climbed up on the dais to get a better view.

It was like the circles the ghadi put around their death pits. But this was much bigger. This room could easily hold a thousand, maybe more. Nate turned around and looked at the place from all angles.

There were ten separate entrances like the one he

had come through. Nate could picture several layers of corridors winding up through the walls like coiled ropes. One entrance was grander than the others, and it directly faced a wide ramp that led down to the dais.

Nate faced that direction and saw the frescoes of ancient ghadi kneeling and making offerings toward the space where the large entrance was. Nate turned and studied the frescoes. Group scenes, many ghadi facing some central figure. This time the central figure wasn't some alien pan-dimensional monster, but another ghadi.

This was their government.

Nate was sure that, where he stood, once stood a ghadi mayor, or baron, or king . . .

"Why come here?" Nate asked quietly.

He looked up and saw that the whole party had come here now. Fifteen ghadi in human armor, looking down on the dais where Nate stood.

Why do you think we came here?

CHAPTER FORTY-FIVE

ABAD KARRIK had been a scholar within the College of Man for many more years than he cared to recall. As he stood on one of the high balconies of the College in the center of Manhome, he felt the full weight of his years. The world around him had upended, and he could feel the established order of centuries eroding beneath his feet.

Never had any temporal power challenged the College in such a brazen and open manner. And never had the College taken measures so severe. In Manhome, tomes of knowledge had been opened that had remained sealed since its founding. Now the shores around the College's great city were red with the blood from the Monarch's army, and the air ripe with the smell of their bloated bodies. Even where Karrik stood, high above everything, the air smelled of death.

Below him, the streets were nearly empty. Those who could flee had done so long ago. Those who remained stayed inside. The mood was one of terror barely kept in check. Those outside the College feared the College, as they should.

Those in the College feared other things.

The Venerable Master Scholar now saw the machinations of the Monarch in smoke and fire, and in the way the waves crashed against the base of Manhome itself. The defection of Uthar Vailen had disintegrated the remaining bonds of respect and trust at the highest levels of the College, leaving only fear and suspicion. Heretics and traitors were everywhere now.

Since the fall of Zorion, the College had imprisoned three hundred "traitors." Dozens from within its own ranks. Far too many to even make a pretense of any investigation.

"What is left?" He stared out at a pillar of smoke where someone was probably disposing of bodies.

"You are left, Karrik, my friend."

Karrik spun around to find the speaker and saw nothing. He called in a harsh whisper. "Friend?" He shook his head violently. "You call me friend when just speaking to you could cost my life?"

The wind responded in a familiar oily tone, *"You exaggerate, and I have no interest in seeing you feed the maw of the Venerable Master Scholar's justice."*

"Begone! I will strike no deals with you or Ghad."

"I ask nothing of you but time."

"Uthar Vailen is no name I wish tied to my own."

"Very well. If your faith is so much in the College, we will speak no more."

Karrik nodded slowly and turned back toward Manhome. Looking down at the empty streets, he saw a body being picked apart by sea birds. He couldn't tell if it had been a scholar of the College, a soldier of the Monarch's army, or some innocent bystander.

"Wait," Karrik whispered, half expecting Uthar Vailen to have abandoned him.

He hadn't.

●   ●   ●

When Uthar left his tent, the Monarch was upon him. "What news? What news?"

The person who, until the fall of Zorion, had been the most powerful man outside the College, reminded Uthar of nothing less than some orphan beggar accosting him for some sweetmeat. Having demonstrated his worthlessness as a person, Uthar was beginning to doubt the man's value as a symbol.

Not yet. There is the loyalty of Ehrid's men to consider. Still five days to travel.

"Perhaps it will please you to know that the College yet weakens itself, even as it counts its victory in Zorion."

"Yes, we can regroup for a counterattack."

Uthar stared up at the sky, which was beginning to darken. He wondered if the gods might be so offended at this man's stupidity that they might strike him dead on the spot.

It seemed, though, that the gods hated Uthar more, and the Monarch remained alive.

"We shall take Manhome, but we shall do so by taking the College."

"How, then?"

If I knew this, I would be in Manhome and you would be in an unmarked grave.

"The Angel of Death seems to have not yet outlived his usefulness." Uthar told the Monarch, leaving the Ruler of Man confused and unenlightened.

• • •

When Yerith walked into Arthiz's tent, the scholar was bent over a map. She didn't know what all the notations were, but she recognized the great arc of the continent, a crescent with a mountainous spine. Near the western tip would be Manhome, and east of that, along the inner curve would be Zorion. Somewhere, between the two cities, and between the mountains and the ocean, was the place they were camped right now.

Arthiz looked up at her and smiled. It was disturbing to see a scholar unmasked, more so to see such an expression wrapped in scarred flesh. She looked down at the map again.

"Thank you for coming," he said. He spoke as if it was really a choice on her part.

"I serve at the Monarch's pleasure." It was impossible to keep the words from feeling hollow. She had seen the Monarch, and heard him. Now she knew she had been serving little more than another mask.

If Arthiz sensed what she felt, he didn't comment on it. Instead, he turned toward the map on the table before him. "Can you read this map?"

"I can see Manhome and Zorion."

Arthiz nodded. "This is where we are headed." He pointed to a cryptic notation next to a small town that sat in the foothills perhaps a day's travel north of Manhome.

Looking at the map, Yerith saw some of the other notes and decided that one set, midway between the two cities, showed their location, and another cluster of marks showed the forces of the College around Zorion.

But there were other marks, farther east of Zorion on the coast, and north of Zorion, in the jungle between Zorion and the mountains. Both marks were close to the fringes of human settlement. "What is over here?" she asked.

Arthiz chuckled. "The subject of our conversation, Nate Black."

He seemed to be pronouncing the name better.

It took a moment for Yerith to gather herself enough to respond. "He escaped?"

"Yes, he escaped. And while we've been cautiously moving, avoiding notice, he has been brazenly doing his best to terrify the scholars of the College." Arthiz tapped the markings on the coast. "A small merchant village. Our pale stranger led the release of over a hundred ghadi."

"Ghadi?" Yerith looked up, shaking her head.

Arthiz tapped the other markings, north of Zorion. "Here, there was a detachment of troops led by fifteen scholars of the College."

"Fifteen?"

"You, of all people, can understand that the revolt of the ghadi is infinitely more terrifying to the College than the revolt of any man. They took a force strong enough to slaughter anything they found. They found the ghadi village where our stranger was hiding and reduced it to ashes."

Yerith felt her heart sink. Nate Black had not escaped the College after all.

Or had he? Arthiz was chuckling quietly.

"What happened?" Yerith asked.

"I cannot be certain, since not one of the College's force survived to tell anyone."

"What?"

"Nate Black, and about a hundred wild ghadi, decimated a squad of the College's best troops, and defeated fifteen scholars trained in the art of combat."

Yerith stared at the map.

"I want to talk to you about Nate Black," Arthiz said.

•　•　•

"We needed to isolate your creature from our students." Osif frowned, staring into a small lamp that was the only source of light in the tent. "It was a dangerous distraction."

"You did well keeping it." Uthar sat on a cushion by the door, alert to eavesdroppers. "You followed a prudent course. I was not criticizing you or Bhodan."

"What do you want, then?"

"I want to understand the heresy the stranger was engaged in."

Osif nodded. "This was your interest in it all along, wasn't it?"

"Yes. If the scholars believe rightly, that stranger held devastating knowledge. Knowledge that might threaten the College itself."

Osif shook his head. "If this is the Angel spoken of in stories, it did not arrive with that kind of knowledge. It told us that it was trying to understand the Gods' Language."

"Understand?"

"It wanted to know what the runes themselves meant."

Some of the rumors that Karrik had related, about a ghadi uprising, and the specter of the Angel of Death in their midst, made more sense now.

"In your opinion," Uthar asked, "how advanced was the stranger in the studies?"

"It showed none of the discipline or aptitude of an acolyte. But it was still adept. It learned to invoke the spells of a first-year student in less than a sixday. Quickly enough to be frightening, but I saw nothing that showed more than a particularly promising acolyte."

"Nothing?"

Osif frowned and looked a little unsure. "When it said, 'Understand the Gods' Language,' I felt that it might actually be able to."

CHAPTER FORTY-SIX

SHORTLY after Nate arrived at the tower, the ghadi began to arrive. The first day, Nate didn't even notice the two or three ghadi that joined Bill's little band. But the next day, Nate saw that half the ghadi were going around unarmored.

They arrived in small groups, by twos and threes, more each day. Some even carried human armor and weapons about whose origin Nate had no way of asking. When he walked among them, the ghadi lowered their heads, and the ones who caught glimpses of him had expressions of reverence and awe.

You poor bastards, if you only knew. . . .

Within a week, a village huddled around the base of the tower. And the ghadi kept coming. Nate looked on the mass of them and wondered what it was he was supposed to do. All the ghadi, *all* of them, seemed to be massing on this one spot. As frantically as he gestured at Bill, he couldn't get the concept, *bad idea,* across to him.

Nate knew that the College wouldn't leave things with the massacre at Bill's village. This time, if the College had any sense, it would be massing an army. And they were just giving the College a centralized target. Nate might have the rudiments of spell-casting now, but even the last confrontation had been pushing his luck more than it should be pushed.

They needed some sort of defense, at the very least. Fortunately, by gesturing and sketching in the dirt,

Nate got the concept of *wall,* and *trench* across to Bill, and within another week, trees were falling in the surrounding forest, and logs were being raised around the perimeter of the new ghadi city.

Soon, groups of ghadi walked the streets with long wooden spears with stone tips. The tips, made from fragments of the fallen tower, glinted white in the sunlight. It was as if Nate was watching an ancestral memory made flesh. Huts of sod and twigs grew up on the hillside, and it seemed as if they grew out of the foundations of some great buried city. The shadows of the ancient, long-fallen Ghadikan, seemed just visible, following the ghadi down the ancient buried causeways that led to the tower.

One day, we will be able to talk. . . .

Nate split his days now. Half the day he worked on the defenses, copying the spells he'd found protecting the doors of the tower, setting them to defend the logs that walled the new city. The other half he spent studying the spell he had found living within the ghadi themselves.

He began to think that if he had a little more time, they might be able to defend this keep.

It was time he didn't have.

• • •

It was long after nightfall, and Nate was in one of the upper rooms of the tower, hunched over the ghadi spell, trying to reverse engineer it. He was pounding his leg in frustration.

Something whispered in the room with him.

"The College is right to be dismayed."

Nate jumped to his feet, spinning around, looking for the speaker. No one. Just cold stone walls . . .

"Who's there?"

"It would do for you to speak in a manner that is mutually understood."

Nate realized that he had been speaking English. It took a moment for the words to come. *"Who's there?"*

"One you know, a friend."

It was hard to recognize the whispering voice. More so since it had been so long since he had heard it.

"Arthiz?"

"Yes. It has taken long for me to find you."

"Where are you?"

"Far enough that only my voice can reach you at the moment."

Nate shook his head, backing toward the wall. He expected an ambush any second. "Why are you talking to me?"

"Stand alone with the ghadi and you will be doomed."

"What choice do I have? The ghadi are all that will stand with me."

"Join me."

"What are you asking?"

"The force you saw destroy the Shadow College, the same force that deposed the Monarch's rule in Zorion, is turning toward your citadel. They only wait to regather their strength. They mean to erase all ghadi resistance for all time. They mean to burn you on a pyre of your own heresy."

"You mean me to abandon the ghadi to that?"

"The heart of Manhome is weakened and barely defended. Grant me your aid and the College itself will crumble. Without the head, the body cannot strike."

"How can I trust you?"

"Do not deliberate too long. The army masses even now."

"Arthiz?" Nate said to the air.

There was no answer.

"Arthiz!" Nate shouted to the empty air.

The room suddenly felt much colder.

• • •

The next day brought Arthiz's envoy. The ghadi stopped a rider coming from the west. Bill grabbed Nate and brought him to the great auditorium to meet the stranger.

The stranger wasn't as strange as Nate had expected.

Nate walked down toward the dais, where a robed figure was guarded by three large ghadi. "Who are you, and why have you come here?"

The figure turned and lowered her hood. Nate stopped, disbelieving.

"Yerith?"

She nodded. "Yes."

"Arthiz sent you?"

"Who should he have sent?"

•   •   •

It took some gesturing to get the ghadi to understand that Yerith was not the enemy. After he got that across, they left Yerith to his care. Nate took her up to the room he used for an office. He cleared some papers off a stool for her and sat down himself.

"Be careful. The furniture here is very old."

Yerith took her seat and looked at him. "You have done this all yourself?"

Nate laughed. "In case you didn't notice, there's about five thousand ghadi down there."

"You control them?"

"If I controlled them, this place wouldn't exist. They gather of their own accord. More every day."

Yerith looked into his face. "You are the Angel of Death."

"Bullshit," Nate said in English. "If the ghadi rebel against the College, it isn't any more than their due. Their slavers burn their homes, steal the children, and slaughter any ghadi too old to be used."

"I know how the ghadi are treated."

Nate rubbed his forehead. "Why are you here, then?"

"The College's armies are gathering. Within a six-day, they will march north; a sixday's march after that, and they will destroy this place."

"So I've been told."

"Come back with me, help Arthiz take the College, and their army will crumble."

"I can't leave them. They massed here because of me."

"They'll die here because of you."

Nate stood up, shaking his head. "They think that somehow I can save them."

"You can."

"Do you think that Arthiz can really take down the College?"

"I think you can."

• • •

If there was going to be a war with the College, Arthiz's proposal made too much sense. The two victories he and the ghadi had won so far had been based entirely on stealth and surprise. With only Nate on their side, they stood little chance against an actual army that included seasoned soldiers and mages prepared to find resistance. Even if the ghadi weren't outnumbered, they weren't soldiers, and couldn't communicate across a battlefield.

Nate knew nothing about warfare outside some novels he'd read, but he could see a massacre coming. If Arthiz could cut into the enemy's rear and do some damage, maybe the attack on the ghadi could be diverted or maybe even aborted.

So he gathered his important papers, and his book of MED code, and left with Yerith.

The ghadi watched him go, without knowing why. Nate had no way to tell them, and the fear in their eyes made him feel sick.

Ghad protect your people. . . .

Yerith packed his papers into the saddlebags on her horse and looked at him.

"What?"

"Get on."

Nate looked at the arcane structure of the saddle and shook his head. "How?"

In exasperation, Yerith helped him up on the

horse's back. Nate felt a wave of vertigo as his leg vaulted over the saddle. The fact that the horse was moving, ever so slightly, made his brain scream at him that he was going to fall. Before he even had the chance to get oriented, Yerith suddenly appeared in the saddle in front of him, vaulting out of nowhere.

"Hang on to me, and don't fall off."

Then they were moving, Nate clutching Yerith's waist so hard that his fingers went numb.

The horse galloped, paralleling the mountains, on a trail only it and Yerith seemed to see. For ten minutes Nate watched trees throw themselves at them, branches swinging down in an attempt to decapitate the riders, before he screwed his eyes shut and buried his face in Yerith's back.

She asked him questions at one point or another, but all Nate could manage was a grunt or two.

The horse had an endurance that was literally supernatural. The few times they stopped to rest, Nate could see that the reins, bit, saddle—everything on the horse, in fact—was marked in the MED language. Among other things, the charms seemed to grant the beast an inexhaustible supply of energy with minimal food and water.

It didn't grant the same benefits to the riders.

When they stopped their breakneck gallop to rest, Nate discovered that stopping was more painful than hanging on. Cramps tore though his legs, an invisible fist squeezing the muscles and attempting to tear them from the bones. He began wondering if this expedition was worth it.

• • •

They somehow compressed a ten-day ride into three.

On the third day their pace slowed enough that Nate could—albeit painfully—straighten up and look around.

They approached a village, surrounded by farms. They passed small thatched cottages, and fields bor-

dered by low stone walls. The cottages became more
numerous as they rode toward a low hill. The hill was
dominated by a single octagonal stone building.

"Is that where we're going?"

"Yes."

Yerith rode them through the town and up a broad
road toward the entrance. The walls were plain and
unadorned. The only windows were narrow slits set
high on the wall. The gate at the end of the road
was barely wide enough to let through a single horse-
drawn cart.

Because of the simplicity of design and the small
entry, it looked smaller than it was. A pair of guards
let them in, and Nate was shocked to see the scarlet
and black livery of the Manhome guard. He was suddenly afraid that he had been tricked back into the
custody of the College. He might have tried to escape
then, if he could have gotten his agonized muscles
to respond.

When they passed through the gate, Nate could see
how large the fortress actually was. The high octagonal
walls surrounded a massive courtyard that seemed to
contain as many buildings as were clustered outside
the walls. There were stables, a smithy, and what
looked like barracks which—judging by the number of
people in armor walking about—were fully occupied.
Central to everything was a large, walled, stone building that echoed the octagonal form of the outer wall.

Yerith dismounted and talked to one of the guards.
While she talked, Nate half dismounted and half fell
off of the horse. It was an effort to get his legs to
hold him upright, but with so many people around,
Nate managed it just to maintain some level of dignity.

"Come," Yerith said. "They're expecting us."

"I'm sure he is." *They are?* Nate said as he opened
Yerith's saddlebags. After a few moments of rummag-
ing, he pulled out his book and the sheaf of notes he
was working on. "But I'm not leaving this."

"Come," said the guardsman. He escorted the two

of them up a stairway that led to the gate of the inner building.

They walked into a long stone hall, at the end of which stood several robed figures in front of a plain throne on a dais. When the guard led Nate and Yerith into the hall, the tallest figure made a dismissive gesture and the others left the hall, leaving him and the man seated on the dais.

"So this is the Angel of Death?" asked the man on the throne. It was someone unfamiliar who couldn't be any older than Nate.

The standing figure turned to face Nate. The scarred face was unfamiliar, but Nate knew Arthiz's voice. "You came."

"I came," Nate said, "because you want to destroy the College of Man."

Chapter Forty-Seven

ARTHIZ SMILED. "Welcome, Azrael." The man butchered the name, but Nate still felt a chill.

"I'd prefer it if you did not call me that."

The young man on the dais vaulted to the floor and walked past Arthiz to get a good look at Nate. Nate noticed a weird combination of deference and annoyance in Arthiz's body language.

"So this is going to preserve the Monarch's rule?" the youth said. "Not terribly impressive."

Nate resisted the urge to say something rude. He got the sense that this guy wasn't the right person to annoy at the moment.

"This stranger has done more to undo the power of the College, simply by uttering that name than I have in twenty years of careful work. While he walks the earth, the College can think of little else."

"Is that why you've asked for my help?" Nate asked. "You think I am the Angel of Death?"

"I know you are," Arthiz said. "All you offer is knowledge, perhaps?"

Nate hugged his book.

"I see your face paler than normal. But those old myths can be read many ways, my friend. I choose to read that you are the instrument of the College's destruction. Don't we share that goal?"

"Do not fear," said the youth. "Those who serve the Monarch will be greatly rewarded."

"Yes," Nate replied quietly, his unease growing.

"Then come, let us talk." Arthiz waved Nate forward, letting the youth lead them into a meeting chamber with a long table.

Yerith stayed behind.

•   •   •

The youth was the Monarch, the Ruler of Man.

Arthiz was Scholar Uthar Vailen, until recently the second most powerful person in the College of Man.

Nate, apparently, *was* the Angel of Death, or some facsimile thereof.

It was all a bit much to take.

"We are forced to move with haste," Uthar said. "Decades of preparation were lost when the Shadow College fell. We can now count on only a few loyal acolytes."

The Monarch smiled, "But you have created the perfect feint in the East. The movement of the ghadi, the rumors of your presence, have been enough for them to send their troops from Zorion into the jungles to lay siege and destroy your citadel. Manhome itself lies unprotected."

"Why do you need my help?"

Uthar smiled. "We do not want to lay siege to the College's fortress. The shores are thick with the corpses of the army that would try." The Monarch frowned at the comment, and Nate wondered whose army had tried.

"We shall bring the College itself down. We need to match the mages that remain behind its walls. We need to defeat the scholars before they can recall any of their force."

"You think I can give this to you?"

The Monarch smiled. "It is the reason the gods brought you here."

•   •   •

It took a while, but they told him much of what was going on here, filling in the blanks of the civil war that was going on. Though the Monarch pulled his punches

in describing how the College got the upper hand, and
while Uthar didn't correct the man, Nate could tell
that he was listening to a major screwup.

It made him worry all the more about the ghadi. If
the Shadow College was a sacrifice to draw forces
away from Manhome—no one said it quite like that,
but Nate could read the subtext—what was going to
happen to the ghadi, who were even more expendable
in a human conflict.

Of course Uthar kept saying how they could bring
the College down before the forces massed against
them, but Nate kept feeling as if the man was just
humoring him.

This probably was a mistake.

Eventually, the Monarch left Nate in Uthar's
custody.

Probably past his bedtime.

"I still don't see how what I know can help you win
a war."

Uthar steepled his fingers. "What you know is
enough to frighten the College of Man. You have
called forces equal to those of mages with many years
carved into their skin."

In some cases, the same forces.

"Don't expect me to pull stones from the sky. I
know little more than a sixth of the Gods' Language."
Nate set down his book. "All I know is from studying
ancient ghadi spells."

"Ghadi spells?" Uthar said, staring at the book.
"That is a history textbook."

"It was." Nate smiled slightly. "My one novel experiment. I created a spell that helps me transcribe
other spells. The text that used to fill this book has
been replaced by my own notes."

"May I see?"

"Yes," Nate pushed it over. "Bear in mind, it won't
mean much to you."

Uthar picked up the volume and opened it. He
turned the pages, looking at the hexadecimal notation.
The script was tiny and precise, forming long columns

that repeated across the pages. Uthar ran his fingers down the columns of numbers. "What is this?"

Machine code. The assembly language of the universe.

"The words, the runes, that form the Gods' Language, just to write them, or speak them, or think too hard about them, is to invoke them. To study what they mean, I use other symbols to represent the runes. Those long columns of characters have no meaning of themselves, but if I know that this represents the third character in a spell—"

"I see," Uthar nodded. "A map. It is a map, so you can see the shoreline without walking to the ocean."

"I think that's a good way to put it."

"I have studied with the College, and without, for four decades. Half that time I have tried to learn beyond the boundaries the College placed around its knowledge, and never had such a simple concept come to me. Name the words of power by something else, see their order, their grouping." He looked up. "You could actually see two or three spells at once, and see all of them, their contents, how the words flow—" Uthar closed the book. His eyes were fixed on the middle distance.

"Tell me," he asked Nate. "How can you see which of the countless runes are written in your code."

"Akin to how you know how to pronounce them. The rune's name comes from its shape, so do these symbols."

It took a long time for Nate to explain. While going from binary to hexadecimal was a near trivial step for him, Uthar didn't have any experience in other base numbering systems, or powers of two. It was, in fact, a measure of the mage's intelligence that he was able to grasp the concept in only a couple of hours.

Uthar shook his head. "Where could I be, what could I know, if I had only had this a decade ago."

"I doubt an alternative notation for the Gods' Language will help against the College."

"Perhaps not . . . But you said you *created* a spell?"

"One."

"You know that the College itself forbids such a practice. It has been long since any man could claim that for even the humblest incantation. All the College knows is what has been written in metal and stone, and carved into skin. I know as much as any, and all I have was written millennia ago."

"I know. I also know why. If you don't study the internal structure of these things, and just make random changes, the result won't be pretty."

"But you crafted a spell?"

"Restricting myself to the part of the language I knew. Inefficient as hell, but it works."

"Show me."

Nate looked up into Uthar's face, at the tracery of scars there. There was a terrible earnestness there, the eyes staring at him with an intensity that matched the ghadi's.

Nate took back the book and opened it to a page near the end, where the pages still carried the words of the history text. In the corner was a short runic label. Nate had "named" each page in the book, to make the transcriptions easier.

Of course, there was only one real target to transcribe, so Nate used the spell named on Arthiz's left cheek. Nate called on his one spell, and there seemed something more ritualistic, darker, to it now than there had been before.

After the words were spoken, the words on the page moved. It was as if the ink had become oil on an already slick surface. It blended, and twisted itself into long columns of figures. Uthar touched the page and shook his head. "This is what?"

Nate pointed at his face, and Uthar touched his cheek as if burned. "You peel secrets from the skin itself."

"And deeper," Nate thought of the long spell that infected the ghadi.

"And you think this cannot help me?"

"In battle?"

"Tell me, can this run likewise in reverse?"

"I don't understand."

"Can this spell carve the runes of the Gods' Language as well?"

"Well, of course it could. It has."

"Then you can give me an army to take Manhome."

•   •   •

It was ironic, for all of Nate's modern sensibilities, it was Uthar who recognized the implications of mass production first. Despite the presence of magic here, an enchanted item was still a rarity. It took inhuman discipline and stamina to engrave anything of any import in stone or metal, because any pause in the creation of the object would destroy the process, and possibly the caster. Even the ritual scarification of the College mages was done by masters with decades of practice. Creating something akin to the translation sphere had been beyond anyone for an age.

Uthar saw that, with Nate's spell, if they had one enchanted sword, they could easily have a thousand. A single protective amulet could embrace a whole army.

Uthar took Nate down to the armory, where three mages waited. They were young, younger than Nate. They had survived the destruction of the Shadow College because they had not yet made it there when the attack destroyed it.

"Teach them what to do," Uthar told him.

Nate did.

Without the pretense and the ceremony, Nate showed them the rudiments. How to name the source and the target, and the words to cast the transcription itself. Nate had to provide the three mages individually named copies of the spell, but that was easily enough done. The three took their paper copies, and the youngest—and the smartest—did something unexpected.

Once Nate had gotten the concept across, that one used the spell to etch itself into his own skin. Nate watched, horrified and fascinated as the long lines of the spell traced themselves in blood and then scarred over. The spell was so long, it took several minutes, even as fine as the lines it drew were.

The young mage stood, the pain clear on his face, sweat mixing with the blood as it dripped down his bare skin.

Then, it was over and the mage handed Nate back the paper. "Now this will always be mine." The acolyte's smile was disturbing, and Nate began to feel that some line had been crossed here.

But they did as Uthar wanted.

In his cache he had three swords that were enchanted. One would cleave through any metal, one would burn anything pierced by its blade, and one's cut was poison to whatever bled upon its steel.

The end of that first day saw thirty such swords. The second saw another hundred.

Shields stacked up that would shatter any blade that cut against them, armor that provided speed and stamina, amulets that protected against hostile magic.

Less than half a dozen artifacts, a treasure that had been beyond any price before Nate had arrived at Uthar's keep, became, in forty-eight hours, an arsenal to supply an entire army.

• • •

Uthar gave Nate a well-appointed room. He had a desk, a lamp, and a bed that was more luxurious than anything Nate had slept in, either in this world or his own. Nate had a chance to bathe, and to dress in new clothes. He was given meals and drink.

And Nate couldn't sleep.

Were ghadi still gathering at the tower without him, or had they dispersed when Nate abandoned them? Every spare moment, Nate thought of the doom that marched on them and knew that he was in large part responsible for it.

I encouraged the ghadi to fight. I showed them they could fight. . . .

Instead of sleep, Nate burned a lamp and studied

the spell he had pulled from the ghadi flesh, the curse that muted them and made them chattel for Mankind. In the odd twists and loops of code, there had to be an answer, something to be undone.

The code didn't like to be studied. It had more twists and jumps than a nest of rattlers. The logic was slick and evil, as if anticipating the eyes that might try to unravel it.

Nate was hunched over the evil spell, when Uthar knocked on the door to Nate's chamber. Nate looked up and saw Uthar standing in the doorway.

"You should sleep. Conserve your strength."

"I don't have the time. Are you ready to move yet?"

"Within this sixday."

Nate pushed his chair away from the desk and looked at Uthar. "You have what you need of me. I should go back."

"You can do more for your ghadi by aiding me."

"I have given you all I've learned, what else is there?"

Uthar nodded. "Then tell me if this is possible— can a man with no knowledge of the Gods' Language cause a spell to be cast?"

"Of course—" *Not?*

Even as Nate was about to say no, he remembered the counterexamples. The daggers the ancient Ghadi-kan used as keys, the traps where moving the wrong thing could immolate the trespasser. . . .

"Yes," Nate said, "given the right artifact."

"Do this for me, then go."

Nate was about to object, but he already saw how it could be done. His transcription spell could read a spell into the air, and he had seen on the weapons how a spell could be targeted by mere contact with the spell-bearing artifact. Combine the two, and you could create an artifact that could cast a spell by merely touching the text of that spell. Nate had outlined two thirds of the code in his head by the time he said, "I can do this."

• • •

Twelve hours of debugging, and Nate presented Uthar a wand. Runes wrapped the wand, microscopically small, spelling out a dormant spell like the booby trap in the ghadi tower door, or the code that awaited an enchanted dagger to open an ancient passage. This spell awaited the tip of the wand to touch the runes of another spell.

Uthar took the wand in one hand, and opened the other. Scars traced the palm, weaving some sort of incantation. Wordlessly, Uthar touched the wand to the surface of his palm. In response, the air around him began to glow, casting a deadly bright light.

Uthar laughed. "You do not know the miracles you work."

The light faded as he withdrew the wand.

"Return to your ghadi. I have what I need to reduce the College of Man into nonexistence."

"Thank you, Uthar."

Uthar waved to a pair of guards. "Show our guest to his guide and his mount."

Two armored men flanked Nate. Their weapons and armor reflected from thousands of intricately carved runes. Nate knew what the runes did, and he would not want to be on the wrong end of these guys in a fight. The College was in for a rude awakening.

Nate followed them out of the great hall and out into the courtyard of the keep. The troops were already on the march, so the keep was nearly empty. Nate expected to find Yerith, but she wasn't to be seen.

"This way, sir," said one of the guards, pointing toward one of the stables across the courtyard.

"Oh, yes." *Sure, you keep a mount in a stable.* Nate hoped the trip back wouldn't be as painful as the trip here.

Nate walked through the dark entrance and waited

for his eyes to adjust. Something was wrong. There was no horse here, the stable was empty.

"What?" Nate said as he started to turn around.

Something solid and heavy fell across the back of Nate's skull.

CHAPTER FORTY-EIGHT

THE WORLD was moving. That was the first thing that Nate was aware of. The second thing was the vast cold blue sky arcing above him, empty of everything but a small, hard sun that hurt his eyes. He raised his hand to shade his eyes, and found himself chained.

"That fucking bastard!" he called out in English, the words coming out more phlegm than voice. Nate sat up, coughing.

He was in the back of an open wagon, on a straw mat in the midst of barrels and sacks of grain. They were moving, and out the rear of the wagon, Nate could see a column of troops following.

"How are you feeling?"

Nate turned and saw Yerith, seated on a chest, in the back of the wagon with him.

"How do you think I'm feeling?"

"You need to understand—"

"Understand what? That I work with this guy and for thanks he clubs me on the head?"

"They couldn't risk your capture."

"And we just let the ghadi die? We let the College slaughter them?"

Yerith shook her head. "If we take Manhome, the army will break." She said it forcefully, almost as if she was trying to convince herself.

"Then why stop me from going?"

She looked away from him. "This wasn't what I wanted."

Nate shook his hands and looked down at his shackles. The manacles and chains were gold, one set binding his wrists together, another binding his ankles. Outside of that, he could move around.

Looking closely at the manacles, Nate saw long runic inscriptions. He looked up at Yerith. "What are these?"

She didn't respond immediately.

"Tell me, I know enough now that I could figure it out, so save us the time."

"Don't. Those are mage shackles. Any invocation will cause them to attack you. I don't know how, but they have killed before."

Great!

Of course, someone had to have built something like these a long time ago. Otherwise, how do you confine a mage short of killing him or performing an extreme mutilation like the College did to Bhodan?

Nate guessed the manacles were preferable.

"This is only until the army takes Manhome."

Nate nodded. "You know this, how?"

"Uthar said—"

"Uthar is a liar. He said I could return." Nate looked out at the column of troops. "Now he's stolen any chance of me getting to them before the College does."

• • •

The army marched fast, aided no doubt by some artifact or other that Nate played some part in distributing. They marched without stopping until several hours after nightfall, and after that they camped in only the most abbreviated fashion—eating cold rations and sleeping on their shields without any fire.

With no lights at all, and a moonless night, Nate wouldn't have known that there was an army surrounding the wagon if it wasn't for the sound of multitudes breathing. Nate stayed in the wagon, even though he was only chained to himself, the straw mat he had looked to be the most comfortable bed available.

Nate couldn't sleep, so he saw Uthar approach. Nate sat up as he climbed into the back of the wagon. "Yerith tells me that you are unhappy."

"You wouldn't be in my place?"

"Perhaps not," Uthar looked out at the army. "Understand me. I had little choice. This is our opportunity to strike, I cannot cede any advantage. Too much is lost already."

"So you deceive me and chain me and kidnap me?"

"I am protecting you. Right now your safest place is with me. Anywhere else and you may fall into the hands of the enemy."

"I was doing all right before I joined with you."

"When Manhome falls, we can part ways, if you still desire it."

Something about the way Uthar said that made Nate feel chilled. "If I still desire it?"

"Consider well. Rule the ghadi if you must, a broken and dying race. But you could also share in the rule of Man."

"What does the Monarch think of this?"

"I am past the point of troubling the Monarch with such ideas. The men here fight for the Monarch, not the youth who holds that title. There are those better suited to fill such a role."

Are you saying what I think you are saying?

Uthar saw Nate's expression and smiled. "Do not think it odd. Those who lead men must always be marked separate, or they do not command respect. But, as I advised you once, do not talk in haste."

"I will consider what you said."

"I do not wish to be an ungrateful host. You have helped me mightily. Can I do anything to ease your stay?"

Nate held up the chains. "Remove these."

Uthar shook his head. "No, I cannot set you free just yet. Not while Manhome is over the next rise."

"Then give me my papers, my books, and my brushes."

Uthar shook his head. "I know what you are capable of, even if you do not."

Nate snorted.

"Perhaps I can abide a more realistic request."

"Is it too much to ask for a blanket, and maybe a ride in a wagon that has some cover from the sun."

"This much I can grant you."

"And I do not want Yerith's company."

"She has done much for you."

"If I'm captive again, I'd be captive alone."

"I am a reasonable man." Uthar stepped away and paused. After a moment he added, "You will see the wisdom of this path."

I am sure, you manipulative bastard.

• • •

Nate had no real hope of getting his freedom, or his papers, or so much as a pencil. He had asked for those first so that his last request, privacy, was more likely to be granted.

He got what he wanted, a berth on a wagon covered from the eyes of the troops, and a blanket to cover what he did.

To someone who composed C++ code in his head, a pen and paper were more a convenience than a necessity. To study the spell on these gauntlets, all he really needed was a loose nail, a semi-flat board, and an absence of prying eyes.

The problem of the gauntlets was a timing issue. When did these manacles do their dirty work?

To find out, Nate transcribed the spell in hexadecimal notation so he could study the thing. That took several hours, hiding his scratches under his blanket. When he was done, he was almost too tired to study what he had written.

Almost. However, as with many a coding problem before, fatigue only sharpened his resolve.

He stared at his scratches and tried to make sense of them.

The chains were triggered when their captive spoke, gestured, or wrote any runes of the Gods' Language. There were several layers to the code. It would burn, becoming more intense based on the number of characters the victim tried to write or speak. If the runes were completed by successfully invoking a spell, a jolt would be sent though the victim, strong enough to kill. There was even code that punished the captive for invoking other artifacts.

It took some long pondering before Nate thought of a possible loophole.

Of course, the wearer of the manacles was free to activate the manacles themselves. In theory, the person wearing these things could simply invoke the punishment routine directly.

Or any spell named the same as the punishment routine.

If Nate was coding this, at the very least he would have tried to come up with a check-sum, or the MED equivalent. However, the mages who wrote this code weren't that sophisticated. Like most security holes, the people responsible for it probably couldn't even see that it was a hole. After all, the wearer wasn't about to compose anything in MED; four runes in and he'd probably be suffering from third-degree burns. The only thing available to cast was the code on the manacles themselves.

At least the only thing in MED.

The author hadn't anticipated that there might be an alternate way to compose a spell.

Nate knew enough now to compose a hack of the manacle's code without writing a single rune of MED. If he wrote code in hexadecimal, there was, in theory, no reason it needed to exist at all in MED until he cast it. Nate already *thought* of MED in his own notation; it required less effort to think about.

As long as the code he wrote matched the beginning of the manacle spell, he shouldn't trigger anything when he cast it.

Shouldn't.

Nate sat in the darkened back of the wagon, contemplating what he was going to do.

Well, this is going to be dangerous.

That was a bit of an understatement. He could kill himself with what he planned on doing. He could easily sit back here and let events roll on, in relative safety. . . .

On the floor of the wagon, he sketched several columns of hexadecimal code to replace the body of the punishment routine.

It was a variant of the one spell he had invented himself. One of the few working spells he could remember entirely. Sketching it out, he worked out how to make it do exactly the opposite of what he had written it to do. The effect was elegant and strangely devastating.

When he was done, he smiled, thinking of the expression on the ghadi's faces when he had left them.

"Okay, guys, I haven't forgotten you."

While he still had light, he began the arduous task of memorizing the new spell.

• • •

Before dawn, Uthar Vailen sent Yerith to fetch the stranger. The attack on Manhome was about to commence, and the scholar wanted the Angel of Death with him and the Monarch, overseeing the battle.

Yerith didn't know what she was supposed to think. This creature, this *man,* had started her questioning things she had been avoiding questioning. She had seen the mass of ghadi that came to serve him. How could it be right to take Nate Black away from them?

She kept thinking of what Uthar had told her, that the College's army would break when the College fell.

What if it didn't?

Was it that easy to deceive herself? Did she believe Uthar because he was right, or because she needed to? Was she, after everything, willing to sacrifice the ghadi to see her revenge against the College?

The choice wasn't like that. This is the only chance

*we had. Without Nate, without the College's forces
far removed . . .*

She was disturbed to find herself thinking Uthar's
arguments as if they were her own.

Nate knew better, apparently. He had seen through
her enough to ask Uthar to keep her away. She
wanted to be angry at him for that, after all that she
had done for him.

Somehow, the only anger she could come up with
was for herself.

She reached the back of the wagon where they had
moved Nate and stopped. Dawn had yet to touch the
sky, and no light made it inside the dark, covered
interior of the wagon. She couldn't see anything, but
she heard something. Even with the sounds of troops
massing around her, the clank of armor and the crunch
of hundreds of boots on gravel, she could hear Nate
Black's strangely accented voice.

The sound of the Gods' Language was unmistakable.

"No!"

Yerith vaulted up into the back of the wagon. Inside, she could barely make out Nate bent over in
concentration, speaking the sacred syllables while staring at his chained hands.

"No, the enchantment will kill . . ." Her words
trailed off. Nate was deep into the spell, sweat rolling
off of skin so pale that it was almost luminous in the
dark. Yerith had seen the scholar's bindings before,
her father had worn a pair in the months before the
College removed him. Nate should not be able to
speak the Gods' Language at all. He should be writh-
ing in pain, and his skin should be charred from the
brands the manacles would become.

But nothing was happening.

How can he be doing this?

Yerith thought of what Nate had brought to Arthiz's army, and remembered the legends of the Angel
of Death.

My Angel can teach you more of my language than any man has ever known.

She was suddenly very afraid.

Nate finished speaking and Yerith expected him to collapse in a final spasm of pain as the enchanted bracelets sent a fatal jolt through his body. Instead, the manacles on his wrists and ankles glowed faintly blue for just a moment. Yerith briefly caught the scent of heated metal, then it was gone.

Nate looked up at her and rubbed the surface of the manacle binding his right wrist. She could see a half smile on his lips.

"Well, you seem to have found me out. Why are you here?"

Yerith took a few steps away from Nate. She couldn't speak for the longest time, she kept thinking of all the tales of the gods and their creatures, and the terrible powers they wielded. Up to now, to her, Nate was just a strange man who resembled a ghadi. Now she saw what he was, a creature of Ghad.

Just talking to such a thing could bring horrible destruction in its wake.

"Well?" Nate asked.

"You're wanted for an audience with the Monarch."

Nate sighed. "Let's go, then."

As he climbed out of the back of the wagon, Yerith caught the reflection of the moon in one of his manacles.

She gasped.

Where the metal had once been carved with the intricate runes of the Gods' Language, there was now only smooth, polished metal.

Chapter Forty-Nine

"WE CANNOT be under attack!" the Venerable Master Scholar Jardan Syn shouted at Scholar Abad Karrik.

The words hung in the air of the meeting room as the dawn light impaled dust in diagonal shafts of air. Through the open windows, Karrik could still smell smoke and death in the air. Also rising in the air was the distant clank of metal, shouting, and running feet.

Karrik replied in a level tone, "All our guardsmen outside the walls are gone. They are either dead or abandoning us for the countryside."

The red demon mask shook, the nose bobbing so abruptly that Karrik thought it might snap off. "The Monarch has no army left."

"The main body of the force bear the livery of the Manhome Guard," Karrik said.

"Traitors. All traitors."

"Sir. If we retreat and recall our army from the field, we can retake the city—"

"You would have me abandon the College and its mysteries to these heretics? No."

"Their force is too small to hold the entire city. The army from Zorion will easily—"

The Venerable Master Scholar slammed his fist on the table. "No. I see your plot. You are with them, aren't you?"

"No!"

"No, Scholar Karrik? You would have me open the

doors of the College of Man to an invading army and abandon our rear to a mass of rebellious ghadi that have tasted human blood. Your plots will see no fruit here. *Guards!*"

The shout received no response.

Karrik sighed and shook his head. "There are no guards, my Master. They have gone to defend the entry to the College. All they do is buy some time. If we escape now—" Karrik's voice was cut short with a gasp as something slammed into his side, above the kidney. He looked down and saw the hand of the Venerable Master Scholar burying a dagger into his side.

As it withdrew, and the blood began to flow, Karrik began to feel the pain.

"I will not abandon my duty or the College of Man."

Karrik clutched his side. "You. Fool."

The blade slammed into him again.

"I will take words from the vaults myself. I will call the sky down on them, I will have the earth open under their feet."

Karrik spat up blood. If there was only a spell he could think of, name . . . but he was too old and too slow, and his thoughts were spilling on the ground with his blood.

● ● ●

The Monarch had set his observation camp on a bluff overlooking the plateau of Manhome. With the wagons, tents, and officers crowding the area, it took a while before Nate recognized the spot—not until it was light enough for him to see some of the half buried white blocks that dotted the site.

He had come almost completely full circle.

Christ, if Yerith could have waited five minutes.

His plan had been to slip away in the dark, but that had gone to shit.

Because of Yerith's appearance, all he seemed to have accomplished with his masterful hack of the enchantment binding him was to terrify her. He might have freed himself to cast whatever he might please, but he was still in the middle of an armed camp. And now he was flanked by two guards and couldn't think of a single thing he could accomplish before someone clubbed him on the head again.

Worse, Nate doubted that Yerith was going to remain quiet about what happened until he had the privacy to cast something useful. She was staring at him now, obviously intimidated, but that wouldn't last.

Fortunately, no one else seemed to notice his newly polished bracelets, and he tried as best he could to cover the lack of engraving with his hands.

"Our Angel is here," the Monarch said finally, after Nate had been standing there for nearly an hour. The guards flanking him took that as a cue and walked Nate up to the edge of the bluff where the Monarch and Uthar stood, watching the city.

"A grand morning," said the Monarch, smiling at him.

Nate looked off at the city-mountain of Manhome and had trouble sharing the sentiment. Fires were burning, throwing hellish billows of smoke into the dawn sky. Flashes silhouetted walls, followed by ominous rumblings. Lightning arced between towers, and explosions would occasionally cause the city to slough off a layer of stone like shed skin, opening a building's interior to the sky like a wound.

"Thanks to you," Uthar said, "each member of our force wields the same power as the most talented scholar. And each is protected against much of what the College can bring against them."

"I see." Nate looked at the city. It was in the midst of tearing itself apart, and all he could think was: *I did this. . . .*

How many people were dying in there who had nothing to do with the College? He had lived through hell at the hands of the scholars of the College of Man. Was *this* what he wanted to see?

Somehow, seeing the walls crumbling on the great

old city, the fire crawling its streets, was different than anything he had imagined.

The wind shifted and he smelled smoke. He wanted to gag.

"Y–you have what you want. You're in the city." Nate shook his head. "Let me go back to the ghadi before it's too late."

The Monarch laughed.

"What is funny?"

"I am afraid it is too late," the Monarch said.

"What do you mean?" Nate felt his gut sinking.

"You have great knowledge and power," the Monarch said, "but strategy is not your forte. The ghadi are as much a threat to the Monarch as they are to the College. It is better to let them deal with the threat. That is why this attack is timed to coincide with theirs."

"What?"

The Monarch shook his head. "In affairs like this, sentimentality is not a virtue. The College's army should be at your citadel as we speak."

"But they aren't supposed to be there for another—"

"We adjusted our estimate to encourage you to come." The Monarch smiled and looked off at the city. "The troublesome ghadi should be exterminated by sunset."

"NO!"

The scream came from the edge of the encampment. Nate turned with everyone else to see Yerith running forward, tears streaking her face, carrying a large fragment of white rock.

"Yerith, no," Nate whispered.

Things slowed and became razor clear. The guards were the first to realize what was happening. The closest ones were the men next to Nate, who bolted forward to intercept Yerith. The guards beside the Monarch were a few steps removed and started to interpose themselves between the youth and Yerith.

Even in her rage, Nate could see that Yerith knew

she wouldn't make the last ten feet toward the Monarch. She started to reach back with the rock in her hand.

The Monarch smiled. It was an almost goofy expression, as if he was watching some play act put on for his sole amusement. As Yerith hurled the stone, he started to say something. "This will not—"

The words were cut short by the white stone slamming into his face.

Nate's guards tackled Yerith, while the Monarch's reached for their ruler. The Monarch stumbled backward out of the reach of his men. He was spitting blood and shaking his head, stunned, his face a bloody pulp.

Uthar stepped forward, a little too slowly, and said, "Watch out."

The Monarch, unhearing, took another step backward.

Over the bluff.

Chaos reigned as everyone rushed the edge of the bluff. No one paid attention to Nate.

Here's my chance, what do I do? What can I do?

He had only moments, with no spell book handy. He began wishing he had scarred himself. All he could think of was the code he had written to transcribe and unwrite spells. That and the damn candle spell.

What could he do with that?

If there was something castable around here . . .

Nate kept backing away from the crowd and tripped over one of the stones from the ancient ghadi ruin.

Nate stared at it.

Is there anything left?

Looking around, Nate saw a circular depression in the earth, not much, but it was ringed by mounds in a concentric pattern. It was almost unnoticeable. If he hadn't seen the layout several times before, he would have ignored it.

Was it buried intact? Is there enough of it there?
Did it have the inscription in the first place?

He didn't have long before the Monarch's demise

ceased being a distraction. If he was going to do it, he needed to do it *now*.

Whispering, Nate cast the spell, drawing out whatever code lived in the rock buried beneath the circular dip in the ground, where the ghadi once had their temple.

In response to his words, the ground around the buried pit erupted in circles of blue-green fire. The light traced the runes of the Gods' Language into the dirt, the clay, and the rock beneath. Nate could feel the power of it as the lines wrote themselves. It was electric in the air.

He wasn't the only one who felt it. Everyone in the area turned toward the buried pit as the force of the transcription caused the ground itself to recede, unearthing the remains of the ancient ghadi shrine. The soil drained down into the great pit, which was now circled in runes carved with fire.

No one moved, the Monarch's fate forgotten.

"What are you doing?" cried a voice from the other side of the pit. It might have been Uthar.

"What I came here for," Nate whispered.

As the guards started running toward him, Nate uttered the short, four-rune name that invoked the spell carved in the rock before him.

• • •

Armsmaster Ehrid Kharyn was the first to enter the doors of the College itself. He led a squad of a dozen men who, equipped by the Monarch with relics of unimaginable power, had fought like an army of a thousand. They had torn through all resistance like a thing out of legend, and there was no question left in Ehrid's mind that the College would, in fact, fall this day.

As he stepped across the threshold, one of his men called to him.

"Armsmaster, quick! Something is happening!"

Frowning, he turned away from the splintered remnants of the siege-door and the crushed bodies beneath it, and walked back outside.

"What is it? A counterattack?"

"I don't know." The man led Ehrid up some stairs to the top of the outer wall of the College's fortress within a fortress. From there, to one of the defensive towers. Here, all of Manhome was spread below them, but the guardsman pointed outward, beyond the city, and back toward the shore. "There."

Ehrid looked, and felt his heart dry up.

Above the bluff where the Monarch had his command, storm clouds had emerged from the middle of a clear dawn sky. They swirled in a vortex that centered on an area of blackness beyond dark, beyond the absence of light. It was a darkness that opened into the abyss between the worlds. And even at this distance, even with no light to perceive it, Ehrid knew that, in the darkness, something moved.

Something older than the world and vaster than the space that contained it.

He had seen it, in old carvings, in tapestries and paintings. Never in his worst nightmares did he think he would live to face it. "May the gods between the worlds fail to take notice of us," Ehrid prayed.

"What is it?"

"The eye of Ghad," Ehrid said. "Let us hope we die before it sees us."

Ehrid descended, assured as ever that the College of Man would fall this day.

It was no longer a comforting thought.

CHAPTER FIFTY

✦✦✦**Y**OUR PURPOSE *is not fulfilled."*

Nate tumbled headfirst into the void before him. Above him, around him—and in some disturbing sense, *within* him—was the presence of the undulating, ever-changing Ghad. Nate was expecting it this time, so he managed to keep his thoughts rational and composed, and his breathing steady.

It wasn't easy, with every fiber of his brain screaming out the sheer *wrongness* of the Ghad-thing enveloping him.

"Your purpose," Nate said to the darkness.

"I give you your purpose."

"Then help me, damn it! If you want the ghadi free, help me."

"Knowledge is all I provide."

Nate clutched himself against the alien thing around him. He could feel that he was leaking away, his self melting like ice in the sun. He grabbed on to the one kernel of emotion he had: anger.

"Bullshit! You brought me here, you can take me there."

"You have your own door."

"What do you mean?"

"You have walked outside the world. Go where you will to return."

What?

Nate looked around, and suddenly he could see

things in—or through—the darkness. He would stare
at something, and it shot into focus.

He saw the Monarch's encampment, the guards restraining Yerith as Uthar placed guards around the pit
where Nate was now absent. Nate shifted focus, and
Manhome came into relief with dizzying speed. He
could see the face of the guardsman who had first
captured him, walking through the ashes of a great
library. An acolyte came from nowhere to attack him,
but the guardsman took a familiar white wand and
touched a phrase that was faintly embroidered in his
cloak. The acolyte burst into flame.

Nate blinked and the image was gone, replaced by
bodies bloated and floating in the shallows at the base
of Manhome.

Blinked and he saw jungles. Then mountains. Then
the streets of Zorion, absent of guards or any authority, an exodus of people fleeing a riot of looting and
rape.

Then the citadel where the ghadi faced the army of
the College. The walls had only held so long with
Nate's protective enchantment. They were falling, and
the ghadi were falling with them.

*"You sit at the center of power. Words you speak
now shall be heard by all you see."*

As Nate watched, he saw the ghadi run from the
soldiers, being cut down by the dozens. What could he
do to help them? He couldn't halt a whole army. . . .

"Unchain my people."

He could. He had shown himself how to erase a
spell. That's all that muted the ghadi, a spell that was
encoded into their bodies, their biology. He had
wasted so much time in studying the spell, trying to
understand it, when all that was really necessary was
to erase it.

As the ghadi retreated in front of the scholars'
army, Nate began to speak the Gods' Language.

Here, in the presence of Ghad, the words flowed
freer than they ever had before, the power behind
them immense and terrifying. He had only been tap-

ping a thousandth, a millionth, of the potential of these words. Each syllable seemed to twist the fabric of the universe as it passed, revising reality to conform to its presence.

I've been programming a Commodore 64, and Ghad just handed me a Sun Microstation.

The words tore through the streets of the burning ghadi village, finding the ancient curse within the bodies of the ghadi, alive and dead. In an instant, molecules and genes revised themselves a hundred million times over. The spell tore through the fabric of the planet itself, finding every corner, and everywhere, all at once, the ghadi awoke.

• • •

The scholar that Nate had once called the Red Skull was leading a squad of guardsmen after a trio of retreating ghadi. He was taking a personal pleasure in the attack. There were still scars where his flesh was healing from the fire that the ghadi's savior had inflicted on him.

He had burned fifteen ghadi already this morning, and he would not be satisfied until he burned the white flesh of their leader.

Until then, seeing the ghadi suffer as he had would have to do.

"Over here!" called one of his guardsmen.

He followed to a makeshift hut where the trio of ghadi—male, female, and a child—huddled in a corner. Behind his mask, he smiled. "You shall see what defying the College means, even for brute animals."

He pushed his sleeves back on arms that were still scarred pink from the burns, and began an incantation that would immolate these ghadi alive. As he started, he felt something odd, as if he—or someone—had already cast a spell. He could feel the fringe of an immense energy brush by him, tantalizingly close. He ignored it, deep in the concentration of the spell.

So deep in concentration, he barely registered surprise when the ghadi spoke.

Then the words choked deep in his throat and he gasped.

The ghadi in front of him were standing, no longer cowering.

Suddenly afraid, he tried to complete the incantation even as he felt the potential evaporate around him. All he could do was cough and sputter. The guardsman was not smart enough, or imaginative enough, to realize what was happening when the ghadi turned toward him.

Five words the male ghadi spoke.

Five words in the Gods' Language.

Five words and the guardsman was on his knees, vomiting blood.

He was frozen, sputtering, unable to speak, as the female ghadi walked up to him and removed his mask. To his horror, she spoke in words that he could understand. "It is humbling to be silent."

He was silent all the way until the end, when they let him scream.

• • •

The ghadi knew.

They had always known.

That part of the brain the curse had shut away was neither broken nor missing. The part that Ghad had created was always there, learning, watching, building an invisible and hateful intelligence that was walled off from everything, even the ghadi themselves.

With one spell, the ancient race, the race hardwired to the Gods' Language, that breathed its runes the way man breathed air, had returned. The race where every member was more powerful than the highest adept of the College of Man had been unleashed.

And they were pissed.

• • •

What the fuck did I just do?

The alien satisfaction around him was suffocating in its intensity.

"You have done well."

Everything began to sink in in full force. He *was* the Angel of Death. Ghad had handpicked him not to destroy the College of Man, but to destroy Man, period. Nate had just restarted the war that had nearly destroyed the planet in the first place.

Ghad couldn't have done better than to drop him in there. He had just the right skill set to completely destroy the balance of power. He had managed to pass off just enough knowledge so Uthar and the Monarch could decimate the College of Man. And now, out of pity and some sense of remorse, he had just unleashed the ghadi on them.

"I have opened the passage back to where you belong."

Nate blinked, and he could see linoleum.

The floor of the Case campus.

Home.

Ghad, you bastard.

Easy now. Just reach over, and it would be over. All of this would be some nightmare. Just let this world disintegrate without him.

Let Man die here while Ghad laughed.

"You've won, haven't you?"

"My ghadi belong to this world, this world to them."

Nate felt sick.

"Go home, Azrael."

Something sank in.

He was still here.

"Wait a minute."

"Go home, Nate Black."

"That's my decision, isn't it?"

Silence.

"You can't do anything, can you? Other than open a gate? I still have to walk through, don't I?"

"Your purpose here is concluded. This world has nothing for you."

"Whatever I do is mine, isn't it? Your power only comes from manipulating others, giving them enough information to destroy themselves."

The darkness slithered around Nate; it felt suffocating and tight within his chest. The intensity of Ghad's presence was blinding in its power.

But that was it. It was feeling without substance, potential without action.

"You haven't won. Damn it, you blackmailer, e-mailing bastard, you haven't won."

"Do not anger me."

"Your threats are empty. Whatever rules you've established, whatever divine game you're playing, all you can do is talk to me."

"Test me and . . ."

Something happened, and the threat trailed off. The slithering darkness suddenly gained another character, another presence. A different voice came out of the void.

"You would void our wager, my brother."

Brother?

"The wager is concluded. You can see my ghadi rise as I have said they would."

"You cannot have this man do other than what he would."

"He has, my brother."

"But he defies you yet."

It sank in what was happening, what had happened. Just like the myths he had read, he had been caught in some sort of game between these deities. "What was it?" Nate muttered.

"It challenges us." said the new voice, the one that wasn't Ghad.

"What wager?" Nate asked again.

"Ghad, my brother, claimed that he could do to my manlings with one person in a year, what my manlings had done to the ghadi in six centuries."

Nate swallowed. It must be Mankin that addressed him, and it began to make sense, this world's attitude toward their "gods." Mankin voiced Ghad's wager without emotion, as if the elimination of Mankind was little more than a loss in a hand of cards.

I can still leave. . . .

Nate kept thinking of Yerith, and Bill, and abandoning them both to a world where they would be forced to kill each other. He thought of Uthar and what the man already knew, how there could easily be an arms race with the newly-awakened ghadi. This world had already been through it once.

But he could buy some time. . . .

It wasn't easy coding the spell in his head with the slithering alienness engulfing him, trying to distract him. But Ghad was right, Nate was at the center of power, and it was as if the heart of the Gods' Language, the superstructure of Ghad's world was open to him.

"What does your Angel do, my brother?"

There was actually an uncertain note in Ghad's voice. *"No, you do not understand what you do."*

Nate ignored everything around him, and spoke a spell of erasure, like the spell that had freed the Ghadi. It only had a few more lines of code, lines of code that were modeled on stuff he wrote when he really was Azrael, when he didn't give a fuck about the consequences of his actions, and back when there wasn't such a thing as knowledge too dangerous to possess.

"What have you done?" Ghad's words echoed pain, as if the thing around him felt the import of what Nate had just done.

"Back where I come from," Nate said, in English, "it's called a virus."

• • •

Armsmaster Ehrid Kharyn, bloodied by confrontations with acolytes and suddenly hostile ghadi, stumbled into one of the last vaults in the College of Man. The shadows down here were long and odd, and he stood in the half-open doorway before the scene made any sense to him.

"May Ghad avert his eye," he whispered, sure that Ghad had done no such thing.

The shadows were cast by a lantern that had tumbled onto the floor and somehow remained lit. Desks and shelves had been upended, scattering books and papers and ancient scrolls everywhere. In the middle of the floor lay the Venerable Scholar himself, neck twisted, demon mask sightlessly staring at the ceiling. Around his throat were the fingers of a ghadi that lay in a pool of purple blood.

The scholar's hand was still on the dagger embedded in the ghadi's flesh.

When he was sure he was alone, Ehrid lowered his weapon and stepped into the room. He knew where he was. Here was the holiest and darkest repository of the College. Everything written in the Gods' Language too dangerous to be etched in skin was kept here. The scholar was obviously down here to find something with which to mount an apocalyptic defense.

I probably owe my life to that ghadi, Ehrid thought.

He knelt down to look at one of the books that had tumbled to the floor. One of the most secret of mysteries, to be defended and secreted by the College to the end of time itself.

He opened the book.

The pages were blank.

He flipped through, and all the pages were blank.

Ehrid frowned and picked up a loose scroll. Before the aged paper disintegrated, he could see there was nothing written on it. All of it—he looked at dozens of books, parchments, scrolls—all of it was blank.

He walked over to the body of the Venerable Master Scholar and removed the demon mask. Looking up at Ehrid was a completely unmarked face, the skin flaccid and completely unscarred.

• • •

Nate sat up next to the pit.

Casting the virus had thrust him out of the netherland between the worlds. It wasn't completely unexpected, but he couldn't help feeling a deep sense of loss.

I guess I'm not going home. . . .

He was still chained up, and as he stood, a number of guards rushed him, and the only thing that kept them from running him through was a shout of "Hold" from Uthar.

Uthar pushed himself through to Nate. His face no longer bore any trace of scar tissue.

"What have you done?" he demanded.

Nate raised his wrists. "Can someone remove these?"

"What have you done!" Uthar sounded frantic.

"Leveled the playing field." It wasn't a local idiom, but it was one of a few English phrases that translated in a way that made sense.

Uthar grabbed him. "You called the presence of Ghad down on us, and now none of the enchantments remain. Even the ones carved into the skins of the acolytes . . ."

"It's all erased."

"What?"

"All documentation of the Gods' Language, every written source, has ceased to be. Even if the words are spoken into the air, they will be undone before any spell is spoken."

The color drained from Uthar's face. "How long?"

"As long as my virus keeps propagating itself," Nate said in English. "How long is forever," Nate added, in Uthar's tongue.

Uthar seemed to cave in on himself. "Why, why would you cause something like this?"

"Basically to keep you and the ghadi from destroying each other, now that they're awake."

Uthar stared at him.

"Also, I think you should get me back to those ghadi. I may be the only person who can talk some sort of settlement with them." *I am their messiah, after all.*

"Negotiate? With the ghadi?"

"You should show gratitude," Nate said, "The ghadi managed to destroy the greater part of the College's army for you."

Things had obviously progressed too fast for Uthar. He couldn't absorb it all. He just kept shaking his head.

• • •

For a while Nate was a prisoner. But he was patient, and eventually Uthar came around when his own people started coming back with reports confirming what he was saying. He was completely convinced when he brought Nate in front of some ghadi prisoners and they genuflected in Nate's presence.

So, the fourth week after the fall of the College of Man, Nate was on a horse, heading back toward the citadel with Yerith. The horses moved at an unenchanted pace, and by the time they reached the ghadi frontier, Nate was actually getting used to riding.

As they approached the citadel, they began to see piles of human bodies, left to rot on the plains. The sky above was filled with the shadows of carrion birds.

"I'm frightened," Yerith told him.

"You didn't have to come with me."

"You couldn't go alone, and what other experts on ghadi did the Monarch have?" Nate smiled at how easily Uthar had slipped into the title. "Do you really think there can be peace here?" She kept looking at the bodies they passed. Some piles were little more than bones now, and Nate saw one skull that still wore half a mask. In a touch of surrealism, the mask was, itself, a red openmouthed skull.

"As long as the gods ignore us," Nate slipped honestly into the local idiom. He looked up and saw riders approaching from the citadel. "We're about to find out."

A party of about twenty ghadi came down and surrounded them, and Nate really wasn't surprised when the one leading them turned out to be Bill.

There was an intelligence in the familiar ghadi's eyes that hadn't been there before—or Nate hadn't recognized before. His voice was old, low, and threatening. "You abandoned us."

"To save you," Nate said. "I spoke the words that allowed you to defend yourselves."

"A great darkness has lifted," Bill said. "But the words of Ghad have been stolen from us."

"You are free," Nate said. "Isn't that enough?"

Bill stared at him. For a short time Nate thought he might have lost all the goodwill he might have had here. But Bill's expression changed slightly, and it took a moment for Nate to realize that it might be a ghadi smile.

"As ancient belief would have it, you have delivered us. We shall show you and your house our hospitality. And we will listen to what wisdom you bring."

The ghadi turned and led them both toward the citadel and the city growing at its base. As they approached, Nate patted the pack on his hip where he kept a book of notes in hexadecimal.

Not stolen, Bill. Only borrowed.